# SUCH A
# PERFECT
# FAMILY

## BERKLEY TITLES BY NALINI SINGH

### PSY-CHANGELING SERIES

Slave to Sensation

Visions of Heat

Caressed by Ice

Mine to Possess

Hostage to Pleasure

Branded by Fire

Blaze of Memory

Bonds of Justice

Play of Passion

Kiss of Snow

Tangle of Need

Heart of Obsidian

Shield of Winter

Shards of Hope

Allegiance of Honor

### PSY-CHANGELING TRINITY SERIES

Silver Silence

Ocean Light

Wolf Rain

Alpha Night

Last Guard

Storm Echo

Resonance Surge

Primal Mirror

Atonement Sky

### GUILD HUNTER SERIES

Angels' Blood

Archangel's Kiss

Archangel's Consort

Archangel's Blade

Archangel's Storm

Archangel's Legion

Archangel's Shadows

Archangel's Enigma

Archangel's Heart

Archangel's Viper

Archangel's Prophecy

Archangel's War

Archangel's Sun

Archangel's Light

Archangel's Resurrection

Archangel's Lineage

Archangel's Ascension

Archangel's Eternity

### THRILLERS

A Madness of Sunshine

Quiet in Her Bones

There Should Have Been Eight

Such a Perfect Family

## ANTHOLOGIES

*An Enchanted Season*
(with Maggie Shayne, Erin McCarthy, and Jean Johnson)

*The Magical Christmas Cat*
(with Lora Leigh, Erin McCarthy, and Linda Winstead Jones)

*Must Love Hellhounds*
(with Charlaine Harris, Ilona Andrews, and Meljean Brook)

*Burning Up*
(with Angela Knight, Virginia Kantra, and Meljean Brook)

*Angels of Darkness*
(with Ilona Andrews, Meljean Brook, and Sharon Shinn)

*Angels' Flight*

*Wild Invitation*

*Night Shift*
(with Ilona Andrews, Lisa Shearin, and Milla Vane)

*Wild Embrace*

## SPECIALS

*Angels' Pawn*

*Angels' Dance*

*Texture of Intimacy*

*Declaration of Courtship*

*Whisper of Sin*

*Secrets at Midnight*

# SUCH A PERFECT FAMILY

## NALINI SINGH

BERKLEY

New York

BERKLEY
An imprint of Penguin Random House LLC
1745 Broadway, New York, NY 10019
penguinrandomhouse.com

BERKLEY and the BERKLEY & B colophon are registered trademarks
of Penguin Random House LLC.

Book design by Laura K. Corless
Interior art: That Wānaka Tree © Richarya/Shutterstock

ISBN: 9780593549797

Library of Congress Cataloging-in-Publication Data

Names: Singh, Nalini, 1977- author
Title: Such a perfect family / Nalini Singh.
Description: New York: Berkley, 2026.
Identifiers: LCCN 2025024278 (print) | LCCN 2025024279 (ebook) |
ISBN 9780593549797 hardcover | ISBN 9780593549803 ebook
Subjects: LCGFT: Thrillers (Fiction) | Novels | Fiction
Classification: LCC PR9639.4.S566 S83 2026 (print) | LCC PR9639.4.S566 (ebook)
LC record available at https://lccn.loc.gov/2025024278
LC ebook record available at https://lccn.loc.gov/2025024279

Printed in the United States of America
1st Printing

The authorized representative in the EU for product safety and compliance is
Penguin Random House Ireland, Morrison Chambers, 32 Nassau Street,
Dublin D02 YH68, Ireland, https://eu-contact.penguin.ie.

# SUCH A
# PERFECT
# FAMILY

# CHAPTER 1

I'd buried Susanne on this day in October five years ago.

My hands clenched on the steering wheel, my chest tight at the sudden, crushing memory of the first woman I'd ever loved. Complex, sophisticated Susanne Winthorpe, lover of red dresses and stiletto heels, who never stepped foot out of the home without her signature full face of makeup—and at least one diamond.

As different from Diya as the sun was from the moon.

The tightness in my chest evaporated as I thought of how my wife's face would light up when I handed her the box of little taster cakes on the front passenger seat. She'd asked me to pick them up from the bakery so we could choose a cake for the reception to take place after our religious wedding ceremony in six months' time; my in-laws weren't satisfied with the fact we were legally married, wanted the whole shindig.

So I'd be getting married to Diya all over again . . . and that was more than fine with me.

My heart doing that thing it did only for her, I made sure to take the corners with smooth grace to ensure the cake box didn't slide off the seat and onto the floor. Water glinted to my right as I passed Lake Tikitapu, which Diya had told me was also called the Blue Lake, the morning sunlight a bright sparkle that had already lured a couple of kayakers onto the water.

I hoped they were wearing wet suits just in case.

The end of October in New Zealand meant spring—brilliant sunshine, crisp temperatures, cherry blossoms and wisteria blooms—but the lakes still felt as cold as ice to my Los Angeles-born-and-bred body. I couldn't figure out how my father-in-law jumped into frigid lake water every morning for a vigorous one-hour swim.

"It's good for the heart, my boy!"

Then Lake Tikitapu was in my rearview mirror, with Lake Rotokākahi, or the Green Lake, coming up ahead. Nestled in the thick green bush in between was a lookout from which you could see both lakes. I continued past, my destination the far larger body of water that was Rajesh Prasad's daily swimming spot.

It didn't take long, the road all but empty today.

I'd already turned into the drive that led to the beautifully landscaped and expansive property that was the Prasad family home when I noticed smoke drifting up above the tops of the native trees and ferns that flanked the path's gentle downward slope.

Smoke in the closest township wasn't unusual—Rotorua was a geothermal city known for its boiling mud pools, hot springs, and geysers, alongside the distinctive scent of sulfur that came and went with the wind. Friends of the Prasads in the city had recently ended up with a sinkhole in their front yard. Small, it mostly blew up curls of hot white smoke—but go deeper and I had no doubt you'd encounter water or mud capable of giving you third-degree burns.

The authorities had fenced off the sinkhole and evacuated everyone from the home while they investigated, and the family involved had been joking about charging people to come look at their own personal piece of geothermal scenery. Beneath the jokes, however, was the fear that their home was sitting atop a disaster waiting to happen.

But the Prasad home wasn't in Rotorua proper. It sat on the edge of the clear blue-green waters of Lake Tarawera, a good twenty-five-minute drive out of the main part of the city, longer if roadworks were in progress. Close enough to be doable for two specialists who rarely had patient emergencies, but far enough to have the feel of a peaceful enclave set apart from the city.

It wasn't that Lake Tarawera didn't feature any geothermal activity—as I'd discovered to my delight when Diya led me on an overnight hike to a hot-water beach on the shores of the lake. We'd walked out of the bush after our hike under the stars to the surreal sight of steam rising off the water, the small boats anchored on the lake ghostly afterimages.

But this smoke . . . it was too black, too dark, too *high*.

My mouth dried up.

I pressed my foot to the accelerator pedal and just glimpsed the Prasads' nearest neighbors—a family of three—running into the drive behind me; their mouths were open, as if they were yelling. Ignoring them, I turned the corner of the drive—to come to a screeching halt behind a bright yellow Mini Cooper.

The cake box slammed onto the passenger floorboard.

"Diya!" It came out a scream as I tumbled from the car in front of the elegant single-level family home that now boiled with fire.

The lake lapped placidly in the background, below a sweep of green lawn that led to a private jetty and boathouse, with the bush-clad hills on the other side casting shadows across the wide swath of water.

The Prasad home was—had been—a showpiece. Huge panes of

glass, polished wood stained a rich black, landscaping heavy with native trees and shrubs, each element thoughtfully put together to create a property that fit the landscape rather than attempting to conquer it. Unlike some of the McMansions I'd seen in lakeside towns, the homes around Lake Tarawera weren't about a display of excess, but about quiet, luxurious beauty.

Tucked in between the newer builds were a number of small and well-maintained cottages from another time, pretty little chocolate-box things with planters that had just begun to overflow with flowers as spring took solid hold.

The Prasad home had been constructed only eight years earlier—from bespoke plans created by an award-winning architect. Even the attached garage and the apartment above it had been designed with care. Stained a black to match the main house, the garage's roll-up door appeared to be wood of the same shade, while the apartment's triangular facing walls on both sides were glass.

That glass was shattered now.

*All* the glass was gone, nothing but shards that burned with reflected fire, glowing pieces of shrapnel on the charred lawn.

Black smoke poured out of the resulting gaping holes and through the roof, which had partially fallen in, while jets of flame shot out through the side of the house that had boasted a grand open-plan kitchen designed for entertaining, complete with a dining area centered around an artisan-constructed table of reclaimed swamp kauri.

Thousands of dollars of precious wood that was now kindling.

All of it to feed a fire that might've stolen something infinitely more precious to me.

The heat scalded my skin even from this distance out, my arm rising instinctively in an effort to shield my face as I moved toward Diya's beloved car in the vain hope that she was sitting shell-shocked behind the wheel. Of course it was empty—and it was parked behind her brother's black Mercedes-Benz SUV and her father's cream-colored Lexus.

"Call the fire department!" I screamed at the neighbors who'd raced down the drive behind me.

I'd seen the building that housed the Lake Tarawera Fire Station, a curve of black with huge barn-style doors on the lake side of the road, knew it wasn't far. Diya had told me it was a volunteer-run station—I didn't know what that meant, whether it was staffed twenty-four seven or not.

If we had to wait for help from Rotorua . . .

"We already called! But I'll call again and tell them how bad it is!" the neighbors' teenage son yelled, while I and the dad—I couldn't remember the stocky man's name—ran toward the fire.

The mother, in shorts and a tank top too lightweight for the chill morning air, her feet bare and her ash-blond hair falling out of a loose bun, turned to shout at her son. "Bring the phone back with you!"

Already some distance away, I barely heard her.

Grit in my throat, a stinging in my eyes. I began to cough well before we reached the wider periphery of the house, the smoke was so noxious. Lifting my forearm to my nose, I blinked rapidly in an effort to see the front door through my watering eyes.

Even though Diya and I lived in the apartment above the garage, I knew she'd be in the main part of the house. She was a creature of family, loved being involved, wouldn't have been able to bear being out of the mix when she saw that her brother and sister-in-law had come to visit.

Especially today. The morning after the party.

She'd have been so excited to discuss the night with her sister-in-law, who happened to be her best friend. And all the while, she'd have been keeping an ear open for the sound of the forest green Alfa Romeo Stelvio Quadrifoglio I'd borrowed from her mother for my run into the city, since my long legs weren't as comfortable in the Mini.

Truth was, I just liked driving the high-performance vehicle Dr. Sarita Prasad called her "midlife noncrisis" car.

"After working my tail off all these years," she'd said to me when I admired it, "I decided I deserved this ridiculously gorgeous thing even if it gives me palpitations that it's worth more than our first house!" Then she'd handed me the key. "Go, have fun. Give it a work-out."

This morning, she'd already been for her morning run when I popped my head into the main house. Still in her running gear, her curly hair up in a ponytail, she'd lobbed the key at me before I could ask to borrow the vehicle, her smile wide enough to carve grooves in her cheeks. She loved that I loved the car as much as she did—it had been our first conversation about the Alfa Romeo that had taken our relationship from awkward acquaintances to the beginnings of true family.

"No, man! You can't go in!" The neighbor's breathless voice from behind me, his hand gripping the back of the long-sleeved gray T-shirt I'd thrown on for the drive into Rotorua. "The fire's too strong! The front door's collapsed!"

He was right, but I wasn't about to abandon Diya. Given the presence of the Lexus and the Mercedes, I knew four other people must've been inside the house when it went up in flame, but helping them would be a thing automatic, a thing I'd do for any human.

Saving Diya was my reason for being.

"Go around to the right!" I yelled at the neighbor. "I'll go left! See if you can find a way in!"

The other man didn't argue, just took off in a wide arc around the burning house while I did the same on the other side. I stayed closer, though, close enough that soot and ash landed on my T-shirt and the heat blazed against one side of my face.

Sweat pooled under my armpits, beaded along my brow.

*Please, baby, please.*

It was a mantra inside my head as I searched frantically for any possible entrance into the house. I knew where Diya would've most likely been—in the large central living room filled with comfortable sofas and the biggest wall-mounted television I'd ever seen. That living room flowed off the kitchen so that it was all one huge area separated only by furniture, plants, and clever placement of artwork.

I could get to that space from the glass door on this side—it was segmented into panels, a line of black demarking each panel, and could be folded back to open up this entire side of the house. The same could be done at the back, to create an indoor-outdoor flow from the lounge to the back patio with its sweeping views of the lake.

But when I turned the corner, it was to see shards of glass scattered across the lush green grass that was Dr. Rajesh Prasad's pride and joy. "This lawn eats better than I do!" Diya's father had joked last week while fertilizing it with the special organic lawn fertilizer he had shipped from a supplier all the way in Dunedin.

Flames poured out of the empty maws of the door panels, hot orange tongues that threatened to lick at my clothing.

My chest spasmed, the coughs I'd barely been managing to control turning into a hacking akin to that of an old man with a four-pack-a-day habit. "Diya!" I screamed when I could catch enough breath to make sound.

The fire's roar, the crash of timber inside, was the only reply.

A small flame carried on a tiny piece of paper landed on my T-shirt, burning a hole in it. Brushing it off, I continued on around to the back of the house even though I knew that it was too late—even if I somehow managed to get in, there was no way anyone inside that house had survived.

Tears streamed down my face, but they were from the grit and smoke. Not grief. Because I wasn't done yet. The lawn led directly down to the lake, the distance a matter of seconds to cover at a run. If Diya had managed to stumble out in that direction, she could've taken refuge in the chilly water.

Even if she'd run out panicked, disoriented, and with burns, it would've been instinct to head that way.

That last shred of hope held tight in my desperate hands, I started to turn the corner—

My knees and hands slammed onto the grass, the knuckles of my right hand grazing the hard edge of the patio stones.

Even the grass felt hot. As did my back, the house and its devouring flames too close.

I didn't care. About the heat, or about the throbbing in my knees. The reason I'd fallen was because I'd tripped over someone. "Diya!" I cradled her in my arms even as I blinked desperately in an effort to see more clearly through the smoke.

She rasped a breath, the honey-brown skin of her face paler than I'd ever seen it, and her floral dress and green cardigan all wet against my skin. She must've doused herself with water in an effort to survive. "Diya, baby, I've got you! Hold on!"

Her fingers clutched at my tee, her eyes pleading as her mouth moved.

Desperation was a scream in her expression.

I'd been about to rise to my feet with her in my arms but now leaned instinctively closer to reassure her that she'd be all right.

But Diya spoke first. Her voice was a ragged whisper, her breath hotter than the fire. "Annie . . . they said . . . about Annie . . . not . . ."

Her body went limp.

"Diya!" But her eyes were closed, her face slack.

"—no way inside!" A coughing male voice. "Oh my God! You found someone!" The neighbor came down on Diya's other side. "Wait, is that . . ."

I stared at my hand at the same time. Even the bleary vision created by the smoke and my watering eyes couldn't obscure the red wetness bright against the pale skin of my palm. "Blood." It came out a rough whisper.

My wife of exactly forty-three days was bleeding.

Bleeding so much that the red on her dress wasn't flowers, but scarlet blooms that grew as I watched. She hadn't doused herself in water; it was blood that smeared my skin where I held her, blood that pasted her clothes to her skin.

"Has she been shot?" the neighbor yelled.

*No. No, there are too many blooming spots. Too many . . . holes in her dress.*

"Stabbed." It came out a soundless whisper.

The woman I adored beyond all reason or rational thought had been brutally stabbed.

Something crashed inside the house, spouts of flame jetting out from the back toward the lake. Turquoise shifted to orange, the lake a mirror aflame. Then the entire house seemed to pulse, the fire suddenly oddly quiet.

Primitive instinct took over. Scooping Diya into my arms, I said, "Run!"

Flames at my back, the world silent, and then . . . a massive boom of sound as the house let out its breath and exploded in all directions.

# CHAPTER 2

Private notes: Detective Callum Baxter (LAPD)
Date: Dec 2
Time: 20:37

Arrived at site of single-vehicle crash on Knox Canyon Road. One fatality: Virna Musgrave (68). Not suspicious at first glance, but the local out walking his dog who discovered the crash—James Whitby (46)—states that Ms. Musgrave drove this route monthly for years without any issues, and that she never exceeded the speed limit.

"If anything," he stated, "she sat at least ten below. Used to annoy the shit out of her neighbors—me included—if we ever got stuck behind her, but she always said we'd thank her one day for teaching us patience.

"She wouldn't have lost control. Especially not on a clear evening like today—it would've still been light out when she went over. I ran down to check on her when I spotted the car, and the hood was dead cold. She'd been there for a while."

He also noted that despite her annoying driving habits, she was a "nice lady" and well-liked by her few neighbors. The Musgrave residence is the biggest property on the road, right at the top.

There were no skid marks, and she appears to have gone over the edge at high speed while going downhill. Seat belt on and her car's a newer-model Jeep that held up well to the crash, so she might have survived if not for the steep nature of the drop—it looks like she took a serious bang to the head and I don't like the way her neck's sitting.

It's possible she suffered a medical event that caused her to go off the road. Have to wait for the ME's report on that. Vehicle to be towed to LAPD forensic facility for further investigation after the techs finish up here.

Case open for now.

## CHAPTER 3

In that endless moment when my feet left the earth, Diya's bloody body clutched to my chest, I saw her as I had that very first time: a butterfly beauty of a woman who laughed with open delight under the colored bulbs strung across the roof of a West Hollywood tequila bar that buzzed with people and conversation.

Her dress had been short and a glittering green so dark it was almost obsidian, her hair tumbled black curls that fell to just past her shoulders, and her presence so bright that she glowed. I hadn't known her name then, hadn't understood that her parents had seen that glow, too, right from the moment she'd first come into the world.

*Diya. A light against the dark.*

Only later had I begun to understand that her candle flame was one with an internal flicker, ever in danger of going out. Sometimes, there was an insubstantial quality to my wife that panicked me—as if she were a will-o'-the-wisp that might slip out of my grasp one moonless night.

I couldn't lose her. Not as I'd lost the others.

I'd woken with my heart thudding night after night during our first weeks together, needing to see her beside me. Her chest rising and falling. The feel of her skin a relief because it meant she was real and not a figment of my need for her. This woman who was as fragile as a dandelion against a storm wind . . . and who burned incandescent.

To not go to her the night I'd first heard her laugh had been an impossibility. She'd seen me weaving my way through the crowd, watched me with those enigmatic eyes she'd made up smoky and smudged that night.

Every step I took had been a step closer to my destiny. Every tiny hair on my body had prickled, my charmer's mouth suddenly dry, and my words jumbled up in my head.

She'd known. So had I.

Strangers to each other or not, this was it. We were it.

But when I'd asked her for her number, she'd told me I better have a good memory before reeling off a long cell number with an unusual country code.

Then her friends had decided to change bars and she'd left me with a smile that was a teasing challenge, the quiet enigma of her morphing into sweet, playful beauty. "Call me tomorrow . . . if you remember the number."

We'd run laughing out of a Las Vegas wedding chapel five weeks later.

———

*I, Tavish Advani, promise you, Diya Prasad, that I will protect the candle flame of you against any and all storms that may come. Nothing and no one will ever get between us. You will ever be my guiding light, the warmth that shows me the way home for the rest of my life.*

*I love you, Diya. Now and always.*

My knees hit the earth. *Hard.* Pain was a starburst in those knees, vibrating up my thighs, but I still had Diya in my arms. I didn't care about anything else.

Rising with a grunt, I began to run again.

Sirens wailed in the distance as the neighbor scrambled up and ran ahead. He was yelling at his wife and kid about a possible survivor. The woman pelted toward me at that, and I suddenly remembered what Diya had mentioned the other day. A nurse—the woman was a senior nurse. Worked in the same hospital at which Diya's parents were consultants.

"It's too close!" I yelled to her when she made a motion for me to put Diya down so she could examine her.

Staring behind me at the fireball of the house, she nodded, and the two of us made our way to the manicured grass on one side of the drive, across from where I'd parked the Alfa Romeo. "She's hurt," I said as I put my wife down with care. "There's blood." I couldn't make the word "stabbed" come out of my mouth again.

If I didn't say it, maybe it wouldn't be true.

"She might've sustained an injury getting out if she escaped through a shattered window." The nurse was taking Diya's pulse as she spoke, now placed her ear by Diya's mouth. "Faint but present pulse, shallow respiration."

She began to open up Diya's cardigan. "Let me see if I can find the main wounds so we can put pressure on them at least—though it sounds like the fire department and the ambulance are almost here. We told them there might be injur—"

Her voice broke off. "Oh my God." A whisper.

The top of Diya's dress was soaked red. Obscene, every bit of white eclipsed, the yellow flowers turned scarlet.

"On her neck." I touched my fingers just above the wound that
bled sluggishly, my hand holding a visible tremor. "We have to
stop it."

"Right." She snapped out of it. "Joseph! Give me your T-shirt!"

Even as her son rushed to obey, I stared helplessly at the saturated
front of Diya's dress and the splashes elsewhere. "Those are knife
wounds, aren't they?" I asked, even as I held the wadded-up T-shirt to
the wound.

I wanted her to tell me I was an idiot, that these were clearly
wounds from going through a glass window. I was ready to believe
anything that would make even a remote lick of sense.

The nurse wouldn't meet my gaze but gave a jagged nod, her
blond hair lifting in the wind coming off the lake.

Running feet, two paramedics coming down next to her.

The fire crew raced past us to assess the situation at the same
time, their heavy gear making their footsteps thunder on the earth
and their shouts to each other blurring into a heavy buzz in my head.

Then one of them yelled directly at us. "Can any of these cars be
moved? We can't get the appliance in!"

It jolted me up. "Yes!" I called back and dug into my pocket before
realizing I'd left the fob in the car.

My fingers painted red streaks on my jeans.

Not allowing the meaning of that color to sink into my brain, I
ran to the Alfa Romeo and pulled another electronic key off the small
bundle. It was a spare to the Mini. Diya had ordered one for each
of her parents so they could move her car out of the way if she accidentally blocked them in and they had to leave for the clinic or the
hospital.

Seeing that the nurse was still crouched down beside the paramedics, I threw her husband the spare fob, and the two of us jumped
into the vehicles to reverse them purposefully into the grassy ditch

on one side. With the fire truck already in the drive, it was easier to do that than attempt to back out.

Two of the fire crew had smashed the window of the Lexus to allow them access to the vehicle's controls. Its alarm shrieked as they put it into neutral to roll it out of the way. As soon as I'd reversed my vehicle, I ran over to smash the window of the Mercedes. The neighbor, seeing what was happening, came over to help me push that car off the drive, too.

It wouldn't budge.

"Fuck! It's the newest model!" Diya's brother had purchased it after I arrived in the country. "Probably has some safety or security features we don't understand!"

The cacophony of the Lexus's alarm going off drilled into my skull, spearing through the roar of the fire.

"It's fine!" the neighbor yelled back before jumping away from the drive. "They have enough room!"

The fire truck rumbled past only seconds later.

Sweat pouring down my face from the heat blazing off the house, and my T-shirt stuck to my skin, I ran back to Diya the instant I could duck behind the truck.

The paramedics had cut open her dress, wiped away the smeared blood.

*Jesus.*

I'd seen those kinds of marks on countless television shows. She hadn't just been stabbed. She'd been attacked with a mindless fury that meant one mark blended into the next. Narrow, like thin lips in her skin . . . except where they were clustered together, her beautiful body mangled and torn.

She'd made me an omelet this morning while wearing yellow pajama shorts and a white tank top, her hair piled on top of her head in a haphazard updo. Without shoes, she only reached the top of my breastbone, a petite woman with the kind of presence that could hold an entire stadium spellbound.

Her laugh as I muttered curses at her fancy coffee machine had become entwined with the smell of the omelets, and with the soft morning scent of her. "Tavish, my gorgeous man, my beloved, it's a machine." Her eyes dancing under a curl that had escaped her attempt to contain it. "Threatening to disassemble it won't miraculously make it work!"

"Oh?" I'd said as the machine began to cheerfully create her favorite latte. "I rest my case. Robot; it's a robot. Probably going to eat our brains in our sleep."

Shaking her head, her smile creasing her cheeks, she'd said, "I had the oddest dream last night. About our old house in Fiji. I could see the mango tree from a window—and then I was trying to dig it up using a shovel." A sudden pause. "Oh drat, I forgot to put spinach into your omelet like you wanted. I'll sauté it as a side dish."

Now the omelet as well as the spinach threatened to leave my stomach. Because my wife's torso was a maze of stab wounds wet and red, the bruising around them barely begun.

I knelt down beside her, took her hand.

Pale, clammy, limp.

"—another survivor!"

The words made no sense, not when the house had *blown up*.

By the time I turned to look over my shoulder, one of the paramedics had picked up his gear and was racing over to join the fireman who was walking over with someone in his arms. Not from the house. From *around* the house.

Long dark hair, a sleeveless navy blue jumpsuit, both dripping wet.

*Shumi.*

Diya's sister-in-law and best friend had done what I'd hoped Diya might have—jumped into the lake as the only safe option. But from the limpness of her in the fireman's arms, I couldn't tell if she was alive or not.

I should've gone to her, checked, but I couldn't—wouldn't—leave Diya. "How bad is it?" I asked the paramedic as he worked on my wife. "She'll be all right, won't she?"

The middle-aged man gave it to me straight. "Look, son, it's serious. More than ten stab wounds from what I've seen so far. I can't tell how deep they are, but they're all in dangerous places. We have to get her to the hospital."

A shadow fell over me.

"Hey, I got you your phone and wallet from the car." It was the teenager . . . Joseph, that was it. Tall and lanky with hair that fell into his eyes and the beginnings of a peach fuzz beard. "I figured you might need it to, like, call people and grab stuff? Your passport was with your wallet, so I grabbed that, too."

"Thanks, Joseph." I stuffed the phone into my back jeans pocket, the slim leather wallet into a front one. The passport I shoved into my other back pocket.

Another ambulance screamed into the street just then, and there was no real choice—I went into the ambulance with Diya, while Shumi was placed in the other one. A second fire truck turned into the drive of the Prasad home even as the ambulance's siren pierced the air, the peaceful lakeside now a chaos of people and vehicles.

Shutting it all out, I held my wife's hand and brushed back her hair. "Don't you dare let your light go out. Don't you *dare*. Not now, not when we've come through the worst of it."

To say that the Prasads hadn't been pleased with our rapid-fire courtship and Vegas elopement was an understatement of magnitudes. Their treasured daughter, who'd only just turned twenty-four, had left for seven days in Los Angeles for a friend's bachelorette celebrations—and returned six weeks later with a husband who was a total unknown to them.

Her family's initial disapproval had dimmed Diya's light, made it flicker in that dangerous way that kept me awake at night, but she'd refused to burn out under the pressure, refused to agree with their belief that she'd made a horrible mistake.

"It'll be okay, Tavish," she'd told me when I'd sat at the edge of our bed with my head in my hands, terrified their words would get to her, thrusting a wedge between us. "My family just needs time." A kiss on my bare shoulder, her body pressed up to my back as she knelt behind me. "But they love me, and once they see how happy you make me, they'll be your biggest fans."

We hadn't quite gotten to that stage, but her parents and brother had thawed enough to throw us a huge party, and preparations were well under way for the "big, fat, totally extra Indian wedding" that would truly cement our relationship as husband and wife in their eyes. The description of the wedding was Diya's, my wife excited about the celebration to come.

"Come on, baby," I said to her today. "We're getting married a second time, remember? No Elvis impersonator with purple hair and diamante eyebrows this time." My voice hitched, my rib cage crushing my heart. "Then you're going to take me on a tour of your favorite spots in New Zealand for our honeymoon. You promised."

"We'll drive to Milford Sound," she'd said one dreamy night as we sat side by side at the end of their jetty while the stars sparkled overhead, the Milky Way so much brighter here than in the glittering metropolis in which I'd been born—and where I'd lived until I'd landed in New Zealand approximately a month and a week ago.

There was a poster in her teenage bedroom inside the main house that featured the lake and the sky, with the Milky Way caught in breathtaking detail by a camera lens. But even with my human vision, I'd seen an enormity of stars that night, the sky studded with diamonds.

"In the rain," she'd added. "Milford Sound is best in the rain—waterfalls coming down all of the mountains that soar over the road as you drive in, the landscape so misty and mysterious that it's straight out of a fantasy movie." She'd leaned her head on my shoulder, warm and happy and so lovely that I didn't know what I'd done to deserve her.

*We both know you have blood on your hands.*

I shoved away the memory of Detective Callum Baxter's accusing words from eight months—and a lifetime—ago. Diya needed me sane and whole to fight for her; I couldn't spiral into the black abyss that had been my life for far too long.

"We're about to pull in," the younger paramedic said.

I made sure not to get in the way as they unloaded Diya and rushed her into Emergency. The staff halted me when I tried to follow her through the doors inside, told me I had to wait because she was going straight into surgery. "We'll alert you once she's on a ward."

Numb with fear, I was still standing in the public area when I saw the second ambulance turn in. I ran out in time to see Shumi being unloaded. Realizing that she'd probably be headed in the same direction as Diya, I waited by the second ambulance until the crew returned.

"Can you tell me anything about Shumi?" I asked, and when they looked blank, added, "The patient you just took in. My sister-in-law."

"Oh right." The woman of the pair, a brunette of maybe forty, grimaced. "I'm really sorry about your family. Do you know who else was there?"

"My father-in-law's car was there, and I saw both him and my mother-in-law before I left the house earlier. The other car belongs to Bobby. That's Shumi's husband." And Diya's protective big brother. "They had to have come together—Shumi doesn't drive."

"Oh man." The brunette glanced at her partner—a wide-shouldered Polynesian man—and got a nod. "Look, don't tell anyone we told you, but she was stabbed, just like your wife."

I shoved both hands through my hair. "None of this makes sense. They're just a normal family." Wealthy, yes, but not Beverly Hills levels of obscene money—or the stalkers and other nutcases that came with that. "Who goes in and stabs a normal family?"

The paramedics said nothing, but I had the feeling of words hanging in the air. "Did she jump into the lake?" I asked, trying to answer one question at least. "Shumi?"

A nod from the man. "Only reason she didn't drown was that she got caught on a large branch that must've gone into the water in that last big storm and washed down by the house. She was unconscious by the time the fire crew found her, so without that branch . . ."

My stomach roiled. "Do you know if . . . if they found anyone else?"

# CHAPTER 4

Private notes: Detective Callum Baxter (LAPD)
Date: Dec 2
Time: 23:15

Death notification made to Virna Musgrave's son, Jason Musgrave. He was distraught and didn't ask many questions. I'll follow up with him tomorrow morning, when he's had time to process the information.

Perez is back tomorrow so we can split up the tasks—all this money everywhere. Jason Musgrave's mansion was the real deal, complete with fancy Italian tiles and all that—I don't know, I get a bad feeling about it. Might be nothing, but we got to make sure we cross every *t* and dot every *i*, or the family's piranha lawyers (it's like the rich get them from the same vicious pond) will fucking eat us alive.

At least the higher-ups aren't leaning on me yet. That'll probably start tomorrow after Jason Musgrave gets over his shock and starts demanding answers.

## CHAPTER 5

No, man, I'm sorry—we didn't see the fire guys bring out anyone else." The male paramedic squeezed my shoulder. "But we left straight after the ambulance that brought in your wife. The cops will have any new information."

His partner nodded. "This is the first place they'll look for you, so I'd stay here."

"I have no plans to leave. My wife's in surgery." I wasn't a man who overshared, but the words wouldn't stay inside, didn't even feel real. How was it possible that I'd kissed my wife good-bye on the drive and left to get cake and come back to blood and fire?

My last image of Diya before the fire was of her in pajama shorts and a navy blue hoodie she'd stolen from me; it swallowed her up, but she loved the thing. Her feet had been in flip-flops, her hair still piled on top of her head as she waved me off. She hadn't had her shower yet, had been planning to do so while I ran the errand.

"I think I'll wash my hair, do the full curls routine," she'd said to me before I left. "You can take me out for a date tonight."

"As long as you wear the green dress." Already in the car, I'd stuck my head out the window. "You know what that dress does to me. Last time around, I married you!"

Her laughter had been wild and sweet, the kiss she blew me the kind of goofy romantic thing newlyweds did. No shadows in her eyes, none of that weight that seemed to crush her at times, no fear inside me that my wife would vanish if I turned away.

Blood—God, there'd been *so much blood* on her.

Something crackled on the brunette paramedic's shoulder, the speaker coming to life to indicate an urgent call for assistance.

I stepped out of their way.

It wasn't until I was back inside the public area of the Emergency Department that I realized why else they'd told me to stay here. I had no idea if the fire was out or if it continued to rage, but the firefighters *would* eventually gain control.

And the situation would shift.

Forensic officers on the scene. Vans destined for the morgue. Bodies . . . or body parts being carried out.

*Fuck, fuck, fuck!*

"Sir." A nurse walked up to me, her eyes a concerned hazel against freckled white skin, and her scrubs a deep blue. "Are you bleeding?"

"What? No."

When she indicated my tee, I looked down to see smears of red. Diya's blood.

This nurse must not have been on the floor earlier.

"I came in with my wife—she was stabbed. Taken straight into surgery. They wouldn't let me stay with her. Diya Prasad." All her legal documentation was still in her maiden name even though she'd decided to take mine after marriage.

"Diya Advani," she'd said, sounding it out. "I like it."

I wasn't sure if she'd even had the chance to begin the change-of-surname paperwork, or what that entailed. She'd mentioned something about updating her driver's license for starters, but neither of us had been in a rush about it. We were married, were one; the rest of it was window dressing.

"Hold on a minute." The nurse left.

She returned to find me in exactly the same spot. For the first time in my life, I didn't have a plan in mind, my usually agile brain on the fritz.

"Your wife is no longer on this floor," the nurse said. "Here are directions to a waiting area close to the ICU, where she'll be brought after surgery."

She put a piece of paper into my hand, as if aware that, right now, I didn't have the capacity to retain too much new information. "I've told the ICU staff where you'll be if they need to get hold of you. Before you go to the waiting area, though, I'd suggest changing." She indicated my long-sleeved T-shirt. "I found a clean scrub top for you."

I took the offered item, suddenly viscerally conscious of being covered in Diya's blood. My skin crawled. "Wait," I said before she could move away. "Will my sister-in-law also be brought to the ICU? Shumi Prasad. She was stabbed, too."

The nurse's eyes widened. "Are you next of kin?"

Another crackle in my brain, another struggle to find the right words. "Her husband . . . was in the fire. Her family's based in another part of the country and I don't know how to get in touch with them. My wife would know, but . . ." I fisted my hands. "I'm the only one here right now."

"You might have to wait for the police in that case." A sympathetic smile.

A woman walked into the ER just then, crying and doubled over in pain, and the nurse had no more time for me. She was gone before I could think up an argument that might get her to divulge Shumi's status or location. Shoving the piece of paper she'd given me into my pocket, I made my way to the closest guest toilets.

Someone had stuck a small sticker to the wall just outside, of curving green against a black background.

One look and I was thrown back to my first local bushwalk with Diya. She'd pointed out the tight curving curl of a fern frond, said, "The koru design I showed you at the airport? It comes from these fronds. It's a symbol of endurance and growth."

A slow smile, her hand sliding into mine. "It's peaceful here, right?"

I'd known why she was asking; she understood that her new husband was a man drowning in darkness who needed the embrace of such nonjudgmental silence. She didn't know the why of my nightmares—how could I tell her what I'd done? What I'd *been?*—but she'd soothed me many a night.

*It's okay, Tavi. It's okay.*

It was only on that forest walk that she'd asked me the most important question: "Who's Joss?"

The name I called out in the night over and over, the guilt that whispered to me like that heartbeat in the creepy Poe story we'd had to study in high school. Only this one was all vicious laughter and the scent of expensive tobacco.

Jocelyn "Joss" Wai had never smoked anything so cheap as a store-bought cigarette.

Diya had protected me from the storms since the very first night we spent together, Jocelyn's vengeful ghost deciding to visit me on the day when I was the happiest I'd ever been.

Back then, far from this land that she called her own, far from the family that cherished and protected her, she'd been the stronger of the two of us. In those nighttime hours after a terror that woke me on a reverberating scream, my fears of her drifting away had seemed foolish, a fanciful whimsy.

Diya had been the most solid thing in the room.

It was only after we came to New Zealand that I'd realized my wife's flame sometimes flickered so low that it came close to extinction. Not even a hint of a smile for days, a black cloud hanging over her head that seemed ready to suffocate her. She'd felt distant, even when she was in my arms, as if she'd gone somewhere I couldn't follow.

*It's fine! I have enough!*

Words I'd overheard when she'd moved into my Venice Beach condo after her original hotel booking ran out five days from that night on the rooftop where I'd fallen in love with my girl in the green dress. I'd thought her family was worried about her financial status after she'd impulsively decided to stay on in the city, and had told her she didn't have to stress about finances.

"I have plenty of money," I'd said, standing on the balcony of that piece of beachfront real estate I'd owned since I was twenty-two. "Please let me spend it on you."

She'd given me an odd little smile then, this breathtaking woman from the other side of the world who'd captured me so completely that I wasn't even mad about it—not when she loved me as hard as I loved her.

"I never thought I'd meet someone like you, Tavish. A man straight out of my fairy-tale dreams." Her fingers on my jaw, the caress so light it was the merest whisper. "I feel so free with you, as if I'm truly seeing life for the first time. No filters, no restraints. I'm myself and I remember all of me."

The pills, so innocuous in their brown plastic bottles . . . those I'd discovered later. I'd grown up in LA, the land of glitter and excess;

my first thought had been that my wife had a party-pill habit. Then I'd seen the labels with complex drug names and started to understand that this had nothing to do with ecstasy or heroin, uppers or downers.

I was holding prescription medicine in my hands.

It didn't matter; my wife owned my heart when she shone bright—or when she fell into the dark.

I shoved through the door into the toilets.

It was hospital clean and hospital cold, hard-wearing tile and icy white sinks. Unable to even look at my crumpled and bloody T-shirt after I pulled it off, I shoved it into the trash can meant for the paper towels used to dry hands.

It vanished in a soft rustle.

With the toilets still empty of anyone but me, I washed my hands and forearms to get rid of any traces of blood and soot, then threw some water on my face, using the paper towels to finish my cleanup. I noticed absently that I'd lost some of the hair on my arms—scorched by the heat from the fire. But no burns as far as I could see . . . until I turned and looked at my back.

A scattering of mismatched red spots across my shoulders and upper back, small indicators of my proximity to the flames, but nothing serious. Not like the lips sliced into my wife's body.

Hands shaking, I pulled on the dark blue scrub top; the color was several shades lighter than the midnight blue Bentley I'd hired to drive us to our wedding in Vegas.

"Black looks good on you, Mr. Advani." Diya's gaze had been sultry as she ran her fingers over the tuxedo that Susanne had had made for me when I turned twenty-one, an expensive gift that had stood the test of time; the tailor had left room in the seams so I'd been able to have it altered when I put on more muscle, settled into my adult body.

Diya, for her part, had chosen a dress of darkest amethyst fitted to the waist, the bottom half an airy flow to the ankles. Sleeveless, with a plunging V-neck, it had made her appear a siren right off the silver screen.

The necklace I'd given her—a jagged icicle of a diamond pendant—had sat perfectly in that vee, but she hadn't needed the adornment. Diya's shine had dazzled brighter than any gemstone as she spun under the kaleidoscope of lights and music and color that was Las Vegas, her beauty so sharply defined that it had scared me for a minute.

A woman that lovely, that fragile, might just one day shatter.

As Jocelyn had shattered. As Virna had shattered.

Susanne . . . her end had been a thing far more torturous and slow.

"I'm Diya Advani!" Diya's happy scream had obliterated the cold chill of my worry, my world as awash in multihued lights as the skies of Vegas. "*Mrs.* Tavish Advani!"

Grabbing her by the hips, I'd lifted her up and spun us both around.

Diya's hair a tumbled fan around her shoulders, her strappy black heels hanging off her fingers, and her body light but so, so *alive*.

My fingers clenched on the cold porcelain of the sink. "Please, baby." The plea whispered out of me.

The door to the toilets swung open.

Gut clenching at the sudden burst of noise, I pushed off the sink. It took all my courage to follow the directions to the waiting area. The main atrium of the hospital proved huge and wide; it was full of natural light due to a high peaked ceiling full of glass panels, while the pillars to my left bore intricate Māori carvings.

A number of people sat talking quietly at tables I could see at one end.

I didn't notice much else, my focus on getting closer to Diya. Going up one floor using the stairs, I went through the doors as the instructions said I should—and realized I'd arrived.

Tucked to the left of the doors, the waiting area was delineated by several large armchairs currently empty of occupants. A sign at one end advised of the hospital's chaplaincy services, while the largest wall held a striking piece of Māori art. The usual hospital signs and a fire extinguisher sat at the far end of the wall, while a water fountain occupied the little corner directly next to the doors.

Despite the fact that the waiting area wasn't a walled room on its own, it sat mired in silence . . . because according to the sign opposite the doors, the hallway led to the Intensive Care Unit as well as the Coronary Care Unit on the left, the Medical Unit on the right.

Not a place where people lingered or wandered past without painful reason.

While a nurse about to enter the ICU did check and confirm that Diya remained in surgery, she refused to share any information on Shumi, and since my mind was going in circles, my panic stretching my skin until I thought it would burst, I decided to keep myself busy by seeing if I could find my sister-in-law's family.

They needed to know what had happened.

The first thing I did was click through to Diya's profile on her favorite social media app. Her smiling face hit me in the gut, the photo one I'd taken right before the "engagement" party the Prasads had thrown us.

Diya's parents might have thawed toward me, but they weren't over missing Diya's wedding. Rajesh and Sarita had convinced us to pretend that we were only engaged, so that they could throw us a full Hindu wedding in six months' time—spread over multiple days, it was to involve a guest list of hundreds and simply couldn't be organized any faster.

*You have no idea who she is or what she needs to be happy. Do you even know that she's kept a wedding-ideas scrapbook since she was sixteen?*

Bobby's voice, his sharp words.

Diya's older brother hadn't been my biggest fan, either, not when we'd first arrived. But I'd appreciated him for his cold bluntness in telling me about Diya's girlish dreams; it'd have devastated me to realize it down the road, when there was no chance of giving Diya the kind of wedding that she'd imagined.

Bobby had been right, too. My wife's face had lit up when I'd agreed wholeheartedly with her parents' desire for a full ceremony, complete with all the traditional rituals.

"Why didn't you tell me?" I'd murmured to her late that night as we lay face-to-face in bed, a thin sheet pulled over our naked bodies. "You know I'd do anything for you."

"You already moved countries for me." A sweet kiss pressed to my fingertips. "I wasn't about to ask you to sign on for what's sure to be an insane and over-the-top production that'll hijack our lives for months."

I'd laughed at her ominous description. "Tell me now. About all the things you dreamed."

She'd turned and picked up her phone, then tucked herself up against me, the little spoon to my big spoon, and started with showing me images of intricate wedding mehndi. "Mehndi is henna," she'd said when I hadn't understood that word. "And, oh, by the way, I always dreamed that my groom would learn a romantic Bollywood dance number with me for our sangeet night. Full choreography."

I'd groaned and buried my face in her curls. "I can't believe I'm agreeing to this, but I'll do it—but only for you."

Laughing, she'd snuggled in deeper and showed me more pieces of her dreams, translating terms and explaining the rituals as she went along. Ethnically half-Indian, half-white, I'd grown up "as

American as apple pie," as my mother used to say on the short-lived sitcom that had kicked off her career.

Cliché words, terrible script. No wonder the show had barely limped through its first season. But while the sitcom had died a quick death, it had made a superstar out of its leading lady before it closed up shop, the "vivacious, charismatic, and startlingly lovely" Audrey Advani.

My father, Anand, had framed the review for her; it still hung in the hallway of their Malibu home, a piece of a distant past when they'd been two young people in love—both on the cusp of the next stage of their careers.

"Audrey and Anand," my father had been known to say when he was feeling maudlin. "We were meant to be."

He spoke fluent Hindi, but only when we were alone—or when he was speaking to my paternal grandparents. The rest of the time, the Advani household ran on English. I'd learned to understand Hindi because of how much time I'd spent in my father's study as a child, but my ability to speak it was middling at best. And when it came to tradition and ritual, of those I knew less than nothing.

"Mehndi," I whispered, having forgotten all about the fact that Diya had decided to get her hands done for the engagement party. She'd spent hours with an artist who'd driven out to the house, her mum and Shumi her willing partners in the day of pampering and preparation.

The final mehndi was an intricate filigree across the backs and on the palms of both of Diya's hands.

I could see part of the design in the photo she'd uploaded last night when she updated her profile image. She was seated at her vanity in a robe of emerald green that she'd closed up modestly so as to not "horrify the oldies," her makeup done and her hand lifted as she showed off her engagement ring while beaming at me.

"Just so you know," she'd told me the moment after I'd snapped the picture, "I'm planning to be one of those obnoxious brides who has her wedding photo as her profile picture for the next ten years. It'll be a pic from tonight until then."

Only . . . she'd never had the chance to upload any of the photos from the party itself.

A broken rock in my throat, I clicked through to Shumi's profile from an older photo where Diya had tagged her. And soon frowned, my shoulders hunching as I concentrated on the small screen. I scrolled and scrolled without finding a single photo of the other woman's family.

Two years down and still nothing.

I kept going despite my stiff neck, until at last I landed on an image of Shumi with a youth of maybe nineteen. The two had the same eyes, the same shape to their lips. The caption read: My baby brother all grown up!

She'd tagged him: Ajay Kumar.

His profile listed the names of their parents. And at the very top of his feed were three photos from yesterday. One featured a slightly older Ajay from the one in the photo with Shumi, the second his parents, while the third one had all three of them in front of a sign for a huge gold mine in Perth, Australia.

Vacation!!

That was the only word in the caption, but the comments seemed to indicate the three had only recently arrived on the far side of the huge red continent. A quick search told me the Perth-to-Auckland flight time was roughly six and a half hours. Add in the available flights, the time it might take them to get to the airport on their end, then travel from Auckland to Rotorua, and it would likely be well over a day before they made it here.

Now that I had the names of Shumi's parents, however, it didn't take me long to find some contact information for them. The first hit was her father's job—he was a partner at an accounting firm, his details listed on the firm's website. I figured that at his level of seniority, there was a good chance they could contact him even on vacation.

The receptionist answered on the first ring, and when I explained who I was and why I needed to get in touch with him, she said a shaken, "Oh my God. I just heard a short update on the radio about the fire, had no idea it was Mr. Kumar's family." A pause. "I should call him, rather than giving you his mobile number."

"Okay," I said dully.

"I don't want to tell . . ."

"It's okay. I will. Just let him know it's a family emergency and identify me as Diya's fiancé from the US"—it was how the Prasads had introduced me—"and ask him to call me."

"I'll do it right now," she said on a wash of relief.

My phone rang with an incoming call only two minutes later, despite the fact that—per my phone's world clock—it was very early morning in Perth.

The sick feeling in my stomach bloomed to burn the back of my throat. This was it. I had to destroy someone else's world now. That was when it struck me that I had no idea of Shumi's status; for all I knew, my sister-in-law was already dead.

A cold wind whispered across the back of my neck as, in the far distance, someone's phone played a ringtone that sounded like wind chimes.

# CHAPTER 6

Private notes: Detective Callum Baxter (LAPD)
Date: Dec 3
Time: 08:10

Spoke again to Jason Musgrave. Man doesn't appear to have slept all night, but he was calm and reasonable until I indicated the possibility that the accident might not have been straightforward. I focused on a possible medical event rather than interference with the vehicle, but Jason zeroed in on the latter.

He immediately began to shout that his mother was healthier than he was, and that if the accident *was* suspicious, we needed to look at "that fucking Romeo who conned her out of at least a quarter of a million! He probably thinks he's in her will!"

Per Jason, Virna Musgrave's estate was in the realm of fifteen million dollars while she was alive. Have made a note to confirm this with her attorney, but an initial search of available databases shows her as the owner of multiple high-value properties.

Case remains on hold until the pathologist gets to her—if she had a heart attack, that ends it. Morgue says she's at the top of the queue since the gangs are having a few days off from shooting each other, and the mayor's made a special request.

Also per Jason, the name of the "Romeo" is Tavish Advani.

# CHAPTER 7

I s this Tavish Advani?" a male voice demanded.

"Yes, sir." One hand clenched tight on my knee, I somehow managed to keep my voice steady as I told this stranger that his daughter was in the hospital with severe stab wounds and that her husband and parents-in-law were most likely dead as a result of a catastrophic house fire.

"Is this some type of prank?" Shumi's father's voice rose. "What kind of sick bastard are you?"

"I wish it was a prank." I stared at the hard-wearing carpet on the floor of the waiting area. "The fire's made the news, so you can look it up online, or just call the police here. They'll confirm. I'm really sorry, sir."

It was easy to default to formal politeness, keep this small distance between us so that his anger and grief didn't mingle with my own to leave me locked in a state of panic. "Diya and Shumi are both here, at Rotorua Hospital. They won't tell me anything about Shumi because I'm just her brother-in-law."

I wasn't surprised when he hung up on me. He'd be checking the news, calling the cops, trying to prove to himself that I was just some dickhead getting my rocks off by making up this horrible story.

I was still staring unseeing at the floor when he called back a bare ten minutes later, and this time, his voice was rough and unsteady. "I spoke to the police. We'll be on the first flight back that we can get on. Ajay—my son—is trying to find seats now. What ward of the hospital should I call? The officer I spoke to didn't have the information at hand."

After I told him, he said, "Thank you, Tavish. I apologize for—"

"There's no need," I interrupted. "This is a nightmare. Just take care of your family and get here soon. Shumi will need you."

"Yes, I'll message you our flight details as soon as we confirm them." A pause. "You're alone there, aren't you, beta?" Concern, care in the term used for younger members of the family. "Your family's in the States?"

"Yes." I had one casual friend, a guy I'd met at the local rock-climbing club, but I'd only managed to get to four meetings so far, so even he was more acquaintance than friend, if I was being honest.

"I'm sorry I don't have any contacts in Rotorua these days that I can ask to help you," Shumi's father said. "We're based in Christchurch, but we'll be there as soon as we can. Until then, I'm sure Rajesh and Sarita must have colleagues who'd be more than willing to help—you know how to get in touch with them?"

"Yes, I have the contact details of their clinic."

The waiting area rang with silence after we ended the call. I was the only person taking up space then and for at least an hour following. A couple arrived at that point, and we all ignored one another with the dull compassion of people lost in our own worry.

Two nurses walked past, their heads bent over some paperwork.

A woman around my own age came through the doors from the

stairs two hundred and three breaths later. Taking a seat, she opened up a paperback with the tired ease of a person who'd been here before, sat this vigil. Only . . . she didn't turn the page, not the entire time she sat there, the open book a mere prop.

I stopped a passing member of staff an endless time later to ask if they could find out if Diya was still in surgery. He returned only two minutes later with confirmation and "No other news yet, I'm sorry." In his eyes was the knowledge of tragedy.

"Thank you for checking."

"One of us will come find you as soon as she's with us," he said, before returning to the ICU.

Unable to sit in the waiting area any longer but not wanting to be far from my wife, I drank from the water fountain, then began to pace the hallway that led to the Medical Unit. It murmured with the soft hush of the nurses' footwear, broken up with the intermittent beeps emitted by various machines inside patient rooms. Laughter sounded at one point, coming from some distant corner.

The wind chime ringtone sounded again, melancholy and quiet and disturbing in a way that had nothing to do with the sound itself.

Shaking off the chill that rippled up my spine, I walked away from the direction of the noise. When my phone buzzed with an incoming message a minute later, I didn't know who I was expecting, but it definitely wasn't Aleki, my rock-climbing buddy.

Hey Tav, just heard the news. You okay, man? They aren't releasing much info, but I figured there can't be two other Dr. Prasads in one family out on Lake Tarawera. I know you're living out there. Just message me back so I know you and your wife are okay.

I stared numbly at the message, my brain not working quite right. Then a nurse walked by, and the movement snapped me out of my frozen state.

Thanks, Aleki. I'm at the hospital with Diya and our sister-in-law. I'm

fine but they're hurt. It took everything I had to even write the latter—
to explain that they'd both been stabbed was beyond me.

The other man replied at once: I'm so sorry, mate. Is there anything
I can do? Just say the word. I know you don't have any of your family in
the country, but I've got a big aiga that'll step up. Just tell us what you
need, bro.

The kindness of his offer closed up my throat. I don't have any
clothes. Do you think you can pick me up a couple of T-shirts? I can pay
you back. Thanks to that kid, Joseph, and his forward thinking.

Don't worry about paying me back, Aleki wrote. I'll go do it now.
And—I've only got a bedroom in a flat, but you're welcome to crash on
our couch if you need it. If you want more privacy, I can ask around—
someone will have a room for you.

This was the first time I'd truly felt that I was in a much smaller
town than the glittering metropolis I'd left behind. I couldn't imagine a casual gym buddy in LA reaching out with this much help.
Thanks Aleki.

I was on my hundredth—two hundredth?—circuit of the hallway
when I turned to see police officers near the waiting area. One in uniform, one out of it. Uniform was an Asian man in his mid-twenties, the
one in plain clothes an older woman with her salt-and-pepper hair tied
back in a bun, her skin the kind of pale that has a pink undertone.

Navy blue suit, sensible black shoes, tall for a woman.

The two spotted me at the same time, began to head my way.
Ignoring the dull curiosity of the three other people who waited for
news about their own loved ones, I quickly picked up my pace to
meet the cops halfway.

"The rest of the family?" I asked before they could say anything.
"Did anyone else—"

"Let's move a little farther down for privacy," the woman said,
and this close, I could see both the fine wrinkles around her mouth

and eyes, and the way the suit fit her. Mid-fifties, but fit and toned. Probably a runner, given the type of sports watch she wore on her left wrist.

Once we were far enough from the waiting area that no one could overhear us, she said, "I'm sorry, but the only survivors we've located are Diya and Shumi Prasad. Do I have it correct that Diya is your fiancée and Shumi her sister-in-law?"

I shook my head, the movement jerky. My bones didn't seem connected, all fluid and out of sync. "Diya's my wife. We eloped. Vegas wedding. Elvis presiding." It came out in staccato pieces, snapshots of the night that had changed my life forever.

Garish plastic flowers, diamante-studded white leather, a grinning middle-aged man who swiveled his hips to the tinny music piped through the sound system . . . and Diya laughing as she clutched a bouquet of real flowers. We'd run out under a rain of rose petals for which I'd paid a premium, pieces of floral-scented heaven that Diya had picked out of my hair later.

"I apologize." A tiny frown between her eyebrows, the detective made a note in the small spiral-bound notebook she'd pulled from her jacket pocket.

"Who . . ." I coughed, cleared my throat. "Who else was in the house?" It was possible that one of Diya's parents had been called to the hospital or their clinic, or that Bobby had dropped Shumi off and . . . what?

His SUV had been there.

If he'd gone for a walk around the lake, he'd have seen the fire, come running.

I was reaching, grasping for any hint of hope.

The fine lines at the corners of the detective's eyes deepened to tiny valleys. "It's hard to tell due to the explosion. Do you know if there were accelerants in the house? Gas bottles for the barbecue?"

"What?" I blinked. "No, I—" A sudden memory flash, of something Diya's father had said that morning. "Maybe fuel for the boat? I think Diya's dad said he'd asked Bobby to pick some up when he next came over—it'd usually be stored in the boathouse, I think, but could be Bobby just left it in the house or on the patio when they arrived?"

"Who's Bobby?"

Another snag in the turntable of my brain, another long pause as I dug up the information. "Diya's brother. Everyone calls him Bobby." I hadn't even known it wasn't his real name until the second time I'd met him. "His legal name is Vihaan. I don't know where 'Bobby' comes from." Probably some childhood thing no one had thought to explain to me.

The cop made another note before taking a deep breath. "It isn't safe for the scene-of-crime officers to go in yet," she said. "The fire was significant and the fire crews want to be certain there aren't any lingering hot spots." She exhaled. "However, they are fairly certain they've come across the remains of at least two individuals."

Ice over my skin, I staggered against the wall, one hand braced on the cold surface. *Which two?* "Did you check with the hospital? Both of Diya's parents work as doctors here sometimes, even though they have their own clinic." I didn't know the system in New Zealand, had no idea if my in-laws were regular consultants or were called in on special cases. "Doctors Rajesh and Sarita Prasad."

"We've checked with the clinic, and the doctors would have been alerted by other staff by now if they were in the hospital—but I'll double-check." Another note in the little book. "Officers have also been to Bobby and Shumi Prasad's residence and received no answer to their knocks—and there are no signs of anyone being home. Is it possible your brother-in-law wasn't at the Lake Tarawera house?"

"No. His SUV was there and Shumi doesn't drive."

A raised eyebrow. "She has her full license and a late-model Audi registered under her name. Are you sure she doesn't drive?"

"I—" Frowning, I shook my head. "No, I haven't known her very long." Only a month and a bit since I'd landed in the country, hardly enough time to draw firm conclusions about any of the Prasads. "Bobby always gives her lifts, so I assumed."

"Did he mention plans to be anywhere today?"

"He didn't say anything last night."

"Last night?"

"The Prasads threw Diya and me an engagement party." It seemed surreal now, the echoes of our laughter and the memories of the women's fancy lehengas and gowns some Daliesque nightmare.

Broken, melting . . . burned.

"I thought you said you were already married."

"Diya's parents said that, culturally, our Vegas ceremony only counted as an engagement because we hadn't yet had a religious ceremony. They asked us not to refer to each other as husband and wife in public for now."

"So there was tension about your marriage?" A question asked in a voice so gentle that it almost slipped past my guard. *Almost.*

"Diya's the baby of the family. They couldn't stay mad at her." The tremor in my voice was real, my love for Diya the purest thing I'd ever felt. "Especially after we agreed to the Hindu ceremony." I squeezed my eyes tight, my breath feeling as if it was stuck in my lungs.

"How did you feel about not being able to call her your wife in public?"

"Diya's an event planner." Never happier than when she was bringing a client's vision to life, whether that was a sixtieth birthday party or a corporate awards night. "She was buzzing to plan the wedding of her dreams." Her parents had all but written her a blank check. "I was happy to go along with it for her—the only thing I cared about was that she was mine."

I held the detective's cool gray eyes. "Sarita and Rajesh hired out this fancy hotel ballroom for the engagement party, and Shumi's a good seamstress—she managed to turn Diya's store-bought outfit into a custom fit when Diya couldn't get an alteration appointment at short notice." Peacock blue and vibrant green, with splashes of pink and details in gold, the lehenga had made Diya appear a goddess.

Diya's dad and brother and I had worn black sherwani suits with their narrow mandarin collars and tunic-style tops, while her mother had donned an elegant sari of gold silk. Shumi, meanwhile, had dressed up in a pink lehenga with gold detailing. The two best friends had coordinated the entire family's outfits, so that the photos would be perfect.

Shumi and Bobby had gifted Diya a delicate hair decoration of twenty-two-karat gold that ran along her part, with the small pendant sitting just below the top of her forehead. Diya had told me it was called a maang tikka. Her earrings and bangles had been gifts from her parents, with more jewelry to come prior to the wedding.

"An Indian bride must wear her weight in gold or the foundations of her family will crumble," Diya had joked as she showed me the heavy gold bangles, but her smile had been soft with affection. "My mother wore these at her own wedding."

A tender look aimed at me. "One day, our daughter might wear these."

"It was a great night," I said, wanting only to see her again, hold her again; she was the repository of all my dreams, all my hopes. "The party went on past midnight—everyone was in a wonderful mood."

"Her brother, too?" A pointed question. "What did he think of you eloping with his sister?"

"He wasn't a fan at first," I said, because there was no point in lying to the cops about something they could easily disprove. "But last night he invited me to join him and his friends on a fishing trip." I'd been so relieved at the sign that he was warming up to me that saying no hadn't been an option, even though the idea of hooking a fish on a line made me vaguely uneasy.

My idea of time on boats was sipping champagne on a yacht.

"He was laughing and saying we'd shoot the shit, drink beers, and buy snapper from the fish shop on the way home and pretend we'd caught it. Shit. Fuck." I slid down the wall to sit with my hands thrust into my hair. "We were all so happy. I don't understand."

The detective's expression seemed to soften as she looked down at me. "While we'll have more concrete details once the SOCOs can get in, right now it's possible that one of the three missing family members wasn't in the house at the time of the fire.

"Since both the doctors had patients they were monitoring and are known to answer their phones at all hours, there's a high likelihood that the missing member is Bobby Prasad. But we won't be able to confirm identities or the number of deceased for some time. There was significant damage and the rubble covers a wide area."

Nausea was a watery taste in my mouth.

*That violent boom of sound. The smoke so black and vicious.*

The forensic team might have only bone fragments with which to work.

# CHAPTER 8

Private notes: Detective Callum Baxter (LAPD)
Date: Dec 3
Time: 11:17

Search on Tavish Advani brought up an upscale address on Venice Beach. It also brought up his connection to Jocelyn Wai and, more specifically, to her death—have to say, I did not see that coming. Neither did Perez. We both thought Jason Musgrave was just throwing out wild accusations due to grief, but man might be onto something.

Have left a message for Detective Gina Garcia, lead on the Wai case.

# CHAPTER 9

I'm Detective Senior Sergeant Rose Ackerson," the cop said at last. "And this is my colleague Constable Jeffrey Wong."

"Tavish Advani." It was reflex, no thinking required—because obviously, they were already well aware of my identity.

"Why don't we head downstairs to talk further," Ackerson suggested after two people in street clothes passed us with curious looks, likely visitors on the way to a patient room. That interruption was followed by a doctor rushing past, his lab coat flapping.

My shoulders locked. "I don't want to be away from Diya."

"The staff member we spoke to earlier said she'll be in surgery a while longer. You'll be back well before then."

Despite her reassurance, it took all of my willpower to get up and walk even the short distance to the doors, then down the flight of stairs to the sprawling atrium . . . which was no longer drenched in sunlight, the world outside far darker than I'd realized. So many hours, Diya in surgery the entire time.

My stomach—empty, I realized, but with no real sensation of hunger—twisted.

We halted next to a wide wall away from any foot traffic.

"You found a change of clothes." Ackerson indicated my scrub top.

"A nurse gave it to me, told me to change. I guess my bloody T-shirt was unhygienic." It felt surreal to talk about clothes while two—possibly three—people were dead and the love of my life lay critically wounded in a surgical suite, while her sister-in-law fought for her life in another room.

Ackerson nodded. "We might need your T-shirt for evidentiary purposes. Is it in the waiting area?"

"No, I put it in the trash can inside the toilets near Emergency."

Ackerson gave her colleague a nod and he walked off in the direction from which I'd entered this part of the hospital. "You really shouldn't have been allowed to leave the scene," she said in a mild tone of voice. "You're a witness to a crime."

"I would've fought you if you'd tried to stop me." I folded my arms. "No way in hell was I about to let Diya go alone in the ambulance when she was bleeding and unconscious." When she could've fucking *died* before ever reaching the hospital.

"I understand that. Were you the one who called Shumi Prasad's parents?"

"I figured they should know." I wasn't liking the direction this was going—her tone might be mild, but the questions held a faint undertone that rubbed me wrong. I knew what my father would say: *Shut up and get a lawyer.* But I also knew how that would look this early into the investigation.

I had to take another tack.

"Do you think I had something to do with this? *How?* I wasn't even there." It didn't take any effort to tinge my voice with disbelief and shock. I might be the son of an Oscar-winning actress, but at this instant, I was also a grieving and angry husband with a wife who might not make it out of surgery alive.

Ackerson ignored my question. "Why weren't you at what—assuming Bobby Prasad was present—seems to have been a family meeting?"

I'd been trying not to think about that, trying not to remember how the Prasads had reacted after they first learned of our elopement. Diya hadn't even told them until we were already on the plane for the flight to Auckland, the tarmac at LAX in constant motion as planes taxied out or rolled into the gate.

Message sent, she'd shut off her phone. "Oops," she'd said with a wink. "Guess the onboard Wi-Fi isn't working."

I'd walked out of biosecurity on this end to three grim faces—and Shumi's squeal of joy as she rushed over to hug Diya. She'd been holding a sparkly balloon with *Congratulations* written on it in silver glitter, which she'd attached to Diya's suitcase.

My new sister-in-law had managed to whisper that "the parents" were "big mad" before her husband and the elder Prasads reached me and Diya. I hadn't needed the warning, not after glimpsing their faces, but I'd appreciated her loyalty to Diya all the same.

"Diya's family is close," I said today to this detective who was looking for a reason to blame the outsider. "Shumi and Bobby—or just Shumi like you said—probably dropped by to have tea or coffee and chat about the party.

"And there was so much leftover food to snack on. Containers stacked up on the counters and stuffed into the fridge." Sarita and Rajesh had told the catering and other staff to take what they wanted, but that had still left multiple unopened boxes, so Bobby and Shumi had taken some, while the rest came home with us.

"Both my mother- and father-in-law had the whole weekend off—available only for patient emergencies. Everyone was at home and able to relax together."

"Except you."

My mind wanted to torment me with thoughts of what could've been, what I could've done had I been in the house that morning. "Diya," I said, fighting past the incipient guilt because it would just make me easy prey for this cop, "asked me to drive to a bakery in the city center to pick up a box of samples in flavors she was considering for our wedding cake."

As we'd walked outside, she'd told me to enjoy zooming around in the Alfa Romeo—she knew I liked to break the speed limit on the winding road to and from Lake Tarawera. The view of the green-clad hills, the deep hues of the Blue and Green Lakes, even the misty fog high up in the mountains—it was nothing like LA, but I was starting to love the lush quiet of it, the lack of concrete barriers and endless hours on the freeway.

"You left your job in LA to move here?"

Heat under my skin, my muscles threatening to bunch at the abrupt change in the direction of the conversation.

No way could Ackerson know about Virna.

She'd died months before I ever saw Diya across that rooftop bar.

"I left the job before I met Diya," I said to the detective. "I wanted a change." The lie would stand; the firm would never air its dirty laundry, never tell Ackerson that I'd been escorted out by two security goons after Virna's son, Jason, threw a tantrum and threatened to pull his considerable investment portfolio from the firm.

"We don't believe the firm is a good fit for you any longer, Tavish." A fixed smile on the white-haired senior partner's face. "I'm afraid the situation with Virna cannot be overlooked." The merest flicker of an eyelash. "What, my dear boy, were you thinking?"

I hadn't been thinking, that was the problem.

*Never shit where you eat, son.*

Too bad I hadn't remembered my father's sage advice until it was far too late.

"Are you currently in employment?" Ackerson's voice held no judgment, but I knew what she was getting at.

It took all of my skill to keep my expression even. "I've only been in the country five weeks—I'm in the process of figuring out what certifications I need. But I have picked up a remote job in the interim—doing stock breakdowns for a business magazine."

Ackerson made another note. "Can I have your current address?"

Once again, I didn't flinch at the abrupt switch in direction—Detective Callum Baxter of the LAPD had done that, too. My father had warned me that it was a way to throw off the target, make him stumble. "We live . . . lived with Diya's parents."

"Traditional setup?"

"No. Just convenience." This cop didn't need to know that my wife hadn't been ready to move out—she'd lived with her parents all her life. Part of it was their overprotectiveness of their younger child, part of it Diya's genuine love for her mother and father—and part of it the sheer beauty of their lakeside property, which had been her home since she was sixteen.

"No rental will ever live up to this," she'd said to me with a sigh one afternoon as we stood at the end of the jetty, watching a lone paddleboarder making her way across the cool water in the shadow of Mount Tarawera.

Her arm had been tucked into mine, her head against my shoulder, her perfume a pretty thing with surprisingly dark notes beneath.

I'd looked down at the black silk of her curls. "Will you mind? Not having all this? At least not straightaway?" I had every intention of building my wife her own personal paradise. All I needed was time . . . and the ability to access the money no one official had yet managed to find.

A year, perhaps even two, and we'd be set for life. *If* I wasn't impatient.

Diya had aimed a joyous smile up at me. "Not a bit," she'd said. "In LA, with you at your condo, that was the first time I'd ever experienced life without being watched over by my parents and brother.

"Even the week we met, while I was with my friends, they knew the hotel I was in, had the itinerary of the entire bachelorette weekend." A pause, her gaze back on the lake. "I know they mean well, but it's starting to suffocate me."

*I told you, I have enough! I'm not answering any more calls if you're going to be like this!*

The pills in the brown bottles, Bobby asking me if I understood Diya's needs, her mother's penetrating gaze on Diya when the black shadows began to gather. And my wife, whimpering and crying in her sleep, with no memory of it when she woke.

My nightmares had stopped after I landed in New Zealand.

Diya's had begun . . . or returned, with a vengeance.

Enclosing those vulnerable truths behind a wall of privacy, I answered Ackerson's question with a different truth. "Diya and I have been looking for our own rental over the past couple of weeks, but there's not that much available in the area, and Diya's business is based here." My wince was real. "Trust me, it wasn't my choice to bunk with my in-laws—I've been living on my own since I left for college."

Pursing her lips, Ackerson nodded. "Yes, my son's having trouble finding a good rental, too. Market's tight." She put away her notebook. "You don't want to buy in?"

It was a clever way to ask about my financial situation. Thankfully, I had an answer for her. "My money's tied up in my condo—plus I don't have a residence visa yet. Honestly, we haven't done all the research, but I'm guessing it'll be easier for us to buy together as a couple once I'm a permanent resident."

"Right." Ackerson put her hands on her hips, pushing back the sides of her jacket. "You still have family in the States?"

"My parents, and one elder brother and his family." Though to call us siblings was a gross overreach; that implied we'd grown up together—simply having occupied the same house as minors didn't count. "My father's helping me list my condo for sale. It's in an excellent area, but I don't want to sell low and quick—Diya agrees we should wait for a good offer."

Blowing out a breath, Ackerson looked straight at me, our eyes locked. "Be honest, Tavish. Do you think one of the family could've done this?"

"Absolutely not." I sliced out a hand. "If you'd seen them together, you'd never ask that. They're *tight* . . . were tight." I swallowed. "Shumi is Diya's best friend. Bobby and Shumi used to come over every weekend for family dinners and barbecues, and Diya spent at least twenty minutes every day just hanging out with her parents after they got home from work. They enjoyed each other."

I'd found it all a bit too much, but I was also aware that my family dynamic wasn't exactly a healthy one. And if it made Diya happy, I wasn't about to stand in her way. "It *was* overwhelming for me," I decided to admit, because one look at the profile of the Advani clan and Ackerson would know the truth anyway. "My family is the opposite. We all do our own thing."

"All that togetherness must've made you nuts."

"They weren't obnoxious about it." No forced invitations, no expectation that I'd come down to hang out each time Diya did. "And it was by the lake—when I needed a breather, I just went for a walk along the edge, or out on the jetty."

I leaned my head back against the wall, staring up at the darkness beyond the atrium's glass roof for a moment. "And I don't want to give you the wrong impression about Diya—she went out with her girlfriends, too. Dinners, chick-flick dates, brunches, that kind of thing."

I'd met three of her girlfriends at the engagement party. I only remembered the name of one—Carolyn something—and had been struck by the fact that I knew less than nothing about her and the two others; Diya didn't tend to talk about them except to mention their names when she was planning to meet one or all three.

In my head, I'd filed them under the more-casual-friend category.

"Did Shumi Prasad often accompany your wife on these outings? You did say they were best friends."

I frowned, flipped through the pages of memory. "I never thought about it, but no, she didn't, especially not if it was at night. She's devoted to Bobby." I'd never once seen her go against him, even in the most playful argument. "Maybe she's a bit more traditional in her thinking? The wife staying home with her husband kind of thing?"

I shrugged, because honestly, I was guessing. I hadn't spent that much one-on-one time with the other woman. "She and Diya did things alone together, though—coffees, getting their nails done." Perhaps Shumi found that acceptable because Diya was Bobby's sister, and thus Shumi wasn't stepping out on her commitment to Bobby and their marriage by spending time with her.

Ackerson's expression shifted subtly, more tension to her jawline, more darkness in her eyes. "You have any other ideas of who we should be looking at? Given the stabbings, the likely accelerant-enhanced fire, and multiple victims in the bright light of day, it's highly unlikely to be a random intruder."

"Overkill," I said, my throat dry. "That's the word they use on the TV cop shows."

"Yes, unfortunately that's the correct description. Because while, at present, we have no way of knowing how the other victims died, we can extrapolate from what we know of Diya's and Shumi's wounds."

*. . . no way of knowing how the other victims died . . .*

My stomach lurched, my mind creating horrific images of what the cops might find of my in-laws. Rajesh and Sarita had both been fit and toned—though Rajesh had started to develop a small belly despite his daily vigorous swims, and Sarita had been muttering about how the sari looked on her taut runner's frame.

"I think I've put on some weight around the hips," she'd said to Diya in my hearing. "I'll have to change my running route, add in a few more hills."

The fire had consumed that troublesome flesh, their bones the only pieces of them that remained.

Swallowing, I said, "From what I saw of how people came up to them when we were out in public together, my in-laws were trusted and good doctors." One woman had cried in the ice-cream aisle of the supermarket while hugging my mother-in-law.

"They even won an award recently for the surgical forums they hold for trainee doctors in Fiji—that's where they emigrated from. I think maybe they even offer a scholarship for one student a year from Fiji to train in New Zealand."

Diya had been born in the tropical island nation, as had Bobby, though neither carried any trace of their parents' unique accent.

"You didn't mention your brother-in-law," Ackerson prompted.

I pressed my lips together.

"No point protecting anyone now, Tavish. You need to tell me what you know."

"Fuck." I shoved a hand through my hair.

# CHAPTER 10

Private notes: Detective Callum Baxter (LAPD)
Date: Dec 5
Time: 14:15

Virna Musgrave's attorney is in the process of gathering details about the current value of her estate but was able to confirm a ballpark figure of "around fifteen to twenty million" as her net worth.

No legal paperwork exists for the alleged quarter-of-a-million-dollar transfer to Tavish Advani, and we haven't yet gained access to Virna's financial records. Interesting thing is that Advani isn't exactly doing it hard, either, not from what we can see on the surface. We'll need to dig deeper.

Time: 20:18

Forensic mechanic refuses to speculate on anything to do with the Musgrave vehicle, but he did admit that he's already spotted signs of tampering.

Case is now a homicide in my books. Perez agrees.

# CHAPTER 11

Diya mentioned that her brother fired some employees recently," I told Ackerson. "Bobby owns and runs that big electronics store in the center of town, has several more branches around the country."

"Elektrik Ninja?"

"Yes. I don't know the reason for the firings, but apparently the people he fired weren't happy about it." I folded my arms, suddenly cold. "They're the only ones I can think of who might've had reason to be angry with any of the family. But it still doesn't make sense that they'd come for *all* of them."

Unless, of course, the Prasads had had a stake in their son's company. Perhaps they'd even been silent investors. Given the family's closeness, that would make sense.

"We'll check that out. People have done worse things when driven by anger."

My nape prickled, and I wondered if I was imagining the glint in her eye. It had to be my paranoia—no way she could've dug up any real information on me so fast. "So the fire was set on purpose?" I asked.

"That's what it's looking like."

"And the explosion? Was that on purpose, too?"

"Fire investigator will work on finding an answer to that question, but it can be complicated—lot of things can set off an explosion." Taking out her phone even though it hadn't made a sound, she glanced at it. "One more question," she said after putting it back in her pocket. "This might be me buying into the stereotype, but a lot of doctors end up with doctor kids. Why not here?"

I gave a hollow laugh. "I actually asked Diya that, because you're right—especially in South Asian immigrant families. If not a doctor, then at least a lawyer or an engineer." My family had been different, only one son set up for success—and in a field most immigrant families would never countenance.

But then, the Advani family had never toed any line when it came to tradition. Sometimes I'd wondered if that was why I felt so rootless, so divorced from life. Then I'd met Diya and understood that I'd been searching for her. She was my roots, was the solid earth under my feet.

"Diya told me that Bobby was determined to make his own way—and he was really good at mechanical-type things from childhood. She said there was tension when he was younger, but it evaporated once his parents saw how good he was at what he'd chosen."

*As for me, I'm the baby of the family. No one ever pushed me too hard.*

The words had been playful, her eyes gleeful.

I hadn't found the little brown bottles back then. And we still hadn't talked about it. Now I told Ackerson the gist of what Diya had said. Let her believe my wife was just spoiled; better that than she start digging into the private pain that tormented the woman I adored.

"Where can I find you if I need to talk to you?" the detective said in response.

"Probably here." I gave her my cell number and had the thought that I'd have to buy a charger—the battery would be flat by tomorrow.

"I probably don't have to tell you this, but the house is off-limits," Ackerson said after inputting my number into her phone. "There's nothing there you can salvage anyway."

Pain shot through my jaw as I remembered Diya's dad watering his prized lawn, her mum pointing out the designer wallpaper mural she'd had hung on one wall of the lounge as a feature. They'd been so proud of that house, of building something so beautiful after coming to New Zealand as doctors from a small island nation whose qualifications weren't automatically recognized.

They'd worked hard to gain the right to practice here.

"What about the cars? Can I get access to one of them?" They were likely damaged from shrapnel sent out by the explosion, or just from proximity to the heat, but hopefully at least one was still in working order.

"The entire property is off-limits for the time being. If you need funds, I can get—"

"No, I have my cards on me." Diya had bought me my sleek black wallet as a gift, even had it monogrammed with my initials in a muted bronze that suited me far better than gold or silver. "When . . . when will you know anything?"

"It's a big scene, a lot to process. It's going to be a while." She passed a slightly crumpled card to me. "My contact information."

After accepting it, I thought of what Diya would want me to do. "The funerals?" My mouth was dry, my hands a second away from trembling. I had no idea how to organize one funeral, much less two and possibly *three*.

"Don't plan anything yet. There's no guarantee when the remains will be released."

*Remains, not bodies.*

I just nodded, grateful that Shumi's parents were flying over. They'd know what to do for the Prasads, the rituals that were to be followed. My in-laws hadn't been heavily religious, but I'd seen a small prayer alcove in the house, caught the distinctive scent of incense two or three mornings a week.

Their faith had mattered to them.

"Wishing your wife and your sister-in-law a fast recovery," Ackerson said, the rote words sounding rehearsed and stiff.

I thanked her regardless, because right now, she was my only way into the investigation.

She paused before leaving. "Keep me informed of your movements, Tavish. I don't want to waste time chasing you down."

My pulse accelerated at what had sounded very much like a subtle threat, but, well-versed in dealing with cops, I just nodded again and stood slumped against the wall for long minutes after she'd left. It was clear that Ackerson considered me a suspect. She didn't need to have any information from the LA cops.

All it would've taken was a simple online search.

The name Tavish Advani had been splashed all over the news and gossip sites three and a half years ago, when Jocelyn fell from her luxury apartment on the ninth floor, her body a shattered doll on the pavement.

*Jocelyn Wai's Boy Toy Lover Taken in for Questioning!*

*Did She Fall or Was She PUSHED?*

*Model, Philanthropist, Socialite . . . Murder Victim?*

Accusations and insinuations like that tended to stick. Especially after they'd been raked up again in the wake of Virna's accident.

If I didn't get my head on straight, figure things out, Ackerson might railroad me right back into a nightmare I'd barely escaped. One of the first things I planned to do was call my father and ask him for the contact of a good local criminal defense attorney. Just in case.

"Mr. Advani?"

I jerked at the sound of the nurse's voice; it was the same nurse who'd found an answer for me when I'd asked if Diya was still in surgery. That he'd tracked me down outside the ward had my heart thumping.

"Is my wife out of surgery?"

"Yes." He held up a hand when I would've rushed past. "But you have to be prepared—she's in a critical state."

"I understand." Happy to get even a glimpse of Diya, I followed the nurse upstairs. The woman with the unread book was gone from the waiting area, but the couple was still there; they offered me small, tired smiles when I passed by—and I realized they must've told the nurse I'd gone downstairs with the police.

"Thank you," I mouthed to them before we turned left to close the short distance to the ICU.

It was easy to find my wife once I was through the doors; the three patient beds I could see were placed in a generous space directly in front of the nurses' station—from where the staff could keep a constant eye on them and intervene at a second's notice. However, that was the secondary level of care—the first would come, I saw, from the nurses seated at the small stations directly in front of the beds.

One nurse to one patient.

The seats and desks for the assigned nurses were higher than the beds, so they could easily monitor their patients.

Each bed also had a curtain that could be pulled fully around it for privacy—as long as the nurses never lost their line of sight.

Only Diya's curtains were pushed all the way back right now.

And Diya, my Diya, looked so small and pale, far too many lines going out of her, far too many machines surrounding her. The intricate mehndi of which she'd been so proud stood out stark and dark, almost as if it was hovering above her skin . . . but for the spots marred by white strips of plaster to hold various lines in place.

Heavier wound dressings covered the side of her neck and the skin by her collarbone on the other side; no part of her body visible above the blanket was free of the evidence of violence. There was even a large, square dressing on the side of her skull.

I hadn't realized she'd been stabbed there, there'd been so much blood everywhere. Her hair must've been matted to the wound. I wondered if the doctors or nurses had had to shave off a patch to check the wound.

Diya would no doubt scrunch up her face when she woke and realized. Then she'd laugh and shrug and probably go hunting for a vintage hair clip to help cover up the spot while her skin and hair recovered.

"Baby, I'm here." I gently touched her foot through the blanket.

"I can arrange something for you if you want to stay here," the nurse who'd brought me in said a few minutes later, "but I suggest you go home and get a few hours of proper sleep. You can talk to the surgeon tomorrow—she had to respond to another patient or she'd be here now. I can tell you that your wife's been placed into a medically induced coma due to . . ."

I wasn't listening, my focus on the rise and fall of Diya's chest, the butterfly beat of her pulse against her skin. She was alive. The woman I loved with all my heart and soul, the woman I'd watched put out seeds for baby birds every spring morning, the woman who'd danced with me in the glitter and glamour of Vegas, was alive.

I wanted to stay with her all night, just watch her breathe, but I knew the nurse was right. I had to start thinking, had to start trying to figure out what had gone so horribly wrong. Not just for Diya, but because right now, I was the perfect gift-wrapped suspect in the multiple murders and attempted murders of the Prasad family.

Sweat broke out over my back, my tongue feeling too fat in my mouth.

Because this time, I was innocent.

# CHAPTER 12

Private notes: Detective Callum Baxter (LAPD)
Date: Dec 11
Time: 10:17

Interview with Tavish Advani. Full record in official file.

Good-looking, articulate, highly intelligent. Cooperated fully, admitted that Virna had given him a monetary "gift" in the range of a quarter of a million, and appeared embarrassed when I pointed out the client-adviser relationship he'd had with Virna.

"I screwed up," he said. "We became friends, and when she offered, I was in a tight spot. She told me it was loose change to her. I still should have said no, but she was so insistent that I allow her to help me."

Not sure what I think of him, but I can see why Virna was charmed. He's barely a couple of months past twenty-six, but he knows how to talk and say exactly the right words. None of that bullshit young asshole stuff—man is smart and smooth. Big difference between running a love con on a rich and vulnerable older lady and murder, though.

Perez says it's a slippery slope. He's definitely got Advani as his number one suspect.

Especially since unconfirmed rumor is that Advani was fired from his job a couple of days ago after Jason Musgrave kicked up a stink at Advani's old investment firm. That job came with a serious six-figure pay packet—which leaves us the question of why Advani was in a tight spot in the first place.

Man should've been swimming in money.

# CHAPTER 13

Aleki had left a duffel bag for me with someone he knew at the hospital, and shot me a text: Hey man, they said you were up in the ICU and I wasn't sure if I could get in. My auntie JJ has your stuff with her at the nurse's station in Maternity. Call me if you need anything—I mean it.

His aunt proved to be a matronly Samoan woman who gave me a silent pat on the hand when she handed over the battered duffel bag. Aleki hadn't just gotten me the T-shirts I'd asked for; he'd bought me a toothbrush, toothpaste, even a razor and some soap, along with a set of sweatpants, a hoodie, and a box of protein bars.

I couldn't think of anyone in LA who'd have done this for me, who'd have been so thoughtful about it. And my family was based in the city.

The people I'd called friends . . . they'd gotten the gloss and shine of Tavish Advani, investment adviser and child of A-lister Audrey Advani. None of them knew *me*. Several had, however, picked up the phone when the Musgrave case hit the headlines.

False sympathy. An avaricious desire for drama and gossip.

Not their fault. I'd chosen to make friends with them, hadn't I? I'd chosen to be the kind of man who surrounded himself with people who boosted my ego with their own status and glamour. Chasing love, my therapist had told me when I'd decided to go get my head shrunk after Jocelyn's death.

"You really have to stop associating with vacuous people who say all the right things and fill up your days with meaningless company," the bespectacled woman had advised. "What you need is the opposite. Not a shallow crowd but one or two people who see you down to the bone and call you on your bullshit."

She would've liked Diya . . . but she would've liked Susanne most of all.

Susanne, Jocelyn, Virna, all had been touchpoints in my life before the luminous supernova of Diya, but it was Susanne who'd left the biggest, deepest mark.

*Remember me after I'm gone, Tav. Be disgraceful now and then in my memory.*

I'd never forget the woman who'd been the making of me.

She'd be so disappointed in what I'd done, what I'd become after her death.

After sending Aleki a thank-you message, I found a room in a motel not far from the hospital.

While food wasn't topmost in my mind, my body reminded me that I hadn't eaten anything since breakfast and it was now after dark. Diya and I had been planning to have lunch together, picking our meal from the leftovers. All we'd have had to do was put a few things on an oven tray, heat them up for ten minutes.

"I can't wait! I saw an entire box of those tiny croissants filled with smoked chicken in the fridge." Diya had rubbed her flat abdomen. "I hardly ate any of it last night because I didn't want my stomach to start pooching. The waist of my lehenga was way too tight to forgive a few pastries."

I'd rolled my eyes. "Baby, your idea of pooching is my idea of sexy."

A scowl ruined by a smile before she'd run to sit on my lap and kiss me like it was the first time all over again. "Mmm, you taste like coffee." Soft, breathy words. "I could eat you up."

That was how we'd ended up back in bed, and she'd been late for her shower. Had that been the moment that sealed her fate? Because earlier, she'd talked about riding along with me to pick up the cakes, but after we'd made love in the morning sunlight that slanted in through the apartment's triangular windows, she'd decided to stay home, do her hair routine.

I hadn't even thought about it, had just told her I'd be back soon. Now she lay fighting for her life.

My stomach lurched, but, aware I had to function if I wasn't going to end up in an interrogation room, leaving Diya alone, I ordered delivery from a Thai place, then had a shower. The food arrived ten minutes after I'd finished; I sat and ate it with methodical focus while skipping through the motel's extensive list of channels until I finally hit on an evening news recap.

The fire was the lead item.

*"Rotorua residents were shocked to hear of a fatal house fire in the Lake Tarawera community earlier today. The house belonged to husband and wife Drs. Rajesh and Sarita Prasad—two of the four partners of the Rotorua Fertility & Gynecological Group. While fire crews were able to stop the blaze from spreading to neighboring properties thanks in part to the Prasad property's extensive lawns, the Prasad house is in ruins.*

*You can't see the property from where I'm standing at the top of the drive, but we were able to get footage from the lake earlier, and as you can see, the damage is catastrophic. Neighbors report finding pieces of the home in their own yards, and we spotted debris floating in the lake.*

*The police have confirmed that they're currently in the process of recovering human remains from the site, though it will take some time before they're able to confirm the identities of the victims. However, from what the neighbors have told us, and what we've gleaned from the shocked and distraught staff at the fertility clinic, it's highly likely that both doctors were inside at the time of the incident.*

*We've also been able to ascertain that two people did survive the fire and are in critical condition in Rotorua Hospital. Unconfirmed reports state that the two survivors showed signs of non-accidental injuries."*

*"Sonia, do I have it correct, there are indications of foul play?"*

*"Yes, David. Police have announced a press conference tomorrow afternoon at four where they intend to share further information. For now, they're focusing on identifying the victims and beginning the first stages of what is no doubt going to be a very complex investigation."*

There was nothing else of note in the rest of the report, but for the images of the house itself. The reporter had found her way onto the lake in time to get footage of the home while it was still burning, then had stuck around to get shots of the blackened and ruined aftermath, with the fire hoses pumping out foam to dampen the last embers.

The house was gone. So was the garage apartment.

All the photos pinned to the huge corkboard in Diya's suite in the main house. All the tiny animal figurines she'd collected since girlhood. All the black-and-white images from her maternal and paternal grandparents' lives in Fiji that her mum was so protective of because they had no backups beyond physical negatives—which had also been in the house.

Gone.

A family's entire history erased from existence.

I switched off the TV and tried to make some sort of sense of it all. I couldn't, my head thick with foggy thoughts when I finally fell into a restless sleep.

———————

Jocelyn sat across from me in the dream, a cigarette in her mouth as she dealt cards with the speed of a Vegas dealer. Glossy black hair in a sleek bun, high cheekbones further defined by makeup, those striking green-black eyes that had first led a sixteen-year-old girl from her humble village in Henan Province, China, to the catwalks of Milan and Paris.

Then later, straight into back-to-back hit movies.

Even at sixty-one, she was considered a timeless beauty and still had a number of deals with companies that wanted her to wear their clothing and jewelry at various high-profile events.

"You don't smoke those!" I blurted out. "You always say they're cheap rubbish."

"I borrowed it from some odious man, love. Every dealer should have a cigarette, after all." She pretended to stub the unlit cigarette on the table before just leaving it there. "How much do you want to bet?" Her accent was "European," as she'd put it—a mélange of her original accent and all the other places she'd lived and worked.

"Calling it European sounds so much better than saying I'm a vocal mongrel," she'd said with a laugh one night as we drank together.

Jocelyn Wai was known for her bawdy humor, but in private, she could go straight to crass.

I'd liked that about her, liked that she had no filter.

"Bet, Tavish," she said again, drawing out my name as she always did until it sounded more like *Ta-veesh*. "Come on, this suey isn't going to chop itself."

Pure Jocelyn. Taking the racial epithets and comments that had been directed her way before power and fame and making them a part of her signature snark.

Too real. Too much.

"I don't want to do this anymore." I tried to push away from the table but the chair wouldn't move.

"Oh really?" Jocelyn's husky laughter drew my attention back to her. "Because of her? The love of your life? That insipid child? Oh, please. You were already bored of her before this unfortunate . . . accident. Such a shame she survived."

"Shut up!" I flipped the table over, scattering the cards. "I love Diya!"

Jocelyn smiled. "You loved me, too, once." Sorrow in her eyes. "What happened, Tavish? Did I get too old?" Her face began to crack and rot in front of me.

"Joss, no! Joss!"

But she wasn't listening, her now-skeletal face focused on the cards she was dealing into empty air. "I screamed as I fell. The air cut like ice against my skin even though it was a warm night. Did you hear me?"

Flames licked around her, the scent of burned flesh in the air.

And suddenly, her face was Diya's, the hands that dealt the cards coated in blood.

"Diya!" I jolted up in the flimsy motel bed, my scream yet reverberating in my throat and the sheet pasted to my sweat-soaked skin.

The clock blinked 3:07 in the morning.

The time of Jocelyn's fall.

When even LA had been silent and quiet, no one awake to hear that scream.

"I wasn't there," I reminded myself. "I was at Danny's apartment, crashed out on his couch because we'd tied one on that night." My heart continued to thunder. "I *wasn't* there." It was a mantra I'd repeated over and over while waiting for Detective Gina Garcia to call me back to the station for an interview.

Hands shaky, I shoved off the sheet and walked into the bathroom. The compulsion to check my buried offshore account using my phone was almost overwhelming. That was my one rule: to never ever access that account using any device that could be traced back to me. Only once I'd successfully maneuvered the money through various channels would it be safe for me to touch.

Until then, it might as well be poison.

I stepped into the shower, turned the water to cold.

"Fuck." The shock snapped me out of the last hazy pieces of the nightmare, shoving my brain from the obsessive line of thought that could land me in a prison cell. "I didn't kill Jocelyn," I said aloud. "I did not kill Jocelyn. I loved Jocelyn."

But not as much as I loved Diya.

I'd never loved anyone as much as I loved Diya.

Not even Susanne.

# CHAPTER 14

Private notes: Detective Callum Baxter (LAPD)
Date: Dec 12
Time: I-should-be-home o'clock

Perez uncovered an interesting fact about Tavish Advani—that fancy condo isn't a rental. It's his. Transferred to his name when he was roughly twenty-two.

Probably courtesy of the bank of Mom and Dad, but Perez is going to chase it down.

Meanwhile, I still can't get a bead on the guy—women definitely like him, but he doesn't strike me as the playboy type. He's more focused, more the kind who could make one woman believe she was his everything, and that's not exactly unusual. Henry over in Traffic marries women like it's his job, gets bored, and moves on.

Only difference with Advani is the money involved. Is he targeting rich older women or does he just end up with rich older women because he grew up in that environment?

I need to talk to someone he actually dated. It's not looking good—so far, he's two for two when it comes to dead ex-girlfriends.

# CHAPTER 15

The next day, I learned that the Rotorua Hospital ICU had a generous visiting policy.

"As long as you're not disruptive," the charge nurse told me, "we're not going to kick you out. If you want to visit after the main doors are closed, ask the security guys downstairs. I'll make sure they know you're to be let up." Her eyes were sympathetic.

"Can you tell me anything about my sister-in-law? Her family won't be here till later in the day, so I'm all the family she has for now."

I was expecting her to stonewall me, but she said, "Her father instructed that you're to be kept updated on Shumi Prasad's status. Honestly, she's much the same as your wife. Since the ICU is full, she's next door, in the Coronary Care Unit, which also functions as the ICU overflow area.

"You can go look in on her when you're ready—it's just through here." She pointed to an internal hallway. "No locked door between the two units, but check in with the nursing staff when you enter so they know who you are."

"Thank you. I'll go visit after I spend some time with my wife."

When I walked over to Diya, I saw that someone on the staff had placed an armchair beside her bed in an act of silent compassion. I also consciously noticed the monitors on either side of the bed and what appeared to be some kind of a mechanical arm on the ceiling.

A hoist, I guessed, to help with patients who needed to be moved. I didn't have enough interest to ask for confirmation, Diya my sole focus.

After pulling the curtain so we'd have at least a little privacy—but making sure I didn't block the line of sight of the monitoring nurse—I sat down in the armchair and held Diya's hand, the intricate filigree of mehndi on it seeming even darker today.

"They say the darker a bride's mehndi," she'd told me, "the happier and more loved she'll be in her marriage."

But my bride lay broken in a space filled with the sound of mechanical breaths, the brunette nurse who watched her—whose name I'd learned was Hazel—rising every hour to record her vital signs. "Any change?" I asked each time.

The answer was the same. "No."

Diya's life hung in precarious balance, a fact her surgeon confirmed when she came by later that day. "How much information do you want?" she asked with a bluntness I guessed might be typical for surgeons.

"Don't worry about detail," I said, because the last thing I wanted to know was how many times she'd been stabbed. "I'm only interested in her overall status. We can discuss the specifics with her after she wakes."

Nodding, the surgeon said, "Overall status is critical. The head wound worries me—we'll be monitoring that constantly. I repaired her abdominal injuries but they were significant, so she's not out of the woods yet. Liver and kidney injuries on their own wouldn't put her in the ICU, but infection is always a risk."

Each word was acid on my skin.

The only good news that day was that Shumi's parents would be landing in Auckland early that afternoon. The Kumar clan had intended to rent a car to drive the three hours to Rotorua rather than waiting for the next flight to the city, but I'd talked them out of it.

"It's a long drive and you're not in the best frame of mind." I'd driven like a maniac after being notified of Jocelyn's death, and almost plowed straight into a concrete freeway barrier. "The last thing Shumi needs is for you to get in an accident. The closest flight to your arrival into Auckland will get you here not that much later than if you drove."

It had been Shumi's younger brother who'd convinced her parents I was right. "We need to be there for Shumi," Ajay had said. "None of us are thinking straight. We shouldn't be driving."

Now I took Diya's cold hand in mine, held it. "I'm here, baby," I said in a quiet tone that wouldn't reach Hazel. "I'll find out what happened." I pressed my lips to her skin, wishing I could give her the life that pumped inside my body so she'd laugh again, dance again.

My wife loved to dance, had pulled me into a dance on the sandy edge of Lake Tarawera just the other night, the only music a faint hint of a guitar being strummed somewhere along the lakefront.

Her eyes had sparkled as she looked up at me. "I never thought I'd meet my soulmate; never thought I'd get the chance to know someone like I know you. I love you, Tavi."

No one knew me.

Susanne had come the closest, but I'd been different then. Younger, more vulnerable.

I hadn't tried to hide myself from Diya . . . but I hadn't wanted her to know about the murky corners, the places where the darkness gathered and churned. Hadn't wanted to scare her, lose her.

"I'll tell you everything," I whispered to her, emotion a thick lump in my throat. "So you really will know me inside out. Just wake up. *Please.*" Rising, I pressed a careful kiss to the undamaged slope of her cheek, then opened up the curtains so all the nurses had an unobstructed view of their patient.

My eye snagged on the vista through the large windows behind her bed as I finished—trees bright with spring green leaves, even a glimpse of water.

*Lake Rotorua.*

I struggled with the disconnect—how could my young, beautiful, and talented wife lie so badly wounded in a place where sunlight slanted through the windows, while a lake lapped peacefully beyond?

"Tavish?" Hazel's soft voice. "Are you all right?"

Turning away from the surreal view, I said, "I have to leave her for a little while. Please take care of her."

"She'll never be out of our sight, I promise. If I have to get up, one of my colleagues will keep their eyes on her."

It hurt to walk away from Diya, but after that talk with Detective Ackerson, I knew I couldn't rely on her to unearth the truth. She'd zeroed in on me. The new husband. The outsider. The man whose last two girlfriends had died in accidents that had emblazoned his name across the headlines.

Before I left, however, I looked in on Shumi. My sister-in-law seemed, to my nonmedical eye, to be in a worse state than Diya, even more tubes going out from her body, even more bandages—including one on her face.

I didn't try to find out if that had been a stab injury, didn't want to know.

Having already asked the ICU staff to contact me should there be a significant change in either Diya's or Shumi's status and received their agreement, I went outside the hospital and called a car using a rideshare app.

If I was going to figure this out, I had to start at the beginning.

"Damn," the twentysomething driver said as he pulled up outside the gates of the Prasad property a half hour later. "Was this your place?" His faded blue eyes were huge as he looked over the steering wheel. "Sorry to hear what happened."

Not saying anything, I got out.

The driver lingered as I crossed the street to stand in front of the crime scene tape that was a visual fence across the property. I could see a police cruiser a bit further down the drive. A couple of cops were sitting in it, but they stayed put when I made no move to step past the tape.

From here, I couldn't glimpse anything of the house.

"Tavish, isn't it?" It was the neighbor who'd run toward the fire with me. "I'm Tim—I know it must be difficult remembering so many new people." He followed my gaze. "We can see the property from our place. Did you want to . . ."

"Yes." I didn't know why; it wouldn't make any difference to my knowledge of the situation, but I had to see.

Tim didn't talk as he led me to his house and up to the back deck using the external steps. That deck would've previously looked down on part of the roof of the Prasads' single-level residence, the rest of the property obscured by trees. Now Tim's family had an expansive view across what had been Rajesh and Sarita's home.

Ash and charred beams, blackened grass and dead trees, that was all that remained. The lake lapped placidly to the left, a silent witness to the horror that had taken place here twenty-four hours ago.

A lone canoeist rowed past, his neck turned to take in the destruction.

Movement. Someone walking through the rubble, a white blot against scorched soil.

"The forensic people have been here since late yesterday—I guess they had to wait for the site to be declared safe," Tim said. "They still didn't go in deep that I saw. I don't know if they worked through the night, but they were here at first light this morning when I took the dog out."

I knew one of those people was probably a fire investigator, while others had to be connected to the police or the ME's office—I didn't know how it worked in this country, who took responsibility for what, but I had enough general knowledge to guess the kind of specialists who'd be looking at the scene.

*Bone people.*

Forensic anthropologists, I think they were called. They'd have to be brought in if the bodies had been shattered into innumerable shards. So many pieces that they couldn't tell if two or three people had been inside that house.

Because Ackerson still hadn't contacted me with an update on the number of fatalities, despite the fact that the forensic teams had been working the site since late the previous day.

"The Alfa Romeo's down there, isn't it?" Tim's face was sympathetic when I made myself look away from the carnage. "Cops say when you can have it back?"

I shook my head. "They're treating all the vehicles as part of the crime scene. I'll need to rent a car. Can you recommend a local place?"

Tim looked over to the room that flowed onto the deck. The kitchen, I realized after seeing the long sink tap in the window. A small rectangle of glass, the majority reserved for the walls that faced the lake.

"Hannah and I were talking last night," the other man said, "and we'd really love to lend you our spare vehicle. It's a beater and we were planning to give it to our boy when he got his license, but he's okay with us lending it to you. No rush to return it. Joseph isn't planning to sit his learner license test until after he finishes up the school year, and then he has to take driving lessons."

The generosity made my hands clench on the balcony railing. "You're sure?"

"Absolutely. And if you need a place to stay, we have a spare room."

I couldn't stand the idea of being stuck with people who'd be watching me with sympathetic eyes the entire time. And if worse came to worst, and Ackerson didn't drop her suspicions, they'd start to look at me with fear or judgment or prurient curiosity instead.

I'd been through it all before.

"Thank you," I said, "but I found a place near the hospital." The nightly fee was one I could afford even with my depleted accessible account, and the family-owned motel was clean and well maintained.

If I did run out of funds, I'd ask my father to transfer me some money. He'd send it, no questions asked, but only up to a point, so I had to be careful with my spending. Because behind closed doors, feared attorney Anand Advani answered to his wife, any money he sent me coming out of his assigned "personal" funds. The rest went into Anand and Audrey's joint account.

And Audrey would burst a vein at the idea of giving her second son a single red cent. Which was why I'd stolen it. Slowly, and with infinite care, over a period of years, until I had a seven-figure sum sitting in that offshore account. I'd also managed to hang on to it through sheer spite even as I flushed the rest of my money down an endless black hole. Because it had mattered that I have the money, *Audrey's* money. A revenge I'd told myself was ice-cold but that had been born in a child's anguish.

Now that emotion-fueled decision could hang me if it came to light.

*It won't,* I told myself. *She doesn't have a clue, will never have a clue. That's the whole point. To make a fool out of her in front of her face and laugh over her grave when she dies.*

Yes, I had a shit ton of mommy issues.

"Oh right, it makes sense you'd want to be close to Diya and Shumi." Tim's smile was open, his eyes searching. "Will you have breakfast with us?"

"No, but thank you." All at once, I didn't want to be near the house, the smell of soot and fire in my every breath. "If you're sure about the car?"

"Of course. Let me get the keys."

The car wasn't as much of a beater as he'd made it out to be—a small gray sedan, it started straightaway and only had a couple of minor dings in the door. It was a few years old, with knobs and dials for the temperature and other controls, and a radio with a limited bandwidth, but it'd get me where I needed to go.

After thanking Tim one more time, I drove out to the nearest mall to grab the charger I needed, along with a second pair of jeans, a pack of socks, extra boxer briefs, and a stick of deodorant.

The last thing I wanted to do was stink of sweat while talking to Ackerson or the other cops; they'd take it as a sign of guilt.

Dumping everything in the trunk afterward, I shut it, then drove right back to the hospital.

The first ICU patient I saw when I walked in was a Māori man whose age I couldn't tell due to his injuries, his body showing signs of some kind of a catastrophic accident. The woman who sat beside him was reading quietly to him from what looked like a doorstop of a fantasy novel.

Her exhausted eyes met mine for a heartbeat, a painful understanding passing between us before I moved past.

Seeing a nurse with Diya when I reached her bed, I said, "Is everything okay?"

"Yes. I'm just checking her dressings." After doing that, she pulled the curtains closed on either side of the bed but left the front open to the view of the nurses' station. "Hazel's on a break, but Maria's monitoring Diya from the station."

I was glad of the droplet of additional privacy. "Hi, baby." I leaned over to lightly brush my lips over the side of Diya's.

I hated the tube that came out of the other side of her mouth because it meant my beautiful wife couldn't breathe on her own. The ventilator hissed, its mechanical breaths a constant pulse interspersed with beeps from other machines.

Her lips were soft, slicked over with something. The nurses, taking care of her. But it wasn't what she would've used. Diya had a very specific five-step skin-care routine for the morning and an even longer one for nighttime. "I'll get you that raspberry-flavored stuff you like. Korean beauty products, right? See? I do pay attention when you tell me these things."

Her hand remained motionless, her hair tangled on the pillow. I tried to smooth it out as gently as I could. "Who's Annie, baby?" I murmured, thinking of how desperately she'd tried to tell me something when I'd first found her.

*Annie . . . they said . . . about Annie . . . not . . .*

But she was silent, and when a doctor walked in, I took the opportunity to ask him about Diya's injuries in detail. It had struck me that I'd been wrong to tell the surgeon to stick to generalities—the exact nature of Diya's wounds might tell me something about who'd done this to her.

"No smoke inhalation that we can determine," Dr. Chen said, his voice far deeper than I'd expected given his near-skeletal frame.

"Your wife must've managed to get out before the fire really took hold. Eleven stab wounds. Six of them were superficial—but five went deep enough to do significant damage. One in particular only missed severing her abdominal aorta by a millimeter."

He pointed to Diya's stomach. "That one caused the worst bleeding, but the ones that hit her kidney and inferior vena cava as well as her liver, along with the one at her neck, are the most dangerous. A little longer before getting her to the ER and it might've been too late." His manner was brusque and pragmatic, taking the emotion out of the situation.

It helped. "How long before you know if she's out of the woods?"

"No way to tell at this stage," the doctor said. "Right now, it's watch and wait. Especially when it comes to her head injury."

My phone buzzed. I'd have ignored it except that I'd just realized the time. "That might be Shumi's family." Taking it out, I glanced at the message. "They're here, coming up to the ICU."

Maybe they would know about Annie, this woman whose name Diya had never spoken until she lay bleeding and dying in my arms.

# CHAPTER 16

Private notes: Detective Callum Baxter (LAPD)
Date: Dec 14
Time: 14:03

Finally got a copy of Virna's will. No unexpected bequests in there—and no mention of Tavish Advani. Bulk of the estate will pass on to her son, Jason, but he's insistent that Advani must've siphoned money from his mother in other ways.

I have to agree on one point: Advani is a financial genius. I did a bit of digging around and there's a reason he held such a high position at his age. Man delivers when he isn't getting into bed with his clients. If anyone knows how to play hide-and-seek with money, it's Advani.

That uptight firm he worked for wouldn't give me the names of his clients, but I managed to track one down after trawling through social media photos where Advani was tagged at various shindigs, and making some cold calls.

Vincent White was more than happy to talk about Advani—he's pissed the man "jumped firms"—I guess that's the cover story for Advani's firing.

"I'm waiting to see where he pops up," White said. "The rest of them are good, but Tavish? Pure genius. Got me returns like no one else—so good that I actually had a forensic accountant go over the books, figured maybe it was some pyramid deal.

"Nope, all straight. Tavish kept precise records of every transaction—which is why I learned he was doing deals for me at like four a.m. to take advantage of various time zones. Man is smart and focused and more than earns his paycheck. Whichever firm he joins, I'll be shifting all my money over there."

Have to say it wasn't what I was expecting to hear, not with Jason's accusations of financial malfeasance. But then, lots of folks are clean at work and messy in private, so maybe Tavish kept his financial messiness to his love life.

Still haven't found anyone he dated between or before Jocelyn Wai and Virna Musgrave, but I have managed to track down a college friend of his. Maybe Emilio Vasquez can shed some light on our enigma of a person of interest.

## CHAPTER 17

Even though I'd never met Shumi's family, I would've recognized her mother at first glance—she was an older version of Shumi: the same rounded face, the same soft lips and big doe eyes that wouldn't have looked out of place on a fifties pinup. Not much difference in their heights, either. Both around five four, with bodies that tended toward curves.

No swollen eyes for Mrs. Kumar, no dried tear tracks, but that was likely because she was holding herself so stiffly that she was permitting nothing to escape. I knew what that felt like—and I knew the crash that would come when she released her anguish at last.

The young man with her, by contrast, had eyes feathered with burst red vessels behind his spectacles, his nose rubbed raw from all the times he'd wiped it.

Shumi's father was a study in grim lines. If not for the circumstances, I'd have pegged him as a beleaguered executive—he had the silvered hair, his neatly trimmed mustache the same shade, and was a short and somewhat stocky man. He wore a suit, as if he'd dressed on autopilot for work.

It was wrinkled from the flights.

"This is Dr. Chen," I said when they reached us. "I'm Tavish."

A nod of acknowledgment from the older man before he looked at the doctor. "Our daughter?"

"Please follow me." He spoke to the family as they walked, while I trailed behind. "Shumi suffered four deep stab wounds alongside three more minor ones." He waited as if to see if they wanted a detailed breakdown of her injuries as I had with Diya, but when no one spoke, he said, "It's a miracle she's alive—your daughter has a strong spirit."

"She always was stubborn," Shumi's mother said, her voice crisp.

"It'll serve her well in this fight." The doctor brought them to a stop in front of Shumi's bed in the overflow unit. "I'll allow all three of you to visit with her today, but please keep it to one or two people at a time going forward. And maintain calm—I know you're emotional, but you won't help her by wailing and weeping."

"We won't startle her," Shumi's father promised, then looked at me. "You'll stay? We'll talk after."

"Of course." I propped up the wall nearby while the three of them visited Shumi. I could hear sniffles but that was about the loudest sound aside from the doctor's retreating footsteps as he returned to his rounds.

The nurses didn't interrupt the family until it was time to change one of Shumi's drips.

All three stepped away to join me.

"You should eat and get some sleep," I said, leaning on what I'd been told. "She's going to rely on you when she wakes—this is the time for you to rest, so you're strong for when she needs you."

Shumi's mother gave a small nod. "He's right. We can't get sick ourselves." Her voice was calm, her words clipped. "Do you know where we could stay? We didn't book anything."

As I told them about the motel, I hoped I wasn't anywhere near her vicinity when she cracked at last—because it would not be pretty. "Place is clean and modern, and there's food delivery from a variety of restaurants. Looks like it's mostly used by families in town to see the mud pools. I can take you—I have a car borrowed from a neighbor."

That was when I realized. "Where's your luggage?"

"A lady at reception said she'd store it when we told her why we were here," Shumi's brother, Ajay, said in a quiet voice. "I guess everyone knows about the fire and everything."

"Yes." It wasn't every day New Zealand woke up to the news of the mass murder—and attempted murder—of an entire family.

My stomach lurched.

My name was going to end up in the articles. It was pure blind luck it hadn't to this point. *Fuck.*

———

It was only after Shumi's family had checked into the motel and I'd helped Ajay carry their luggage over to their family suite that I said, "Do any of you know anyone named Annie?" It was a long shot, since they were in-laws, rather than part of the immediate Prasad family—I wasn't surprised when they frowned and gave me confused looks.

"No, is that a friend of Diya's you want to contact?" Shumi's mother asked. "You should get Ajay to help you look online. He's very clever with the computer." A fond smile on her face, she patted her son on the arm.

Who surprised me by saying "Actually, I might have seen an Annie on Shumi's friends list. Let me have a look." The clean-cut male pushed up his spectacles. "Mum, Dad, you go in and shower. I'll be right in."

"Don't be too long, Ajay beta," his mother said. "Tavish is right. You have to rest."

Ajay nodded and pulled out his phone. But instead of opening any social media apps, he shot a glance over his shoulder at the open door of the suite, then nudged his head for me to start walking back to the car.

"It's not Annie," he said after we were away from the door. "It's Ani."

I heard the difference in pronunciation at once, realized that was what Diya had actually said. The *A* part of the name was more like an *uh* sound. Take the *m* out of "money," and you'd have the right pronunciation. Of course my fucked-up brain would make that comparison when I could've as easily used a word like "honey."

"Ani," I said after telling my grief-manic brain to shut up. "You know who that is?"

Brown eyes stared at me from behind the smudged lenses of his spectacles—paler eyes than Shumi's, set in a more angular face. "How come you don't already know?"

Ajay shook his head almost as soon as the words were out of his mouth. "I forgot. You two met and fell in love in the space of, like, a month, right? My mum heard from Sarita auntie," he said in explanation of how he knew. "They aren't"—a quick pause—"weren't super close, but I guess she wanted Mum to know in case people started to gossip and make up things."

*Sarita auntie.*

It felt odd to hear composed and sharp-witted Dr. Sarita Prasad being referred to as an auntie. Dr. Rajesh Prasad had no doubt been Uncle Rajesh. To simply use the first name of an elder was just not done in large quarters of the Indian community.

Even my publicly ruthless hard-ass of a father was Uncle Anand to some. My mother, by contrast, *hated* being auntied—and it had nothing to do with different cultural expectations. "Just call me Audrey," she'd said to my paternal cousin when he'd been only seven. "'Auntie' makes me feel so *old.*"

That was the one thing Audrey Advani couldn't bear: the march of time, the relentless wrinkles of age. My mother would probably have a standing appointment for Botox injections if she didn't understand that a great actress needed a face capable of a subtle and intense range of motion. So instead, she got fillers and wore makeup with religious fervor.

I wasn't sure I'd ever seen her naked face.

"I guess you and Diya haven't had time to talk about everything," Ajay was saying.

Memories unraveled inside me, an endless photo-booth strip, preserved in cerebral celluloid forever. We'd spent hours night after night murmuring chapter after chapter of our stories to each other until one of us finally couldn't fight sleep any longer. We'd been in a hurry to catch up on all the years that had gone before we walked into each other's lives.

But . . . eleven weeks wasn't enough to share an entire lifetime's worth of memories. And some secrets we'd both kept. The knot in my abdomen was proof of that. As were the brown plastic bottles that had melted in the fire. I'd never asked and she'd never told, but I'd looked up the drugs, gone down the list of possible reasons why they might've been prescribed.

*Anxiety.*

*Depression.*

*Intrusive thoughts.*

*Hallucinations.*

*Schizophrenia.*

*Bipolar disorder.*

*Psychosis.*

Did Ackerson know about those medicines? Would she attempt to pin the blame for the murders and the fire on my beautiful, luminous star of a wife?

My tendons twisted, tight enough to snap.

"Tavish?"

"No," I said to Ajay's quiet query, forcing my voice into calm. "We were still learning each other, and now . . ."

The other man's eyes grew glassy. "Yeah." Coughing, he looked away and took a deep breath. "Anyway, Ani was Diya and Bobby's adopted sister."

My stomach dropped. This wasn't a random memory Diya had forgotten to mention; it was a core facet of her identity.

# CHAPTER 18

Private notes: Detective Callum Baxter (LAPD)
Date: Dec 19
Time: 11:08

Second interview with Tavish Advani was more frustrating. He came with his lawyer, who happens to be his father—Anand fucking Advani. Same Anand Advani who got Celia Byers off for the murder of her married lover. Woman was covered in blood and had the gun in her hand. Jesus.

Tavish didn't say much during the interview, with Anand blocking most of our questions. We couldn't hold him. Have nothing on him. Can't actually blame the man for shutting up—Jason Musgrave's poisoned the well there with how he's been shooting his mouth off in the media.

At least the journalists have the good sense not to leak Tavish's name—no proof, but I'd say they probably got their hands slapped by their bosses after Advani senior threatened them with a lawsuit if they crossed that line. Not that it matters; the implications are all there in the headlines—especially now that they've dug up his connection to Jocelyn Wai.

Gina Garcia's still on leave, so I'll have to wait a bit longer to get further background on that case.

And still no word on where all his money is going.

It definitely didn't go toward financing his condo—at least not openly. Perez was able to confirm it was purchased by a corporation, which then transferred the deed to Advani's name, free and clear. He's trying to see behind the corporate setup, find out where the money actually came from, because he doesn't think it was Mom and Dad after all.

Says he's not getting "happy family vibes" there. Gotta agree. Audrey Advani is seen a lot with her elder son, Raja, but neither of us has been able to find a recent photo of her with Tavish. Then again, could be the corporation is Daddy Advani's baby. He's certainly showing up for his boy.

Perez's theory is that Tavish Advani is funneling "ill-gotten gains" through various corporations to clean them up. If he is, he might've outsmarted us— we'll have to pull in the finance cops if Perez has no luck.

Time: 14:00

Got a call back from Emilio Vasquez, Advani's old college roommate. Apparently they're still in touch online but not really close after Vasquez relocated to New York. Per Vasquez, Advani was always "choosy."

"Could have any girl he wanted," Vasquez said. "It wasn't just the looks. Don't want to sound like an asshole, but I'm not exactly ugly. But Tavish . . . he just knew what to say to the girls, how to make them feel important and beautiful. Hell of a thing to watch. I figured maybe it was the acting genes—you know, from his mom.

"I used to be happy to go out as his wingman because he'd attract the women and sometimes I'd get lucky after a disappointed girl turned to me as a consolation prize. I didn't mind. I was a dumb college kid who wanted to get laid."

Per Vasquez, Advani didn't have a steady girlfriend that he knew of in college, but— "He was definitely seeing someone off campus. He took a gap year toward the end of our course, so I wasn't with him for that. But before that, he used to vanish all the time on weekends and come back grinning like a man who got real lucky. When I asked, all he'd say was that her name was Suzi, Suzi W."

Suzi W.

It's some kind of starting point at least.

# CHAPTER 19

I only know bits." Ajay thrust both hands into the front pockets of his jeans, his shoulders hunching up. "Shumi mentioned her to me once, said how sad it was that baby Ani had died at only three, or I would've had an in-law close to my age. Ani was two years younger than Diya."

"She died as a child?" It made more sense now that Diya hadn't mentioned her to me; to her, it would've been a lifetime ago.

Except that she'd said Ani's name as she lay bloody and wounded in my arms.

*Ani . . . they said . . . about Ani . . . not . . .*

"I don't know how she died." Ajay pushed up the bridge of his glasses. "Shumi only ever mentioned her in passing, and I was a teenager at the time and not interested in finding out more. But I remember that Shumi said how she couldn't imagine what it must've been like for Rajesh uncle and Sarita auntie to lose a child, even if she was adopted."

"Do you know why they adopted her or from where?"

"It was local—back when we all lived in Fiji."

I frowned at the mention of the group of Pacific islands that—as I'd learned after meeting Diya—had a significant ethnically Indian population due to the vagaries of history. "All of you? For some reason, I thought Shumi was born here."

"No, and neither was I. We were neighbors with the Prasads out in the boonies. That's where Bobby and Shumi first met." A slight smile. "God, she's always been crazy for him."

The smile faded. "But I wasn't even two when Ani died, so I don't know any other details. I'm sorry." He removed his hands from his pockets, then didn't seem to know what to do with them. "Why are you interested in Ani anyway?"

I didn't see any point in lying. "When I found Diya, she mentioned her."

"Oh." Tears appeared in his eyes; Ajay hadn't inherited either his mother's intense ability to lock away her emotions or his father's grim resolve.

"I guess it'd be natural to think about her sister when she was so hurt," he said, "especially if she knew her parents were gone, too. And probably Bobby, too. God, can you imagine what Diya and Shumi must've seen?" His voice cracked . . . and I noticed for the first time that he always used Shumi's name, rather than the word for elder sister.

Diya had never used Bobby's name except when first introducing him, always referred to him using the word for brother—"bhaiya." It was just how she'd been brought up. But Ajay had clearly not been taught to refer to his sister with similar deference.

Probably nothing, just a difference between two families, but it struck me as odd, especially as both had come from the same small region. Some things were just expected when you grew up in the same culture in the same area.

"Ajay, beta!"

Ajay looked up at the sound of his mother's voice. "I better go. They're not doing as well as they're pretending." He held my gaze, his expression pleading. "I know they're coming off as stiff and—"

"It's fine." I squeezed his shoulder. "I get it. I can be like that myself sometimes. I still haven't cried even once—I'm scared that if I do, I'll be useless."

All the passion leaching out of him, Ajay turned to walk back to the motel rooms. His shoulders were hunched in, his hands thrust into his pockets once again, the height of him truncated by the curve of his spine.

As I watched, he stood in the open doorway to the two-bedroom suite and took a deep breath, as if bracing himself, before he walked in. Poor kid. Only twenty-one if I had my mental math correct, and having to handle his parents' grief and worry on top of his own.

Getting into my vehicle on that thought, I drove back to the hospital, but there was no change in Diya's status, her face serene in her wounded sleep. As I sat beside her, my hand on hers, I thought about what she'd actually said. It hadn't just been Ani's name, hadn't just been a moment of her life flashing before her eyes.

She'd been trying to tell me something.

*Ani . . . they said . . . about Ani . . . not . . .*

I couldn't make any sense of that, but it was all I had. And I knew I had to follow that fragile thread—even more so after I was called into the police station for a formal interview by Detective Ackerson.

I'd forgotten to make that call to my father, forgotten to get a lawyer. No matter. I could handle this first interview on my own—all I had to do was keep my cool and remember what Dad had told me prior to my first ever conversations with the cops in LA.

"Never flinch," Anand had advised after Jocelyn's fall, his brown eyes as hard as granite. "Cops are like wolves on the hunt. A single drop of blood and they start to smell victory."

I'd almost asked him if he'd learned that lesson from his wife. In the realm of film and television, my mother was an actress touted as the best of her generation, her reputation one of warmth and kindness. Behind the closed doors of my parents' strikingly modern Malibu home? The mask came well and truly off.

Audrey not only scented blood, she drew it with vicious efficiency.

Of the three men who lived or had lived in that home, it was my brother, Raja, alone who'd experienced Audrey as she was to the outside world. Ironically enough, in the end, my childhood had proved a gift—no cop could come close to the cold manipulation that was Audrey's stock-in-trade.

"So." Detective Ackerson's tone was polite, even kind, but her eyes drilled into me in the confines of the interview room. "You're doing contract work for a finance magazine."

"Yes."

"Were your in-laws aware of the downgrade in your employment status?"

I hated this windowless box of a room marked up by God knows what, my mind pushing to shove me back into the hellish seven-hour interrogation by Detective Gina Garcia that my father had told me I needed to white knuckle because if the case went to court, we'd have evidence of my cooperation as Jocelyn's grief-stricken lover.

*Give it up, Tavish. We both know you two had a volatile relationship—what went wrong that night? Did she do something that drove you to push her off the balcony? Provocation can be looked at as a mitigating factor, but you have to be honest.*

Gina Garcia was the kind of tough-talking cop who didn't let up. She just kept on pushing, her questions unrelenting. Drops of water wearing away stone.

But I'd walked out of her interrogation room and I'd walk out of this one.

"Sarita and Rajesh understood that I had to establish myself in my career here and that it could take time," I said without acrimony. "They did the same when they moved to New Zealand."

It had been a slender strip of common ground between us, Dr. Rajesh Prasad going as far as to slap me on the shoulder and say, "It's hard to change countries and start all over again—it makes me feel good that our Diya's found a husband who loves her enough to make the effort."

It had been the night before the party, the two of us out on the back patio. The sun had set, the water motionless under the dark orange light that was already fading to charcoal at the edges. "I do, sir," I'd said as two black swans took to the water, twin ripples in their wake. "Love Diya. And she wants to live here, so that's what we'll do."

He didn't need to know that Los Angeles had become hostile ground to me after Virna's accident. The world of wealth and fame in which I existed had seemed far more angered by her death than by Jocelyn's. For Joss, they'd wanted lurid stories and endless gossip. For Virna, they'd demanded justice.

Hypocrites.

"Care to tell me why you left your previous position?" Ackerson asked in a calm tone, her expression neutral, nothing accusatory about it.

*Talk to me*, it said, *I'm no threat at all.* Too bad for her that I'd played this game against far more experienced foes and won.

I just had to hold my nerve.

# CHAPTER 20

Private notes: Detective Callum Baxter (LAPD)
Date: Dec 21
Time: 14:27

Lunch with Gina was productive. Turns out the gossip rags weren't making things up—Gina did look at Advani as a suspect in the Jocelyn Wai case. But Wai's fall was eventually ruled an accident.

Off the record, Gina stated that she doesn't buy the accident theory, but her hands are tied. "Advani had a rock-solid alibi. Didn't even have to rely on his drunk friend to back him up—the friend's apartment complex is high-end, has security cameras in all the public zones.

"It showed him coming over, the two of them going out to buy beers, then Advani opening the door to accept a food delivery. No sign he ever left the building. And no sign he ever reentered Jocelyn Wai's after he walked out earlier that night—her building had even more cameras. We checked his phone location anyway, but nada. It was at the friend's place the entire time.

"If he did it, he's a brilliant psychopath. Scariest thing is he was only twenty-three and maybe six, seven months, when Jocelyn died. If you're right about him being involved in Virna Musgrave's death, that's two women in the space of, what, three years? What's the word for an unmarried black widower?"

As for motive—that's tricky, because there's no financial one. He wasn't in Wai's will. But Gina estimates Wai spent probably half a mil on Advani over the course of their relationship.

"They lived large, were snapped at all the hot spots, and I don't think he was paying for it—that would've wiped him out, even at his salary. No, our boy has a way of hooking up with wealthy women, and having those women show him a good time—then die on him. You know how he got his Venice Beach condo, right? Look up Susanne Winthorpe."

I expected Suzi W to be some hot stripper or dancer.

Yeah, got that one really, really wrong.

# CHAPTER 21

I left my job because of the impossible hours and asshole bosses," I said to Ackerson, the lie so generic it told her nothing. "Being a junior in those firms is brutal. A constant churn of burned-out twentysomethings. I wanted more out of life—I was deciding what to do next when I met Diya. Seemed like a sign from the heavens to take a big leap and head out here."

No one from DeJong, Greyson, & Wijesinghe would ever refute my statement, not when it said nothing many others hadn't said before. In their line of work, reputation was everything, discretion the name of the game—and burning people out was a badge of honor rather than a black mark.

"Our caliber of clients," portly Greyson had said to me when I began at the firm, "do not wish to do business with a firm known for its loose lips. Keep them zipped.

"Doesn't matter if you learn that Mr. Smith needs more investment income for his secret second family out in San Diego, or that Ms. Rock Star is screwing her entire crew of backing dancers every

Wednesday and needs to pay off a blackmailer. None of your business. Your business is their money and keeping them happy so they never want to switch to another firm."

If the firm hadn't bowed to pressure from the LAPD, they sure as hell wouldn't do it for a cop in another country. Detective Callum Baxter might suspect I'd been fired, might even have a source in that poisonous dickwad Jason Musgrave, but it meant nothing without official confirmation. Even that official record, if ever opened, would simply show an elegant resignation letter.

DeJong, Greyson, & Wijesinghe hadn't survived this long by being anything but ruthless. Fighting my forced "resignation" would've just left me with a permanent stain on my name in the circles that were my livelihood. This way, if any future employers ever reached out, HR would just say the firm and I weren't "a good fit"—though privately, the firm *had* no doubt gotten the word out among their top-tier friends to steer clear of me.

It didn't matter how good I was at making money, I'd shit the bed when I'd become not only romantically involved with Virna, but financially involved.

I'd never again work in those gilded halls.

"Do you know if your wife has a life insurance policy?" Ackerson asked.

I'd been ready for her to resort to her tactic of switching topics, but not for this particular question. My answer was startled—and honest. "I don't think so? We never discussed life insurance, so if she has a policy, it'll be from before we met."

"How about a will?"

"Yes, we did it a couple of days after our wedding."

"Why the rush?" Ackerson leaned across the table, her tone sliding into abrasive. "You're both in your twenties, plenty of life left to live."

I lifted my shoulders. "My father's a lawyer. He suggested it."

"Odd thing for a man to suggest to newlyweds."

I shrugged again and left it at that, even though Ackerson paused and stared. Poor Ackerson. She had no idea I'd grown up in this environment—and while the game player was my mother, it was my father who'd taught me how to withstand it. Because Anand Advani had been caught between his slavish devotion to his wife and his paternal need to protect his second son since the day of my birth.

"People want to fill silences," he'd said to me when I was nine, and freshly emotionally bruised after an interaction with the woman who only had enough love in her for one son.

"Long pauses are a favorite tactic of anyone who wants to get information out of another person—just wait until the other party cracks from the awkwardness or gets nervous. Don't fall for it again, Tavish. Don't show her your heart." A pause. "Or you won't survive her."

Today, I deliberately *didn't* maintain the eye contact. Some cops read that kind of contact as a challenge and got aggressive. But neither did I look around as if unable to settle. Rather, I looked down at the table as if lost in thought.

*There's no such thing as justice. It's all legal chess. First one to check-mate wins.*

My father's words. My mother's thoughts.

The problem was that my former employer wasn't the only other player in this game. If Jason Musgrave got wind of the murders of the Prasad family, and of my involvement with Diya, Ackerson would have herself a font of nasty innuendo and accusations.

If I could've murdered anyone, it'd be the man who'd done all he could to make my life hell. The only problem was that I'd be the chief suspect as soon as the bastard turned up dead—or went missing. Still, it was nice to dream.

"I'll need a copy of the wills."

"We did one together. Never got around to putting it in the Prasads' safety-deposit box." Despite my cooperative tone, my mouth was dry, my temples beating with a pulse that felt so big I was afraid it was visible. "The lawyers in LA will have a copy. I can get their name from my dad—he set it up. We just turned up and signed."

"And your wife was fine with all this?"

"Why wouldn't she be?" I scowled, my frustration real. "Look, I don't know what you're getting at, but there's nothing weird in the will. Just the two of us giving our stuff to each other, and a few sentimental items to our friends or family."

Though when Ackerson read the will, she'd see that it was Diya who'd made ninety percent of the sentimental bequests; I'd put only one name in there, the bequeathed item a particular piece of art from Susanne that I thought should go back to the Winthorpe family. "Most of the assets coming into the marriage were *mine*."

I knew I'd made a mistake, that I'd spoken too much, when her eyes gained a sudden feral spark. "Balance has changed now, though, hasn't it?"

"What?" My brain was lagging, my nerves eating up my thoughts.

"The Prasad family's lawyer has confirmed that the doctors left everything to their children in equal shares. One of those children is most likely dead, his body all but obliterated. The other is clinging to life—but Diya Prasad has already become the beneficiary by being the sole survivor. If she dies, it all goes to you."

My face burned, my leg threatening to pump up and down. Of all the possible avenues on which Ackerson could've pinned her suspicions, the financial one was the absolute worst.

*Susanne. Jocelyn. Virna.*

My history could bury me.

"What are you getting at, Detective?" I channeled my father's cold and hard "asshole lawyer" demeanor. "In case you've forgotten, *I wasn't there* when Diya was attacked and her family killed."

"Thanks to the fire, there's no way for us to pinpoint the exact timeline," was the curt response. "For all I know, you attacked everyone, then began a small fire that you knew would take time to get going."

I furrowed my brow. "What?"

"Act stupid," my father had advised me at thirteen, after my mother had nearly broken me despite everything he'd already tried to teach me. "People who hold you in contempt will just give up if they think you're not worth their energy." Hope in his tone. "It's also a useful tool in life—folks often forget to watch their words around those they see as less intelligent."

It had never worked with my mother; Audrey was already well aware that I could do complex math in my head and that I'd never had to study for a single exam in my life. Socially, I'd far outpaced my brother, so I couldn't even fall back on a lack of emotional intelligence—I'd had to develop a whole different set of tools to deal with her.

But Detective Ackerson wasn't my mother. "You just said Diya only inherited everything because she's the sole survivor. Now you're saying I tried to murder her, too?" Confusion in every word, the simulacrum of emotion a little trick I'd learned from a mother who'd found great delight in making me believe she loved me . . . only to laugh hysterically when I fell for it.

*Good grief, Tavish. Pull yourself together. It was just a little joke.*

I'd been six years old and the "little joke" had involved the promise of an outing to the park. She'd sent me to my room to get changed . . . then waved good-bye to me from the car as she left for the park with Raja in the passenger seat.

My rage was a hard kernel of ice lodged in my soul.

"And," I added, "if you think my relationship with Diya has to do with money, I'll have to disappoint you. There are plenty of rich older women in LA who like to spoil handsome young men. I never had to marry one to live the lifestyle."

A calculated gamble to bring up my highly publicized past before she could. Taking ownership rather than allowing her to bludgeon me with the fact that I'd once lived off charm born of an insatiable need to fill the hole in my heart that was an old and bitter thing. I no doubt needed far more therapy than the few sessions I'd allowed myself, but what was the therapist going to tell me that I didn't already know?

More important than that, I'd broken the loop when I fell for Diya, my flickering candle flame of a wife, so dazzling and bright, and full of mysteries.

"Your wife have any idea of how you funded your luxurious life in LA?" Ackerson blustered when I refused to buckle.

"Detective." I gave her a tired smile. "My salary at my previous job was four hundred thousand dollars per year, with bonuses built in. I could fly back today and walk into another job, probably for half a million." I'd always been good at bluffing—that was why I'd won a million at poker my first time out at real tables.

Slaps on my back, the rush not of the win but of what it made me. *Important. Seen.* All of it wrapped around the toxic need to feel the same again, the hunger inside me without end.

The casinos, of course, had been happy to roll out the red carpet, happy to help me chase the high, day after day, week after week.

"My future earnings potential is many multiples of whatever Diya has inherited," I reiterated. "I know how to make my money make more money. The women I dated? I did so because they were beautiful, sophisticated, and interesting."

From the way Ackerson blinked quickly before shifting the papers in front of her, she'd had no idea of my salary—or was doing a good job of pretending that she hadn't. Because a second later, she looked up and said, "Tell me about Virna Musgrave."

The world narrowed into a breathless spiral. But I was my father's son. "It's easy to tear apart a reputation without evidence," I said with a slumping of my shoulders. "The media doesn't care. Not when it sells advertising space and gains clicks. I took you for a good detective, not a tabloid muckraker."

A flush of color on her cheekbones, a slight pinching around her eyes. "That doesn't answer my question."

"Virna was a friend who gifted me a chunk of money. Despite her framing it as a gift, I insisted to her that I'd pay it back as soon as my own investments matured. Unfortunately she died in an accident before we could put our agreement on paper."

"If it's that simple, why is the 'accident' still under investigation, with you as the main person of interest?"

Oh, Ackerson *had* been busy. "Do you know who inherited Virna's millions? Her son. Who then contributed an entire million of that to a fund that supports retired cops and firefighters." I didn't break eye contact. "She gave me a quarter of a million. A big sum, yes, but nothing compared to Jason Musgrave's staggering inheritance.

"She was also talking about gifting me ridiculous diamond cuff links as well as a luxury trip to the Maldives for Christmas. Not only am I not the one with the most motive where Virna is concerned, I inherited *nothing* in her will. It'd have been far better for me if she was alive and showering me with a continuous array of gifts."

Leaning toward her, I said, "You ask me, Jason was getting angry about his mother using her money to spoil me even though that was literally small change to her. That was *his* money as far as he was concerned. His fucking inheritance. I heard him yelling that at her one day—told the detectives in LA about it, too, but he's the poster child for charity and philanthropy after that donation; they don't care to look too hard at Jason."

I'd definitely surprised Ackerson this time; the tell was subtle—a minute twitch of her left eye—but I had it now. She hadn't known about the donation. Most people didn't. My father had told me to keep the information in my back pocket in case things went from bad to catastrophic.

But Ackerson wasn't ready to admit defeat—and she was a far better detective than I'd realized. "Let's talk about Susanne Winthorpe."

A ghost whispered in my ear, the scent of her signature Baccarat perfume in the air.

# CHAPTER 22

## SUSANNE

S usanne closed her menu and looked up at the handsome young man who'd come to pour her and Cici water out of a silver pitcher coated with a fine layer of fresh condensation. He performed the service with panache, spilling not a drop.

"Would you like to order a glass of wine to go with your lunch today, Mrs. Winthorpe?" he asked, well aware of her habits by now. "We have a beautiful crisp white that just came in from a small but excellent winery in Napa that I believe you'd enjoy."

"Oh, why not, Tavish, you've twisted my arm. And for my friend, an oat milk latte, single shot." Lowering her voice, she mock-whispered, "Cici doesn't approve of my midday drinking."

Cici rolled her brown eyes but waited until Tavish had grinned and left the table before saying, "Really, Sue?" She compressed her lips, the exquisite deep pink of her lipstick dynamite against the rich brown of her skin tone. "He's barely out of high school and you're flirting like you're a tiger."

"Cougar, darling, that's the vernacular." Where Susanne's expat family had sent her to a boarding school stateside, Cici's parents had chosen to have her educated in Singapore. At a top private school, of course, but it wasn't the same, was it? Though there was also Cici's disdain for all things modern. Including new terms in the language.

"And why not?" Susanne asked after a sip of the water. "I'm filthy rich, very well-preserved in the looks department thanks to a lifetime of moisturizer and a dynamo surgeon, and in the market for a hot fling." Sad to admit, but her pale white skin hadn't held up anywhere near as well as Cici's—not that anyone could tell, not with all the maintenance work she had done on it on a monthly basis.

Susanne's face was as fresh as a daisy.

Cici, who'd been born with a rule book in tow, pressed a bejeweled hand to her heart. "You are sixty-seven, Susanne. Act your age."

"Doing that is why you have all those grays, dearest Cici."

"Don't come crying to me when you put your back out getting frisky with that young man."

Susanne almost snorted with laughter. This was why the two of them were friends, despite their diametrically opposed personalities and lives. Cici might be a contented grandmother who babysat her grandchild out of choice, not necessity—a grandmother for whom lunch out with Susanne was the high point in her social calendar—but she'd never lost the sharp wit that had bonded them as young girls plucked out of their lives in the US and placed in the hothouse beauty of Singapore.

"It'd be worth it," Susanne purred after she'd recovered. "I didn't marry a strapping young man like you, my dear heart, never got the chance to be adventurous in bed." Her husband had been in his forties when they'd fallen in love, twenty years her senior, and while she didn't regret it, she did regret not sowing some wild oats.

"You're going to do what you're going to do." Cici tapped one nail on her wineglass, her manicure a classic French tip. "Just make sure he has permission from his mother."

Susanne was still laughing when the gorgeous waiter with his golden-brown skin and intelligent dark eyes, his jaw square and his shoulders broad, returned with their drinks. "Thank you, darling," Susanne purred. "So, how does a lady go about asking for your number, Tavish?"

His smile made his eyes sparkle . . . and her heart skip a beat.

Well now . . .

# CHAPTER 23

I spent time with Diya that evening, the curtains pulled to shield us on either side, and the nurse on duty having gone to watch from the main station, so we could have a bit more privacy.

"I kept a secret from you," I told the woman who'd pulled me out of the black spiral of lingering grief and endless need without ever knowing what she'd done.

Because I hadn't told her.

It was all but silent in the ICU now, the lights lowered for the evening, and the nursing rounds done for this hour. No one would disturb us while I made my confession.

"About my past," I clarified. "But only because I fell so hard for you—I just wanted you to give me a shot without preconceptions, and then it got too difficult to tell you."

I swallowed then, and told her. All of it. From start to finish.

It felt like a boulder rolling off my shoulders. "Ackerson must've got word about the condo from Baxter and Perez in LA." Because despite the detective's posturing, she hadn't actually known much about me and Susanne. Not many people did; Susanne had been the kind of wealthy that didn't end up in the media, the kind of wealthy that ran generations deep.

Quiet, refined, private.

When Ackerson confronted me with the fact that my condo had been a gift from Susanne, I'd admitted it without hesitation. "She gave it to me when I was twenty-two, said I wasn't to argue because she could more than afford it." In truth, her words had been far more emotional, a prelude to a final good-bye, but Ackerson didn't need to know that.

I'd then named the full figure of Susanne's estate and watched Ackerson's mind go blank with the enormity of it.

That number didn't give Ackerson even a glimmer of my complex and life-altering relationship with the first woman who had truly seen me as who I was, and not as who she wanted me to be. So strange that it had ended up that way, when we'd begun the relationship as a flirtatious game.

Today, I spoke to another woman who would know me—because I was through with hiding things from her. "I have to dig up something else for Ackerson to sink her teeth into, or she's going to find a way to pin the blame on me. I can see it in her eyes—she's fallen for what my father calls the 'too many coincidences' theory. Susanne, Jocelyn, Virna, and now you. How unlucky can a man be?"

No one could guarantee that either Diya or Shumi would ever wake to clear my name.

Picking up my wife's hand on a wave of terror such as I'd never before felt, I pressed a kiss to the back of it, the mehndi a stark reminder of dreams turned to ash. "I love you, D."

Then I considered what I had to work with.

The answer was dispiriting: *Ani*.

A memory from another lifetime spoken of in a moment of awful pain and confusion.

It could be nothing. But it was all I had.

The question was what to do with it. Ajay had already told me what he knew, but I hadn't broached the subject with his parents after he'd cleared up my mistake about the pronunciation of the name.

Now I messaged him: Do you think your parents would talk to me about Ani?

The three moving dots that indicated he was typing a response appeared almost at once, but his answer when it came at last wasn't what I wanted to hear: I already brought it up with them, said Diya had mentioned Ani before she lost consciousness. They told me Ani died in an accident as a child. They said it was very sad and everyone was devastated, and that she and Diya were close, so that's probably why she mentioned her. I don't think there's any other reason—they sounded sad about Ani even now, but that's all.

I blew out a breath between compressed lips. Thanks for passing that on, I wrote back, then stared down at the floor, my hands between my knees.

*Ani . . . they said . . . about Ani . . . not . . .*

That wasn't just a memory. Who said what? What did it have to do with a little girl who'd died almost two decades ago? And why was it so important that Diya had struggled desperately to speak even as her blood pumped out of her violated body?

The Prasads had no close extended family in the country, no one who might know the story of Ani's life and death. And neither Shumi nor Diya could speak, tell me what role a lost child played in any of this.

The person with the wind chimes as their ringtone received a call down the hallway, the music of it haunting enough to raise the hairs on my arms, goose bumps that chilled me from the inside. I couldn't understand why they'd have such a sad ringtone—especially here, in this place.

*Fiji.*

The word was a whisper against my ear, so real that I jolted up from my slouched position to look at Diya, certain I'd find her awake. But she lay unconscious, the ventilator constant in its mechanical breathing, while the name of her birthplace echoed inside my skull.

The wind chime ringtone sounded again.

Rising, unable to bear the pain in the music, I went to walk toward it, ask the person to silence their phone . . . but all was quiet. And though I stood in the hallway between the ICU and the CCU for a long minute, it didn't sound again.

Rubbing at my arms to get some warmth back into my flesh, I returned to Diya's bedside. "I can't just go to Fiji," I said to my wife.

It'd be insane to fly to another country on the strength of such a vague droplet of information . . . but whatever it was that had tormented Diya in that moment when she'd spoken her dead sister's name, it had to do with the place where Ani had lived and died.

"Our house is in the back of beyond," Diya had told me while showing me the black-and-white photos her mother had so cherished. "Used to be sugarcane fields all around us, a lot of farmers in the region. Not sure what the crop is these days, but it's still mostly farmland. No intensive development."

In an area that rural, people would remember the family of doctors who'd lost a child.

"It's only a three-hour flight," my wife had shared with a nostalgic smile. "Available throughout the week. We'll go after you're more settled here.

"It's so peaceful," she'd added, "the breeze that comes off the ocean like a kiss on the skin. The beach near the house is hidden, only really used by locals—pure white sand and coconut palms, water clear enough that you can see tiny tropical fish swimming around your ankles in the shallows. You'll love it, Tavi."

My heart twisted and twisted until the agony threatened to send me to the ground. The only thing that kept me upright was the knowledge that if I didn't fix this, if I didn't get Ackerson's attention off me, then Diya would wake to a husband accused of multiple murders.

Taking out my phone, I looked up the travel requirements for a US passport holder who wanted to go to Fiji, found that I didn't need to get a visa. That hurdle passed, I began to search for flights.

There was one the next morning at nine, complete with a single empty seat.

My gambler's heart saw that as a sign.

I booked the fare, locked in my return flight two days later. Ended up having to pay for a seat on a charter flight for my return connection so I could make my international flight on time. That done, I found Ajay—seated at Shumi's side—and told him about my decision to head to Fiji. He looked surprised but promised to keep an eye on Diya.

I also found Hazel, the nurse who was most often with Diya during the day, and told her. "I don't want to go, but I have to." It was the truth, the idea of leaving Diya wrecking me. "Has to do with preparing for the final rites. I don't know when the police will say it's okay to have funerals, but I need to be ready." The staff, I'd come to learn, had a deep understanding of different cultural practices—part of the reason for the generous ICU visiting policy was to respect the needs of the local Māori population.

I felt bad taking advantage of that understanding, but I had no choice.

Hazel gave me a sympathetic smile. "I understand. We'll take care of Diya until your return. I'll make sure to speak to her, keep her mind active, and so will everyone else."

Her sincerity only made me feel more like shit. "Thank you. I'll only be gone for two days."

I couldn't afford to be out of the country longer without making it look like I was running away. Right now, if Ackerson even noticed I was gone, I could play it off much as I'd done with Hazel, say I'd gone in preparation for laying Diya's lost family members to rest—specifically to fetch a sentimental item from the family estate in Fiji.

Because that estate was still there, still in Prasad hands.

Diya had shared that the property's value had skyrocketed after their sleepy seaside village began to attract the attention of scouts from the companies that set up resorts. "But my parents won't sell," she'd said with a faint smile that held an edge of sorrow I'd mistaken for wistfulness. "Too many memories there."

I hadn't known about Ani then. Now that I did, I understood all the layers of Diya's statement. She'd have told me about her baby sister, I realized. She'd already been dropping hints, building up to sharing this awful, dark part of her family's history.

"I'll find out about Ani," I promised Diya before I left. "You just hold on for me, D."

The first thing I did after I was out of the hospital, however, was call my father from the privacy of my car. Perhaps I was paranoid, but I didn't trust that the cops hadn't bugged my motel room.

After hearing what had taken place, Anand Advani said, "For fuck's sake, son, can't you ever keep your nose out of trouble?"

My hand tightened on the phone. "You really think I could do this? Murder an entire family?"

"It doesn't matter what I think except as your lawyer—and as your lawyer, this looks bad. Most people don't have even one suspicious death attached to their name. You already have two even before your in-laws are factored in. You know what the number is to be termed a serial killer? Three."

There was a reason Anand Advani was considered a vicious ass-hole by those who'd come up against him in court. But I didn't see him that way. To me, my father was a weak man in thrall to a woman who saw him as a trophy, and who'd probably mourn his death, when it came, more for theater than out of any true emotion.

My mother loved only two people on this earth: neither my father nor I were on that list.

"Can you help me find a local attorney or not?" I asked the man part of me loved even as I pitied him. Because for all his faults, he'd stood by me when the shit hit the fan . . . and he'd never once asked me if I'd killed Jocelyn or Virna.

He didn't know about Susanne.

"Let me make some calls." The sound of air being dragged in, exhaled. He was smoking again. "That cop—Baxter—he's still sniff-ing around. Called me to ask what you were doing on the other side of the world. Didn't believe me when I said you'd run off and had a quickie Vegas wedding, so I sent him a copy of your marriage certif-icate."

"He reply?"

"Sent a message saying we have an extradition treaty with New Zealand. I told him that was nice, but that I had paperwork for Jason Musgrave's seven-figure donation to a certain fund related to the po-lice and just how fantastic it would look in a defense brief."

"Baxter didn't strike me as the kind who'd toe the company line." In fact, he'd struck me as the exact opposite—a dogged cop incapable of letting a case go.

"Might be he wasn't clued in. Now he is." A shrug I could hear in his voice. "Regardless of what Baxter does or doesn't know, the hierarchy will understand that the instant I file a case, the media will descend on them like rabid dogs.

"No matter if the fund is a wholly separate entity from the force, Musgrave's donation just has the rotten smell of corruption about it—and you know how popular the department is after that gangland case that fell apart." I could almost hear his satisfied smile. "I'll email you a list of non-extradition countries anyway, just in case."

Pressing my head back against the headrest, I smiled at the inside of the car roof. "Thanks, Dad."

"Don't say I never do anything for you." Another drag of the cigarette. "You need money?"

"No." I still had twenty-five grand in my official accounts, mostly thanks to my father forcing me to go cold turkey on the gambling after Virna's death.

That first million I'd won? My salary? The balance in my main savings account?

Gone.

Aside from the twenty-five thousand—a remnant of my final big win—all that remained was the money I'd taken from Audrey. And by the time my father forced me to quit, *not* touching that money had been taking its toll on me in sleepless nights drenched in sweat, the need to be back at the tables a constant gnawing in my bones. His intervention still wouldn't have worked if I hadn't met Diya . . . if she hadn't become my new addiction.

"Your mother called." Another drag of his cigarette. "They're filming the new show out in the desert. Says the sand gets between her teeth, in her hair, on her lipstick." When I stayed silent, he said, "Raja's boy is babbling now. Pretty sure he almost said 'Anana' the other day. That's me."

My lips curved, my eyes on the dark gray of the parking lot.

"How's the pregnancy going?" The second pregnancy so soon after the first had been a surprise, but Raja and Elizabeth seemed happy with it.

But my father paused. "Fine, I guess. I'll find that lawyer for you."

I didn't luxuriate in the hint of trouble in paradise after my father hung up. My brother might be Audrey's narcissistic reflection, but I liked his wife and my nephew. Elizabeth's only flaw was that she loved Raja.

I drove out of the parking garage.

Rain hit the windshield soon afterward, blurring the golden light thrown by the streetlamp under which I'd stopped when the traffic lights up ahead went red. In the hazy light, I glimpsed the ghostly image of a stunning woman with high cheekbones and lush lips, her hair a wavy mass of ebony against skin that would make Snow White jealous, and her curves legendary.

Even more legendary was her sultry voice.

Audrey used to sing Raja to sleep even when he was eleven or twelve, while I listened with my ear pressed to the wall between our bedrooms. And she used that same voice to campaign for the care of abused and abandoned children.

"No child should have to live without love," she'd said in one interview. "Every child should know they're treasured, their dreams important."

I guess all that goodness got cloying after a while and she'd decided that not loving me would be her outlet. It had been an active thing, my mother's lack of love for her second-born, not simple emotional neglect.

"I should've never given in to Anand's begging and had you," she'd told me while doing her makeup one day when I must've been seven at most, her tone offhand. "Raja was all I ever wanted or needed. We had five years as the perfect little family before you came along."

The wipers swiped back and forth as the traffic started to move again, and I allowed them to swipe away the memories of my strange mirage of a childhood. Smiling appearances before the media, my mother's arms around both her children.

Those photo ops had been some of the only times she'd touched me.

But Audrey Advani no longer mattered. Not when the love of my life lay in the hospital after using what might've been her last moments of consciousness on this earth to give me a message I couldn't decipher.

*Ani . . . they said . . . about Ani . . . not . . .*

# CHAPTER 24

Private notes: Detective Callum Baxter (LAPD)
Date: Dec 28
Time: 01:02

Everyone's on vacation and too busy to reply to my requests, but I have managed to confirm that Susanne Winthorpe is dead.

Christ.

That makes three women. Three dead lovers.

What the hell are we investigating here?

# CHAPTER 25

Half of me was convinced Ackerson had put me on a no-fly list, but I got through customs and security in New Zealand without a hitch, then onto the flight. But it wasn't until after the plane was in the air that I relaxed.

A bare three hours later and we were on the runway in Nadi, Fiji's largest airport.

The humid heat of the tropical country hit me like a damp wall when I stepped off the plane. The air was as thick as molasses and somehow slower, the scent of the earth different in a way I couldn't explain. As if all that lush tropical vegetation had permanently altered its chemical composition.

No one rushed ahead of me, most of the male passengers in shorts, and shirts featuring hibiscus blooms or palm trees. Many of the women wore strappy sundresses and had pulled out sun hats in readiness for hitting the outside world.

Tourists.

Hardly any locals on this midweek flight, to my eyes, though I did spot a couple of little old Indian ladies in light saris, and a small group of native Fijians in black shorts and white tees bearing the name of a local rugby sevens club. The latter was a game with which I had little familiarity, but that Rajesh Prasad had followed with near-religious fervor.

My jeans weren't going to cut it in this heat, but they'd have to do.

An airport staff member in uniform, a red hibiscus bloom over her ear, pointed the passengers toward the immigration line. Unlike when I landed at LAX, no one was impatient, and a number of people chatted to each other as if they were in no rush to be anywhere.

I shifted from foot to foot.

And heard Diya's laughter in my mind as she teased me about my need for constant forward motion. "Island time will drive you crazy," she'd said one night, after we'd been talking about her childhood home. "But resistance is futile—things will happen when they happen, so just relax and enjoy life."

As it was, the line moved along quickly enough even with no one in a hurry. When the officer, with his dark skin and tight curls, first saw me, he said, "Bula. Coming home?"

Funny, how I'd never thought I'd be asked that question on island soil at the far end of the Pacific. Hadn't ever thought about visiting Fiji at all; my grandparents had immigrated from India, my only knowledge of this land due to seeing its name splashed across my mother's favorite bottled water.

"First-timer," I said. "My wife's from here."

"You'll be back," he predicted before returning my passport and waving over the next person.

I had no luggage to pick up, nothing to declare, and was soon exiting into the arrivals area, where people waited for their relatives. A little girl in a pretty pink dress was jumping up and down as she peered at the stream of arriving passengers, her hair pinned to the sides of her head with barrettes. Dressed up to fetch someone important to her.

Her father stood next to her, smiling indulgently.

Skirting past the others milling around, I found the sign pointing out the direction for the domestic terminal, from where I was to fly to the more rural of Fiji's two big islands. The walk took me a minute, if that, the international and domestic terminals side by side.

I barely noticed the palm trees or the cabs lined up at the stand.

The ninety-minute wait for my flight almost drove me insane, but the journey on the small commuter plane was mercifully short—and the descent into Labasa Airport a breathtaking glide over endless sugarcane plantations. The tall gray-green leaves waved in the breeze, the airport nowhere in sight until we were suddenly landing on the tarmac.

Even from this lower vantage point, all I saw were the sugarcane stalks in every direction, as if we'd been dropped from the sky into the middle of the fields. Unlike in Nadi, there was no skybridge when the plane taxied to a stop. Instead, staff wheeled over stairs, and we were directed to disembark directly onto the tarmac.

I was braced for the tropical warmth this time, but it was worse when my feet hit the tarmac, the sticky black of it reflecting the heat back at me.

"Bula!" A smiling member of airport staff standing on the tarmac directed me along the safe pathway to an entrance. His skin was as dark as cocoa beans, his smile beaming white; the lack of any sweat stains whatsoever on his clothing shouted local louder than even his Fijian greeting.

Meanwhile, I was pretty sure I was melting.

This was the smallest airport I'd ever been in, but it moved fast because of that.

When I stepped out on the other side, I found my face brushed by a breeze that felt like a silent welcome to this place that lived in my wife's heart. The sugarcane in the distance rustled, creating a *hush-hush* sound that was just a touch rough.

"I love fresh sugarcane," Diya had told me when talking about her birthplace. "Have you ever had it?"

When I'd shaken my head, she'd said, "You strip off the hard outer shell, then just chew on the white flesh inside. It's thready, so after you chew out all the juice, you spit the husk out and take another bite. It's not the same as having sugarcane juice—half the fun is in the chewing and holding the cane in your hand."

A delighted grin, no hint of the shadows that had swirled around her only a week earlier. "Watch out for the leaves, though—they're tough, can cut your palm if you're not careful."

Pain settled again in my heart, stung at my eyes as the sugarcane rustled on.

"Taxi?" A question asked by an Indo-Fijian man in a pressed shirt and trousers who was leaning up against his vehicle not far from me. His body partially blocked the TAXI sign emblazoned in faded black lettering on the door.

"No, thanks." The rental car I'd booked from New Zealand was meant to be waiting for me outside, but I saw no sign of anything but other cabs or locals doing a pickup run.

Taking my no with good grace, the cabdriver turned to speak to another driver, the two of them flowing between languages so easily that it took me several minutes to realize that one was speaking Fijian, the other Hindi, both also throwing random English words in the mix.

Neither seemed to have any trouble understanding the other.

Five minutes later, and the original cabdriver had customers in his vehicle and was away, while I was still standing there.

A tic beginning in my jaw, I dug out my phone and called the rental car company. Sweat dripped down my neck, the breeze not enough to counter the heaviness of my jeans or the weight of the humidity.

Los Angeles heat was as dry as the Mojave, my body unprepared for the water in the air here.

"Sorry, sorry," the owner said, his voice languid. "Car's on the way. Only ten minutes. Island time, eh."

Grinding my teeth, I confirmed the registration number and description of the vehicle so I could spot it as it pulled in, and was thankful that at least they'd given me the four-wheel drive I'd asked for when I'd booked over the phone from Auckland Airport.

When the rental did finally arrive—a good twenty minutes later—it proved to be far less shiny and new than implied, and the air-conditioning was broken, but it drove well enough, which was all I needed. In the interim, I'd managed to grab a sandwich, a banana, and an ice-cold Coke, as well as a paper map; now I threw everything but the Coke onto the passenger seat after placing my duffel on the passenger floorboard.

Then, my drink secured in the cup holder, I headed out.

I still had a three-hour drive ahead of me. The distance to travel itself wasn't far, but Diya had described gravel roads and dirt tracks when she'd shown me a map of where her family had lived before they moved to Nadi so her parents could work in the hospital there, some years prior to their shift to New Zealand.

"Beautiful, *beautiful* place," she'd said, "but getting there is a nightmare, especially if it's been raining."

That map had gone up in flames, but I remembered enough to get myself pointed in the right direction out of the airport. Once I reached the general vicinity, I'd have to ask the locals and hope. The heavens opened up right then, blurring the sugarcane fields interspersed with tin-roofed houses, many with bougainvillea running riot in brilliant splashes of pink and purple.

The rain was gentle rather than torrential, but it did cool down the world to a bearable temperature. Coconut palms waved in the breeze, papaya trees with their unripe green fruit tucked close to the top stood sentinel beside homes, and I could see hibiscus blooms growing wild, all of it against a backdrop of mountains everywhere I looked, the landscape an undulating beauty of lush green broken up by bursts of wild color.

It was paradise.

My jaw ached from how hard I was clenching it.

An hour into it—along a smooth sealed road—and after the rain had passed as if it had never come, I pulled over in front of a decrepit-looking shop with a faded Fanta sign in the window, and a front path bordered by what might've been zinnias.

Against the sun-bleached shop, all its signage long faded, the zinnias were bursts of intense pigment that made me glad I was wearing sunglasses.

But I slid them off the second I entered the cool semidarkness of the shop. The proprietor had covered over the windows with signage that faced outward, blocking the sun. No AC, but a ceiling fan spun lazily overhead.

The combination worked surprisingly well, the inside of the shop cool enough to be comfortable even for me.

The owner was seated behind a screen of iron bars, the cigarettes and the cash register behind him. Despite the bars, which reminded me of certain parts of LA, he shot me a friendly smile. Around my age, he was Indo-Fijian, his skin dark and his short-sleeved shirt a pale blue. When he opened his mouth and spoke, I recognized the words but couldn't respond to them.

"Sorry," I said. "English?"

"Yes, I speak English." His expression remained cheerful. "Grow up overseas?"

"Yes," I said, because it was simpler to allow him to believe that than to explain that I had no connection to this nation or its people beyond my love for Diya.

The shopkeeper nodded. "What do you need?"

"Directions," I said, and expected to be told to buy something in return, but the man was happy to help me out.

"The Prasad place?" he said at one point, after I indicated the general area of Diya's family home.

I stared at him.

He laughed. "My cousin-brother's uncle Ravi is the caretaker there. It's easy to find. Just follow this way."

Taking out a piece of paper, he sketched a map on it that had such landmarks as "the coconut tree that split in two in the big cyclone" and "Ali's old house before he built his new one in town—it has grass growing through the windows" and "the river bridge with blue arches."

"How long from here?" I asked. "I was told about three hours from the airport."

He made a face while looking in the direction of the rectangle of light that was the open front door. "With the rain before . . . the tracks might be muddy. So, yes, I would say two more hours."

Two more hours until I might have some semblance of an answer as to why Diya had gasped out her dead sibling's name in what might well have been her last conscious moments on this earth.

# CHAPTER 26

## SUSANNE

Susanne turned in bed to watch her young lover on the carpeted floor beside it.

He was doing push-ups while clad in just his boxers, giving her a lovely view of his rather delicious musculature. He'd turned twenty a week earlier, and last night had been their private celebration—she wasn't gauche enough to flaunt him to her social circle even if he was so pretty.

The signet ring she'd gifted him sat on the bedside table, beside the new phone she'd bought him only a couple of months after she'd first asked him to join her for coffee. It had been a year now, and she knew full well that she was what the younger generation called a sugar mama. She had no argument with the arrangement—he was, after all, definitely keeping up his end of the bargain.

"Come back to bed, darling." Her body sighed with need. You'd think at her age, it'd be quieting down, but it turned out that she'd never gotten to full revs with her dear husband.

This was all an entirely new experience.

*A sharp grin from the twenty-year-old who was currently holding a plank without effort. "I have to maintain my strength to keep up with you."*

*Chuckling—and pleased by the charming comment—she let him finish his workout while she sat up in bed and considered whether to buy him that vehicle he had his eye on. Perhaps in six months' time. She was having fun, and so was he. No need to overdose when they could stretch it out.*

*She'd be seventy in two more years. God. Perhaps she might lose the itch by then, and he'd surely have moved on. Could be she'd give the vehicle to him as a parting gift, a shiny trophy for him to drive around in—she'd enjoy imagining him so handsome and young and suited to the fast car.*

*"How are your studies going?" That was another thing she liked about Tavish—he was very, very clever. Studying business and finance, and not just studying, but interested. And that made him interesting. He could talk investments with her over breakfast, and pump her to orgasm at night.*

*Truly, he'd be her perfect man if only he wasn't almost five decades her junior.*

*"Aced the latest exams." He bounced to his feet. "I'm a bit bored, to be honest, but I need to have these credits to get the kind of job I want."*

*She also loved that he had all these plans, young Tavish Advani; he might enjoy having a woman spoil him, but he was planning to become a man who could spoil himself. Some younger woman would one day find herself with a very successful and driven husband. "With an eye to setting up your own investment firm down the road?"*

*Another one of those wide grins before he prowled over the bedspread toward her, strong and gorgeous and aroused. "Of course, Susanne with an s. You know I play to win."*

*Smiling, she let him lower her to her back, and was proud that she'd kept herself toned and fit enough that he had no trouble with the physical aspect of things. If she'd been a more emotional type of woman, she might have made the mistake of falling in love with him. But she wasn't a stupid girl.*

*Still . . . it was nice to pretend even as she faced her own mortality in the mirror every day. And especially this week, when her left leg was giving her enough pain to make life irritating.*

*His hand on there, massaging gently even as he put his mouth to her breast.*

*A little more, Susanne thought as her back arched, just a little more of him and of life, of youth.*

# CHAPTER 27

A ny dust that had coated the road before the rain was gone, everything fresh and shiny. A small Fijian boy wearing blue shorts and a green T-shirt waved at me as I passed a village. I saw him race across the road in my rearview mirror, to retrieve a ball that he'd kicked to the other side.

No other cars even in the far distance, the road empty but for the two of us.

I turned the corner . . . and there was the tree split in the middle. As instructed, I took that exit off the main road. And kept on following the shopkeeper's instructions as the landscape became ever more green and rural.

I hit the gravel road fifteen minutes into it, but the car hugged it with ease, no hint of a wobble. I was suddenly glad it wasn't as shiny and new as advertised. It meant any fresh dents caused by stones flying up wouldn't be noticeable even on close inspection.

Around me, I saw only crops I couldn't identify, interspersed with patches of verdant forest.

No houses or people.

When I did eventually stop, it was because I was getting a spinal adjustment from the potholed and bumpy road and needed to stretch out my back. Unclipping my seat belt, I pushed open the door to get out. The air felt cooler than it had by the shop, all that green cutting down on the heat.

A small and scuffed-up blue truck loaded with what looked to be freshly cut taro—a root vegetable to which Diya had introduced me—rumbled over from the other direction while I was stretching, and stopped right beside me. The man who leaned out was Fijian, somewhere in his twenties, his hair tight curls buzzed close to his skull, his skin bronzed, and his T-shirt a faded gray.

"You break down, brother?" he asked. "Gonna be dark soon. I'll give you a lift home."

"No, car's fine. My back just needed a rest from the road."

His laugh was huge and warm. "You should drive this truck, man—thing is twenty years old. It's all bump, bump, bump." But from his grin, he didn't much care. "You American?"

"Accent that obvious?"

Another grin. "Where you going?" he asked with a bluntness that would never fly in a city but was likely expected in a place this small and rural.

"The Prasad place," I said, using the same verbiage as the man in the shop.

The truck driver frowned for a minute. "Ah, right, big place by the water. Nice, man, nice." Lifting his hand, he said, "Got to get these ready for the morning market."

*Big place by the water.*

It could've described the home that had gone up in flames. The Prasads re-creating the home they hadn't been able to let go of even after so many years in another country? Because of Ani? Was she buried here?

I frowned. No, that couldn't be it. The family preferred cremation. I knew that because Diya and I had found it morbid that it was in the boilerplate wills we'd signed, each of us having to put down what we'd prefer when the time came.

"We don't bury our dead," Diya had said, her gaze pensive. "The idea of being buried underground in a small box . . ." She'd shuddered. "I'd far rather burn up and be done with it."

The comment haunted me.

Jumping back into the car, I continued on.

Thirty minutes later, right when I thought I must've passed it already, I saw the top of a large house just emerging from the thick green foliage in which it nestled. I spotted banana palms, along with flowering vines and a tree with huge glossy green leaves, among many others.

The foliage was so dense that all I could see of the house was the tip of the roof even as I came closer and closer . . . and that was when I realized why the shop owner hadn't told me to turn off at a certain point. Diya's family home was right at the end of the road, only the ocean beyond it on the far side.

I felt cobblestones under me as I brought the vehicle to a stop in a front yard draped in the thick shadows of early evening, and when I stepped out, I saw that the grass had been kept under control.

By that caretaker? The cousin-brother something?

The two-story house, while free of the encroachment of what felt like a forest now that I stood inside it, was shuttered and silent and in urgent need of maintenance. Large flakes of paint had come off the frontage, while mold grew on the upper level.

The tropical environment might've done even more damage over the years if the building hadn't been formed of concrete—I'd seen a couple of similar structures on my drive, houses far more stable than the dwellings of rickety wood and corrugated iron that dominated the rural landscape.

This was a rich person's house.

The entire property was also a haven of cool, the tropical heat ameliorated by both the plantings and the breeze coming off what I knew to be a secluded beach behind the house. Not visible from ground level as with the Lake Tarawera property, but only a short walk through the foliage.

Despite its beauty, however, this place felt desolate, a ruin in the making.

"Hello!"

Heart kicking at the sudden interruption, I looked over to my right—to see a skinny Indo-Fijian man with hair so flawlessly deep brown that it had to be dyed, and a matching pencil mustache. He'd come from somewhere beyond the banana palms to the left and wore a short-sleeved tan shirt with what might've been Fijian tapa prints on it, jeans, and flip-flops.

His thinness accentuated his wrinkles, but he wasn't that old. Forty-five maybe.

And unlike me, he seemed perfectly comfortable in jeans.

"Hi." I held out my hand. "Are you Ravi? I think I met a relative of yours over at the store about two hours from here?"

"Oh yes, yes." He pumped my hand. "I saw him at Kushma's niece's wedding just last weekend."

I had no idea who Kushma was, but smiled politely. "I'm Tavish Advani," I began, preparing to explain my link to Diya.

But the man's face lit up, and, wrapping his free hand around our already clasped hands, he pumped even harder. "Namaskaram, Mr. Tavish! You are the businessman from America!" His speech was a seamless mix of Hindi and English that I had to focus to understand. "We heard Diya beta got engaged!" His face fell as fast, his hands breaking away. "Is she . . ."

So, the news of the fire and the deaths had reached this isolated place. "She's in the hospital," I said. "Shumi as well."

He shook his head, eyes looking down. "So sad. The crime is terrible these days."

I didn't say anything to that. "I came to get something from here. I thought . . . for the funerals—an important piece of the family's past." I'd thought about what to say, decided to leave it open-ended because surely there had to be *something*.

He made the slightly nasal *ha* sound that meant yes. "I know the one you mean," he added, linking my vague description to the specific. "Dr. Sarita never took it with her the times she visited. Leaving a part of herself to watch over baby Ani. But yes, you should take it for the funerals. It was her mother's, you know."

I couldn't believe he'd just handed me such a brilliant opening. "I don't know too much about Ani. She was a sister who died young?"

"Cousin-sister," the caretaker explained, hyphenating cousin the same way the shopkeeper had done—the usage was one I'd heard before; it was cultural, cousins addressed the same way as siblings except when clarifying the relationship to others.

"I was working in Suva then," Ravi elaborated, "but baby Ani's parents died in a car crash. Terrible, just terrible. So young, both of them. Hitesh was Dr. Rajesh's only brother, and so of course Dr. Rajesh and Dr. Sarita were going to look after baby Ani."

He turned, began to walk up the stairs to the covered porch of the house. "Come, I have the key—I always keep it with me when I do my evening stroll, sometimes just go in and walk around, make sure everything is tip-top. You staying here? We keep it clean."

"If you think it'll be all right? I'm only here two nights."

The caretaker shook his head again. "So sad. House is too big for one person. We can put our boys in one room for the night so you can have a bed."

"Thanks," I said, having the feeling the offer was sincere. "But it might be nice for me to stay here. I can tell Diya about it when I go back . . . maybe it would help her wake up." My throat choked up, the last words barely audible.

Ravi blinked rapidly before clearing his own throat. "I'll ask my wife to make you dinner, bring it over. You okay with spicy? Kushma likes using spice, but she leaves it out for her friend from Australia, so no problem if you don't like it. She can make the recipe a different way."

"No, I love it."

Taking an old-fashioned iron key from his pocket even as I spoke, Ravi put it into the lock, turned. "Some caretakers, they just don't do the work. They know the owner maybe won't come back for years.

"But the doctors are a good family—they pay us well to be here full-time, and even pay our kids' school fees every year and buy their textbooks, their uniforms, all they need for school. Dr. Sarita always says education is the key to a bright future. We take very good care of everything."

He tapped the outside wall. "I told them, it needs paint, but they wanted to have a look personally, decide what to do—but they're so busy it's been two years since I told them and they haven't managed to come here."

It didn't escape me that he was using the present tense in relation to Diya's parents. Hope? After all, their deaths hadn't yet been confirmed . . . even if the likelihood of survival was less than minuscule. "So they didn't visit regularly?" I'd just assumed they had, with how much they talked about Fiji.

"They used to." When he pushed open the door, it went inward without making a sound. "But last three years, only once. I think they did special doctor stuff, got busy."

I had a vague memory of Diya mentioning extra certification but couldn't recall the details. Not that it mattered now. "I don't know how you'll be paid until Diya wakes up," I said. "Everything's a mess."

Ravi waved it off. "It's no problem. The lawyer pays us from the rental money of their other house in Fiji. He'll work it out."

No wonder Ackerson thought this was about money. Diya's inheritance kept increasing. "I didn't know they had another property here."

"In Nadi," Ravi said. "Just a small one—would've been baby Ani's. Was her parents' place. After Ani died, Dr. Rajesh thought about selling it but couldn't. Too painful. Last memory of his brother and family, you know?"

Inside, the Prasad house was cool and dark.

"I'll open the curtains so you won't have to in the morning." Ravi was already doing so. "Most days, we keep them closed to keep out the sun, and we put up the shutters, too, during hurricane season. The upstairs we only fully open up when the family visits. Dr. Sarita likes the view of the water from up there."

A sudden pause, as if it had hit him that Sarita and Rajesh would never again wake in the upstairs rooms of this old house, never again admire the view of the Pacific Ocean rolling in to shore. There was only so far you could go on hope when both doctors had been missing since the morning of the fire.

"Kushma," he said in a quick, shaky burst, "she airs out the house properly once a month, checks nothing's gotten inside, cleans the dust. I do all the outdoor work, keep the plants tidy, make any repairs." He pushed open another set of curtains. "Here you go."

The gray light of dusk poured over furniture from another decade that was worn but still nice enough for a family home. Comfortable.

A rich person's house, but not a showpiece. A true home. Small knick-knacks sat on the shelves, and I spotted a pile of seashells on a windowsill, a stack of books on the coffee table.

"Here, I'll turn on the light."

No dust motes danced in the air in the creamy light that poured from the ceiling bulb, Ravi's wife a conscientious housekeeper.

"It really feels like they were preparing to come back."

"They always said they'd retire here—nothing like home, Dr. Sarita always said, and Dr. Rajesh would smile and nod. Even though they were so successful overseas, they never got too important to remember this place. They always brought my boys chocolate from New Zealand, said they'd sponsor them to study there later on if they got good marks in school."

The talkative man angled his head to the right. "I'll show you the prayer place." A pause, a touch of awkwardness. "You know about being clean before you touch the prayer statues? Full shower. And no eating eggs or meat while handling things?"

"Yes, my grandmother was Hindu." She hadn't managed to pass on her religion to her son or grandson, but I'd been around her enough to pick up a few things. "I won't touch anything until I've showered."

As in the Lake Tarawera house, the prayer alcove had been custom-built, a generously sized rectangle of space nestled in the wall. It held a number of small brass statues of gods, and the shallow clay oil lamp that was the genesis of Diya's name. Tucked into the corner were several photos of a chubby-cheeked little girl along with a young couple.

"Baby Ani and her parents," Ravi said. "Whole family, just gone. I think that's what killed old Mr. and Mrs. Prasad." He indicated the black-and-white photos on the other side. "Lost their younger son and daughter-in-law and then, only seven months later, their grand-daughter.

"He had a heart attack not long after, and she just went in her sleep a month later. Five people, gone in less than two years. Everyone still in mourning for Hitesh and his wife, but then another funeral, then another and another. Bad, bad time."

The tragedy of it crashed over me like the ocean I could almost hear, but held within it was the realization that Lake Tarawera, too, had involved five people. As if this family's terrible losses came in multiples of five.

Music. A faint wind chime melancholy in its timbre.

My arms prickled with goose bumps. "Is that someone's ringtone?" I asked, though I hadn't seen any signs of a third person in the vicinity.

"No, that's Ani," Ravi said. "That little baby never left here. I think she plays under the mango tree."

# CHAPTER 28

## SUSANNE

*T*he results came back." Susanne sipped the special juice Tavish had made for her that morning in an effort to help settle her stomach. He'd used lots of fresh crushed ginger, and it felt good in her throat.

Beyond the metal railing of the apartment balcony, Singapore glittered and thrived, the water a silvery glimmer of light in the distance.

The sun was warm on her skin, the humidity just right.

She'd wanted a long vacation in the place where she'd spent so much of her childhood, and—with what was happening—Tavish had deferred a semester and come with her.

"What did they say?" He dragged over his chair so that he sat facing her rather than on the other side of the metal table on which he'd put the pitcher of juice. "Suzi, tell me." He took her hand, began to do that massage thing on her palm that always made her feel good.

Eyes closing, she leaned back in her chair and smiled. "I'm glad I picked you up that day." She met his gaze. "I thought I'd sow a few wild oats before settling down into life as a sophisticated old lady. We've had fun together, haven't we?"

His throat moved. "Yes. I thought we were having fun and that was it, but . . . I really like you. I wish we'd been born at the same time."

"Sweet boy." She managed a little more of the ginger drink, then put the glass down on the table. "It's lung cancer. Bad, but not terminal . . . yet."

His pupils flared in front of her. "You'll fight it," he said, and while it sounded like an order, his voice was raw beneath.

She didn't think he was pretending; he was too young, too unfinished. "I don't think so, Tavish." Susanne had lived the reality of a long, devouring illness with her husband, would wish that fate on no one.

Her forever-laughing man had become a ghost of himself, a querulous stranger whose eyes had begged her for surcease. "I'm choosing to live as I've always done, go out as myself in my home rather than a shriveled creature in the hospital."

"Susanne, no."

"I've always gone my own way, darling, you know that."

Tavish blinked and looked away. It warmed her that he would grieve her.

"Will you stay with me?" she asked. "Not to be my nurse—dear God, no. I'll hire someone for that when needed, but to be what you are to me. My friend and lover. We'll stay here, in the place where I spent the happiest years of my childhood."

She touched the side of his face, his skin smooth since he'd just shaved. "It's selfish of me to ask. You won't graduate with your class."

"I don't care about that. I care about you." Rough voice, his Adam's apple moving as he swallowed. "Of course I'll be here." The sunlight sparked off the signet ring on his finger as he squeezed her hand. "Whatever you need, I'll be here."

In that moment, with this boy who had become so much more to her than a lovely flirtation, Susanne realized that she'd been lucky. She'd loved and been loved by two good men in her life. Not the same way—how could a relationship that would never even reach the five-year mark compare to one of decades?—but loved all the same.

# CHAPTER 29

The wind chimes sounded again, a faint nocturne that penetrated under the skin and took root.

*Not a ringtone at all. Never a ringtone.*

Fighting back the chilling whisper but unable to stop the cold from spreading through my veins, I said, "I didn't know about Dr. Rajesh's brother and parents."

"He didn't like to talk about it. How his big family became so small." Expression somber, Ravi pointed out a particular statue after first putting his hands together in prayer and saying a string of words under his breath.

"That's the one you need," he said. "Dr. Sarita's mother gave it to her before she passed. Don't take the one beside it, though—Dr. Sarita bought that after baby Ani passed away. It's for Ani, and Dr. Sarita always said that Ani's soul is here, where she died."

"I won't touch it," I promised, suddenly not sure I'd ever seen any pictures of Ani in the family home in Lake Tarawera. It was possible that she'd been in the collection on the piano, but I'd never paid too much attention to that—especially as, most of the time, I'd been trying to be polite and make conversation with Diya's family while being very aware that they hadn't yet made up their minds about me.

After partially closing the intricately carved doors of the prayer alcove, Ravi led me down the hallway. "You want an upstairs room?"

"Downstairs is fine. No need to open up anything extra."

"This room is great for the morning light." He showed me one that faced the frontage, and all that thriving tropical foliage. "I'll ask Kushma to put sheets on the bed." He pointed up. "No air-conditioning here, but you have the fan and the windows. Usually a nice breeze coming from the ocean."

Able to feel that breeze through the glass louvers as soon as he flipped them open, I said, "This is perfect, thank you" . . . just as the wind chimes sounded again, louder this time. More real.

Not ghost music, but an actual physical object.

Wanting to kick myself for falling victim to the atmosphere and Ravi's dramatics, I drew deep of the salt-laced air. Then I turned to the caretaker. "Ravi, can I ask you about Ani?" I had to take the chance. "The family doesn't talk about her and I really can't ask Diya or Shumi after all this. I don't want to put my foot in it by accident."

Ravi's already long face fell. "Yes, such a sad thing. Come with me—I'll show you the tree Dr. Rajesh planted for baby Ani. Ashes went in flowing water as is proper, but he always said this was Ani's place, and he put the tree there for her."

As we walked out into the dark gray of oncoming night, the sky erased of even a touch of the orange-pink I'd seen on my drive, he said, "I don't know so much about how baby Ani died—everyone just says accident. But Kamal who lives up the road, he was the police who came to handle it. He'll know."

"The blue house?" I asked, because that was the only house I'd passed before reaching this one.

Ravi nodded. "Lives with his wife and son and daughter-in-law." Coming to a stop in front of a large tree with narrow green leaves from which hung countless curving yellow-red fruits, he said, "Dr. Rajesh told me Ani loved mangoes. This tree? It gives the sweetest fruit." He plucked one off, held it out. "Here, for you to taste."

"Thank you." Something had been niggling at me about the mango tree since Ravi first mentioned it, but right then, it was the size of the tree that struck me. A *lot* of years had passed since Ani's death, and yet hers was the name Diya had spoken right before she lost the battle with consciousness.

A wind chime silvered by time hung from one of the lower branches.

"Diya beta put that there," Ravi said, following my gaze. "Just before the family moved to New Zealand. They'd been in Nadi for a few years by then, so Kushma and I were already here as caretakers. Dr. Sarita said Diya found it at the market one day and brought it home for Ani."

Diya and Ani.

Two girls.

One clinging to life, one long dead.

Forever entwined.

"I think I'll go talk to Kamal tomorrow," I said to Ravi, something about the wind chime story disturbing to me. "Since I'm here . . . and, well, I don't think I'll ever ask Diya. It's going to be hard enough for her to wake up and realize that she might've lost her entire family. I don't want to bring this up."

A sad nod of understanding. "You can go to his place anytime— he's home all day. Smokes and goes for walks, but never too far. I'll go ask Kushma to make up your bed now." He handed over the key.

"Just give it back to me before you go. I live in a wooden house to the left, behind the bananas."

"Is there running water to the property?"

"Yes, from the tank in the trees. Good you reminded me—I'll go turn on the flow on that end. Only take half a minute. And don't worry—I don't let it sit. Plenty of rain around here, easy to keep it refreshed in case the family decides to visit unexpectedly.

"Dr. Rajesh had me put in a filter," he added. "So it's safe to drink, but the doctors always said to boil it anyway. Kushma will also put some bottles of water from the shop in your kitchen, in case you don't want to bother with boiling and cooling."

After Ravi left to walk to the tank, I turned and went back to the house, the mango in hand. It felt as if it had gained in weight in the time since Ravi handed it to me, and I suddenly found myself wondering if Ani's ashes hadn't been given to water, if she was buried under the tree, her blood and bones part of its veins . . .

I left the mango on the kitchen counter.

Abruptly aware of how sticky my skin felt, I decided to have a shower in the large bathroom down the hall from my room.

There was no soap stocked inside, but the water was ice-cold and pure, the droplets that fell from the old-fashioned showerhead fat and round. Though I'd shivered when it first fell on me, I found myself lingering, letting the water soothe me, wash away all the pain and stress for a short window of time.

When I finally got out, I realized I'd forgotten to bring my duffel in with me. No towel, no fresh clothes.

And Ravi's wife was meant to be making up the bed for me.

I opened the door a crack and said, "Hello? Anyone in here?"

Silence, the ripple of a curtain in the distance.

I called out again, just in case, but if the mysterious Kushma was inside the house, she wasn't answering. Hoping I wasn't about to scandalize the caretaker's wife, but loath to put on my sweaty, dusty clothes—oh, how Susanne would've laughed at my predicament—I kept an ear open as I walked naked down the hall.

But when I peeked into the bedroom, it was to see the bed neatly made up. On the end sat a stack of towels, beside that a small basket that held soap and other toiletries. She'd clearly been intending to stock up the bathroom for me before realizing it was already occupied.

Grateful for her and Ravi's help, I used one of the towels to dry off, then hitched it around my hips and walked to fully open one of the larger windows. The air was cool against my body. This, I thought, would be the most comfortable time of the day to hang around outside. Could be Kamal would be happy to have a visitor at this time, but all at once, my bones ached from exhaustion.

It wasn't about the amount of time that had passed since the fire, but the sheer weight of the stress I'd been under. Tonight at least, I could sleep, free from the threat of Ackerson swooping down on my head—or the media discovering the identity of Diya Prasad's American fiancé.

My hands squeezed the window ledge.

———

I'd expected to spend the night tossing and turning despite my tiredness, but I slept for nine straight hours, as if my body just shut down. No dreams. No haunting wind chimes. No fear. Maybe it was the invisible but efficient Kushma's cooking—she'd sent dinner over with her eldest son, who'd told me to leave the dishes on the porch table outside where I'd eaten.

Those dishes were gone when I walked outside into the comfortable morning air, and when I stepped down to stand on the grass, I could almost feel the thunder of the surf in the distance. I considered walking to it, watching the ocean under the morning light . . . but it felt like a betrayal to Diya.

"I can't wait to show you Fiji!" Kisses pressed to my jaw that made me grin. "I'll be Mrs. Tavish Advani to the whole world by then! We'll walk hand in hand to the beach. It's so beautiful, Tavi, better than any Caribbean resort, trust me."

My fingers curling into my palm, I headed back inside to do a workout using my own body weight; I'd started exercising as a kid in order to burn off the rage I couldn't acknowledge. Not then. Now I just liked it.

As for the rage . . . I'd dealt with it.

I'd just walked back outside after a quick shower to freshen up when Ravi appeared with a tray. "Bula! I thought you'd be awake. Breakfast for you. I know Diya beta likes bread, but we didn't have any fresh, so Kushma made you roti, and eggs from our chickens— she made them with onions and chili, but she said she can do an overseas-style omelet for you if you want."

My heart twisted—Diya had made eggs for me that way, taught me how to roll them up in the flatbread called roti, so that it became a savory wrap. "It sounds delicious, thank you."

Ravi put down the tray but didn't stay to chat, saying he had to get his boys to school. "It's a long drive every day, but education, you know."

When I took the lace cloth cover off the tray, I discovered coffee and a plate of sliced papaya and what I thought might be guava, as well as the roti and eggs. I was glad for the absence of mango. Though the coffee was instant, it still provided the necessary caffeine hit, but I slammed into a roadblock when I tried to eat the eggs.

Diya's laughter in the kitchen of my condo, the way she'd told me to watch as she flipped the egg "like a maestro"—only to splatter it all over the floor.

We'd laughed like lunatics while cleaning it up, just two people who were stupid in love. My wife had been so different back then, so full of a radiant light. Coming home to New Zealand, I realized with the gift of distance, had stolen a piece of that light from her, replacing it with shadows black and ominous.

*Why?*

Was it the same reason she'd spoken Ani's name when she thought she was dying?

Was it why her parents were dead? Because official confirmation or not, I knew the senior Prasads had to be dead. What other reason could there be for two respected doctors to vanish off the face of the planet on the same day their home burned to the ground?

Head chaotic with questions to which I had no answers, I ate the fruit and roti, then buried the eggs in the backyard, so as not to insult my hosts. I made a note to drop the mango under the tree, too, just another fallen fruit.

"What'll we find if we dig up your metaphorical backyard?" Callum Baxter's hard green eyes drilling into me in that tiny interrogation room where he'd held me for far too many hours. "How many women have you scammed?"

Dropping broken foliage over the small area I'd dug up to make it blend in with everything else, I went inside to wash my hands . . . and only realized I was gritting my teeth when I looked in the mirror. "Fuck you, Baxter, you piece of shit."

He hadn't won then, and he wouldn't win now, not even in my head.

# CHAPTER 30

Private notes: Detective Callum Baxter (LAPD)
Date: Jan 1
Time: 01:07

I can't believe we're into the new year and Tavish Advani is walking around free. Fuck, he's probably at some New Year's party now. Meanwhile, I'm still trying to track down how and when Susanne Winthorpe died.

Their names haunt me.

Virna Musgrave.

Jocelyn Wai.

Susanne Winthorpe.

All dead.

All with only one man in common.

I'm going to get that bastard if it's the last thing I do—that's my goddamn New Year's resolution.

# CHAPTER 31

A grizzled man of maybe seventy sat in a rocking chair on the front porch of the blue house a five-minute drive from the Prasad home, a cigarette hanging from his mouth, and his head a shining baldness but for two silvery stripes down the sides.

"Kamal?" I asked after exiting the car when he just watched me with dark eyes that didn't blink enough for my liking.

Cop, definitely a cop.

"I'm Tavish," I said when he didn't respond. "Diya's fiancé." As far as I knew, the Prasads hadn't told anyone that we were already married, and I'd honor their wish with the people here until Diya woke and we could talk about what to do going forward.

Stopping in his rocking, he took the cigarette out of his mouth. "You bring them home." He coughed after that raspy order given in heavily accented English. "Sarita and Rajesh and Bobby. Ashes should be scattered on their home water."

Kamal clearly had none of Ravi's hope when it came to the three missing family members. "Diya will make that decision," I said. "When she wakes up."

His expression twisted. "Bad?"

"Bad."

Exhaling, he got up. And though his back was a little bowed, he walked easily enough as he turned to go into the house. "Yash's wife made lemonade."

Taking that as an invitation, I walked up to take the other chair on the porch. The view from that vantage point was of the gravel road and what looked like farm fields beyond it. I couldn't tell the crops from this distance but could see what looked like a tractor working the land on the fallow far edge.

"Beans," Kamal said after walking out with a single glass of what looked like cold lemonade and putting it into my hand.

He was still smoking his cigarette, the scent of nicotine drifting my way on the warm but not unbearable morning air.

I thought of Susanne, of how she'd taken such pleasure in what would end up being her final cigarette, drawing in long drags and making smoke rings with her mouth as she exhaled. Where Jocelyn had smoked with an addict's passion, Susanne had managed to avoid that pitfall, had only smoked around me maybe five times overall.

Each cigarette had been a slow display of pleasure.

That night, she'd been wearing the glittering red cocktail dress she'd chosen for our date to a bar as sophisticated as she was, her lipstick perfect and not a strand out of place in the elegant twist in which she'd put her hair.

I had loved her so much. Enough to kill her.

Nothing else could've made me do what I'd done. Only love of the kind that was a vine around the heart that couldn't be removed. Susanne had been inside me. Where Diya now lived.

"Thanks." I took a sip of the drink in an effort to push away the memory of what I'd done, sighed at the tart sweetness. "Tastes fresh."

"She uses those. Good girl. Knows how to make it right." He pointed at a tree on the other side of the porch, heavy with tiny yellow citrus fruits. "So, why're you here? Shouldn't you be with Diya and Shumi?"

The fact that he'd added Shumi's name to the list told me that he was well up on the news.

I gave him the same excuse I'd given Ravi, but he didn't buy it. "You could've done that later. I don't know how the police in New Zealand do things, but I know they'll be looking at the forensic evidence—and that includes any remains. No funerals anytime soon."

"No." I drank a little more. "The thing is, Diya said something about Ani when I found her after the fire. I didn't know if it was important and there was no one there who'd tell me—Shumi's parents said they didn't know anything, and her brother didn't have much information."

Kamal snorted. "Those two. Of course they know. But Ajay wasn't even two when it happened." He tapped the ash from his cigarette into a dented metal ashtray on the little table between us. "It's old history. Nothing to do with now."

"It was on Diya's mind after she was hurt," I insisted. "And, honestly, she's not doing well. She's still in the ICU. If there's something she needs me to do so she'll be at peace, I want to." It was a stab in the dark, the latter, but I'd spotted the yellow string tied around his wrist, caught the scent of incense coming off him—Kamal was religious, and for the scent of incense to be strong enough to cut through the acrid puff of nicotine, he had to have prayed that morning.

It would matter to him that Diya not pass on in distress.

Another puff before he crushed out the butt in the ashtray. "They were just children. No point in making anything of it."

My heart thundered, and though I wanted to push, I stayed silent, both of us watching the tractor.

"My son, Yash," Kamal said at last. "I wanted him to become a police officer like me, but this is what he wants to do. Stupid. How's he going to emigrate overseas driving a tractor and growing beans and whatnot?" A shrug. "His wife works in a bank, so maybe she'll talk sense into him."

Leaning back in his chair, he began to rock again. "They were playing outside, Bobby and Shumi and Diya and Ani. Nobody much watching over them—we didn't, not back then. They knew not to go into the water alone, and usually just climbed trees or ran through the fields trying to find gooseberries."

The images were the stuff of hazy, happy childhood memories, but Kamal's face was grim.

"No Ajay," the older man added. "He was a little too young, but even if he hadn't been, that mother of his wouldn't have allowed it. She had all the control, with her husband off in Suva for work most of the year. I always said he'd grow up weak with a mother like that—woman had him tied to her apron strings from the day he was born." A glance at me, a silent question.

"I've only just met him," I said, thinking of how Mrs. Kumar had called him back to the motel room. "He seems okay on the surface."

Kamal's lip curled. "I pity the woman who becomes his wife. Ajay will always do what mummy says—she made him that way." The rocking increased. "I wasn't home that day, was at the station house by the koro. You would've passed it on the way here."

I remembered the small blue-and-white building across from the village where I'd seen the boy running for his ball, nodded.

"It was Sarita who called me. She was at home after a night shift at the little clinic they used to run, having a sleep while her mother- and father-in-law looked after the children. Rajesh was on day shift."

"They all lived together?"

"Yes." Picking up the cigarette packet on the table, he slid out another slender tube, put it to his lips, but didn't light it. "Shumi came running home, said Ani was hurt, so of course Sarita's in-laws woke her. She was a doctor. But there was nothing anyone could do—baby Ani was dead."

Diya must've been so scared and confused, I thought. "What happened?"

"In the report, I wrote that she fell against a rock while playing, smashed her head." He lit the cigarette now, cupping his hands around it with the ease of a longtime smoker. "Big crack in the head." A shake of the hand to douse the match, the first puff of new smoke. "Her lips were blue by the time I got there."

The visceral sensory memory of backroom poker games pushed aside the echo of Susanne enjoying her last cigarette. The nicotine had been so thick in the air at some of those games that it had been a visible cloud—but I'd never indulged. One self-destructive addiction was more than enough. "But you don't think it was an accident."

"It wasn't." Flat words. "There was another rock nearby. Blood and hair on it. The Prasads were a good family, Sarita a dedicated young mother. And what use was there in punishing a child for being angry for a moment?" Another puff, while my mind tumbled. "The Prasads did good thing after good thing for the locals. And they'd suffered so much already. No reason to ruin their name."

So this small-town cop had covered up the murder of a child. Even knowing the consequences of his choice, I wasn't sure I wouldn't have done exactly the same. "How did you . . ."

A shrug. "It wasn't hard. I was the senior policeman, and it was believable. No morgue here, so we had to drive her to Labasa and the doctor there knew me since I was a young officer, accepted what I said. Terrible accident."

"Weren't you afraid he'd do it again?" It took all my strength to keep my voice even. "Kill someone else?"

"He?" Taking out his cigarette, Kamal stared at me. "It wasn't the boy. Little Diya got jealous of her cousin-sister being gifted a new doll and hit her. She was so small herself, had no idea what she was doing." He sighed. "She was standing there with the doll in her hands when I got there, her dress all splattered with blood. Yellow hair and blue eyes, I remember that doll had yellow hair and blue eyes."

# CHAPTER 32

## SUSANNE

*N*othing tasted right anymore, not even the ginger drinks Tavish made her with such care. Susanne sipped this one nonetheless, unwilling to hurt his feelings.

"You're in pain." He tucked another pillow behind her. "How bad is it?"

Sighing, she put the drink on the bedside table. "It feels as if my spine is crumbling inside me." She hadn't been to the oncologist again, already knew what he was going to tell her—the cancer had spread, likely to her bones. "Be a sweetheart and open up the curtains a bit more."

Tavish moved to do as she'd requested, Singapore a spread of glittering buildings and water on the other side. "You should see Dr. Chua," he said when he turned back to face her. "This is moving too fast. He said you'd have longer."

Oh, but he was having a hard time handling her mortality. "It's too late now, Tavish," she said gently, and patted the spot beside her on the bed. "I can feel the disease eating at me in greedy bites."

He came, picked up the drink. "Have a little more," he coaxed. "You're losing so much weight—I tried to bulk this up with protein powder and honey."

Susanne took another sip to please him but couldn't stomach the taste. Nudging it away, she said, "I'd have had maybe a twenty-five percent chance of beating this if I'd started aggressive treatment straightaway, but I chose another path, and unfortunately, I gambled wrong."

It wasn't that she hadn't had some good time after the diagnosis, just that the time had been too short, the end of her life a sharp and jagged descent rather than a gradual slope. Now the only thing left to discuss was how she would spend her final days.

In pain, slowly losing control of God only knew what function.

Or . . . "Tavish, my sweet boy, I need you to do something for me."

# CHAPTER 33

A rattle from inside Kamal's house that felt like a drum in my head, the world too loud, too bright, the words the older man had spoken bile in my throat.

*It wasn't the boy.*

*Yellow hair and blue eyes . . .*

*. . . her dress all splattered with blood.*

A thin and wrinkled woman in a loose floral dress followed the noise onto the porch. "You need to take your medicine." She shoved a bottle into Kamal's hand with those words spoken in Hindi, her tongue as sharp as the edge of a knife.

Grunting, Kamal said, "Fine, *I'll* get the water."

My mind was still roaring when the woman spoke after her husband was gone. "Only English?" The question was hard and flat.

I somehow managed to comprehend what she wanted to know, and found the right words to string together in my grandparents' mother tongue. "No. I . . . understand Hindi. Speaking . . . not . . . so . . ." I just shook my head at the end.

That seemed to be enough for her, however, because she began to speak in rapid-fire Hindi it took all my concentration to follow. "I never thought it was Diya beti—or that it was about a doll. She used to play for hours with Ani, shared all her toys. Diya loved Ani." She sniffed. "That brother of hers, now, he was a bully. No surprise after the way his own father bullied him."

I stared at her, my focus snapping back into brilliant color. "You . . ." Halting, I fought to find the right words. "You . . . think . . . Bobby . . . hurt Ani?"

"Not my place to say. I'm not the police officer." She picked up the ashtray and threw the butts into a little trash can under the table.

"Please," I said.

Rubbing her back, she rose. "I'm just saying Diya beti didn't talk too well even at five. They wouldn't take her at the school even when they took other children her age, said she had to start talking properly first. But Bobby sahib, oh, he could talk and talk—and that Shumi, she thought he was better than a movie star."

A roll of her eyes. "The girl would've parroted anything Bobby told her to say. And I know my husband likes to talk about the blood on Diya's dress, but the poor child could've just been standing there when it happened. Or the boy could've put it on her on purpose. He was vicious even back then, and Diya didn't talk at all for days and days after."

"Meera!" A yell from inside the house as the tractor trundled over to this side of the field. "I can't find the other pills!"

The woman turned on her heel but pinned me with her gaze before stepping inside. "They'll find out it was that Bobby who killed his family. They haven't found his body, have they? That's what it said on the news. Only signs of two people in the doctors' house. And the boy was so angry on the inside. Poor baby Ani just got in his way and he scared Diya into staying quiet."

She waved her hand at me. "You go now. Kamal will sleep again after his pills. Come later if you want, but he didn't keep any papers if that's what you're after. Just what's in his head, and the stubborn old goat won't budge from the idea that it was Diya who did it."

I rose shakily to my feet.

Was that it?

Bobby had lost it again?

Was that what Diya had been trying to tell me? That he'd done the same thing to the family that he'd done to Ani all those years ago?

Just lost it, gone psychotic.

I'd never seen the other man act the bully, but then I'd only known him a matter of weeks. Anyone could put on a mask for that long.

"Hello!" Yash called out from the seat of the tractor he'd brought to a standstill parallel to the road. "Come to see my father?" His biceps pushed against his black T-shirt, his beard short and neatly trimmed, and his smile friendly enough. "He's in a good mood, isn't he?" An amused laugh.

Shoving my brain back into gear, I walked over to the edge of the field so we could speak without shouting. "I'm Tavish, Diya's fiancé."

"Oh." His smile faded into somber quiet as he leaned forward on the steering wheel before flowing from his first language into what was most comfortable for me. "How are they? Diya and Shumi?"

I folded my arms. "In the ICU." It was all I could say and even that came out gritty and painful.

Dark eyes pinched at the corners, Yash just gave a clipped nod. "Cops have any idea who did it?"

"No, but your mother seems to think it was Bobby." No filter, my brain in shock.

"Yeah, Amma might be right." A vein pulsed at his temple. "We were in school together—Bobby and me—when they lived here."

Lifting his left arm, he showed me a small scar on his inner forearm. "He did that. Cut me with a sharp rock when I wouldn't give him some jalebi Amma had got me from the market."

"Everyone else seems to have a high opinion of him."

"Ask people his own age if you want the truth. Not his friends. The others." He put down his arm, rubbing absently at the scar with the fingers of his other hand. "He knew how to play nice for adults, too, be the perfect eldest son. No one ever believed us when we complained about him."

"Your mother mentioned that his father was abusive."

"Never yelled or anything that I saw, but back then, it wouldn't have mattered." Yash shrugged. "Doctor, you know. Big important man. Never spotted any bruises on Bobby, either, but one time I saw him crying because he'd scored ninety-seven percent instead of a hundred percent on a test.

"Not angry tears. Scared tears. A kid can tell, yaar." He rolled the *r* in that last word the same way I'd heard my father's friends use it when speaking to him; the direct translation was "friend," but used this way . . . maybe "bro"?

"He punched me in the mouth when he realized I'd seen him," Yash added. "Told me he'd kill me if I told anyone else."

"I never saw any hint of that in their adult relationship." If anything, Dr. Rajesh Prasad had struck me as an indulgent father . . . but I'd only ever watched how he related to Diya—she was my wife, my priority.

"Wouldn't know about that." The other man sat back up. "I hope Diya and Shumi make it. Tell Shumi that Yash Dayal says hi. Always thought it a shame she fell for that bastard."

My instincts caught more than the obvious bitterness. "Your mother seems to think she was always sweet on him."

"Rich doctor's son, yaar, all the girls wanted him." A hard wave before he carried on with his tractor, and I got into my vehicle.

Despite his apparent need for rest after his pills, Kamal was back in his rocker by then, his wife beside him. Neither waved as I pulled out.

———

I finally met Kushma when she brought me lunch. A slender woman with silky hair worn in a bun whose English was broken at best, she laughed without malice at my halting attempts at Hindi but seemed pleased that I wanted to put her at ease.

"Bobby?" she said in her preferred tongue when I asked about whether she'd known him growing up. "I was too old, already married by the time he was in high school." Despite the words, her gaze was thoughtful.

"I did know him a little before," she said a few moments later. "After I finished school and couldn't find work, I used to come help clean the house with my amma. The doctors were so busy with the clinic and Mr. and Mrs. Prasad-ji, the elder ones, they were already looking after the children. So the doctors hired Amma to clean."

I invited her to sit at the table, but she waved it off to remain on her feet. "Bobby was a nice boy," she said, the tray on which she'd brought me sautéed okra, dhal, steaming jasmine rice, and home-made mango pickles tucked under her arm. "Funny, too—he used to do the dialogues of Dr. Sarita's favorite actor. That's how everyone started calling him Bobby."

I absorbed that unexpected little piece of information with dull resignation for something that couldn't help me.

"He even helped us mop sometimes," Kushma added. "But mostly he was at school when we came, so I didn't talk to him much. He always had a lot of school papers in his room—he studied hard."

She had nothing much more to tell me when it came to Bobby, and when I asked about Ani and Diya, all she said was, "Oh, such sweet babies, they were. It was so sad what happened to Ani."

"Would anyone else know more about the family?" I dared ask.

Kushma, already heading down the stairs, shook her head. "Most of the doctors' friends went overseas already, and other people they knew from around here moved away to work in the cities."

Despite the fact that Kushma hadn't told me anything useful, she had given me one idea: *papers.*

I spent the rest of the day methodically searching the house for hidden journals, notes, paperwork of any kind that might shed light on the events that had taken place close to two decades earlier.

All I found was a box hidden in the closet of the upstairs master bedroom that held a small stack of photos, a bracelet of tiny black-and-white beads small enough to fit a child's fragile wrist, and a birth certificate . . . for Annika Sonakshi Prasad.

*Ani.*

———

If I'd imagined I'd sleep easy again a second night, I was proven very wrong.

The house creaked and groaned, the wind chime shivered its sorrowful music, while the ocean's pounding surf sounded like it was right on top of me. I tossed and turned, snatching bits of sleep here and there.

Only to fall into the past.

I dreamed of Susanne and how she'd been at the end, so emaciated beneath her glamorous makeup that she'd been bones and tendons held together by skin gone translucent. She'd done a stellar job of hiding the ravages of the cancer our final night out. No one at the bar to which we'd gone to drink her favorite champagne had blinked an eye at a woman they'd probably taken to be fashionably thin.

But Susanne had been far beyond thin at that point.

"I'm ready to die, Tavish." A phantom whisper from the past. "And I'm going to do it on my own terms. A raised finger to the universe."

Husky laughter that morphed into a hacking cough so terrible it jerked me to wakefulness. "Fuck."

Susanne's hollow eyes stared at me from inside my memories, the pill bottles scattered all around her as she lay on the cotton throw of her bed dressed once again in that glittering red dress she loved, her makeup flawless.

I'd never seen her that way, her nurse the one who'd discovered her body, but I'd read the coroner's report.

And I knew Suzi W.

It wouldn't have been pajamas or underwear for her. Only sophisticated, independent beauty, all the way to the very end.

"Nothing that'll make me vomit, dear," she'd told me when talking about her requirements for a painless drug-induced death. "How utterly embarrassing to go out with such a lack of style."

Shoving off the thin sheet I'd been using as a blanket, my boxer briefs my pajamas, I picked up my phone to look at the time: four a.m.

I should've tried to go back to sleep, but I got up and walked out onto the front verandah instead . . . and realized that I'd never been in darkness such as this. The only light came from the small bedside lamp I'd turned on in my room. A soft glow that was already attracting moths, their fluttery shadows as powder soft as their wings.

The rest of the world was pitch-black. No streetlights, no car lights, nothing but a blackness broken only by the starry pinpricks above. Even the wind chime had gone silent, the surf a distant thunder my brain had finally learned to tune out at some point during my fitful sleep.

Something croaked so close that I jolted.

More croaks came from everywhere all at once.

Then the lawn started to move.

Frogs. Tiny frogs going about their nocturnal business.

This was definitely not the city.

No, this was the place where a provincial cop had covered up a little girl's death because the assailant had also been a child—but the child on whom he'd pinned the blame had been the wrong one. Diya was petite even now. She would've been tiny back then, certainly not strong enough to bring down a rock on another child's head with enough force to crack it.

Kamal had to have known that, too, so why had he never looked at Bobby?

*. . . a good family . . . ruin their name . . .*

Good old-fashioned chauvinism?

My brother, Raja, had never once been held to account for anything, but neither had I—at least when it came to my extended family. Inside the family, of course, it was a whole different story.

Raja had put the blame on me plenty of times when we were children. Though his subterfuges had been about petty matters, I could see how the same sense of entitlement could lead to the belief that the eldest son didn't need to be held responsible for anything . . . not even murder.

It was always someone else's problem.

Bobby, six years older than Diya, would've been plenty big enough to do what had been done to Ani. And Shumi, his ever-devoted follower, would've never betrayed him. No, she would've done exactly what he wanted.

*Oh, you choose, Bobby. You always choose the best options.*

*Sure, my love, we can leave if you want.*

*Of course, darling!*

Those last words, I'd heard over and over again. Bobby loved his wife's masala chai and had requested she make it at least three times in my vicinity. It had struck me because all three times, they'd been guests in the Prasad home . . . but Shumi had never been treated like a guest.

The Prasads treated her as they did Diya—like a daughter. She also referred to them as Amma and Pitaji, which to my ear seemed more formal—or maybe just more traditional—than the Mum and Dad that Diya always used, but the affection between the elder Prasads and Shumi was clear. That part had given me hope that one day, I, too, would have a similar relationship with my in-laws.

Bobby, on the other hand, had treated his wife like she was at his beck and call. And Shumi had appeared more than fine with that. She'd jumped up to make the time-consuming chai at a moment's notice—beginning with hand-grinding her special mix of spices.

The fact that she'd had all the ingredients at hand in the Prasad pantry had told me how often Bobby sat chatting to his parents while Shumi worked in the kitchen. And still, I might not have noticed any of it consciously if I hadn't had to force down more than one cup of chai—which I hated with a vengeance.

"They'll take away your Indian card," Diya had said with a giggle when I confessed to her after the first time Shumi handed me a cup of the chai she'd made with such love. "Are you sure you're even half-brown?"

"Ha ha." I'd tickled the bottoms of her feet in vengeance, sent her squealing.

Despite her teasing, however, she'd grabbed my chai the next time it was thrust on me and gulped it down while no one else was watching. "The things I do for love," she'd whispered afterward.

What, I thought around the pulsating ache in my heart, had Shumi done for love?

# CHAPTER 34

## SUSANNE

Connelly West, attorney-at-law, pushed up his reading glasses even though he already knew the contents of the will verbatim. His small audience waited in silence.

"Mrs. Susanne Eliza Winthorpe was of sound mind when she updated and verified this last will and testament four months ago. She insisted on recording herself in the process so that no one would dare imply that she'd—and I quote—'lost her marbles at the end.'"

A sniffle of laughter from the red-eyed woman Connelly knew to have been Susanne's dearest friend. "That sounds like Sue."

"It does," Susanne's nephew said, his face florid and his suit ill fitting.

The much younger man who sat behind the two, next to another woman, said nothing, but his expression was stark. Susanne had planned her own funeral and given Connelly that plan during the same session in which she'd updated her will. "If I give the responsibility to anyone else, Lord knows who will browbeat them into pomp and ceremony. With you, it's a legal imperative and they won't dare interfere."

Connelly had enjoyed Susanne as a client and appreciated her as a woman of strong character.

As it was, she'd wanted no pallbearers or lengthy speeches aside from the one she'd taped herself, so Connelly hadn't seen her young man speak, but he'd recognized Tavish Advani from Susanne's descriptions of her lover, a man who, she'd told him, had turned out to be of far deeper character than she'd ever imagined when they first met.

Connelly remained taken aback by the age difference between the two, but with Susanne being who she was, Advani clearly had to be more than looks. Susanne assuredly wouldn't have permitted him to stay with her in her last months if he'd been nothing but a pretty face.

That her young man had remained by her side when so many much older men vanished without a trace when their wives and girlfriends got sick? Yes, Connelly was predisposed to like Tavish Advani.

"First of all," Connelly began, "she's left her New York apartment to you, Cici." He knew none of the group would want him to read out the legal verbiage. "While it's yours to do with as you wish, she thought you might want to pass it on to your granddaughter in time, as she's a city girl like Sue."

Cici laughed again, the sound wet. "She's right. It's like my child gave birth to a younger version of my best friend. Only nine, and she's already putting on shows and telling us about how she's going to be on Broadway."

Susanne had said that Cici wouldn't argue for more, that she wouldn't even expect this much, and Connelly was pleased to see that Sue had been right about her friend. It wasn't often that he saw the better side of human nature at these readings. People—especially people with money—became grasping and venal creatures when more money was on the table.

"She's also left you some of her jewelry," Connelly continued. "The exact items are listed in an appendix, but she asked me to assure you that they are all tasteful pieces that will not shock your neighbors or give you the vapors."

"*I am going to miss her so much.*" Soft words from Cici, even as the man next to her moved with greedy impatience while attempting a sympathetic expression that came across as a grimace.

"To her nephew, Harold," Connelly said, meeting the man's gaze, "she leaves fifty thousand dollars in a lump sum."

Harold's mouth parted. "That's it?"

"It's considerable," Connelly said mildly. "Susanne has specifically noted that she assigned you five thousand dollars for every time you visited her in the last fifteen years. She intended for you to receive her dear husband's prized Rolex, but after you made it clear you found it old-fashioned and 'fusty' on your last visit, she decided to donate it to an organization of which Mr. Winthorpe was a patron."

Harold had the grace to flush beet red and shut up.

Had Susanne had her way, she'd have left her "idiot nephew" the grand total of nothing. Connelly was the one who'd suggested she give the atrocious man a nominal amount in relation to the entirety of her estate, and that she put her reasoning for it in writing. It would make it much harder for him to challenge the will when it was clear that he hadn't been forgotten—he'd just been left a minor bequest on purpose.

Susanne had hooted as she wrote out the reasoning in her flawless penmanship. Because back then, she'd had all her usual fine motor control, the disease that had stolen her life too soon not yet visible on the surface. "There's a reason you're my lawyer, Connelly," she'd said. "You understand petty."

"'To my niece, Grace,'" Connelly read past the unexpected lump in his throat, "'I leave my diamond wedding set and my emerald necklace.'"

Grace sobbed. "Oh, I always said I'd borrow those for my engagement and wedding. She remembered." More tears. "I'll cherish them, save them for my own children. They'll be precious heirlooms."

"'Also to Grace, I leave the sum of a hundred and fifty thousand dollars, plus another fifty thousand dollars. The hundred and fifty thousand is in *special thanks for Grace stepping in as my nurse during my decline, since she refused to accept the generous salary I offered her at the time.'"*

Again, words written so Harold couldn't challenge them.

Grace was sniffing into her tissue, far more overcome by grief than her apoplectic cousin. While she wasn't thinking about the value of the jewelry Sue had bequeathed her, Connelly had no doubt that Harold had done the sums and figured out that Grace had just inherited well over half a million dollars.

"'And to my dear friend Tavish Advani,'" Connelly read, "'I leave a sum of ten thousand dollars for his friendship in my darkest hour.'"

Harold, who'd fisted his hands on his thighs, suddenly had a smug smile on his face. Tavish said nothing. Clever boy. No reason for the others to know that Sue had made her main bequest to him while she was still alive: the purchase of a condo in his name, free and clear, right on Venice Beach.

There'd been a transfer of money, too, to ensure he could live well in that location.

"I'm not being a foolish old woman, Connelly," she'd said with the ease of long acquaintance. "He's made my final years a sheer delight. Family helps because of obligation, but he's spent time with me because he enjoys me as I enjoy him. I do this of my own free will—I want to give him the same joy he's given me."

Connelly had offered her what advice he could, but he had to admit he'd been impressed by what she'd told him of the young man's actions. Though Susanne had refused to permit Tavish Advani to act the nurse, he'd sat by her bedside during the worst times, and read to her.

"Rollicking romances and no skipping the sexy bits," she'd said with her wicked smile. "He's made me laugh over and over, and for that I can never repay him."

Now Connelly completed reading the rest of her will. "There are no bequests to her domestic or other staff, as she preferred to give those to them before her death."

"She would." Cici's smile was thick with affection and memory. "Would want to be sure they were treated well."

"As for the remainder of her estate, that she has bequeathed to a charitable trust that helps provide a way to live in dignity for those suffering with cancer, who—in her words—'do not have the kind of resources I had in my life.'"

That done, Connelly answered any questions, then farewelled the group. He'd just finished tidying his papers and was rising to fetch himself a cup of coffee when he happened to pass by a window that looked down on the square outside his office.

Tavish Advani was standing there with a crying Grace. His expression was solemn, the hand he had on her lower back comforting but respectful. Grace leaned into him, her body crumpling.

The tall and strong young man absorbed her weight without impact.

Connelly frowned . . . and wondered if Harold wasn't the only one who'd done the math on Grace's new financial status. Not only was Grace now rich by most standards, but she was also nearing forty, was single, and had nothing of Sue's confidence.

All it would take were a few kind words and a smile from handsome Tavish Advani, and she'd fall like ripe fruit into his hands.

# CHAPTER 35

My hand clenched on the verandah railing, the night balmy around me and the air heavy with a scent I couldn't quite identify. It wasn't the ocean, was thicker, sweeter than the salt-laced whispers I caught when the wind turned.

*But Bobby sahib, oh, he could talk and talk—and that Shumi, she thought he was better than a movie star. The girl would've parroted anything Bobby told her to say.*

How could Shumi have lived with herself all this time knowing that she'd put the blame on Diya's innocent head? Even more so when Diya loved her so much, saw her as her best friend? How could Shumi have *protected* Bobby after he'd done a thing so vicious that it was beyond comprehension?

I wanted to shake the other woman, make her speak the truth. Because I knew that there was no point in telling any of this to Ackerson. The original police report was a fabrication, and no one had to tell me that Kamal wouldn't say anything on the record. Neither would his wife. Because Kamal had committed a crime by filing a false report, and no matter what his wife might say to my face, what she'd say to the authorities was a whole different scenario.

Ani's body was long gone.

I wondered now what Diya remembered of the murder. She'd only been five. My memories from that age were fuzzy at best, over-written by things other people had told me they remembered about me.

The sole crystalline memory I had was of standing outside the living room, watching through the crack in the door as my mother surprised Raja with a mass of toys she'd bought him on her latest shopping spree.

Toy after toy, gift after gift, for her "best boy."

It had been my birthday.

That was why I remembered. Because later that same day, I'd been excited to get my own haul of gifts from her. Instead, I'd been given a bakery cake that the adult me knew must've been ordered by the nanny who looked after me most of the time, and three generic "little boy" toys that the same nanny had likely ordered online.

Funny, what the mind chose to remember.

*Ani . . . they said . . . about Ani . . . not . . .*

My throat grew tight, choked up. Because my wife *did* remember enough about what had happened to Ani to be distressed about it. Yet, how many times over the years had she been told that she'd done that awful thing?

Had the lie overwritten her childish memories of the truth?

Did she believe herself a murderer?

The horror of it twisting her up until maybe it had become the reason for the medication she'd tried to hide from me. What she'd been told was the truth tangling up what she knew to be the truth, until she could no longer separate them, her memories a field of bro-ken shards that didn't fit together no matter how hard she tried.

SUCH A PERFECT FAMILY

My poor sweet Diya. "I'll fix it," I vowed as that thick, sweet smell laid itself on my tongue.

*Mangoes.*

*Ani's tree.*

My fingers tightened to bone whiteness. "I'll make sure the blame falls on the person who deserves it. Not on you and not on me."

This time, there was no Kamal to hush things up, and no Sarita and Rajesh Prasad to allow the lie to exist even when they, too, had to have known it *was* a lie.

Diya had been *five years old.*

———

I was already up and showered by the time first light crept through the curtains. I'd tucked the religious statuette Ravi had suggested I take in a clean facecloth from the pile Kushma had left me by the bed, then put that safely in the middle of my duffel, where it'd be protected on all sides by my crumpled clothing.

But as I went to leave the house, I hesitated and returned to the prayer alcove to pick up the photo of the smiling couple with the little girl. It was a posed shot probably done in a mall or in a photographer's home studio, complete with a fake background that looked like Venetian canals. The woman had dimples and shiny black waist-length hair that she'd allowed to fall over one shoulder, while the man had black curls and a thick mustache.

Their little girl was laughing in the picture, her dimples an echo of her mother's.

I wasn't a kid person, but I could see that Ani had been a beautiful baby. Also a happy one in this picture, her hands caught in a clapping motion as she sat on her mother's lap, while her father stood behind them with his hand on his wife's shoulder. He was wearing a crisp white shirt and dark pants, while she wore a rich pink sari over an aquamarine blouse.

The photo had faded, but not enough to wash out those brilliant shades.

Her mother had put little Ani in a white dress that poufed around her, and put two golden barrettes in her fine hair. I knew it had been the mother. The way she held Ani, it said this little girl was her heart and soul.

They could've been any young family that had dressed up to get their photo taken.

Turning it without thought, I saw a single line of text written in blue ink in neat cursive writing: *Annika's first photoshoot!*

Annika. A grown-up name that would've meant only her family sometimes slipped and called her baby Ani after she became an adult. But Annika had never grown up, would always remain baby Ani in everyone's minds.

Heart heavy, I tucked the photo back where it belonged, in this sacred space created by a family that had been mourning three lost lives. That didn't absolve Sarita and Rajesh of what they'd done, the terrible weight they'd put on Diya's fragile shoulders to protect their only son, but I could feel horror at their choice and sadness for them at the same time.

The house seemed to whisper in melancholy as I closed and locked the door behind me. As if it knew that its owners were never again coming home except as ashes. "Diya will come back," I promised the spirit of the house. "She'll open you up and let the sea winds sweep in."

With that, I turned toward the banana grove, intending to hand Ravi the key.

The wind chime began to play.

I froze, staring at the unmoving leaves of the mango tree, and of the banana palms. There was no breeze to move the slender metal tubes that hung from the chime, not even the whisper of one. The morning was a still photograph broken only by the metallic shimmer of the chime dancing . . . and the faint echo of a little girl's laughter in the air.

*That's Ani. That little baby never left here. I think she plays under the mango tree.*

# CHAPTER 36

Private notes: Detective Callum Baxter (LAPD)
Date: Jan 8
Time: 20:11

What interests me about Susanne Winthorpe is that, according to an off-the-record chat with her oncologist, her cancer wasn't terminal, but she went from diagnosis to death in under a year. She did refuse treatment, but even without treatment, she should've had a good couple of years at least.

The Singaporean authorities ruled her death a suicide, and if there was an autopsy, I haven't yet been able to get hold of the report. Whatever they found in an autopsy—if there was one—it didn't change their conclusions. And I can't run any further tests. Her body's gone, cremated as per her wishes.

How hard would it be to find a way to poison an already dying woman? Weak immune system, probably not preparing her own food. And Advani was staying with her for the last months of her life. On the flip side, why take the risk if you knew she was a dying woman anyway?

Impatience might be the answer. He was barely twenty-two when she died. Could be he got sick of being stuck at an invalid's side, got sick of pretending to care. He'd already missed his final year of university—though apparently he managed to do enough courses remotely that he did get his degree only six months after he should have. Not the same as partying it up with your class, though, is it?

So maybe there was resentment there, too.

I asked her doctor if he had any of her blood or tissues left, anything on which we could run further tests, but no luck. He barely saw her after her diagnosis—just for a bit of pain medication and that was about it.

End result is that I still have nothing except some disturbing circumstantial evidence.

Susanne Winthorpe (Advani aged 19.5–22): Died by suicide. Would've otherwise died of natural causes (untreated lung cancer) per the official record.

Jocelyn Wai (22.5–23.6): Dead of a fall ruled accidental due to drug intoxication (a mix of ecstasy and alcohol), her case closed with nothing in it to force a reopening.

Virna Musgrave (25.7–26.2): Dead. Vehicle tampered with; likely homicide.

That gap of over two years between Jocelyn and Virna worries me. Who haven't we found? Who else is dead?

Time: 23:17

I forgot about Susanne Winthorpe's niece. The lawyer mentioned her, said she acted as Winthorpe's nurse at the end—and that she appeared close to Tavish. Fuck, I hope the woman is alive.

# CHAPTER 37

My phone rang on the way to the airport. The name on the
screen read Ackerson.

I ignored it, not ready to talk to her when—in the prac-
tical sense—I was in no better a position than when I'd sat
across from her in that interrogation room. Ani's story couldn't help
Diya until she woke up and was ready to talk about it, and it couldn't
help me at all.

As for Shumi . . . was it possible that after Bobby had attacked
everyone with such murderous violence, she'd break, tell the truth?
Who knew? Right now, there wasn't any way to know if she'd even
wake up. I could only hope she did. Because her memories of Ani's
murder *mattered*.

Three years older than Diya, she'd have been eight at the time,
old enough to remember all of it. Even if she refused to talk of what
had happened at the Lake Tarawera house, if she admitted what
Bobby had done to Ani, it'd shine a spotlight on his violent nature. It
would also put this tragedy in the territory of an annihilation driven

by old emotion and old secrets, instead of a cold-blooded crime with a financial motive that put me in the crosshairs.

I squeezed the steering wheel in lieu of smashing my head against it.

I'd been such a self-destructive idiot all those years after Susanne's death! What had I seen in the dopamine rush of gambling away every dollar that had come into my hands? It'd be easy to keep on blaming Jocelyn for the part she'd played in dragging me deeper and deeper into that world—because she had, oh, she had. Witty, sarcastic, fascinating Joss had wanted a fellow addict at her side, one she could control.

Her little toy whom she'd delighted in breaking . . . until he'd broken her.

My chest heaved, my breathing choppy.

The therapist I'd seen, under duress from my father after Callum Baxter put a target on my back and zeroed in, had been a sanctimonious old prick, but he'd said one thing that stuck with me: "You're looking for validation, Tavish. Each time you win, you get that rush. False validation, but validation nonetheless. You've been searching for it all your life."

Well, fuck that. I was done with being a mess because my mother was a narcissist who could only love one child, the one she'd so carefully molded in her image. I almost felt sorry for Raja at times. My brother had never had a chance to be anyone but who Audrey wanted him to be; he didn't even enjoy acting as far as I could tell, but Mommy dearest wanted him in the land of make-believe and so Raja trudged on with a string of mediocre guest appearances, his life funded by Audrey.

Unfortunately, my decision to shrug off the strangling chains of the past came too late, the damage already done. A fact that became crystal clear when I found Ackerson waiting for me in the busy arrivals hall of Auckland Airport late that afternoon, a uniformed officer at her side.

Lips pinched, she said, "I told you to stay close."

I hitched the duffel over my shoulder, trying not to notice all the people staring in our direction. "I went to fetch a religious relic for the funeral rites. I wanted to have it ready for Diya when she wakes. So she can do right by her family."

"I'll need you to accompany me to the station."

I smiled. "Sure." Soon as I was in the back of the marked police cruiser, I sent a text to the criminal defense attorney my father had hooked me up with—he'd shot me the man's details two hours after we spoke.

Still trying to protect me as he hadn't when I was a child.

The lawyer was waiting at the station when we arrived. Broad shouldered, with rich black hair cut with flair, his skin the same shade of brown as mine, he wore a suit fitted to his body with such perfection that I knew it had to be bespoke.

A greenstone pin glinted on one lapel, the design intricate.

"Kia ora, Detective Ackerson," he said with a beaming smile. "Andrew Ngata. You'll remember me from the Piri case. I'll be sitting in on this interview with my client."

Ackerson's face flushed a scalding pink, a balloon about to explode blood. "You don't need a lawyer," she said to me. "This is just a chat."

"You picked me up from the airport with a uniformed officer and put me in a cruiser in front of the public," I said, my tone tight. "Sorry if I'm pissed off. I want to be by my wife's side, not here while you waste time looking at the wrong man."

The balloon pulsed.

My lawyer touched me on the arm. "Detective Ackerson is just doing her job, Mr. Advani. Let's keep this cordial."

*Let me do the talking* was the unspoken order. Since there was a reason my father was paying this man's significant three-figure hourly rate, I obeyed.

Once in the interview room, Ackerson raised her eyebrows. "Funny how you had your passport handy for your jaunt to Fiji. I'd have thought it was at the house. We know the Prasads had a safe—thing came through the fire."

Only after Ngata gave me a small nod did I say, "I wanted to ask the bank if I could open up a local account." It was the truth. "Figured my California driver's license might not be enough ID so took my passport along."

"What did the bank say?"

"I blew it off. Wanted to get home to Diya, thought we could come in together later in the day."

Ackerson set her jaw, her next questions hard and flat. I let Ngata head them off for the most part. She'd met the cooperative Tavish Advani; now it was time for her to meet the Tavish Advani who was the son of one of the most successful criminal defense attorneys in Los Angeles.

It soon became obvious that she had nothing beyond my lack of solid employment and apparent lack of money. The staff at the bakery where I'd picked up the cakes had verified my alibi—God, that cheerful interaction where they'd teased me about the wedding madness to come seemed about a million days in the past—but with no way for Ackerson to know the exact time of death, she continued to insist that I could've done it before I left.

"I had a very interesting conversation with Detective Callum Baxter yesterday," she said at one point. "He had a lot to say about the Virna Musgrave investigation."

"Which isn't your bailiwick, Detective," Ngata inserted with unflinching calm, his faint smile chiding.

But Ackerson didn't back down. "Perhaps not, but it does give me an excellent idea of your client's predilection for violence. Though it seems he usually chooses older women."

"Oh, for Christ's sake! Why don't you look at the bully in the family?" I yelled, having waited until the right moment. Growing up with a narcissist for a mother had taught me how to manipulate people without them ever being aware of it; it was all in the timing.

Ackerson sat back. She was too smart to smile, but it was clear that she thought she'd broken me. "Clarify that," she said.

"Bobby." I fisted my hand on the table. "Ask his classmates how he was as a boy. Not his friends, the *other* children. He sure as fuck was a controlling bastard of a husband.

"Check with Shumi's doctor, because even if she never made a police complaint, she probably needed medical attention at some point." The latter was another gamble, but one with a good chance of paying off given all the information I had about Diya's older brother; a boy who enjoyed bullying other children wouldn't think anything of bullying his slavishly devoted wife.

If anything, he'd probably enjoyed it even more. After all, he'd known Shumi would never call him out on it.

That betraying twitch of her left eye, the signal that I'd startled her. "Are you saying Vihaan 'Bobby' Prasad was an abusive husband?" she said, even as Ngata said my name in a tone that told me to shut up.

"Yes." I leaned forward. "Which you'd know if you'd done any actual investigating rather than deciding it had to be the outsider who did it." Despite my words, I wasn't so sure of her motives anymore, because just before, when she'd mentioned Virna, her voice had risen. Not by much, but enough.

How old was Ackerson? Fifties? Younger than Virna by more than a decade, but close enough to feel a sense of kinship with her. Out to nail the man she thought had scammed, then murdered a rich older woman desperate for love.

Gut instinct stirred, telling me to push on that vulnerability, but I stayed on the track I'd already laid down—letting her believe that I was ignoring my lawyer because I was a hotheaded idiot.

"That was rage, what went on in that house," I said. "I don't feel strongly about any of the family except for Diya! They're just people to me, people I tried to get along with for her sake, but people I didn't really know. Why the fuck would I stab my sister-in-law? Shumi was *nice* to me!"

"On that subject," my lawyer interjected, "have you located Bobby Prasad's remains?"

"The scene is still under forensic investigation."

A faint smile from Ngata. "So it's possible the younger Prasad committed this crime, then walked out to start a new life. I assume you're keeping an eye on his bank and phone accounts for signs of life?"

"Don't tell me how to do my job, Mr. Ngata, and I won't tell you how to do yours."

"I want to go see Diya now." I got to my feet.

Ackerson didn't argue, and I walked out with my lawyer. Who sighed once we were out on the sidewalk, under the bright green leaves of some tree I couldn't identify. "You're supposed to let me speak. Anand assured me you know how to keep your mouth shut."

There was little traffic on the road just then, and what looked to be pale orange poppies—interspersed with small white flowers I couldn't name—bobbed their heads in the plantings on the median. A woman pushed a stroller on the opposite sidewalk, while an elderly man stepped out of a café with a take-out cup in hand.

As I watched, he unhooked the lead of a scruffy brown dog from an outdoor chair, and the dog sat up, tail waving.

People carrying on with their lives as if mine hadn't gone up in flames only days past.

"I know, I know," I said to Ngata. "Sorry, but she's so focused on me that she's missing the giant elephant in the room."

"You got away with it this time, but don't do it again." He squeezed my shoulder. "And be careful what you say to her. She puts on the thick tunnel-visioned cop act, but that woman has a top-tier closing rate—and her cases are winners for the prosecution, so she isn't just about closing cases; she gets the evidence, locks her suspects down tight."

"I'll remember," I said, shaken.

I'd fallen for the idiot cop act, had come close to treating her with the very contempt my father had warned me about.

"You have to be extra clean at this point." Ngata's gaze was suddenly as hard as granite. "Your identity hasn't leaked to the media yet—not in terms of your past in the States—so keep a low profile and stay away from Ackerson. The instant she approaches you again, you call me. No more cozy little chats. Got it?"

"Absolutely."

I stewed on the possibility of media exposure on my cab ride back to the airport to pick up my car from the parking lot. My history made for damn good newspaper inches—and if it had been bad in the metropolis of LA, how much worse would it be in this small city inside a small nation where the Lake Tarawera deaths were still headline news?

A sudden whiff of sulfur on the wind, a reminder that Rotorua was a place where the earth boiled . . . the land itself on fire deep below the surface.

# CHAPTER 38

Finally pinned down that two-year gap in Tavish Advani's love résumé. Man wasn't dating. At all. Grief from Jocelyn Wai's death? Possible—though from all appearances, they didn't seem to have a true-love type of deal. Not like he apparently had with Susanne Winthorpe.

I just got off the phone with her best friend, one Cecilia "Cici" Summers.

She couldn't say enough good things about Tavish. "I teased her about dating someone so young, but when it came down to it, Sue was right—he made her final months so happy. She loved being with him, though in the end she *was* sorry for ever having come into his life. He took it so hard, you see. Was broken up about her loss. She'd started it all as a lark, a little hot fling, as she'd say, but she ended up becoming his first real love."

I didn't know how to bring up how quickly he'd moved on, but I didn't have to. Cici did it herself. "That terrible relationship he was in with Jocelyn Wai?

All the partying and drinking? Grief, that's what it was. He was looking for Susanne in her, poor boy—had no idea that Jocelyn was a piranha. We didn't run in the same circles, but I heard through the grapevine what she was like—a hard, hard woman, that one, taking young lovers and using them up, then throwing them away."

Never thought of Tavish Advani as the victim; Cici is right about Jocelyn's track record. Her boyfriend before Advani was a B-list actor in his twenties who died of a cocaine overdose during their relationship (though she was out of the country at the time). That type of toxic relationship, though, it can lead to violence.

Gina's a good cop—if she thinks Advani had something to do with Wai's death, I believe her. Knowing something and being able to prove it in court are two different things—especially if you have a DA who doesn't like to file anything but slam dunks.

Cici states that Advani always comes to the memorial dinner she holds for her friend at a "glitzy place Sue would've loved." She also has no qualms about Susanne's final days. "Sue died as she lived—on her terms. Never doubt that, Detective."

Susanne's niece—Grace Green—had nothing bad to say about Tavish, either, and she was in the thick of it during Susanne's decline, literally lived in a self-contained suite in the same apartment.

She was also adamant that Tavish never made any moves on her. I'm not sure I believe her. I might pay her a visit in person, see if she'll open up further.

# CHAPTER 39

The first thing I did when I got to the hospital late that afternoon—after stopping at the motel to shower off the long journey home—was kiss my wife on the cheek, then sit with my hand on hers for a long, long time. Willing her to wake, to look at me with those eyes that saw me, loved me.

"I'll always be there for you, baby," I told this fragile candle flame of a woman who owned my heart. "Doing that . . . being there for you . . . it saves me." She filled up the well of emptiness inside me with her need, and I was more than okay with that.

"It's all about Ani, isn't it?" Diya's moods, her need for medication, her endless need for *love*. "What did your family do to you?" Because this was what I'd realized in Fiji—me and Diya, we'd been drawn together because we mirrored each other's scars, each other's damaged psyches.

The machines beeped, the ventilator breathed rhythmically, and the nurses walked past on soft-soled shoes. But from my wife, the woman I loved to my core, there was only a wordless silence.

Swallowing, I released her hand to reach into the duffel I'd put beside the bed. I was careful in how I handled the statuette. "I got this from your mother's prayer alcove." After unwrapping it, I placed it on a small table beside her bed, where it wouldn't be in the staff's way.

"You weren't the one who did anything wrong, Diya. I know." I brushed a strand of hair off her cheek. "I believe you." If there was even a chance she could hear me, then I needed her to know that she wasn't alone any longer; I was in her corner in this fight, wasn't going to allow anyone to ever again blame her for Ani's brutal death.

A stir at the foot of the bed, in the space I'd left uncurtained so the staff could monitor Diya from the nurses' station.

I glanced up to see Ajay.

"Hey, I wondered if you were back." Shumi's brother walked to the other side of the bed, his expression drawn as he looked at my wife. "Hi, Diya. It's Ajay. Just came to chill with Tavish."

Lowering his voice afterward, as if he didn't want Diya to hear, he said, "My sister's the same. It's so hard to see her that way. I've always been a homebody, but she was out and about all the time—she joined so many clubs in high school that I barely saw her all week. She used to come home after dark."

Shumi hadn't struck me as that socially active, but then, I'd only known her through the lens of her relationship with the Prasad family. Just because she'd been a stay-at-home wife didn't mean she actually *stayed* at home the entire day. But what did it say if she had? If that involved and busy girl had become confined to her home?

Everywhere I turned, there was so much I didn't know. But Ajay might be able to answer at least some of my questions. "You want to get a coffee?" I asked. "I need something to eat, too."

He glanced down the hallway. "I should ask my father if he needs anything."

"Sure. Your mom resting?"

A quick nod, his eyes not meeting mine. "She's finding it hard to see Shumi in that condition."

"Yeah." It went a way toward explaining how little time she seemed to spend at the hospital—though truth was, I didn't understand how avoidance was any better. Wasn't she haunted by thoughts of her daughter while alone in an unfamiliar motel room? Better, to my mind, to be surrounded by her family in the busy environs of the hospital.

"Dad's tougher," Ajay added. "Or he puts on a good front, anyway."

We arrived in the ICU overflow unit to find Shumi's father on his laptop in one corner of her spacious curtained area, phone to his ear as he dealt with some issue at his workplace. His voice was a discreet murmur.

When Ajay mouthed the word "coffee," he shook his head and waved us off.

I waited until we were near the elevator to say, "Must be hard for him to have to handle work even when he's so worried." The other man hadn't actually looked worried to my eyes, but I knew a certain age and personality of male tended to shove all emotions down deep. Even more so in a patriarchal culture like my father's.

Still, there seemed something . . . not quite right about Shumi's family. Another case of one favored child, one ignored one?

If so, Ajay was a lot more likable than Raja.

Or I was projecting my own issues onto the Kumars. Might be Shumi just wasn't close to her family, far preferring to nest in with the Prasads as another way to make herself the perfect wife for Bobby.

"Dad's so senior." Ajay pushed the button for the elevator. "They rely on him and I think he feels guilty not being available even at this time." He rubbed his face. "The immigrant work ethic is sometimes the immigrant sense of guilt at being forever grateful for the opportunities afforded us. Your dad the same?"

"Yeah, he's a workaholic, but I think he's just wired that way," I said, thinking of how happy my father had always looked tucked away in his office. "I'm third-generation. It was my grandparents that immigrated from India—so I'm now the slacker Westernized grandson."

Ajay's smile was startled. "Trust me, if you're in finance, you're no slacker."

So, Shumi had spoken enough to her brother that she'd told him about me. "Actually," I said, "do you mind if we walk to the café? I'd like to stretch my legs."

"Sure."

We were already descending the stairs by the time the elevator dinged to announce it had arrived.

"What's it like, having such a famous mother?" Ajay asked, his tone a little hesitant. "If you want to talk about it," he added in a rush. "I mean, people must ask you about it all the time."

"It's definitely . . . interesting," I said with a practiced laugh. "Especially when I was eleven and she was doing the action movies where she was in a string bikini half the time?" During those peak years, she'd been one of the few actresses who could command serious award-winning roles alongside those of a sex bomb. "I *could not* go into the bedrooms of my friends without needing eye bleach. They all had posters of her on the walls."

As always, the funny anecdote made my audience laugh and relax. I never mentioned the rest of it—the posed photo op where she'd hissed at me to "fucking smile" as she kissed me on the cheek, the way she spent long hours "going over lines" with her buff male co-star, the argument I'd overheard between my parents where she'd suggested I'd do better in boarding school.

It was one of the only times in my life when my father *had* stood up for me, but these days I wondered if Audrey had been right. At least at boarding school, I'd no longer have been an outsider inside my own house.

"How was the trip to Fiji?" Ajay asked, instead of pushing for more as most people back home tended to do—it wasn't as bad now, Los Angeles a city obsessed with youth, but Audrey Advani still cut a sexy and striking figure even in her late fifties.

"Tough." No point or need to hide that. "Diya always said she'd take me, show me around the family home. Going there without her felt wrong." I paused on the stairs, a busy member of staff passing us with quick feet. "I spoke to their neighbors. A former police officer named Kamal, and his wife and son."

Ajay frowned before snapping his fingers. "Oh yeah, Uncle Kamal. We haven't visited since I was fifteen, but he was a crusty old man even then. Can't imagine he's improved."

I chuckled at the apt description. "No, exactly the same. He mentioned that your sister's always been fond of Bobby." The present tense just came out, both my conscious and subconscious mind ever more convinced that Bobby was alive.

It was the only thing that made sense.

"Man, isn't that the truth. I was about five when the Prasads moved to New Zealand, but I remember how she shut down at the thought of not seeing him again. Biggest crush I've ever seen, and she was only, like, eleven."

"She must've been happy when your family got to come, too."

"Oh, it was like fireworks inside her when our dad told us that our application had been accepted. But for that one year after they left and we were still in Fiji, she was a ghost, just drifting around. Wrote so many letters to both Diya and Bobby."

The hospital café was quiet this near to closing time, but the staff hadn't yet started cleaning their machines, so we were both able to grab coffees. I also ordered a large filled panini from the cabinet and was told they'd bring it to the table once they'd toasted it in the oven for me.

"Shumi ever date anyone else?" I asked once we'd taken our seats.

The barista started making our coffees while chatting to her co-worker, who was taking my panini out of the cabinet.

"She wasn't interested in anyone else," Ajay said. "Happiest day of her life was when Bobby asked her out." He took a little serving sachet of sugar from the small pot of sweeteners on the table and began to turn it around by the edges. "Before they became a couple, and after our family moved here, we all used to hang out. Me and Diya and Bobby and Shumi.

"Aunt Sarita and Uncle Rajesh were deep into studying for their local certifications, while my dad was working long hours, so Mum used to babysit us all when we weren't in school. I think they were glad when we immigrated, too—we were familiar, you know? We even had rental houses down the road from each other."

"One big happy family."

"I'm sure I was there on sufferance—big age gap. But still . . ." His expression grew soft. "Those were good times. Diya and Bobby used to spend so many nights at our place. Bobby bunked with me, and Diya with Shumi, and everyone knew to behave even when Shumi and Bobby hit their teens and the hormones kicked in."

Round and round went the sugar packet, the younger man's focus on it extreme.

"Otherwise," he said, "the hammer would've come down and ended the whole deal. The worst we did was sneak out of bed at night to raid the chocolate cookies or the leftover Diwali sweets."

His smile faded. "Bobby was a great big brother to me. Patient in a way I didn't appreciate until I was an older teenager myself."

Yet another avatar of the boy who'd given a classmate a scar he carried to this day. "I heard a few difficult things while I was in Fiji—about him being a bully." I twisted my lips, bit them a little, a man uncomfortable with what he was saying. "It just struck me as off. He always seemed like a good guy."

The barista came over at that moment with our coffees, the conversation on pause until after she'd left. But Ajay didn't say anything even then, concentrating on tearing open sachets of sugar and pouring them into his coffee.

"I'm sorry," I began. "I didn't mean—"

But he was shaking his head. "I hero-worshipped him, so even if he was a bully to others, he could've seen me as a mascot, I guess." His hands tightened around the cup. "I could understand if he was different with other kids—his dad was tough on him."

"Yeah?"

A small nod as he began to stir in the sugar. "Rajesh uncle expected him to be perfect. Best grades, first fifteen rugby team, top achievement certificates across all subjects. My parents were ecstatic when I pulled a B in my worst subject, but Rajesh uncle used to lose it if Bobby ever came home with less than an A in anything."

I thought of what Kamal's son had said about catching Bobby in tears because he'd received ninety-seven percent on a test. "Beatings?"

"No." Ajay looked down at the table. "I don't really know the facts. I just kind of heard my parents talking."

"They're all dead now, Ajay." I made my voice gentle, suddenly piercingly aware that Ajay at twenty-one was far softer and less experienced than I'd been at the same age. "And I'm not going to spread rumors. You might as well get it out—it's obviously on your mind."

"Yeah. Just thinking about how we were . . ." He choked up, right as a member of the café staff delivered my toasted panini, with a side of fresh green salad.

After thanking her, I began to unroll my silverware from the paper towel in which it had been wrapped. Giving Shumi's brother space.

"Dad was saying to Mum that Rajesh uncle had locked Bobby up in this space under the stairs that they had in their rental. It was a cubby meant for storage, I think, but a boy of Bobby's size could just fit in there. There was no light."

He swallowed hard. "I saw one of those slide locks on it when I went over the next time, and it was on the outside."

"*Jesus.*" No wonder Bobby had turned out twisted. "Did they hurt Diya, too?" Rage ran molten in my blood, any sympathy I'd felt for the elder Prasads obliterated.

"No, I never heard that. She was younger and, honestly, she was a girl. Overprotected, not as much expected of her." He winced. "I feel bad talking about them like this."

Frowning, I swallowed the bite of food in my mouth. "Sarita didn't strike me as that kind of traditional." But then, neither had I imagined she'd stand aside and let her husband brutalize her son.

Ajay took off his glasses, began to clean them using the edge of his T-shirt. His face was suddenly young and exposed without that fragile shield between him and the world. "That's just it," he said. "She wasn't, not with other women and girls." He put the glasses back on. "She was so disappointed when Shumi gave up her engineering career after getting married to Bobby."

"*Engineering?*" I almost dropped the fork I'd been using to eat the salad. "I had no idea." In all honesty, I'd thought Diya's sister-in-law sweet but a bit vacant. She seemed to have no interests of her own aside from Bobby.

It was cruel to think it, which was why I'd never given voice to it, but she'd struck me as a loyal golden retriever type. Cheerful and nice to be around, but without any original ideas. Happy to go along with others' plans, or to help out with someone else's hobby—whether that was drawing mandalas with Sarita, or helping Diya source images for the inspiration boards she put together for her events.

Honestly, it made her a good friend—as long as you were okay making all the decisions.

Ajay gave me a tight smile. "Shumi's crazy smart. Always has been. But Bobby came first—and he didn't want her to work. As for Sarita auntie . . . I think after she lost Ani, she kind of obsessed about protecting Diya. Never let her do sleepovers, always drove her even if Diya just wanted to walk to a local park with friends, made her share her location on the phone. Rajesh uncle was the same. They wanted her close to home, to them, all the time."

*No! I'm a full-grown woman, not a dog with a collar!*

Another snippet of an argument I'd heard while at the condo. I hadn't been able to understand the context then, but now I realized that Diya must've turned off her location so her parents could no longer track her.

She'd already told me that the only reason Rajesh and Sarita hadn't found a way to stop her from coming to Los Angeles was because the friend whose bachelorette weekend it was—Risha Patel—was a former exchange student who'd lived with them for a year.

"They couldn't say no when Mr. and Mrs. Patel invited me personally on Risha's behalf, all expenses paid. The Patels are both senior partners in a law firm, and they're older than my parents. It would've been a terrible insult for them to say no when the Patels had entrusted Risha to us for a whole year."

So they'd allowed Diya to go—so odd to think of it that way when she was a twenty-four-year-old woman. But they'd checked in with her multiple times each day—and then, when she'd moved in with me and turned off her location, they'd blown up her phone.

Their suffocating protectiveness was no surprise—they had to have known that Bobby's unstable anger could turn on another vulnerable member of his family. Only—I frowned inwardly—Bobby had seemed equally overprotective of Diya. He'd called or messaged as often as Sarita and Rajesh.

Then again, as evidenced by the fact that colorless Shumi had apparently once been driven enough to study engineering, I barely knew my in-laws.

Masks took time to even see, much less tear off.

I knew that better than anyone.

"You're the best chameleon I've ever met, Tavish." Detective Baxter's lined face looking at me from the shadows where he'd stood waiting for me to exit a black-tie event I'd attended after my father advised me not to hide, not to act suspicious in any way. "Do you even know who you are when you aren't becoming your latest target's fantasy?"

# CHAPTER 40

## GRACE

*G*race walked out of the hospital to find Detective Callum Baxter waiting for her just outside, in the covered area where patients often went for a smoke. Snow had fallen again that afternoon, small drifts of it on the concrete.

The Los Angeles cop was wearing the biggest jacket she'd ever seen. Had to be a California native unused to East Coast cold. For her, this was a balmy winter, her own jacket a lightweight wool that she'd thrown on over her scrubs.

She'd have recognized Baxter even if he hadn't sent her a snapshot of his ID. The man looked like some casting director's version of a cop—wrinkled jacket that had seen better days, slightly dissolute look, grizzled face.

"Ms. Green," he said, holding out his hand.

"Detective. And please, call me Grace." She nudged her head to the right. "There's a sort of park area where we can walk—the hospital keeps the paths clear of snow so the patients can get some air if they want."

Hands in the pockets of his jacket, he fell in beside her. "Thank you for meeting me."

*"Well, you came a long way."* Grace had been startled when he'd told her he was flying over to talk to her in person, couldn't imagine that his police department would've okayed the expenditure. Which meant he'd paid for it on his own—a cop certain enough of himself that he was willing to put money on the line. *"Why are you so interested in Tavish?"*

*"He's had three women with whom he's been involved die,"* the detective said flatly. *"He's also done well financially out of all of those deaths."*

Grace shook her head. *"Did you ever stop to think that both those things can be explained by the fact he dates wealthy older women? People who might die for various reasons anyway?"*

*"Yes, but I'd be a bad cop if I didn't investigate."*

Sighing, Grace smiled at a patient who was seated on a bench, her eyes on the snow-covered gardens. *"My aunt left me a luxury condo in Paris, and another one in Los Angeles. If you're looking for who did the best out of her death, it was me."* Her throat thickened, the loss one she wasn't yet over—might never be over.

Aunt Susanne had been one of a kind.

Seeing from his expression that she'd well and truly surprised Detective Baxter, she said, *"It wasn't in the will. She didn't want certain other family members to be able to challenge the gifts, so she transferred both properties into my name a year prior to her death, which meant that—unbeknownst to me—I was already the owner at the time of her death."*

It meant all the more because Aunt Susanne had done it after she got sick but long before she asked Grace to be her nurse. Her aunt had just liked her enough to give her the properties, and for Grace, who'd never been the popular girl, never had her aunt's charisma, the knowledge was worth more than the monetary value of the gift. *"Aunt Susanne's lawyer got in touch with me the day after the will reading."*

Stopping below a tree denuded of all its leaves, a skeleton facing the sky, she turned to the detective. *"She bought the condo for Tavish around the same time—though she gave the deed to him personally a couple of months* before she passed, not through her lawyer like with me. Tavish told me about it." Her throat grew thick as she thought of that conversation between two people who had loved Susanne Winthorpe.

"And I can tell you that Aunt Susanne was in full control of her faculties right up to the very end." It angered her that anyone would seek to infantilize her powerhouse of an aunt. "He didn't influence her, if that's what you're getting at."

From the way he was rubbing at his face, she'd just smashed a great big axe through his theories about Tavish. "A nineteen-year-old with a woman in her sixties, there's something off about it. Don't tell me you don't agree."

"Yes, and I told Aunt Susanne he was too young and she was being predatory." Grace wanted to laugh as the detective's face fell again at her switching around of the players. "I was right—and wrong. He was very vulnerable—but he was also very able to handle my aunt, in a good way."

What she didn't add was that she was sure he'd learned to be that tough on the inside due to his mother. Audrey Advani might be America's favorite siren, but Grace had always felt as if it was all an act, a thread of meanness beneath the surface. "My aunt and Tavish had fun together."

The detective's eyes narrowed. "You're awfully interested in defending him."

"You think I have a crush on him?" Hugging herself, she said, "I'm gay, Detective." Hard even now to say those words aloud. "It took a letter from Aunt Susanne—she'd put it in with the deeds to the properties—for me to admit that to myself. My mom, Aunt Susanne's sister, died when I was a teen, and my paternal family is very conservative. I grew up being taught that it was a sin to be gay."

She rubbed her hands over her arms, even though she knew the cold was inside her. "I'd tell you if he tried anything on me, but the truth is that Tavish and I still meet to talk about Aunt Susanne. We both loved her."

He had more questions for her, and none of her answers seemed to satisfy him. When he did finally give up and leave, she took a few minutes to walk *around the snowy garden on her own . . . and she thought about how Aunt Susanne had made her leave the apartment the week of her death, how she'd booked Grace an all-expenses-paid tropical vacation because Grace "needed to get out of the sickroom and drink some margaritas" . . . and how she'd ordered herself a respite nurse from a service.*

*She'd made sure neither Tavish nor Grace would find her.*

*But Grace had found something else. A single tiny pill on the floor of the condo after she was permitted to go in to fetch an outfit for her aunt to be cremated in—Aunt Susanne had left instructions on what it was to be, of course.*

*Grace had been crying when her eye caught on the pill lying on the carpet just under the bed. She was a senior nurse, one with a degree in pharmacology. She'd recognized the pill and she also knew that there was no way Susanne could have gotten her hands on it herself—her aunt had lived in a world without those connections.*

*Susanne Winthorpe wouldn't even have known how to get her hands on cocaine, much less something this exotic.*

*If the cops had discovered this pill or anything connected to it, the coroner wouldn't have ruled her death a simple suicide so quickly, with no autopsy necessary. Which meant Aunt Susanne had made sure to get rid of any evidence before she ingested the pills . . . except for this one that had fallen and become lost in the rich dark of the carpet.*

*The pills in the bottles found around Aunt Susanne's body? Theater to cover the actual drug she'd taken to die.*

*Grace had walked out with the pill, later dropped it in a public toilet and flushed it away.*

*Grace and Tavish, they had a bond nothing could break.*

*Not after those hours they'd spent together in Singapore as Susanne screamed in pain and the night wouldn't end.*

# CHAPTER 41

A jay turned the half-empty cup around and around in his hand. "I think Rajesh uncle punished Bobby in other ways, too. But I don't know the specifics."

"Look, Ajay, I don't know if I should say this . . ."

The other man looked up, his eyes shiny behind his spectacles. "It's okay. I know Bobby hurt Shumi."

My heart kicked.

Lifting a hand, Ajay dashed away the tear that had begun to fall. "I tried to talk to her when I noticed bruises on her the last time she visited us without him, but she said it was fine, that I had nothing to worry about. She was always so conscious of not damaging the Prasad family's reputation. They were so important in the Indian community. Everyone looked up to them."

*. . . a good family . . . No reason to ruin their name.*

"At least you tried." Quite unlike Kamal and everyone else involved in covering up Ani's murder.

"One time," Ajay added, "we all went camping together when Bobby was maybe sixteen? Shumi fell down a gravel embankment. Scraped up her legs, bruises everywhere. She said she wasn't paying attention and slipped, but I know she was out walking with him. I saw them leave together—I might've been a little kid, but I know what I saw."

"She still didn't tell on him? Even though she could've been badly injured?"

Ajay shook his head. "I don't know the hold he had on her, but she really didn't see any other men or boys. Always just him. Even after he got in trouble when he was sixteen, and my parents weren't sure about him despite his family, she stuck to him."

The hairs on my arms rose. "What kind of trouble?"

"No one ever told me anything. Too young." Frustration under his apparently careless shrug. "Just heard my parents telling Shumi that maybe he wasn't such a good boy after all, and she should distance herself. She said she didn't care, that she wanted to be his wife. They weren't even dating then."

A woman like that wouldn't flip on her husband even if he was dead. She'd lie to protect the only thing she had left of him: his memory as a good man. It would be her word against Diya's. Diya, who'd married her husband on a whim, a man who was linked to the deaths of three women.

I clenched my abdomen.

I'd never forgive myself if the mess of my past affected the woman I loved with everything I was. If Susanne had taught me about love that was generous and kind and loyal, then Diya had brought the lesson home.

She loved with all of her, no holds barred.

"You think it was Bobby, don't you?" Ajay met my eyes with that stark question. "That cop, Ackerson, she was here asking about you while you were in Fiji."

"I'm an easy target. Not a pillar of the community, just some stranger from overseas." Better to stick to that line as long as I could; I wasn't going to be the one to spill open the can of worms that was my link to Jocelyn and Virna. Those two at least I could understand, but I hated that Detective Baxter had added Susanne to the list.

I had *loved* Susanne.

"I wanted to tell Ackerson about Bobby hurting Shumi"—Ajay's voice was a whisper now—"but . . . she loves him so much."

Every ounce of my attention coalesced onto him, onto this moment. "You should." Ajay's independent corroboration of my insinuation that Bobby had been violent could dig me out of this hole. "Not for me, but for Diya. If they come after me, then Diya's the one who's going to get hurt. And she's been hurt so much already."

"I know. She was always the opposite of Bobby, you know—so sweet and gentle. One time at camp, she used her spending money to buy me ice cream after I dropped mine on the ground right after I'd gotten it. I know it's a silly thing to remember, but it mattered."

His Adam's apple bobbed. "I thought it had to be Bobby the instant Dad told us what had happened. He was so angry inside, even though he did a good job of hiding it."

"You got over the hero worship."

"I wish I had." Taking off his glasses again, he put them on the table and rubbed both hands over his face. When he dropped them, his expression was raw. "But I wanted so much to believe Shumi when she said that he hadn't touched her, wanted him to stay my hero." His shoulders shook, tears streaming down his face.

I didn't know what to do, finally got up to sit next to him, my arm around his shoulders. He leaned a little into me and I thought, *Fuck, he's so young.*

I wasn't sure I'd ever been that young.

I'd certainly never had anyone attempt to comfort me when I cried. I didn't blame my brother—Raja was who he'd been molded to be. As for my mother, she'd always been that person. My father had known who she was when he married her; yet not only had he married her, he'd had two children with her.

"Why did you want a second child?" I'd demanded of him at thirteen, right after I'd swept a glass full of whiskey off his desk.

The smell of expensive alcohol a sickening mist in the air, my dad had pressed his hands onto the desk and sighed. "I didn't want Raja to be lonely. I thought you two would be best friends."

That was when I'd understood: I'd been created as a distraction to entertain Raja so that my father could have his wife's full attention. Deep down, Anand Advani was the one I blamed for what had been done to me—and what I'd become as a result.

Ajay sniffed back the last of his tears. "I'm glad Diya has you." Breaking contact, he used a paper napkin to wipe his face, then put his glasses back on. "Do you think Ackerson will answer if I call now? It's after work hours."

"I don't think she's the kind of cop who turns off her phone." She struck me as a woman with little to no understanding of work/life balance. That was probably what made her the caliber of cop Ngata had warned me against underestimating.

Ajay got to his feet. "I'll call her before I head upstairs." His hand was tight around the back of the chair. "My parents . . . they won't like it. They want to pretend everything was perfect, that their daughter married into a good family."

"You're doing the right thing."

As Ajay walked out toward an exit and the night air, his phone already in hand, I considered the most important piece of information I'd learned during the conversation: Bobby had gotten into trouble bad enough in his youth that Shumi's parents had tried to talk their daughter out of an infatuation they'd previously indulged, or at least not opposed.

I had to unearth the details of that trouble. And I had to figure out some way to discover if Bobby *was* alive. If Ackerson was as good as my lawyer had indicated, she had to have all his monetary resources under surveillance. But the man had been a successful businessman for a long time.

Chances were he had a cash reserve.

But he'd also have to hide himself. The media had put the faces of the three likely victims online, and he was a good-looking man, the kind of man people noticed. He might've done something drastic like shave off his hair, I supposed, but even then, he'd have to be careful. If I was him, I'd hide until the heat eased up and the news cycle moved on.

Where?

His businesses had moved real goods. Goods needed warehouses. Not just offices. *Warehouses.*

----

Three hours later, the night dead silent around me, I walked up to a large warehouse in an industrial area on the edge of the city. The company did have other warehouses in other cities, but I had no way to get to those without arousing suspicion.

I had to start here.

The entire area was dark but for the anemic street lighting, the forklifts and trucks of the various businesses parked for the night, and the lights off behind security fencing. All the fencing bore the signs of various security firms, but I didn't see any actual guards as I walked over from where I'd parked the car some way down the street. Live guards probably weren't worth it for most of the businesses.

But they were for Bobby's.

I ducked back, barely avoiding the scythe of light that was the security guard's flashlight as he patrolled the Elektrik Ninja warehouse.

"Come on, boy!"

A huff of sound, then four feet scrambling behind him.

A *dog*? The security guard had a fucking *dog*?

Anxiety was a twisting snake in my gut. I could talk my way in and out of most situations, but I was no expert at breaking and entering. And I certainly wasn't good enough to avoid both a live guard and his canine companion.

On the flip side, would Bobby hide out in a place as secure as this? He'd have as hard a time slipping in and out without being spotted. Or maybe he wasn't slipping out at all, had prepared everything he needed before the massacre of his family, and was just hunkered down in a space to which no one else had the key?

Could be he'd kept an office in there that none of his warehouse managers could enter.

I stood paralyzed in the shadows, trying to figure out my next step. If only Ackerson could see me now.

Paranoia had me spinning around, searching for any hint of a tail. Would Ackerson do that? Just tail a random suspect as Baxter had tailed me so many times, an obsessive presence hovering on the edges of my life? If she was doing it, she was a ghost. Nothing moved nearby, and I'd glimpsed not even a hint of another vehicle on the road behind me when I'd parked.

*Maybe your car is bugged*, said the part of me that had learned to watch my back.

If it was, they might know I was lurking around the business, but what would that get them? Nothing.

Metal clanged, a gate was scraped back. A minute later and powerful headlights speared the night. I sank deeper into the shadows as a van trundled out. It emerged right under a streetlight, so I saw the doggy face hanging out one side, tongue lolling.

The dog saw me, too. Or scented me. It barked.

The security guard grumbled something at the dog that quieted it before jumping out and going to close and lock up the gate. He was back in his car a minute later, the red of his rear lights soon vanishing into the distance.

Not a full-time guard, just one who did the rounds at various properties.

It was possible he'd be back again sometime tonight, so I had to be fast if I was going to do this. And at some point in the last quarter of an hour of standing here, I'd apparently decided I was—because I was moving before I'd consciously processed the decision.

The gate was heavily padlocked, but I'd figured on that. It wasn't as if the fence had barbed wire on top—it was basic chain link. Climbable. Even if I was caught on security cameras, all they'd see was a figure in jeans, their face shadowed by a black hoodie with no branding or markings to make it stand out, and covered by a disposable face mask I'd grabbed from the hospital.

Now I grunted through that mask as I landed on the concrete on the other side of the fence.

The entire area was motionless, not even a rat skittering across the neat frontage.

Running quickly to the warehouse building itself, I began to look for an entrance. It was sealed up tight. Not only that, it had warning stickers on every door and window that bore the logo of a security company—same logo as on the guard's van. The place was wired to sound an alert on break-in.

Of course it was.

I wanted to slap myself. I really wasn't good at this breaking and entering thing. My expertise was in financial sleight of hand, and *only* when it came to Audrey. I'd been scrupulous with the money that belonged to my clients, focusing all my skill on making them more money.

But I was here now, and I wasn't about to give up. And . . . how fast would the security company respond to an alert anyway? This wasn't a central location, and they weren't cops, with the ability to run red lights. Even if they got that same guard to turn back around, it had been at least five minutes since he'd left.

If I waited a few more minutes to hopefully let him drive further away, I might get ten solid minutes.

Good enough.

In the meantime, I found a suitable projectile in the dumpster—a cracked mug someone had thrown out. At least I'd been smart enough to grab a set of disposable gloves from the box on the wall of the ICU.

I wouldn't be leaving any fingerprints.

The mug had WORLD's BEST BOSS written on it in big black letters. Be ironic if that had been Bobby's mug. Or maybe the better term was "poetic justice," I thought as I decided I'd waited long enough, and threw it toward a window that looked into a little public-facing office. Likely a pickup zone for people who lived locally and didn't want to pay shipping costs.

No alarm shrieked, but the alarm pad inside the door was flashing red when I crawled through the window. It had alerted the security company.

I ran into the bowels of the warehouse.

# CHAPTER 42

Private notes: Detective Callum Baxter (LAPD)
Date: Feb 18
Time: 10:23

Forensics finally fucking emailed me the full report on Virna Musgrave's car. Our boy Tavish may have made his first mistake. I don't care if Grace Green thinks the sun shines out of his ass—he did this, and I'm going to nail him for it.

# CHAPTER 43

There was no sign of life anywhere inside the echoing vastness of the warehouse, and I realized the stupidity of my entire plan about two minutes into my heart-pounding run through the long alleyways between metal racks stacked up to the ceiling with various goods. Purple toasters, sleek white heat pumps, and an endless array of table lamps of every variety, a blur of shiny boxes peopled by perfect faces.

The place was too damn big and too damn dark. Bobby could be standing one rack over and I'd never know it. But even more important—there was nowhere to hide in here. No special office as I'd imagined. Bobby couldn't have stayed here without being spotted, and there was no way countless employees would've kept his presence a secret.

Giving up, I was about to run back and out before I was busted when I spotted the small room tucked into the back right corner of the warehouse. Unlike the pickup area out front, this one was a full cube, with a door and windows. Sweat sticking my T-shirt to my skin under the hoodie, I turned the handle on the door.

It opened with ease.

Pushing my way inside, I looked around for anything that might be helpful. Invoices littered the desk, anchored by a mug still half-full of a thick black liquid that might've been coffee. Yellow sheets of paper sat on another end, carbon copies of the delivery drivers' logs. More papers were stuffed into the filing cabinets in back, while files sat spine out behind the desk.

I frowned, my eye caught by the red lettering under the mug.

I carefully moved the mug to another pile. Even if I forgot to move it back, there was no chance the person who worked here would remember exactly how they'd left this mess of a desk.

**OVERDUE!**

That was the red stamp, the edge of which I'd glimpsed. On its own, it didn't mean much. Even businesses this big sometimes slipped. A human input error and a supplier didn't get paid in time. It happened.

Except . . .

I flipped quickly through the pile of invoices.

**OVERDUE!**

**OVERDUE!**

**OVERDUE!**

The entire stack blazed red ink, and when I looked at the dates, I saw that they went back at least two months. The wall clock ticked, the second hand sounding like a hammer. Realizing I'd passed the ten-minute mark three minutes ago, I grabbed a handful of invoices out of the pile, then closed up the office and ran.

I was expecting to hear voices at any second, see headlights spearing through the windows, followed by the sound of a police siren, but the world was as silent as when I'd entered. Shimmying my way out of the window, I didn't dare linger to catch my breath and—after shoving the papers into my waistband—quickly scaled the fence.

I was literally two meters down the sidewalk when headlights turned into the street. Sliding back into the dark between the streetlights, I watched as the security guard turned into the drive and stopped in front of the gate.

No dog this time. Different guard.

I waited only until he was inside before making my way to the far end of the street and my own vehicle. Sweat was a sticky paste along my spine, had broken out along my forehead, but I didn't dare rip off the mask and pull off the hoodie until I was well away from the area, with no signs of pursuit.

The papers I'd thrown onto the passenger seat taunted me, but I didn't try to look at them at the few traffic lights where I had to stop. I wanted the time and light to examine them properly.

The drive to the motel seemed to take forever.

I spotted no lights in the suite occupied by Shumi's family, and hopefully, Ajay wouldn't have looked for my car when he returned to the motel. If he had, I'd just say I'd gone to see Diya.

Once inside my room, I stripped down to my briefs and let the air cool down my overheated skin. At least I'd had the good sense to leave a couple of soft drinks in the small fridge, and now opened a cold Coke as I sat down on the bed to go over the papers I'd stolen.

The first overdue invoice was for a small bill from a plumber who seemed to have come in to fix an issue with the employee toilet in their flagship Rotorua store.

I set it aside.

Big businesses often pulled this shit, keeping up their bottom line while drawing out payments to smaller players, well aware of who held the power in the situation. What was the plumber going to do? Not do business with what was probably a major client that *did* always come through on the bills even if they took their time?

The next two invoices were similar. I was starting to think I'd wasted the entire night when I realized the amount of zeroes on the bill now in my hand. I whistled through my teeth as I read it through. It was an invoice for the rental on the Rotorua warehouse.

Elektrik Ninja was *four* months behind.

The next invoice was from a major supplier and it bore a curt coda: *All shipments on hold until invoice paid.*

My temples throbbed. Why had these been on what I assumed was the warehouse manager's desk, rather than going to Bobby at his much nicer office at the flagship store? Because the warehouse manager handled any bills related to the warehouse? No, that didn't explain the plumber's bill. Maybe the entire senior team had just gathered there for an emergency meeting after the fire.

Whatever the reason, one thing I knew: Bobby had been about to lose everything.

A flash of memory, Rajesh slapping Bobby on the shoulder at the party as he told a friend how proud he was of his children. "Bobby's built his own life, and he never rode on my coattails even when I wanted him to! Now Diya's going to be settled with an accomplished life partner. I'm a very lucky man."

At the time, I'd just been annoyed that Rajesh was ignoring Diya's success as an event planner, had held my tongue only because I'd been standing with another group nearby, not actually part of that conversation. But now I thought back. Bobby had smiled and shaken the hand of his father's friend, nothing in his expression giving away the panic that had to be churning inside him.

His entire identity had been about his success as a self-made man. Men like that didn't like to admit to failure. In the worst cases, they decided that the only way to escape what they thought of as their shame was to ensure there was no one left alive to witness it.

———————

Before finally falling into a fitful sleep, I sent Ackerson an anonymous tip via a throwaway email address: *Bobby Prasad wasn't as successful as everyone thinks. Look at his business accounts. He couldn't even pay his rent! His shops would soon have nothing to sell because no one was going to extend a further line of credit to such a loser!*

I'd deliberately written it in a mean-spirited tone as might come from someone passing on gossip. But I couldn't base all my hopes on Ackerson following that thread and realizing that Bobby had likely murdered his entire family to save himself from the humiliation of having to admit his failure.

I hadn't mattered, wasn't important, could live.

Yeah, that logic made sense.

He might even have killed himself, his body in pieces in the ruins of the house.

No way to know. The obsessive searching I'd done on such murderers—who I'd learned were called "family annihilators"—had thrown out an even mix of those who ended their own lives alongside those of their families, and those who walked away to begin a whole new life.

As if now that they'd erased their family, they'd also erased their shame and worry.

My mind was still struggling to comprehend the cold psychopathy of the entire thing when I woke the next morning. But I couldn't afford to be distracted by my horror at what Bobby had done. I needed more to bolster my case, had decided to focus on Ajay's comment about Bobby's teenage trouble. I knew it was flimsy, but it was all I had.

Hopefully, the more incidents I could add to his pattern of antisocial behavior, the better I'd look in comparison.

The only problem was that I had no idea where to start my research.

Standing in front of the motel bathroom's chipped sink as I finished shaving, I thought back to the engagement party.

My mind flickered with a collage of images.

How Diya's father had smiled indulgently at her, how her mother had brushed back her hair now and then.

*Love.*

Yet they'd allowed the blame for Ani's violent death to be placed on her head. Protecting their bigger, stronger son because he wouldn't make as sympathetic a subject as Diya. Blame the innocent little girl, sweep the whole thing under the rug. Even if that meant giving her a psychic wound that festered until she needed medication to fight it.

*Richard—that's it!*

My mind snagged on the name of the husky blond man with a small red birthmark near his left cheekbone whom Bobby had introduced as his fishing buddy.

"Known each other since the first day of high school," Richard had said. "Bobby's uniform was ironed, his hair in this real tight cut, and I thought for sure he was going to be a swot."

They'd both laughed then, because the next day, they'd turned up to try out for the school's junior rugby team, ended up together in the scrum, and that was it. A friendship that had lasted through school and differing career paths.

Richard hadn't gone to college, I thought with a frown, trying to follow that thread to lock down a way to get hold of him. He and Bobby had been chatting about how Bobby would invite him and his— "Apprenticeship!" I tapped a fisted hand against the cold porcelain of the sink.

Bobby had groaned that the apprentice electricians had been a bigger hit at the college parties than fellow students like Bobby. "I shot myself in the foot inviting you lot," he'd said with a laugh. "All the girls wanted the buff blue-collar guys, not the nerds."

But when I grabbed my phone and looked up "Richard + electrician + Rotorua," I got several hits and all of them came with a face attached that wasn't of the man I'd met.

I tried to remember who else I might've seen chatting with Richard.

A vague memory emerged, of neighbor Tim in an enthusiastic discussion with the younger man. Could be nothing, but at least it was a start. But first, I had more important business.

# CHAPTER 44

Private notes: Detective Callum Baxter (LAPD)
Date: Feb 23
Time: 09:06

Bastard must've been born under a lucky star. The partial fingerprint on the fucking critical engine component isn't enough for a match.

Time: 19:09

Perez thinks we missed something. Because either Tavish Advani is a master criminal . . . or we're looking in the wrong place. I can't see it. Advani fits every single parameter. He has the motive. He had the means—access to Virna's house and vehicles. And he's got a track record of dead lovers.

Man is also the kind of smart that's dangerous.

Virna had no enemies, and her son has his own millions. He didn't need to kill Mom to get his hands on the inheritance. There are no other suspects.

# CHAPTER 45

My wife lay unmoving, but the tube down her throat was gone, the ventilator silent.

"She doesn't need it anymore," said the senior nurse who was there when I arrived, her face holding a smile. "That's excellent improvement, given her injuries. Your wife's a real fighter." She made a note on the chart.

"Do you think the doctors will bring her out of the coma soon?"

"They've already started the process—her team is very concerned about the brain injury and wants to assess her while she's conscious."

"That's from the stab wound to her head?" I said, unable to comprehend how Bobby could've done that to the sister he'd kissed so lovingly on the forehead before our engagement party.

*Can't believe you got married by Elvis, kiddo. What a story for your grandkids.*

The nurse glanced up from the chart as Bobby's affectionate comment floated to the surface of my memories. "No"—she frowned—"from the blow she took to the skull."

The words reverberated around my own skull.

"Could you tell me more?" I asked, thinking back to that first conversation with the surgeon, when I hadn't asked for details. Later, when I had wanted to know, the Kumars had arrived before Dr. Chen finished going over everything. "Truth is, I wasn't . . . all there, immediately afterward. I didn't absorb what I should have."

Expression gentling, she pointed to the bandage on the left side of Diya's skull. "She was either hit with something there, or fell against a very hard surface. She hasn't shown any signs of a buildup of pressure, so her prognosis is excellent, but traumatic brain injuries can be unpredictable."

*There was another rock nearby. Blood and hair on it.*

Sound telescoped into an echoing void as I remembered what Kamal had said about the murder weapon that had taken Ani's life. A rock, smashed into her tiny head. It couldn't be a fucking coincidence that Diya had been attacked the same way.

Had that been the start, the knife only coming into play when Bobby realized two adult women were a lot harder to smash to death with a rock than a little girl? But for even that to work . . . the elder Prasads must've already been dead. Else the four of them could've brought Bobby down—and at least one would've been able to call emergency services.

He must've separated the group somehow, attacked them one by one.

". . . poor thing, though," the nurse was saying when I tuned back in. "To wake to what's happened. At least she has you and her sister-in-law."

"It's going to be tough," I managed to say past the roar in my head, "but we'll get through it together."

I took Diya's hand after the nurse left. "I love you. You're my one and only, Diya. Always and forever. If you can hear me, then know that when I married you, I had no idea who you were or any inclination of your family's wealth."

She was the most impulsive decision I'd ever made.

"I would've been happy living in a shack with you." Then I leaned in close and whispered, "But we'll never have to. I have money stashed offshore." My heart pounded at admitting even that much aloud, but I wanted her to know I could take care of her, give her anything she needed.

Kissing her on the cheek, I said, "We'll talk more when you wake, baby. I love you."

Ajay was walking down the hallway from the CCU when I went to leave. He shook his head at me. "Ackerson has ice in her veins—the way she spoke to me . . ." He set his jaw. "Asking me if I knew who you were, or that you knew how to wield charm like a weapon. As if I was some teenager with a crush."

*Fuck.* That really wasn't what I wanted to hear. "Thanks for trying."

"She really has it in for you." Open expression, clear worry. "She kept asking about you even when I was trying to tell her about Bobby abusing Shumi."

"Some cops are like that," I said as he glanced at his smartwatch. "Your mom?"

A tight nod. "She gets worried if I don't check in with her regularly, and I left early this morning—I was walking in that park opposite the hospital. Have you seen it? They have a thermal footbath for visitors. Was kind of nice this morning being there alone, with the mist curling all around me."

I let him ramble, sensing his embarrassment at having his mother checking up on him. "Diya and I went there after I first came to Rotorua." It had been my first glimpse of the molten heart of the city—the park had more than one fenced-off mud pool, with warning signs everywhere telling people that the temperatures inside were deadly.

Ajay's watch buzzed again.

"She must be terrified after what happened to Shumi," I said in an effort to ease his discomfort.

"Yeah," he said, not meeting my gaze.

. . . *that mother of his wouldn't have allowed it.*

The relationship between Mrs. Kumar and Ajay might explain the distance Shumi kept from her parents; per Ajay, his sister had once been a girl of stubborn determination and drive. Could've been oil and water with her and their mother.

"Are you leaving?" Ajay asked after aggressively *not* replying to his mother's messages. Thrusting his hands into his pockets, he squared his shoulders. "You're doing something, aren't you?"

"I have to, with Ackerson out to get me. I'm going to talk to Bobby's friends, see if I can dig up anything that my lawyer can use. I mean, maybe they saw what he did to your sister?"

"He was good about appearing a nice guy on the surface." Voice dejected, Ajay ran a hand through his hair. "But you should definitely try. You never know."

"I don't suppose you know the names of any of his friends?"

"No, sorry. I kept my distance from him after I figured out about Shumi." He frowned. "Though . . . back when we were younger, he used to hang around with this one big blond guy. Rugby team, I think." His watch buzzed twice in a row.

Shoulders falling, he said, "I better go."

We parted without further words, and when I looked back, I saw him pulling out his phone to return the message.

My own mother, meanwhile, didn't care enough about my life to even know, much less give a damn, that my in-laws had been murdered and my wife was in a coma.

Which of us was the pathetic one in the end?

Turning away, I left Ajay to his call and made my way to the car. En route, I sent Aleki a message thanking him for the home-cooked boxed lunch that he'd dropped off for me with the ICU staff—they'd handed it to me when I came in. The other man, I'd realized, was a genuinely good guy, someone who could become a lifelong friend if I gave it a shot.

If I didn't sabotage it before it got too deep.

*You don't trust love, Tavish.* Susanne's voice. *I can't blame you after your childhood, but really, darling, you must allow people in or you'll not only end up sad and lonely, but you'll spend life in the shallows. And that would be an utter and dull waste.*

"I'm trying, Suzi W," I whispered to the ghost that haunted me. "I'm trying so fucking hard."

With Diya, there was no question: I was in fathoms deep.

Once safely in my car, I set about scanning and memorizing the list of non-extradition countries my father had sent me.

Squeezing the steering wheel afterward, I said, "I'm not leaving you, Diya." But I had to be prepared . . . just in case.

I wasn't about to end up in a cage.

# CHAPTER 46

Private notes: Detective Callum Baxter (LAPD)
Date: Mar 2
Time: 10:08

Chief's ordered me to shelve the Musgrave investigation, put it into the cold case files. He's even got the powers that be to let up on the pressure—we can't give Jason Musgrave what we don't have.

And because the chief knows me, he's also just assigned me a multiple murder involving three young dance graduates, making sure I won't have time to work the Musgrave case on my own. He knows I'd never shortchange the dancer case—man, they were just kids.

He thinks I'm obsessed, that I need some distance at least. "Take a few months, Baxter, then maybe I'll give you some time to work it again. But for right now, it's cold."

Maybe he's right.

Or maybe Tavish Advani is charming another old lady right now.

CHAPTER 47

The caution tape still fluttered at the top of the driveway down to the Lake Tarawera house, but the scene looked a lot different from when I'd last been here. Flowers, masses of them, lay on the grass shoulder along the road on either side of the drive.

Thankfully, however, there were no looky-loos or media vans—I'd been planning to just drive on past if that was the case. This remained the biggest crime that had taken place in Rotorua in a decade or more. Even the national media was continuing to update the public—though right now, those updates just consisted of reporters finding new ways to say that "the two survivors of the tragic incident remain in the ICU."

My history hadn't yet leaked. Possibly because of the prevailing view that the deaths and fire must have resulted from a family issue—the few times where I *had* been mentioned, it had been as Diya's "American fiancé," a man who was newly in the country and thus an outsider to the family drama.

The fact that Bobby had been the CEO of a major company, while his parents were both senior doctors, had given the media more than enough meat to chew on—add on Diya and Shumi being two beautiful women in critical condition, and they had plenty to fill airtime and column inches.

It helped that pretty much no one had my contact details, so the reporters couldn't get in touch with me unless they staked out the hospital. Which, so far, they hadn't been crass enough to do—that, or I'd managed to avoid them due to the erratic nature of my visiting schedule.

Whatever the reason, I knew it wouldn't last much longer. Some reporter no doubt already had the goods on me but was waiting until it would no longer be considered bad form to report what might otherwise be seen as tabloid gossip. I had to use what little time I had to clear my name. If Ackerson refused to listen, then I had no hesitation about leaking the information to the reporters.

I'd watched my father wield information like a scalpel, knew it could sway far more than juries.

Parking the car on that thought, I walked over to read the cards attached to the bouquets.

*I didn't know you, but I'm praying for you. May God in heaven bring comfort to those left behind.*

*Dr. Prasad, you saved my baby's life along with my own. I'll never forget you.*

*You were such a kind and generous family. I'll always remember our days at the beach together when the kids were younger. I'm sorry we drifted apart as they grew.*

That last one was just signed with a single name: Janet. But I made note of it nonetheless before crouching down to read more of the notes pinned to the array of bouquets.

The oldest flowers had begun to curl and wilt . . . though if they'd been out in the sun for days, they should've been in worse condition. Maybe someone was coming around and cleaning up the dead bouquets.

*Hey, Dee. Stay strong. Love you to the moon, babes.* —*Kalindra*

A honey-skinned and curvy woman with freckles across her nose, Kalindra hadn't been at the party, but Diya had pointed out a photo of her in the collection she had on the wall in her old bedroom. They'd been friends in high school, but Kalindra's move to Wellington for college had gently frayed their friendship until it was now more a case of fond memories than day-to-day reality.

Still, I'd see if I could talk to her, since she would've been around when Bobby was younger. I'd also touch base with the three friends of Diya's who had come to the party; though she'd met them through her work, the friendships not deep like the one she had with Shumi, it was possible she'd mentioned something to them that might help.

*Dr. Prasad, thank you, thank you, thank you. You treated me with warmth and dignity and just the most incredible kindness when I needed it most, and you will live forever in my memories. I'm so sorry for what happened to you and your family, and I hope the surviving members manage to come out of this with whole hearts.*

There were several other notes in a similar vein, and for most of them, I couldn't tell to which Dr. Prasad they were addressed. The more specific ones were evenly scattered, which just confirmed that

Sarita and Rajesh, whatever their shortcomings as parents, had both been well respected by their patients.

> *Diya, I only got to spend time with you when you organized my twenty-first, but I thought you were the sweetest person ever. I'm hoping with all my heart that you recover quickly. —Mackenzie*

> *Bobby, fuck, man. I can't believe it. I know you're kicking ass up there. —Dan*

I began to notice a pattern. While many of the notes referred to the entire family or specifically named Diya, Bobby, Sarita, or Rajesh—either as doctors or by name—I'd found no mention of Shumi so far. Not by name. Only in terms of her relationships to the others.

> *Bobby, you were a great boss—I'm rooting for your sis and wife.*

> *Diya, I'm praying for you and your sister-in-law.*

> *Sarita & Rajesh, I promise I'll be there for Diya & Bobby's wife.*

The woman who'd joined endless clubs during high school seemed to have made no real connections in her adult life. It fit with the picture I was building of her relationship with Bobby. Stay-at-home wife. Controlled by her husband. Kept inside the home and not allowed any friendships except with her husband's family.

Another small thing to add to the pile of evidence against Bobby.

"I *thought* that was our car on the road." Tim's voice, the slap of his flip-flops against his heels having announced his presence before he spoke. "It's nice, all these flowers, don't you think? Joseph comes

233

over every afternoon and weeds out the ones that are wilting. Just started doing it on his own. Makes me proud, that boy."

Grateful the other man had initiated contact, I rose from my crouch. "He comes from kind parents."

"How's Diya?" His eyes searched my face in a way that made me wonder if he'd been doing some online searches of his own.

My chest tightened. "She's fighting."

"Good, that's good." He shifted from foot to foot.

Yeah, Tim knew something.

Keeping my expression tired, just a man in a tough situation, I said, "I'm trying to put together a few things for the funerals in case the police release the remains soon." Charred remnants of people I'd celebrated with less than a week ago.

The other man stopped fidgeting. "Is there anything we can do to help? Just ask."

Whatever he'd heard, he remained too much a good guy to hang me out to dry. "I was hoping to get in touch with family and friends," I said. "I don't suppose you remember any names? I already have Rajesh's and Sarita's hospital colleagues—the ones who have access to the ICU have been by to see Shumi and Diya, and they've passed on the wishes of the others.

"Many other folks have left flowers and cards at hospital reception, but usually with no contact details. People . . . they don't realize that no one in the family who has that information is alive or conscious."

Tim blew out a breath. "Oh Jesus, I never even thought about that."

"It's not a normal situation," I said. "Hard for any of us to process."

"I'll ask Hannah about any contacts she might remember, but to be honest, we were just neighbors. Don't get me wrong—we were good neighbors, always helped each other out, but it wasn't a deep friendship. Frankly, I was surprised to be invited to the engagement party, but then I saw how proud Sarita and Rajesh were and I figured they just wanted to share that with everyone. Was nice."

"So you didn't really talk otherwise, except for neighborhood chat?" There went my chance to track down Bobby's rugby-playing friend.

"A little more than that," Tim corrected. "Like when they found out Joseph was good with mechanical things, they suggested he think about engineering. Sarita said he should talk to Bobby's wife—well, that knocked me for six. Never would've pegged her as an engineer!"

"I didn't know myself until recently."

"Joseph said she was lovely, supersmart. Talked him through options and possible pathways." He stared at the caution tape. "She told him she wasn't practicing because she and Bobby were planning to have kids and they'd both decided the kids should have one parent at home."

He shifted his feet again. "I mean, he grew up with a mum who worked all the time—you have to, don't you, when you're a young doctor? I can see how he would want different for his kids, but real shame about his wife giving up a good career."

I thought of Shumi's cheerful presence melded with her absolute inability to refute any request or decision made by Bobby. If he'd asked her to quit, she'd have written her resignation letter that night.

"Sorry I couldn't help with any contact info," Tim said.

"What about Bobby's friend Richard?" I persisted, trying my luck because—quite frankly—I was desperate. "I thought I remembered you talking to him at the party."

Tim's eyes lit up. "Yes! Fishing, we were discussing fishing. He's an electrician, gave me his card when I mentioned we were looking at getting a few electrical upgrades."

Five minutes later and I had that card in hand and was back in the car.

Tim hadn't invited me inside this time.

The first thing I did once alone was search for my name online. Hits populated the screen . . . but they were all from back home. Nothing local.

"Ackerson," I muttered, certain that she was the reason for Tim's sudden change in behavior. It didn't matter. I had what I needed.

I called Richard.

Answering on the first ring, the other man told me to come to a place called Sulphur Point. "It's just around the way from my jobsite at the Government Gardens. I'll take a break so we can talk. Been working nonstop since it happened," he said. "Helps to keep my mind busy. Otherwise I start spiraling, thinking of how it could happen to anyone. Partying one day, gone the next."

It didn't take me long to drive to Sulphur Point—per my phone's GPS, it was only five minutes from the hospital. I'd been here before, I remembered when I parked in the small empty lot beside the wooden walkway that led people on a path that passed mud pools, native birdlife, and smoking craters in the earth.

The thick smell of sulfur filled the air as I stepped onto the walkway. A large red sign to my left listed the dangers in the area, including hydrogen sulfide gas and fumaroles—holes in the earth that emitted dangerously hot steam—but when I walked further along the path, I found myself gazing out at the edge of Lake Rotorua, this part a thick, misty blue that looked unreal: white paint stained by a droplet of blue.

Steam curled up from it, betraying the heat in the water.

Birds sat on the water much further out, where the temperatures were no doubt more normal.

Diya had brought me here, eager to show me her city. "Sorry

about the smell, but this place is incredible!" she'd said, holding her nose before she released it with a laugh. "I swear you go nose blind after a little while, barely even smell the sulfur. Still, I'm glad Mum and Dad built over by Lake Tarawera even if it is a little bit of a drive!"

I'd chuckled at the idea of that scenic roughly thirty-minute drive being considered anything but a pleasure cruise. "Babe, you're talking to someone from LA, the land of freeways and gridlock."

Her eyes had sparkled at me as she reminded me of a drive we'd taken in LA—she'd wanted to go to one of the big outlets. That part had been fun. The return trip, however, had ended up with us sitting in traffic for three hours . . . while Diya pulled snacks out of her purse like some magician.

Never before had I enjoyed gridlock.

Hearing the crunch of gravel, I turned back and reached the little parking area just as Richard was getting out of his work van. His hair was matted down as if he'd been wearing a hard hat, and dust coated his upper arms and the part of his legs visible between the end of his work shorts and the thick socks he wore with steel-toed boots.

"I took a minute to grab us a couple of cold Cokes, and pies since it's time for morning tea anyway."

"I'll take the Coke, but I haven't quite gotten into meat pies, so I'll leave that to you."

A sharp grin as he handed me the soda. "You're missing out. A good meat pie is a real treat." He grabbed his own drink and one of the pies before nudging the door shut and locking up the van. "Lot of expensive gear in there, can't be too careful."

"I can hold your drink while you eat," I offered, but he shook his head.

"Nah, let's walk to that bit with the view of the lake." Opening up the Coke, he took a long swig, then held it in one hand while—having folded down the brown paper bag halfway—he ate the pie with the other.

"Sorry I haven't been to see Diya," he said as we walked past the warning sign. "I wasn't sure they'd let me in."

"They wouldn't. She's still in the ICU."

An easing of those big shoulders.

"I'm trying to put things together for the funerals in advance, help Diya. But I only really met people at the engagement party . . ."

"Oh, no worries. I can help you with that. Bobby and I still play the odd game of rugby with a social team, and I can round them up to help with whatever you need. I might also have a few contacts for his parents' friends—met some of them when Bobby and I hung out as kids."

"Thanks."

We stopped at the spot with the view to the lake, arms braced on the wooden railing. "Look, Richard." I held his gaze. "Thing is, the police are investigating, and they're saying some stuff."

His jaw tightened. "About the Prasads? That's bullshit. They're a good family!"

*A good family.*

For whom reputation was everything.

"I know. But they're insinuating things about Bobby. About him being violent." I didn't imagine it—that slight flicker in Richard's eyes.

He knew something.

# CHAPTER 48

Private notes: Detective Callum Baxter (LAPD)
Date: May 15
Time: 23:18

Chief has kept me busy with multiple cases, but I still can't help returning to the Musgrave file even if it's only late at night, for a few minutes. I hate knowing someone got away with cold-blooded murder. Yeah, I still think it's Advani, and even Perez can't argue with me there, but we have nothing.

Only good news is that Advani doesn't seem to be dating anyone new.

Because one thing I know—if he hurts another woman, then it's on me. Because I didn't stop him.

# CHAPTER 49

I'm trying to push back on the police's insinuations about Bobby," I told Richard, "but they act like they know something I don't."

"Fuckers."

"Yeah, well." Steam rose from the stony moonscape in front of us. "Is there anything I should be aware of? In his history? I'm scared this will leak to the media and I want to be prepared to fight back."

Richard took a big bite of his pie, chewed with too much concentration. "He was my mate."

"I know. But he's dead now"—or doing a good job of playing dead—"and we've got to look out for him. No one else will." My voice came out rough. "Most of all, we have to look out for Diya and Shumi. They're the ones who'll suffer the most under a media barrage."

Pie finished, Richard scrunched up the paper bag and thrust it into his pocket. "Cops are probably thinking about what happened to Rhiannon," he said after taking a long gulp of his Coke.

My skin prickled. "Rhiannon?"

"It would've been back when we were about fifteen, I think. No, sixteen. Bobby's and Shumi's families have been tight for years, and they used to go to a beach campsite every year during the summer. Set up a big tent each, have a shared barbecue, sit and relax while the kids played type of thing. I went one year, and I think Diya had a school friend come a couple of times, too, but mostly it was just the two families."

My tendons were so tight they vibrated, but I didn't interrupt, not wanting to startle Richard out of his flow.

"Rhiannon was this kid who used to go there every year with her parents, too. Not sure exactly how old she was—maybe not quite as old as Bobby, but pretty close. All of them were friends, used to spend the time playing, swimming, climbing the sand dunes. Kid stuff."

"Sounds idyllic."

"Yeah. Bobby was always buzzed about it—his dad used to hire him one of those four-wheelers from around when he was fourteen, and he loved roaring up and down the beach on that. We did that together that time I went."

I could imagine it—one of those long New Zealand beaches that seemed to go on forever into the horizon. Flags fluttering where the lifeguards had set up a safe swimming zone, but the other sections free for four-wheelers, or for surfers who wanted to be away from the swimmers and were confident in their ability to cope with the wild waves.

Salt in the air, a kind of sun-kissed glow to the people.

"Rhiannon drowned." A slap of cold water thrown on the halcyon images in my mind. "They found her body tangled up in some buoy ropes way out in the water."

"Jesus, how awful."

"Neither of the families ever went back to the beach." Richard took another drink. "I mean, would you?"

I shook my head. "But what's Bobby got to do with it?"

"Her parents went on television, gave this big interview. They didn't name Bobby—probably couldn't, because he was a minor— and that meant they couldn't name the Prasads, either, because it would've identified him.

"I reckon that was the TV people, because they did bleep out a couple of names. My oldest sis later said that Rhiannon's mother was on social media talking about it, too, no censorship."

"About what?"

"Rhiannon's mum said that Rhiannon and Bobby were in a relationship, that they did the long-distance thing after the previous summer, but that the summer Rhiannon died, she'd decided it wasn't worth it when they only met in the summer weeks. She broke it off."

I frowned, my fingers tight on the can of Coke. "Surely she wasn't saying that Bobby killed her daughter because of a summer fling? They were kids."

"Most people said that privately, but no one said it to the lady's face—I mean, she was grieving, right? Anyway, she said that her daughter was on the swim team, the best swimmer of the entire group, and there was no way she'd have drowned unless someone helped her."

Finishing off his soda, he crushed the can in one hand. "That television interview, her husband sat there mostly silent, but she cried and said how the police had hushed it all up because the boy's parents were important doctors and she was a checkout operator, her husband a mechanic."

Richard shook his head. "I mean, it was crazy talk, but that's probably what the cops have dug up." His expression grew dark. "Easier to blame a dead man than look for whatever psycho it was who went into that house and did that."

I nodded, but my mouth was dry, my heart racing. That was two dead children I'd now connected to Bobby.

"Sorry, man, I have to get back to the job."

"Right, sure. Thanks for taking the time to talk to me." I chewed over his words as we walked back to where we'd parked. "One more thing, Richard, and this is really awkward . . . but Shumi's family is saying Bobby abused her."

Richard's jaw worked. "He would never lay a finger on her. He was super traditional in that way—that the man is the one who looks after his woman. Back in high school, he used to be a favorite with the girls for how he helped them carry their books or opened the doors.

"We'd laugh at him, but he'd grin and say, 'You suckers aren't getting kissed under the bleachers, are you?'" A sudden smile. "He was right. He had so many girlfriends all through school."

"Not Shumi?"

"Her parents sent her to a girls' school about half an hour from our coed one, and he was a teenage boy. Never cheated on her after they did officially hook up at uni, though."

I wasn't so sure of Bobby's fidelity given everything else I'd discovered about him, but Richard had already been confronted by too many uncomfortable truths. I waved him off with, "I think I'll walk along here a bit longer." The surreal landscape with its whiff of sulfur and deadly hazards suited my mood.

Finishing off my Coke, I dropped the can in the trash before I began to walk.

When my phone rang a minute later, I glanced down to see my lawyer's name. "What's Ackerson saying now?" I asked Ngata when I answered.

"I've got sources, and those sources are telling me she's attempting to request all kinds of financial records about you from the US. Is there something I should know?"

My stomach twisted, sweat breaking out along my spine. "I used to have a gambling problem," I said. "Pissed away everything I earned and took out a mortgage on my condo—when it sells, I'll only clear a hundred grand." No point hiding that when Ackerson had to have received the tip from Baxter in LA.

"But I've been clean since before I met Diya." Mostly because my father had made it plain that the cops would otherwise use my addiction to convict me of murder.

*Two very rich women are dead under suspicious circumstances, and you're bleeding money,* he'd said. *I'd fucking convict you, too. Shut. It. Down.*

Even though the program to which I'd admitted myself was top-of-the-line, it hadn't been easy to fight the urge . . . but then I'd met Diya, and she'd become my new addiction.

I was fine with that—she was the kind of addiction who could get a man through life.

"This isn't good, Tavish," Ngata said. "It just increases what Ackerson sees as your financial motive. Talk to your father, get him to transfer you a wad of cash. No way for anyone to know if it's a gift or a loan—and it's an indication of your resources."

"I saved Diya," I reminded him. "Don't let Ackerson forget that."

"She's going to say you were forced into it because of the neighbor who was with you."

I fisted my hand. "I can't wait for my wife to wake up and tell that cop she's full of shit."

"I hope for your sake that one of the women does wake up. Call your father."

Frustrated and angry after he hung up, I strode back along the pathway while smoke curled up from the stone all around me, a small private hell.

*Ani.*

*Rhiannon.*

*Shumi.*

Three women Bobby had hurt. Two dead. One barely clinging to life. If those three existed, so would others. And now, thanks to Richard, I knew of one woman who would've tried to keep track of the boy she blamed for the murder of her child.

---

Rhiannon's mother wasn't difficult to locate with the details Richard had given me. Her hyphenated surname had been in the papers, and it wasn't a common one. When I did a social media search, she showed up as the third hit down—her profile picture was of the same smiling teenage girl I'd seen in the newspaper articles, but the other images on her page were of an adult woman with deep lines on her thin face.

Only fifty but I'd have pegged her as more than a decade older. Grief and anger left marks.

Her location was listed as Auckland . . . and there, on her profile, was a link to a website: Justice for Rhiannon.

When I clicked through, I found myself on a badly designed site that I could tell hadn't been updated on the back end for some time. But someone was still writing a post on it every year on Rhiannon's birthday.

I began to read one at random.

My sweet girl would've been twenty-one today if only she hadn't had the bad luck to fall in love with a psychopath. Everyone tells me I shouldn't say these things, but I don't care. It's the truth and the truth needs to be spoken. Maybe they've gagged me with their rich people lawyers against saying his name, but I know. You all know.

My girl could swim like a fish. And you're telling me she drowned on a clear day when the sea was all but smooth? I saw him after. He'd been swimming, too. Said it was with his sister, but he was a teenage boy, didn't want to be hanging around with his kid sister.

He drowned my Rhi, my sweet girl. She was such a strong swimmer that he had to have held her under or done something else to her. She used to swim out to that far buoy and back without problem.

His sister was an adorable thing, though. Rhiannon loved her, used to make a special batch of cookies for her right before we went down each summer. "For my little Dee," she'd say. "My adopted baby sister."

I don't know how one child in a family could be so sweet, and the other a monster. I still have the letters that little girl wrote to my girl after each summer. She loved that Rhiannon was a dancer and would always be excited for Rhiannon to teach her new steps.

He was always around them, though. Always watching. I should've known, but who thinks these kinds of things about a kid? Who could know that he was a murderer?

Sarita and Rajesh.

The answer to the writer's final question.

After baby Ani, how could they not know? But I couldn't ask them. Rhiannon's mother, however, was alive—and Andrea Smithy-Carr had listed her personal phone number on the website, in case anyone had information about her daughter's death.

I considered whether to call ahead, decided against it. I didn't want her to talk herself out of it during my drive. It had been more than ten years, after all—and I was Bobby's in-law. Better to call once I was within Auckland's borders, give her less time to over-think.

The GPS told me the drive to Auckland would take roughly three hours. If I left now, I'd get there before five. Even if I ended up spending a couple of hours with her, I could still make it back to Rotorua tonight.

Stiff muscles were a small price to pay for critical information.

I wasn't the least surprised when I spotted a police cruiser an hour into my drive to the country's biggest city. I made sure to stay exactly at the speed limit no matter if traffic was flowing faster and kept passing me. But whichever cop Ackerson had asked for a favor suddenly put on their lights and siren anyway; I was getting ready to pull over when the cruiser raced past me, on its way to respond to an incident.

If another cop was shadowing me during the drive, I didn't see them.

I made only one stop—for gas, and to use the toilet. As a result, my muscles were already tight when I pulled over at the southern border of the sprawling city of Auckland to call Andrea in the hope of getting her address. If it ended up being on the far northern end of the city, then I wouldn't make it back to Rotorua till after midnight—rush hour had already begun, and Auckland was like LA in the sheer spread of its borders.

It was only as I input Andrea Smithy-Carr's number that I realized I'd been stupid in my desperation—the number on the website could've long ago been disconnected.

"Hello." A woman's voice.

"Is this Andrea? Rhiannon's mother?"

A long, long pause. "Who is this?" A harsh edge now.

Relief kicked me like an angry horse. Dropping my head against the headrest, I said, "I want to talk to you about Bobby Prasad."

She sucked in air. "That bastard is finally dead." Her voice held nothing but contempt and satisfaction.

"Yes," I agreed even though I wasn't too sure of that, "but he still hasn't paid for Rhiannon's death. Have you seen how they're memorializing him in the papers? Smart young businessman, employed hundreds of people, brilliant member of the community."

"It's all lies."

"Could we meet and talk? I think you'll be interested in what I have to say."

It was a testament to the intensity of her faith in her convictions—or perhaps a testament to her obsession—that she didn't ask me anything about myself, just gave me her address. Luckily, it ended up being only twenty-five minutes away from where I'd parked, and I was soon in what looked to be a family-style neighborhood of old wooden houses.

No fancy landscaping, but the lawns were neatly cut and scattered with brightly colored kids' toys. A few houses boasted basketball hoops attached to garages, and one had a Persian carpet hanging over the verandah railing, as if they'd been expecting sun, only to be hit by a cloud-heavy afternoon.

The scents that drifted through my open window told me someone was cooking dinner, and it involved a combination of spices unfamiliar to my tongue. Two kids who looked to be around seven or eight rode bicycles beside their T-shirt-and-tights-clad mothers; both women were laughing, delighted by some inside joke.

The group of four stopped in front of another house, waved to the older man who was out there washing his car.

A little black dog with a white muzzle ran out to greet the kids, its tail wagging.

Hands tight on the steering wheel as the small group retreated in my rearview mirror, I realized I was nearing Andrea Smithy-Carr's home. Slowing down, I soon found myself pulling up in front of a small house with peeling gray paint and an overgrown lawn.

# CHAPTER 50

Private notes: Detective Callum Baxter (LAPD)
Date: Jun 10
Time: 13:07

Had an extra hour today so pulled out the file again, to see if we'd missed anything. There's one thing. That neighbor who found Virna Musgrave? He mentioned that he'd had a guest staying with him that week who'd just left—that was why he was walking his dog later than he usually does. He'd dropped off his friend at the airport.

We never interviewed the guest. Seemed no reason to since they were gone well before the accident, but since it looks like this file is staying cold, I might as well see if I can track them down to tie off the loose end. Wife says she'll divorce me if I don't give up the obsession, so I'll have to do it while at work— can't even mention the name Tavish Advani at home without riling her up.

# CHAPTER 51

A board mounted on two thick posts stood amid the weeds in Andrea Smithy-Carr's front yard. Hand-painted on it were the words *JUSTICE FOR RHIANNON*. Below the blocky header flowed tiny writing in what looked like marker pen that had been traced over and over as it faded. From what little I could read, it was a diatribe against the authorities for covering up the murder of her daughter.

I'd already figured out that Andrea Smithy-Carr wasn't exactly stable, but I hadn't realized the depth of her obsession until this instant. But I was here now, and she was opening her front door even as I set foot on the mossy and cracked path through the grass, so she'd clearly been watching for me.

A brace covered her left leg to the knee.

"Don't mind the grass," she said. "The boy who cuts it has been sick this past week."

The grass was knee height; it hadn't been mowed for months. Given that this seemed like a friendly neighborhood to the outside eye, I wondered if her neighbors had been put off from helping her because of her unrelenting obsession—the board, for one, was an eyesore for a street that seemed to be trying its best to keep up a certain level of appearance.

But I just nodded. "I'm Tavish."

"Andrea." Gait halting but stable, she invited me into the house.

The carpet was a dingy and faded beige, and the furniture had the appearance of charity shop goods, but no dust covered any of the surfaces, and—alongside the delicious smell of fresh baking—I could smell a lemony scent I associated with cleanliness. The fireplace was empty and filled with pine cones, the mantel above it lined with trophies that had been polished to a shine.

The trophies sat alongside photos of a smiling black-haired girl.

"Rhiannon won those." Andrea pointed at the trophies. "Swimming and dance."

"She was talented."

"Would've been on the national team if she'd been allowed to live." Her face was hard when I glanced at her, but she said, "I made scones. I'll put on coffee."

"I can help. Your leg . . ."

She waved me down. "Almost healed now." From the slow way she walked toward the kitchen, however, I figured that for a significant exaggeration. "Just got home from the rehabilitation unit two days ago. They bunged me in there for *five* days."

At least that cleared up one small fear of mine: Andrea Smithy-Carr might be unstable, but she was physically incapable of having harmed the Prasads. "What happened to your leg?"

"Fell," she called out from the kitchen. "Stupid little hole in the backyard. Must be a rat or something. I'll be putting poison out, don't you worry."

I made noises of sympathy while thinking about that little dog.

Then, while she made the coffee—instant, it looked like from what I could see of her movements—I took careful note of the photos and trophies but found nothing in them to answer my question.

"Let me," I said when she walked in with a tray.

Smiling, she accepted the offer. "Your mother raised you well."

My mother didn't raise me at all, but I knew how to play this game and gave her a gentle smile. "Those scones look great to this starving man." She'd split them in half and put whipped cream and jam in separate little pots—she'd also provided what looked to be vintage cake plates for each of us.

At some point, I realized, Andrea had been a wholly different woman.

"Dig in," she said after I'd placed the tray on the coffee table, her faded eyes bright all at once. "I hardly get visitors these days after Roger buggered off with his mistress." She sat down in an armchair, while waving me to the couch opposite. "People think I'm a crazy lady. The neighbor kids run past my house like it's some witch's cabin."

Startled by her awareness of how she was viewed, I looked her full in the face. "I don't think you're crazy. I think you saw what no one else did—and because no one listened to you, two more innocent people are dead and another two badly wounded."

She slammed her fist against the arm of her seat. "I *knew* it. He was behind the fire, wasn't he?"

"I'm trying to prove that." Though I hadn't eaten anything since a quick protein bar this morning, I didn't reach for the scones, instead holding her gaze as I said, "I want to tell you who I am, want to be honest from the start. I'm Diya's husband."

Her pupils expanded, but I spoke before she could. "The police are trying to blame me for the fire even though I wasn't anywhere near the house at the time. They don't want to blame rich and successful Bobby Prasad, and I'm new to the family, from outside the country. But I know he beat his wife, and when I learned about Rhiannon, I had to talk to you—you're the only person who might understand."

Andrea's breathing was jagged now. "Of course it was him." A whisper, as if in revelation. "His parents must've seen what he was at last, and he lost it on them."

The funny thing was that she might even be right—the inciting incident *could* have been the fact that Rajesh and Sarita had somehow gotten wind of Bobby's financial troubles. Not a planned crime, but one born in the moment. That would explain the chaos of it, and how Diya and Shumi had managed to make it out alive.

"I need to know if you'd be willing to speak to the detective in charge," I said to Andrea after a sip of the weak but hot coffee. "She doesn't believe me, but you've been saying Bobby was dangerous since day one."

"Yes, yes. I want to show you something." When she bustled off as fast as she could on her hobbled leg, I ate a still-warm scone I'd made up to my liking.

It actually tasted good instead of turning to dust in my mouth—because unhinged or not, Andrea would make a great witness against Bobby. People would understand that it was a mother's grief that had driven her to this sad facsimile of a life. Her husband's desertion would only intensify the sympathy.

I was eating a second scone by the time she returned with a white cardboard box. Rectangular, it was bigger than a shoebox but still clearly only big enough for documents alongside small physical items.

Sitting down across from me, she put the box on the clear part of the coffee table. "I've been keeping records. Just in case the day came when people finally began to pay attention. And now here you are."

I put the half-eaten scone aside as Andrea began to take out newspaper clippings. Some were so yellow and faded that I was scared they'd fall apart, others new enough to leave newsprint on my fingertips. All had to do either with Rhiannon's death, with Bobby, or—most recently—with the Lake Tarawera fire. She'd even saved the newspaper notice of Bobby and Shumi's wedding, and the publicly available financial reports from his company.

It was the kind of box kept by a stalker.

Nothing in it could help me, but I listened intently as she went through it piece by piece, just in case. It was dark outside and my head was pounding when she said, "Do you see? It had to be him. It's all right here."

"Yes," I said, before glancing at my watch. "I'm so sorry, but I have to make the drive back to Rotorua—I don't like to leave Diya alone too long."

"Oh yes, that lovely girl. I have her letters, too, but not in this box. Hold on."

Interested now, I did wait, and she soon returned with a group of letters stored neatly inside a clear plastic file folder. "Little Diya and my Rhi were pen pals." She smiled. "I loved that they were doing something so old-fashioned, used to get Rhi pretty stationery for it." A pause. "I was so proud of my girl for being so kind to a younger child who idolized her."

Taking out a letter, I smiled at the rounded childish writing on the first envelope, and at the stickers placed on every part of it aside from the spots for the address and stamp. The letter inside was a single sheet full of girlish excitement about a movie that Diya was going to see with her brother and Shumi, and about how she missed

Rhiannon *sooooo* much, and wished they could hang out together all the time.

We'd be best friends every day instead of just in the summer!

My heart ached.

Andrea took my hand, squeezed, and it wasn't until then that I realized I was crying. "She'll be okay," she said, her voice trembling with years-old grief. "If there's any justice in this world, that sweet child will be okay."

———

I was exhausted when I arrived back in Rotorua, but I stopped by the ICU regardless. Security knew me by name at this point, even asked about Diya. When I made it to her, I wanted to believe that she looked better, had more color in her skin, but knew I was likely just seeing what I wanted to see.

Afterward, I went to check in on Shumi—the Kumars had let the staff know I had their continued permission to visit, and to be updated on my sister-in-law's medical status.

The nurse with her—a warm woman who had been kind to me from day one—looked up from charting Shumi's vital signs when I entered. "Hi, Tavish."

"Hi, Maria. Any updates?"

A shake of her head. "Her poor brother asked the same—he only left two hours ago after I told him he had to get some sleep. And Mrs. Kumar can hardly bear to see her daughter like this—she was in and out for two short visits today, and looks like she isn't eating. Such a sad situation."

Nodding, I touched Shumi's hand for a moment. "Hey, Shumi, it's your favorite brother-in-law."

The nurse continued to write on the chart. "Were you two close?"

"Never got the chance. I only came into the country a short time ago." I took a deep breath, the medicinal air familiar by now. "Do you think they'll remember everything when they wake up? From the day of the fire?"

She was compassionate enough not to tell me that they might never wake up. "I'm not sure. Diya did have that head trauma, and Shumi almost drowned, according to the paramedics . . . We'll just have to wait and see."

A silvery shimmer of wind chimes, a child's laughter.

I jolted to look in every direction around us. "Did you hear that?"

"No, what?"

The night was as quiet as Ani's breath.

"Nothing." Heart pounding, I dug up a faded smile. "I think I need some sleep, too."

---

I expected to spend the night haunted by ghostly wind chimes, but instead, it was another, far more familiar ghost that came to visit me.

"Joss," I breathed out.

Breathtaking, selfish, dangerous Jocelyn Wai smiled at me, ready for her pound of flesh. "You didn't think you got away with it, did you, my young lover? I swore I'd haunt you forever for what you did to me. It hurts when you fall that far, that fast. I felt my bones break when I hit the pavement."

# CHAPTER 52

## JOCELYN

*T*avish, top me up." *Jocelyn held out her tumbler.*

"*This is your third whiskey of the night,*" *her handsome, dark-haired lover said as he splashed the amber liquid into the fine crystal.*

"*What? Only three?*" *She leaned her head against the tall back of her antique armchair and laughed at his stern look as he capped the bottle and put it on the mantel.* "*I'd hardly know you were Audrey's son, with how uptight you can be.*"

"*Audrey hardly knows I'm her son,*" *was the droll response, Tavish leaning one arm against the mantel.*

*The man wore a suit well—this one was a dark gray she'd had custom fitted to his slim but muscular frame.* "*You know what she said to me?*" *Jocelyn said after a sip of the whiskey.*

"*Who? My mother?*" *A cocked eyebrow.* "*Let me guess, she tried to talk you into casting Raja in your next project. Just FYI—he's into Botox now, could stand in at the wax museum as one of the exhibits.*"

*Jocelyn laughed again, this time from deep in her belly. God, but he was clever, his words sharp enough to draw blood when he wasn't watching them—and he'd learned not to watch them with her. Charm grew boring very quickly, but that kind of vicious sharpness? Oh, it was delicious.*

"No, that was the last time," she drawled afterward. "I had to remind her that I only helm my own productions once a year—the rest of the time, I'm a gun for hire, just like her."

"Oh, I bet she loved hearing that."

Jocelyn shrugged; she didn't much care for Audrey the fucking Saint of Hollywood. "She said I should be ashamed, that I was old enough to be your mother. I pointed out that she'd been bouncing on younger cock only a month ago."

Tavish gave no indication of a reaction to the crass reference to his mother. "It's only because you're leading the Oscar stakes," he said. "She doesn't usually keep track of my life."

Jocelyn was never gladder that she hadn't had kids than when she ran into the unhappy and self-destructive children of her peers. She generally didn't sleep with them, either. Tavish, however . . . he might be messed up, but he wasn't self-destructive in the true sense. He was out for number one.

Jocelyn had always followed the same philosophy. "Did you win in Vegas?" She'd been annoyed to miss the jaunt.

"A little."

"Truly, Tavish, why am I wasting so much of my skill on you if you'll just piss it away?" She put down the whiskey. "Bring out the cards. I'll show you how to beat the house until you fucking own the house."

A tightness to his lips, the first indication of anger she'd ever seen in him.

Quite frankly, it thrilled her the same way the poker tables thrilled her. The unpredictable danger of it, the awareness of dancing on the razor's edge. "Oh, Mr. Tavish Advani doesn't like to be told what to do." She smiled with all her teeth. "Well, tough luck—I'm the boss bitch in this relationship. Now, come sit at my feet like the little puppy dog you are."

That was the first night she ended up with his hands around her throat.

The high was better than poker or cocaine.

# CHAPTER 53

I woke myself out of a nightmare, my throat so raw that I knew I'd been screaming. It would've been Joss's name. It always was.

The clock blinked 3:07.

*I saw the concrete coming at me, felt it fracture me to pieces. Just like that fire fractured your in-laws. Funny how that happens around you, isn't it?*

My entire body revolting at the poisonous echo of her voice in my head, I ran to the bathroom and threw up what little I had in my stomach.

Afterward, I sat in bed, just staring at the door as I waited for the night to end. The nights when Joss came for revenge . . . they were the worst ones. And she didn't let go once she had her hooks in me—just like in life.

To escape, I'd had to tear those hooks from my flesh.

I didn't even know when my tired body kicked me back into the dark . . . but it wasn't Joss waiting for me on the other side.

I stood in the grove where Ani had died, even though I'd never set foot in it.

A little girl stood looking up at me, blood dripping down her face and a doll clutched to her chest, her eyes huge pools of black. "Bhaiya, you killed me," she said in a small, high voice . . . and that was when I realized I was Bobby. Young, with scraped knees and scratched-up arms from all our play.

"I'm sorry," I said, my pulse a lump of muscle in my mouth. "I'm so sorry."

Her face smudged, morphed, and suddenly, I was sitting across a table from Jocelyn, the cards scattered in front of us. "I wasn't that bad, was I, Tavish?" she was asking. "Not bad enough to murder."

"I didn't hurt you." Sweat broke out all over my skin.

A very feline look. "You know that's a lie, love—you've always been so good at those. Audrey's true son, a man who acts through life itself." She picked up a tumbler of whiskey. "I've begun to think that you believe your own lies—that's why you're so good at it. You convince yourself of a whole other version of events."

I plunged to the ground, the hard concrete rushing up at me so fast that I knew I'd die, my face shattered to pieces and my bones shrapnel. "JOSS!"

I stared at the door to the motel.

It took my brain several long seconds to figure out that I was still sitting upright in bed, not falling from the balcony of Jocelyn's luxurious suite. Where Susanne had been about sophisticated glamour, Jocelyn had been a proud maximalist.

Velvet, tassels, everything gilded, her home should have looked tacky but it had instead looked like the den of some old-world vampire who'd collected only the best things through time. I'd been part of that collection, a "pretty boy" she'd met at a high-stakes poker table in Las Vegas.

"Don't tell me I'm too old for you," she'd purred in my ear in the elevator up to her penthouse suite. "I saw the way you looked at me from the other side of the table."

I'd lost the game to her, and that night, I'd lost a piece of my innocence. Because Joss hadn't been Susanne, who had made me. Joss had been the opposite, her intent to break me in ways that I didn't understand until it was almost too late.

Her death had freed me.

Swinging my legs off the bed, I took long, deep breaths and reminded myself of that. Jocelyn wasn't around anymore to tempt me with "just a little taste" of things bad and dark and destructive. I'd never understood why she did it, why she went all out to destroy those around her.

Joss smiled at me from across the room . . . and I realized I was still dreaming. Walking over to me dressed in the long black gown in which I'd last seen her, her hair slicked back in a perfect updo, she leaned down in a wave of musky perfume to tap me on the jaw.

"Make me a villain if you want, Tavish"—a sultry whisper—"but you know the truth: Of the two of us, I'm the only one who's never killed anyone."

———————

My face as haggard as if I'd been on a bender, I walked into the ICU the next morning to find an alarm going off and medical staff rushing about. My heart shoved into my throat, but all the patients I could see, including Diya, seemed stable.

It was only a half hour later, when a harried-looking nurse came to log Diya's vitals, that I said, "Jack, what happened? Before?"

The sandy-blond man's eyes widened. "You don't know? It was your sister-in-law."

"What?" I jerked to my feet. "No. I've been with Diya all this time. Figured I'd stay out of the way."

"She went into cardiac arrest," the nurse said. "No one has any idea why—her heart wasn't touched during the stabbing. But she is badly injured, so it's not out of the realm of possibility that her heart just gave out under the pressure, though the doctors are thinking she's had a reaction to a change in medication."

My mouth went dry. "Could someone have messed with her meds, given her something they knew would hurt her?"

Jack's expression closed up, an acute alertness in his gaze. "Why would you ask that?"

"The cops still aren't sure there are three bodies in the house, not just two," I whispered, quick and low. "And Shumi's husband beat her."

"Christ." Open shock. "Do the police know?"

"I tried to tell them, but—" Shrugging, I stroked my hand over Diya's hair, my fingers trembling. "Diya and Shumi are the only witnesses to what happened in that house. I'm terrified Bobby is alive and about to come after them."

The nurse's breathing was faster now. "Look, don't worry. It was probably a genuine medical reaction, nothing more." He took a deep breath, was calm again by the time he began to take Diya's pulse for the chart. "I feel even worse for her now, though. I didn't realize she was an abuse victim."

"All hidden. Shame's a big thing in Indian families." Enough to silence a woman who'd once held a high-powered job and had endless interests. "With the Prasads being so notable, and with how much she loved them, I don't think she would've wanted to rock the boat."

"I can imagine. What a mess." He touched my shoulder. "I'll give the other staff the heads-up to keep an eye out for Bobby Prasad. Just in case."

After Jack left, I went to look in on Shumi . . . to find her alone but for Ajay; as with Diya, the nurses were keeping an eye on her from their station. He was dressed in jeans and the same checked shirt he'd been wearing the day he arrived in New Zealand; his expression was stark, his voice shaking as he described the events of that morning. "I was the only one here. Mum and Dad were having breakfast near the motel. I didn't know what to do, Tavish."

I hugged him.

Arms clenching tight around me, he clung to me and sobbed, a young man who was doing all he could to be there for his sister. "It's okay," I said, over and over, until at last he was able to breathe again, speak again.

Drawing away, he took off his glasses to wipe the backs of his hands over his eyes. "My parents will be here soon," he said, almost as if he was apologizing for their absence. "They love Shumi so much."

I just nodded, the Kumar family's relationship dynamics not my business except for the fact that they went a long way toward explaining why Shumi had attached herself to Bobby from such a young age—and why she'd never turned on him even when he hurt her. To her mind, his controlling nature might well have equaled love.

Because even when they weren't dating, they'd spent time together.

*Shumi fell down a gravel embankment. Scraped up her legs, bruises everywhere. She said she wasn't paying attention and slipped, but I know she was out walking with him.*

It was attention, after all—of which, it was becoming clear, Shumi had received precious little from her mother and father. One preoccupied with her golden boy, the other a workaholic. "I'll stay with you until then," I said. "You want me to get you coffee?"

"Yeah, thanks." A shaky smile. "I'm so glad you're here, Tavish."

It was just over twenty minutes later that I returned to Diya, thinking of how desperate Mrs. Kumar had looked as she checked that Ajay was okay after the fright he'd had. All the while, her brutalized daughter lay unmoving in the ICU bed behind her.

"I wonder if either she or her husband ever think about how they set Shumi up for abuse," I said to Diya. "I know she's your best friend, but she's broken inside, sweetheart. I don't know if she'll tell the truth about what happened the morning of the fire." Because to do so would be to betray the one person she believed loved her. "You have to wake up, D. For me."

A twitch under my hand.

"Diya?" I jolted up, staring at her.

Her eyelids fluttered.

"Baby, come on, baby, wake up."

A sigh, another flutter, then a little sound.

# CHAPTER 54

Private notes: Detective Callum Baxter (LAPD)
Date: Aug 17
Time: 16:12

Still haven't talked to the friend who stayed with James Whitby prior to Virna's accident. Whitby was happy to provide her name and contact info, but turns out the woman is a professor who studies remote tribes or something and has been incommunicado in the Amazon since the start of June.

Per Whitby, "She'll come out when she comes out. Never ended up missing yet."

Not much I can do but wait.


Time: 23:09

Decided to drive by Tavish Advani's condo, and Jesus, he has a woman living there with him. I was hoping it was just a hookup when I spotted her out on the balcony, but I managed to chat to a neighbor of his who was returning from a party, and he confirmed that the woman moved in recently—he couldn't give me an exact date.

I have to warn her.

# CHAPTER 55

I t took Diya four hours to fully wake, and even then, she was groggy and lost.

Ackerson had got wind of her stirring consciousness and was hovering near the monitoring station, but the head nurse stood her ground and said the patient needed to see a familiar face first.

Now the nurse and Dr. Chen kept Ackerson at bay as Diya focused on me at last. "Hi, baby," I said, fighting to keep my voice from shaking. "You're in the hospital. You're fine."

When she tried to speak, nothing came out.

"I have water." Picking up a water bottle into which the nurse had placed an extra-long bendable straw, I put the straw to her lips.

Diya managed to take a sip or two before whimpering, "Tavi, it hurts."

My heart broke. "I know, baby, I know." Dr. Chen had warned me that she might wake in pain since he had adjusted her pain medication to assist her rise to consciousness. "If you press this button"—I touched the pressure switch taped to her finger—"you'll get a hit."

I'd been told it was controlled, so there was no risk of an overdose. Her finger moved.

It took several minutes, but the fuzziness finally faded from her eyes, the lines from around her mouth. "Why?" she rasped. "Hospital?"

My throat dried up. "Baby, what do you remember?"

I could all but feel Ackerson straining at the seams, wanting to take over, but I'd also heard what the doctor had said: If she made *any* attempt to question the patient, Chen would ban her from the entire ICU.

"I . . ." Diya's eyes welled up, her breathing shallow gasps. "Fire. Fire everywhere. I can't . . ."

"Her vitals are starting to deteriorate," the doctor warned in a quiet tone.

"Shh," I murmured to my wife. "You're fine. The fire didn't burn you." I stroked her hair, careful to avoid the side where she'd suffered a head injury. "It's all okay."

A shaky smile. "Really?"

The vulnerability in her voice twisted me up. "Just rest now. We'll talk about everything else later."

She hesitated. "Tavi? Was I alone in the fire?"

I chose the answer that would cause her the least pain. "Shumi was with you—but she's in another room in the hospital, just down from you. She's not burned, either."

Diya's brow furrowed. "I can't remember . . ." Her fingers clenched on mine, her other hand starting to rise to her head only for her to put it back down when the line on the back of it tugged against her skin. "Why can't I remember?" The pulse in her neck jumped, her breathing ragged. "Dark, it's so dark. Smoke. Fire. I can't breathe. Tavi. I can't—"

The doctor gave me a sharp look.

"Shh." I leaned down to kiss her nose in that way that always made her smile. "Everything's fine. You'll remember after all the medicine's out of your system. Sleep now. The more you rest, the better you'll feel."

Turning toward me, she said, "I'll remember?"

"You'll remember," I promised, but later, after she was asleep, I stood with the doctor in the hallway outside the ICU, Ackerson beside me, and learned the truth.

"It's possible she'll never recall what happened that day," Chen said, his large hands in the pockets of his white coat. "Could be because of psychological trauma, or it could be physical—she did sustain an injury to the side of her head."

"Are you saying her memory's gone?" Ackerson demanded.

"Nothing is guaranteed. She *has* just regained consciousness." He looked at me. "Do you have any further questions, Mr. Advani?"

"I guess . . . just . . . what do I do? About telling her about her family?"

"Play it by ear. Right now, she's in an extremely vulnerable state, but if she becomes distraught when she realizes they're not visiting her, then tell her—we're keeping her in the ICU for the time being, so you'll have staff nearby to help deal with the aftermath."

Once he'd left, I slumped into one of the armchairs in the otherwise empty waiting area.

Ackerson came down next to me.

I was expecting her to grill me, but she said, "Why did you go speak to Andrea Smithy-Carr?" in a quiet voice.

So, she *had* put a tail on me—or she'd bugged my car. I didn't really care. "Because I think Bobby was behind the fire, behind everything."

Then, despite Ngata's command that I not have any conversations with the detective without him, I told her all of it. From the death of baby Ani, to Shumi's teenage fall and adult bruises, to Rhiannon's mysterious death, to the allegations of bullying. Whether she believed me or not, I'd done everything I could—and now that Diya was awake and alive, *she* had to be my focus.

"They blamed a five-year-old for another child's violent death?" A stunned shock that felt real.

"Easier to sweep it under the rug than if it was a boy of eleven." I looked at her. "Especially in that time and place."

Lips tight, she stared at the wall across from us. "We've conclusively identified Sarita and Rajesh Prasad's remains."

I'd known inside that Diya's parents were dead, but it still felt like a punch to the gut. "Bobby?"

Instead of answering, she said, "His business was on the brink of bankruptcy. We just gained access to his business accounts today."

I thought of the sea of red on those invoices, remembered again how proudly Rajesh had spoken about Bobby's business at the party. "The family didn't know that."

"Detective Baxter is convinced you killed Jocelyn Wai in a rage."

"I wasn't there," I said tiredly, concentrating on being here, in this moment, rather than in the dark hours before Joss's fall. "He has all the security camera footage that shows I *couldn't* have done it, but he zeroed in on me after Virna's death and can't bear to be wrong."

"What about Virna, then? Lot of money involved there."

Leaning back against the wall, I let the past tumble through my head. "I was still gambling then; pissed it all away." Ackerson had likely dug up the gambling by now, or Baxter would've clued her in, so better not to hide it. "But I always needed *more*. So if it had been about money, I'd have been better off with her alive."

I leaned forward with my forearms braced on my thighs. "I wasn't in her will—and she'd gifted me that quarter of a million, so it wasn't as if I was in debt to her. Her death held no benefit for me."

"It wasn't? About money?" Softer voice, softer words.

I considered my earlier belief that Ackerson's anger was rooted in sympathy for the women she thought I'd conned. "You know who my mother is, right? Beautiful, striking Audrey Advani. Stunning at sixty-two and still an icon."

"She knew Virna Musgrave?"

"Not as far as I know." I smiled at nothing. "I was answering your question, Detective. About why I was attracted to Virna, to Joss, to other older women." Chasing love that would never be mine. "My therapist said it was an attempt to make up for the lack of maternal love in my life."

So pat, so easy. But sometimes, it was that banal.

"Audrey is a good mom to my brother, but she has a small heart—she only had enough love in it for a single child."

Just like Mrs. Kumar.

Which was why I understood Shumi's choice to stay with a man who hurt her. I'd stayed with Joss, hadn't I? Because when she wasn't being cruel, she could be a loving, attentive woman of sharp intelligence and wit.

"I never thought I'd fill that void inside me until I met Diya," I continued. "It ended that night." Under sparkling colored lights reflected in the enigmatic darkness of her eyes. "I don't need the validation from women like Jocelyn and Virna anymore."

"It's a good story."

I shrugged. "Not really. It's a dumb one. You'll probably find one like it in every fancy neighborhood in LA. Lot of poor little rich kids left to the nannies." Mine had been named Inez, at least for the first three years of my life. I barely remembered her, because I'd apparently called her "Mom" once in Audrey's hearing, and that was it.

No more nannies, just a string of babysitters that changed at Audrey's whim.

She wouldn't love me, but she wouldn't permit *me* to love another maternal figure, either.

"I'm only interesting because I had the bad luck to be involved with Joss and Virna." My laugh held no humor. "You know what the most ridiculous thing is? Baxter thinks I tampered with Virna's car—but I don't even know how to change a fucking tire, much less where the brake lines are or whatever it was that was done to Virna's car."

I liked to drive fast cars and learn about their specs—that was the extent of my mechanical knowledge.

"I know you think I have it in for you," Ackerson said, "but I'm a good cop. I looked into Bobby, and into any disgruntled employees of his, along with any patients who might have held a grudge against the doctors."

I sat back up so I could look at her. "And?"

"There's no sign—not a single one—of it being an outsider. The Prasads had external security cameras, and that footage was stored remotely. We got access to it this morning."

I hadn't known that—the cameras must've been all but invisible. Diya had probably taken them so much for granted that she hadn't even thought to mention it. "Then you know I wasn't there when it happened." It would be the second time in my life that security cameras had saved me from a cell.

"You could've still started a slow blaze and left." She held up a hand before I could explode. "But that's looking less and less likely."

Taking out her phone when it buzzed, she glanced at it before putting it away. "I'm not out to ruin an innocent man's reputation, Tavish, but look at it from my point of view—you've now been involved with at least two women who died under suspicious circumstances, and your current wife is in the ICU."

I turned the full force of my attention on her, smiled in the way that made her the center of my world . . . and saw her pupils dilate.

"See?" I whispered. "I don't need to kill women for money. If one kicks me loose, there are a million more out there I can seduce with little effort. I'm really good at it—guess Mom gave me something after all."

*You're the best chameleon I've ever met . . . Do you even know who you are when you aren't becoming your latest target's fantasy?*

# CHAPTER 56

Private notes: Detective Callum Baxter (LAPD)
Date: Oct 29
Time: 18:07

I tried to warn that young woman, but Advani made damn sure she was never alone where I could get to her. I should've tried harder, even if it got me pulled up on a harassment complaint. Now she's lying in the ICU.

FUCK.

I think Ackerson in New Zealand will get the bastard this time, but I'm still going to close up the last open thread on the Musgrave case. That damn loopy professor who was staying with James Whitby before Virna's car went off the road finally came out of the Amazon. I've set up a call tomorrow morning—Perez is going to sit in, though asshole is more interested in asking her about living in the jungle than believing she can tell us anything probative.

Three likely dead, two in the ICU . . . it's my fault. I should've stopped Advani in LA.

If only I could figure out how he did it with Jocelyn Wai. How does a man who wasn't there make a woman fall off a balcony?

## CHAPTER 57

Diya sobbed in my arms. She'd woken screaming for her mother, and in the end, I'd had to tell her that Sarita was gone, as was Rajesh. I wished we could have had more privacy for that terrible moment, but she still needed the attention of the ICU—and the other patients had their own problems, weren't concerned about us.

"Bobby, too?" she'd asked, teary-eyed, after I'd told her about her parents.

"No one's heard from him since, but they haven't found conclusive proof that he was in the house." At least not that anyone had told me—or had been revealed to the media.

Her tears were unending, her pain so extreme that Chen suggested a mild sedative. As she was hysterical, I had to be the one to make the call.

"It won't knock her out," he said when I hesitated. "Just soften the edges. She'll remember your conversation."

"I just don't want her to wake up to unknown horror time after time."

"She won't. The sedative I'm suggesting will just give her a therapeutic distance from her emotions."

Unable to see Diya in such agony, I nodded.

It took five long minutes for it to start to work, but the effects were obvious—Diya's tears turned softer before stopping, but she wasn't vacant, as I'd feared. She just seemed a touch slower to react—but her mind was all there. "Is Shumi really alive?" she asked me dully.

"Give me one minute to prove it to you." I shot Ajay a text asking him to come over.

Diya's face lit up the instant he appeared in the ICU. "Ajay!"

"Hi, Dee." His smile was so huge it creased his face. "It's so good to see you."

"Shumi?"

"She's starting to exhibit signs of coming to consciousness, too." A glance at me, the overhead light sparking off his spectacles. "I didn't want to interrupt you, but she began to make small sounds a few minutes ago."

"That's great news." I wasn't stupid enough to believe that I'd convinced Ackerson of my innocence—but Shumi could, *if* she remembered what had taken place at the Lake Tarawera house *and* was willing to talk. "You'll tell us when she comes out of it fully?"

"Absolutely." He gave Diya a hug made awkward and all the more endearing by the fact that he was attempting to avoid pressing on any of her bandaged wounds. "I'm so happy you're okay."

After the younger man left, Diya chewed on her lower lip. "I want to remember what happened, but there's a fuzziness over everything."

"Don't push it." Walking over to her bed, I sat on one side, my hand holding hers. "I'll ask the doctor to go over your injuries when you're ready, but you either were hit on the head or fell against something during the fire."

Her free hand—trailing an IV line—lifted to the side of her skull, a featherlight touch against the bandage there. But when she spoke, it had nothing to do with her own head injury. "I was thinking about Ani," she whispered. "I remember that. I was thinking about Ani."

Her pulse jerked, her breath faster.

"Shh." Not wanting her to spiral back into the dark, I moved so that I was seated beside her, my arm around her—like Ajay, I was careful of her injuries, but being able to do this, hold her so close, God, fuck, it meant so much. "I'm here, baby. You don't have to be afraid."

"I was hurt," she murmured, leaning into me, "like Ani was hurt. That's all I can remember thinking."

I didn't push her for more. Not when she was so wounded and barely holding it together. I just held her until she asked to lie back down, then sat with her as she fell into a disturbed sleep.

Every so often, she'd whimper, and it was always the same name. *Ani.*

A chill of certainty began to spread through my veins. I'd been wrong about the inciting incident for Bobby's rage. It hadn't had anything to do with his upcoming bankruptcy. No, I had the strong feeling that for whatever reason, Diya had confronted him with Ani's murder, breaking the silence held by the entire family for almost twenty years.

"Ani," Diya whimpered again. "No! No! *No!*"

Her eyes snapped open, both hands flying to the sides of her head. "Stop, stop!"

"Baby, wake up." I cupped her face as one of the monitors began to beep. "You're in the hospital. *Diya.*"

Dark, dark eyes stared into mine, her pupils so huge they nearly eclipsed her irises. "The wind chime, Tavi, the wind chime won't stop." She sobbed, her hands clutching at my wrists. "Please, please, make it stop! Ani, I'm so sorry! *Ani!*"

# CHAPTER 58

## JOCELYN

Another loss at the tables?" Jocelyn raised an eyebrow as she put down her empty whiskey tumbler. "Tut-tut, my dear, this losing streak is starting to make you unattractive." Jocelyn didn't know why she was being so spiteful to Tavish except that it was a way to crack that armor of easy charm he wore like a shield.

The same things that had drawn her to him—his intelligence and composure—now irritated her, making her feel like she was on the outside looking in.

As she watched, he smiled at her. "You're in a vicious mood, aren't you, Joss?" Walking over, he cupped her cheek, kissed her softly on the lips. "I wouldn't be a loser if you hadn't dragged me deeper and deeper into the world of high-stakes gambling."

"So it's my fault you have no self-control and no skill?"

He stepped back, shook his head. "No. But I don't think I can play your games tonight." The curtains closing over his eyes, shutting her out. "I'll see you tomorrow when you're in a better mood."

"*Fuck off, then.*" *She wasn't about to beg any man to stay.* "*Get out!*"

*He was already at the door. Opening it, he stepped out into the hallway before glancing back.* "*You look beautiful in that gown.*"

"*Fuck you!*" *Picking up the glass she'd just put down, she threw it at him.*

*It smashed against the doorjamb.*

*He stood there, hands in his pockets, his smile sad in a way that infuriated her. She knew all about Susanne—oh, he never talked about her, but Jocelyn had connections, had heard all about their fucking love story.*

*But he wouldn't give her that, give her what he'd given Susanne Winthorpe.*

*Screaming, she walked over and slammed the door in his face, then kicked off her heels and poured herself another drink.*

*She was on her fourth one when she walked into the bedroom to find candles burning on the decorative hearth . . . and a neat row of brightly colored pills on her bedside table. Her mouth watered, her hand already reaching for them before she realized Tavish must've put them there.*

"*I shouldn't have been such a bitch,*" *she mumbled to the room as she swallowed one dry and let the drug work its way into her system with unhurried ease.*

*The hit was intense when it came, made her sway languidly as she danced to inner music while the breeze from the open balcony door swept over her. She really shouldn't have been so nasty to Tavish. He'd clearly meant for them to party tonight—even though the boy had always previously refused to sample drugs, no matter how much she tried to tempt him into a taste.*

*Undoing the button at the back of her neck, she let her long black gown fall to her feet, then made her way to the bathroom . . . to be greeted by countless other candles and a full bubble bath on which floated rose petals as red as blood.*

*She'd come in here to remove her makeup but now ran her fingers through the bubbles. She could've been in that bath with her lover right now if she hadn't been so vicious to him.*

*Going back to the room dressed in her panties, she picked up her phone and called Tavish. When he didn't answer, she sent him a message:* Sorry for being a bitch. Thank you for the romance and the chocolates.

*That was what she'd always called her little fun-time pills—but they were better than chocolate to her. And she couldn't resist when they were in front of her, which was why she only bought two at a time. But gorgeous Tavish had given her five, and Jocelyn saw no reason to resist temptation.*

*Not when she'd fucked up her night so royally.*

*At least this would make her feel good.*

*A faraway horn drifted in through the balcony doors as the second dose made its way into her system. She danced again, but she was already getting hot as she always did when she partied. That was all right. It was why she had a balcony. She'd go out there for some fresh air after she'd indulged a little more.*

*Just one more chocolate, one more hit of happiness.*

# CHAPTER 59

Shumi still wasn't fully conscious by nightfall, her body and mind trapped in a twilight space that was silent purgatory.

Her entire family was camped out in her room, but when I looked across at her mother from the doorway, I glimpsed only a kind of resigned tightness in her expression. Playing a role, being what the world expected of mothers.

"Would you like food, coffee?" I asked them. "Diya's in a deep sleep so I'm going to head out and hit up a fast-food joint." My appetite had returned with a vengeance with my wife's awakening, my entire body suddenly, wildly alive.

To my surprise, Mrs. Kumar got up. "I'll come with you," she said. "I need to get away for a while."

Neither her husband nor Ajay made any move to stop her, and we were soon driving through the night-shadowed streets of Rotorua. I didn't know what to say to her, so kept my silence . . . and as my father had taught me, the silence weighed her down until she had to break it, had to speak.

"You think I'm a bad mother, don't you?" Words formed into hard little pellets. "I see the judgment on your face."

I'd been extremely careful in all my interactions with her—and I knew how good I was at hiding what I wanted to hide. "Mrs. Kumar, I don't know you," I said with open awkwardness. "I've been focused on Diya all this time."

She was stiff in the passenger seat for a long minute before she seemed to fold in on herself. "I'm sorry." Words so tired they were near inaudible. "I just . . . I could never bond with my daughter. That makes me sound awful, but I tried. I just *couldn't.*

"It wasn't about Shumi being a girl and Ajay being a boy like some people whispered. I *wanted* a little girl, had all these baby dresses already picked out for her, was ready for us to do the mother-daughter things I saw other mothers with girls doing, but when she came . . . I felt nothing."

It took effort to see past my own experience of emotional neglect. "Postpartum depression?"

"Yes, I think so, looking back. But I'm not educated like Sarita was—I was a village girl. I didn't understand that anything was wrong, just thought I was a bad mother. It did get better after a while, but by then, she was four and she knew deep inside that I didn't love her."

Her sobs were loud in the car, and even though we'd arrived at the fast-food restaurant, I didn't go into the drive-through. Pulling into their small parking lot instead, I said, "I'm really sorry."

This woman wasn't Audrey, who'd made a conscious choice to neglect me.

"I blame myself," she said at last, after she could speak again, "about how she got so hung up on Bobby. He paid attention to her when she was little, used to help her if she fell, small things like that. It sounds like nothing, but for a child who knows her mother doesn't love her . . . it was everything."

The waterfall of her words wouldn't stop.

"She followed that whole family around like a little pet. She'd do anything for them—but at least Rajesh and Sarita and especially Diya were nice to her. I was happy she had a best friend in that house, even if Diya would never see the reality of who her brother was, what he did to Shumi when they were alone."

Digging out a tissue from her bag, she wiped at her face. "I tried to get her away from Bobby after that girl died at the beach, but it was too late. She had no respect for me and no desire to follow my wishes. Later, when I saw the bruises on her, I told her that people who love you shouldn't hurt you, and she just laughed in my face and told me I should've taught myself that lesson."

Another bout of tears . . . followed by a painful silence.

"She's alive," I said to her. "You have a chance to be there for her if you really want to be." I hadn't forgotten what the nurse had said, about how disconnected Mrs. Kumar seemed when it came to her daughter.

"Yes." She shoved the tissue back in her bag. "Let's get the food. I know everyone's hungry. And Ajay likes the sugary drinks they do, the ones with all the ice cream and chocolate. We have to make sure we order that."

# CHAPTER 60

## DIYA

*D*iya sent off the email to her favorite baked goods supplier—it was an order for a "cupcake cake" for a sixteenth-birthday bash. The birthday girl was the only grandchild in two very loving families, her sweet sixteen looking to be bigger than many a wedding.

Still, the girl didn't seem spoiled—she'd been fun to work with when it came to selecting cupcake flavors and the style of decoration. But it was a good thing Diya had taken care of all of that before she'd made the impulsive decision to stay on in Los Angeles.

Teenagers might be fine with texting and video calls, but their parents wanted actual meetings with the event planner they'd hired to make their girl's day "just perfect."

Having ticked off that task, she scanned down the list to see what else was outstanding.

Her phone buzzed.

She glanced down, unsurprised to see Bobby's smiling face populating the screen. She'd taken the photo the day of his wedding, happy that he'd now be focusing all his attention on his new bride. Shumi seemed to like the jealous intensity of his attention, and Diya was more than ready for the other woman to have all of it.

But, no, Bobby hadn't backed off an inch when it came to Diya.

She declined the call as she'd declined multiple others in the past hour.

But of course her neurotically overprotective brother couldn't let it go. He sent her a text: I'm coming to LA to bring you home.

Face hot, Diya picked up her phone, her fingers flying over the keyboard: Good luck finding me in a city of millions. And don't try to ask Risha— she thinks I already flew home. She purposefully hadn't told her friend about the change in plans, not wanting to put her in the middle of this mess. Risha was one of the few true friends she still had, and she couldn't lose her as she'd lost Kalindra and Rhiannon and Violet.

Don't be stupid, Dee, Bobby replied. You know I'm only looking out for you. Mum and Dad are worried sick—Mum found your extra meds, knows you're about to run out. And, Dee, you know what happens when you don't take your meds.

Diya wanted to scream. I hate you all. You're my jailors, not my family. I. HATE. YOU!

# CHAPTER 61

I went to Fiji," I confessed to Diya at five the next morning, the staff having allowed me to sneak in because Diya was wide-awake when I called the ICU to check on her status. I needed to buy her a phone so she could contact me when she wanted, would do so as soon as the shops opened today.

"You did?" No sedative today, her eyes going wide as she sat up in bed sipping at the hot coffee I'd grabbed for her from a drive-through. "Why?"

"You said Ani's name when I found you." I put one hand on her leg, above the blanket. "I was just looking for an answer, any answer, I guess."

Her face fell. "I'm sorry I didn't tell you about her." Looking away, she bit down on her lower lip. "I don't feel good when I think about Ani."

"You don't have to say anything." I squeezed her leg. "I didn't go to the beach, though—I thought we could go together, and you could show me around like you promised."

She turned back to face me, the hollows in her cheeks too prominent, as were the shadows under her eyes. "Ani died." A wet shine to her eyes. "We were playing and she fell and she died."

It made sense to me that her family had reshaped things that way for the five-year-old she'd been, turning a murder into an accidental tragedy. So she wouldn't ever give away what they believed she'd done, tell others of the stain of blood they'd *put on her*. "It wasn't your fault," I said, because I thought she needed to hear it. "You know that, right?"

A jagged nod. "But after Ani, they became so suffocating. Always watching, always calling if I was even a minute late home from school. I couldn't just hang out with friends, could barely even make them." Tears rolled down her face. "Bobby used to follow me on dates sometimes!"

I frowned. "He followed you?"

"He said he wanted to be close by in case anything happened and I got scared and needed an out, but it just made me feel like I couldn't *breathe*. I used to get so mad at them for it." She began to cry in earnest. "And now they're all gone, Tavi. My brother, Mum and Dad, they're *gone*."

Gathering her into my arms after managing to put her coffee on the table before she spilled it, I just held her while she sobbed for her lost family . . . sobbed so long and hard that the nurses got worried and called Chen, who'd been about to head home after a night shift.

He gave her something to calm her, and I sat with her until she closed her eyes once more in sleep, her wounded body needing rest to heal.

"Tavish." Chen appeared at the end of the bed. "Can we talk?"

"I thought you'd gone home after seeing Diya, Dr. Chen," I said when I joined him in the hallway.

His bony face tired, he said, "I wanted to talk to you about this first—I've had a look at your wife's records. She's been treated for mental health issues since she was a teenager, including severe depression."

Scowling, I set my feet apart as I folded my arms across my chest. "Sure, but you can't blame her for her current state. This is not a normal situation."

"No, that's not what I meant—I want us to be proactive here, treat her mind as we're treating her body. I'm going to arrange for a mental health practitioner to come speak to her."

Unable to forget how she'd cried and cried, powerless to stop, I knew the doctor was right—she needed to talk to a professional. "Look, I have a feeling her parents pressured her into getting medicated, so whoever you find, make sure it's not someone who's going to push drugs on her. She won't be receptive. Not now."

"I'll talk to them myself to drive home the fact that it's to be a therapeutic conversation only."

"Thanks." Unfolding my arms, I pushed my hand through my hair. "My sister-in-law, Shumi? She's still not conscious?"

He shook his head. "It's worrying since she appeared to be waking, but with the near drowning . . . it's difficult to judge her true status. We have to wait and see."

---

The day passed as slow as molasses. Diya slept for large portions of it, while I kept her company and went for occasional walks around the hospital. My wife was to be moved out of the ICU the following day, her status stable enough that she no longer needed the same level of care, but Shumi would remain for the time being.

Ackerson came in at around two to interview Diya and had to deal with me there because Diya wouldn't let go of my hand. As it was, she didn't remember anything more than that there'd been a fire, and that she'd been afraid.

The detective attempted to nudge her memory using various methods, to no avail. She finally gave up when Diya said she was tired and needed to sleep.

I wasn't surprised when Ackerson asked me to step into the outside hallway with her.

"Ngata," I said the second we were alone. "Seriously, if you want to talk to me, wait till I can get my lawyer here." I just wanted to be with my wife, not answering questions I'd already answered ten times over.

"It's not about you." Ackerson's mouth was tight. "Were you aware that your father-in-law wouldn't permit your wife to move out, even after she reached adulthood? That it wasn't strictly her choice to remain at the Lake Tarawera property?"

Another truth Diya hadn't yet shared with me, our relationship too new, the two of us yet learning each other. "No, but honestly, that's not unheard-of with some Indian fathers," I said with a shrug. "And how could he stop her anyway? Yeah, he could turn on the parental guilt, but she runs her own business, has her own income."

She tapped her pen against the notebook she'd pulled out when talking to Diya. "That business is barely breaking even. Most weeks, she can't cover even her most basic expenses. Her parents funded her entire life—and used that money like a leash. They threatened to cut her off if she tried to move out."

A storm of nothingness in my head, a buzz. "Don't you dare try to pin this on her. Even if they were controlling her before, she has me now. We were *actively* looking for a rental place of our own, and regardless of what you might think of my prospects, Detective, I can support both of us."

Hands on her hips, she tapped her foot. "So you don't know anything about the threat of financial disownment?"

"No—and even if they said that during a fight, they'd never have gone through with it. She was too precious to them." Never would Rajesh and Sarita have allowed their daughter to stumble through life without a safety net. "Who told you that nonsense?"

"A reliable source."

"Fuck that. My wife's best friend is currently in the next unit over, and her family is dead. And Diya's not the kind to blab family business to just anyone. Whoever told you is shit-stirring."

I could see her struggling to decide something. Finally, she said, "Do you know Kalindra Renata?"

"Diya's old school friend?" I snorted. "She wasn't even at our engagement party. If she's passing on that so-called threat, it must've been from back when Diya was a teenager."

A deep furrow between her eyebrows. "Ms. Renata says she and Diya talk every week on the phone for at least an hour, and have since Diya returned from the States and reinitiated contact. She wasn't at the party because Sarita and Rajesh Prasad didn't like her. She got caught smoking in high school, was suspended."

"I'm calling bullshit on long heart-to-heart calls," I said, because protecting Diya was a primal compulsion—but the truth was that I had no way to know for sure. We hadn't been attached at the hip. She'd gone out for hours at a time to talk to suppliers, check venues, all the things an event planner needed to do.

"Even if there was some threat," I added, my face hot, "I hope you're not implying Diya murdered her family because of it. She was *stabbed*, and those weren't self-inflicted wounds."

"I'm just trying to get my finger on the intricacies of the family." Ackerson showed no signs of backing down. "It's difficult. The parents don't seem to have been close to anyone—friendly, yes, well-liked and respected professionals, but so far, I haven't managed to unearth a single deep friendship.

"My Indo-Fijian colleagues tell me that's unusual in their community, where even unrelated people can become family over time—especially so when we're talking new immigrants. The Prasads seem to have made no attempt to forge connections within that tight-knit group."

I knew she was right. It was why Los Angeles had a Koreatown and Little Armenia among other neighborhoods. Because people sought the comfort of the familiar, others who could make a new land feel like home. It had been years before I'd realized that the man my paternal grandfather called his brother was no blood relation whatsoever; the two had just met on their first day in America and become fast friends.

"Maybe they were just snobs," I suggested, though I had a bad feeling in the pit of my stomach that this was about hiding a single terrible family secret.

*Ani.*

A secret so damaging that the family had become a closed bunker.

"They invited plenty of doctors and other professionals to the engagement party."

"But they didn't talk to any of those professionals," Ackerson insisted. "Even Dr. Rajesh Prasad's closest colleague—one of the two other partners at the firm—could tell me nothing about his so-called friend that wasn't public knowledge. Said he always felt as if he was being held at arm's length. The Kumars, too, are in the dark about the family's internal dynamics."

"You have to know I'm not the person to ask. I barely knew them." Sarita talking about her love of beautiful high-performance cars, Rajesh telling me about his lawn, all I had were fleeting snapshots . . . and the horror of what I'd learned in a tropical nation of aquamarine seas and palm trees. "Could be their real friends are back in Fiji, and they stay in touch via email and during the times they visit."

No one would've done what Kamal had done and covered up the murder of a child just because the Prasads were a respected family. There'd been more there, a bond of friendship of some kind.

"If you think of anything else, call me," Ackerson said.

"Sure." Despite my agreement, I had no intention of dropping my defenses and becoming friendly with the detective; in all likelihood, she was probably playing me. Baxter had tried that, too, right back at the start.

*Look, just talk to me, Tavish. I'm not here to stitch you up—I just want to know what happened to Virna.*

However, once I was back beside my wife, the rhythm of her breathing deep and even in sleep, I thought about what she'd told me of her family's controlling tactics—and what I'd learned on my own.

Kalindra cut off because she was a bad influence. Risha acceptable only because she'd lived under their control while in this country and was otherwise on the other side of the world. Shumi permitted because she had, as her own mother had so callously put it, followed the entire family around "like a little pet."

Not a woman who would've gone against Rajesh and Sarita.

The other friends, the ones I'd met, had all been shallow acquaintances.

*I* wasn't a shallow acquaintance, wasn't a person they could control. And Diya . . . Diya trusted me, had slowly been giving me more and more pieces of herself.

I'd focused on Bobby to the exclusion of everyone else, but the elder Prasads were the ones whose entire existence was built around the fact that they were pillars of the community, admired and loved by their patients and respected by the public. Mum and Dad to two successful children.

A good family. The perfect family.

Frowning, I thought of what Ackerson had said about Diya's event-organizing business being a losing proposition. My wife, in contrast, had very recently mentioned something in relation to *growing* her business. If I was remembering right, it had been about a week before the fire.

"I have some good news," she'd said with a huge smile after she'd checked her emails.

"Oh? Tell me."

"So, I was meant to have a business partner as of May this year. Idea was to merge my operation with her bigger one, with me the junior partner—it would've pushed me into a whole other sphere as far as the size of the projects was concerned. Alone, I'm stuck in an overfilled niche and there's no growth potential.

"But she got assaulted back in April, hurt bad, ended up basically closing her business; she used to have a little office in the town center and everything. I felt so awful for her—she was so good, Tavi. I was looking forward to learning from her, delighted that she wanted to take me on board."

"How's she doing now?" I knew my wife's heart, had figured she'd be watching over her friend.

"I didn't know until now—she just fell off the radar. I managed to get in touch with her family, and they said she needed space and time and I didn't want to overstep. But I did send her little care packages and cards so she knew I was thinking about her."

"I'm guessing she got back in touch?"

"Yes." A beaming smile. "She's nowhere near ready to go back to work, but she said she's been looking at our past plans again, and she's still excited about the idea. So fingers crossed." She'd held up the crossed digits. "Honestly, I'm just happy to hear from her. I've missed her."

Taking out my phone, I began to search for a serious mugging in Rotorua in April, throwing in the words "event planner" as part of the search.

*There.*

Emblazoned across the local newspaper were the words

### No Suspects in Brutal Kuirau Park Assault

The resulting article named the victim as Violet Long, a thirty-year-old event planner who was starting to become well-known for her wedding work and who'd even been in the running for the well-publicized upcoming wedding of a national television celebrity. A photo provided by her family showed her to be a Eurasian woman with blunt-cut bags and a sleek bob, her face the kind of plump that just made her prettier.

> . . . Ms. Long was attacked after agreeing to meet a new client near the thermal footbaths in Kuirau Park at four p.m. on the seventeenth. Ms. Long tried to reschedule the meeting to another location given the heavy rain that week, but the client was insistent on the park, as they intended to get their wedding photos taken there and had no other free slots in their schedule.
>
> "They'd never spoken on the phone," Ms. Long's mother, Jenn Long, stated. "It was an online query, then they communicated by text. It sounds silly now, but that's how all the young people do things these days—Violet told me almost none of her clients like to talk on the phone until well into the process. And, well, it was daylight, wasn't it? Who even worries about getting assaulted in broad daylight in a busy public park?"
>
> Ms. Long was hit over the back of the head with a blunt object when she reached the footbaths—which were other-

wise empty, due to the weather. Police say there are indications that someone tried to push her head into the thermal water, possibly in an attempt to drown her, but were interrupted by a group of teens who'd decided to visit the baths despite the rain.

The teens didn't see anyone but are sure they heard the sound of running feet.

Police are asking anyone with information on the case to contact them at once. "This attack displays a dangerous level of premeditation," Detective Tawhai stated. "The perpetrator lured Ms. Long to the site with the promise of a lucrative work contract, then lay in wait. They clearly used the weather to their advantage."

Police have been unable to trace the perpetrator's phone number and say it was likely an unregistered prepaid mobile. Ms. Long remains in hospital.

I read several more articles on the assault, but the information was all much the same: A rainy day. Everyone in wet-weather jackets with the hood up, or with umbrellas blocking their vision. Take a chance that no one else would be around even at four in the afternoon—no harm, no foul if someone was; just call off the meeting for some made-up reason and reschedule for another attempt. Otherwise, attack Violet, then lose yourself in the park.

Just another person in a hooded jacket.

That cop who'd been interviewed was right. The entire thing showed a psychopathic level of planning *and* confidence.

Whoever this was, it hadn't been their first crime.

*Ani. Rhiannon. Violet.*

The connection between Bobby and the first two women was crystal clear, but Diya hadn't said anything about Violet ever being involved with Bobby.

*His sister was an adorable thing, though. Rhiannon loved her, used to make a special batch of cookies for her right before we went down each summer. "For my little Dee," she'd say. "My adopted baby sister."*

*I never thought it was Diya beti—or that it was about a doll. She used to play for hours with Ani, shared all her toys. Diya loved Ani.*

*I feel so free with you, as if I'm truly seeing life for the first time. No filters, no restraints. I'm myself and I remember all of me.*

A sick feeling in my gut, a dawning awareness that I'd got it all wrong, that this had nothing to do with finances and pride . . . and everything to do with making sure Diya never *ever* forged a bond outside the closed family unit. Because then she might feel safe enough to remember . . . and tell about the killing that had begun all of it, destroying the foundation of the perfect, beautiful life the Prasads had built in the aftermath.

Which meant . . . she *had* remembered at some point, had tried to talk about it. Only for her family to shut her down, tell her she was wrong, that it hadn't been like that. It had driven her mind to fight itself, and then had come the medication.

Diya had said something the morning of the fire. Something important. Squeezing my eyes shut, I struggled to think back to what felt like another lifetime. She'd been making me the omelet and . . .

*I had the oddest dream last night. About our old house in Fiji. I could see the mango tree from a window—and then I was trying to dig it up using a shovel.*

"Oh God." Had she brought up Ani's death that morning? Was that what had set everything in motion?

Wind chimes whispering down the hallway, a cold touch on the back of my neck.

I swallowed hard, my mind full of images of Rajesh's powerful body cutting through the cold waters of the lake, Sarita putting on her jogging gear for a fast circuit.

# CHAPTER 62

Private notes: Detective Callum Baxter (LAPD)
Date: Oct 30
Time: 11:07

Fuck, fuck, fuck!

# CHAPTER 63

After asking Ajay to keep an eye on Diya and message me if she woke and was looking for me—I still hadn't managed to get her that phone—I left the hospital to meet Aleki at a small coffee shop by his work.

"Hey, my man." He hugged me, a big wall of gentle, kind Samoan in a business shirt and pressed black trousers.

"Hey, Aleki. Thanks again for all you've done."

"No thanks between us." He picked up a coffee from the table. "I had our orders made to go. Gotta start walking back—still have that asshole manager who watches the clock to make sure we're not a minute over our break time." He took a sip of his own coffee. "You cool with walking and chatting?"

"Sure."

"Glad to hear your missus is awake."

It had taken me a few chats with Aleki before I'd figured out that "missus" in the local vernacular didn't necessarily mean married, just together. "You have no idea how relieved I was when she opened her eyes." I drank deep of the coffee—the ubiquitous Kiwi flat white, for which I'd acquired a taste after Diya introduced me to it.

Aleki slapped me on the shoulder. "I can imagine, man. So, you want to know about Violet Long, huh?"

I'd reached out to Aleki after all my online searches had come up blank—Violet Long's business website was down, and she no longer had any social media presence. I didn't even know if she was still in Rotorua, but I figured it was a small city, and with Aleki being around roughly the same age as her, they might've crossed paths. Or at the least, that he could point me in the direction of someone else who would know.

I had no intention of asking Diya for her friend's information and bringing up that past trauma. Not here. Not now.

"My wife was close with her before the assault. I thought I'd see if I could touch base with her, see if maybe she'd want to visit with Diya." It was a flimsy reason, but it was all I had. "She's going to be moved out onto a ward soon."

"It was brutal, what happened to Violet—it was in all the papers, how bad she was hurt." He shook his head. "I don't know her, but the papers mentioned that her dad is a plumber."

Shit, I'd seen that in one of the articles I'd found and totally glossed over it when I'd already tracked one man down by his profession.

Aleki stopped in front of a building. "This is me. But anyway, my cuz's mate Silas is a plumber, too, so I asked him if he knew about Violet Long's dad."

Digging into his pocket, he took out a piece of notebook paper on which he'd written the details of one Greg Long, Plumber & Drainlayer. "He said not to hassle Greg if he doesn't want to talk," Aleki said as he handed over the information. "Man's still broken up about what happened to her—but I figured he'd be okay with you calling."

"I promise I won't push if he wants privacy."

"I better go—but hope you get in touch with your missus's friend."

After saying good-bye to Aleki, I made the call to Greg Long. I'd have preferred to meet him in person to make my case, but he probably had no office and worked out of his van like a lot of independent tradespeople.

"Greg Long," he said when he answered the call, his manner matter-of-fact.

Aware that he'd no doubt been hounded by reporters at one point, I said, "This is Diya Prasad's fiancé, Tavish." No one in Rotorua didn't know Diya's name by now, and Violet had likely mentioned her potential business partner to her family. "I'm trying to get in touch with your daughter. Diya's regained consciousness and I know she misses Violet."

I paused, but when the other man didn't say anything, added, "No pressure at all for Violet to come see her—I just figured maybe they could chat on the phone. And honestly, I'm just trying to find something that'll make my wife happy." I might be a gold-standard liar, but the latter was a hundred percent true.

A rough exhale from Greg. "Ah damn, it's awful what happened to that whole family. It meant a lot to Violet that Diya invited her to your engagement party even though my daughter's retreated so much from the world." Pain twisted through his words. "Her mum and I really thought she was going to go—we were ready to drive her, pick her up, the whole deal, but she backed out at the last minute."

"Diya didn't mind," I said, though I hadn't known that she'd invited Violet. "She just wanted Violet to know she still considers her a friend."

"She's been a good one," Greg Long said. "I see the cards and little packages that come in—my girl always smiles when she sees that handwriting." An added roughness to his voice. "Look, let me talk to Vi. I have your number now, will pass it on to her. Whether she calls or not . . . I can't guarantee anything."

But Violet Long did call, only ten minutes later. "I messaged her," she said in a soft but melodic voice that was slightly slurred. Even as I wondered if she'd fallen into alcohol addiction after her assault, she said, "Diya. After I heard she was alive—but then they said she was in a coma? So I didn't know if I should keep trying."

"Her phone was in the house."

"Oh God, of course it was. I didn't think. Does she have a new number? I'm still in the process of working on my anxiety when it comes to going out"—a tightness there, an anger that I hoped was directed outward and not at herself—"but I'd love to talk to her."

"I'm buying her a new phone today and will send you the number." Having taken a seat on a bench beneath a leafy tree, I stared out at the late-afternoon traffic as I spoke to her. "Violet, I know you must've been asked this a thousand times over, but do you remember anything about the person who made the appointment?"

"Why?" A single sharp word heavy with new suspicion, no hint of alcohol intoxication, so maybe the slur was a speech impediment.

"I'm clutching at straws," I said, flexing my hand on my knee. "It just seems too much of a coincidence to me that both you and Diya came under such significant attack within a space of, what, six months? Could someone have a vendetta against the two of you? An angry business rival?"

A gasp. "I didn't even consider that." Hearing the tremor in her voice, I knew I'd just set her therapy back months and felt like a shit.

But Violet rallied. "Honestly, I can't think of anyone. We hadn't officially started working together. I was much more established, so Diya was going to come on as a junior partner, and we were working out what that would look like."

"So no meetings with clients, things like that?"

"No, it was mostly just the two of us getting together to hash things out. We already liked each other, but with a business, you need to have everything spelled out. We spent hours huddled over the table in my apartment, working on our long-term plan and where we saw the business going."

"Why did you want to work with her when you were so much more successful?"

"I needed a partner to expand my capacity. Diya's a bad businesswoman—and I say this with love—but as a creative, she's a dynamo. I was prepared to handle all the business aspects for a larger share in the partnership, and she was happy to give me that larger share in order to increase her overall income.

"Please don't think I was going to cheat her," she rushed to add. "Diya would have tripled her income in the first year, just with the clients I already had lined up. And we'd agreed that we'd renegotiate the split three years down the road, once we saw the impact she had on the overall business. Not just a verbal agreement—it was to be part of our contract."

Money again. Always money. Because money meant a lot of things. "Did you ever meet anyone else connected with Diya?"

"You mean her vendors? No, that would've come later, after we'd agreed. We're all a little protective of our contacts."

"No one more personal?"

"We ran into her mum once, while we were heading into a café. She seemed lovely, was excited when I mentioned how successful I thought we'd be together. It's so sad, what's happened."

*The teens didn't see anyone but are sure they heard the sound of running feet.*

An image flashed into my mind, of Sarita throwing me the keys to the Alfa Romeo while dressed in her running tights and top, an athletic woman who'd have no trouble outpacing a bunch of startled teens.

# CHAPTER 64

## DIYA

Hi Rhi!

I can't wait to see you! Only six more weeks! It's going to be so fun. I don't know if Mum will let you show me how to do makeup on myself, but I'm excited to watch you do it! It sounds so cool, the set you got for your birthday. Your mum is so nice.

I read the book you sent me. It was exciting and a little scary, but I read it every night till I finished. I like stories about secrets.

I have a secret. A really big one. I'll tell you, though, because I know you won't tell anyone else. We did the pinky promise. When we're at camp, we can go for a swim together by ourselves, and I'll tell you.

See you soon!

Love,
Your friend, Dee

## CHAPTER 65

Shumi came to full consciousness the next day.

I didn't see my sister-in-law the first day—given her groggy state, the doctors would only permit her immediate family. The second day, however, both Ackerson and I managed to get in—and with a few patients having recently been moved onto a ward after they no longer needed the unit's level of care, Shumi was the only patient there.

I waited a short distance away while Ackerson spoke to her with her father by her side.

"I'm very sorry to tell you, Mrs. Prasad," Ackerson said in a tone that was gentler than I'd ever heard from her, "but we believe we've identified your husband's remains alongside those of his parents."

The air whooshed out of me.

I'd been hoping he was still alive—because, no matter what, that gave Ackerson a perfect suspect and took the spotlight off me.

A soft feminine wail, while Shumi's father demanded, "How can you be sure? There was so much damage."

"The lab will attempt DNA tests, but the nature of the remains means that can't be guaranteed. He was identified through dental records."

Ackerson sounded truly sorry when she said, "There really is no doubt. Vihaan Prasad—Bobby—had an emergency root canal done in Japan while on a business trip five years ago. The dental experts tell me the Japanese style is visibly different to ours. His dentist also had more recent X-rays, which we were able to use for identification.

"Added to the fact that his car was on the premises, and the lack of any activity on either his business or personal accounts, as well as his phone, it's conclusive that he died in the incident. But as I said, the team will make every attempt at a DNA match for the survivors' peace of mind."

Shumi was sobbing but trying to speak in between, nothing of her words making sense.

Ackerson was more patient than I expected but didn't leave the room even when Shumi's father asked her to. "I need to get your daughter's witness statement while it's fresh in her mind," she replied.

At last, Shumi stopped sobbing. "Why didn't Diya tell you?" A piteous question. "Why do I have to say?"

"I told you, beta," her father said with an edge of impatience in his tone that made me want to shake him. "Diya is hurt. She can't remember."

"I don't want to say." Shumi's voice was almost swallowed up by her tears. "I *won't* say."

"You have to," her mother butted in. "We know what he did to you, beta." Tears in her voice. "Please, Shumi. You don't have to protect him anymore—I'm so sorry you thought you couldn't come to me, but I'm here now. I'll always be here."

"No, no, I won't." Shumi's breathing was fast and shallow. "We were so happy. We were all so happy."

"I know," Ackerson said in that same unexpectedly gentle tone. "But three people are dead, Shumi. Including Rajesh and Sarita, who I'm told treated you like a cherished daughter. And your best friend remains badly wounded."

Sobbing, Shumi said, "Can I see her? Can I see Diya?"

I was ready for everyone to say no, but Ackerson instead stepped out to talk to the staff, and they made the arrangements to wheel Diya over from the ward for a strictly short visit. The two women both burst into fresh tears at seeing each other, but there was an edge of hysterical happiness to it, the relief of two survivors coming face-to-face.

"Shumi, what happened?" Diya asked after the tears had passed. "All I can remember is the fire . . . and . . ." She pressed a hand over her abdomen. "I hurt here. So much."

Shumi just shook her head, keeping her silence.

"Please," Diya begged. "Please tell me."

Tears rolling down her face again, Shumi turtled in on herself. "I want to be alone now. I don't want to talk anymore."

———

No one stopped me when, two hours later, after Diya had fallen into sleep, I made my way to Shumi's bedside. Everyone else had already attempted to talk to her, but she'd shut down.

However, she was awake—and alone right then.

"I know you're protecting Diya," I said in a soft tone between us alone, the realization having come to me when she'd looked at Diya with agony on her face after my wife pleaded for answers.

Huge brown eyes holding my own. "She shouldn't know," Shumi whispered. "She should have her memories."

"She already knows deep inside," I said. "And, Shumi? It's eating her up to not have any answers."

Shumi bit down hard on her lower lip. "I don't want to say, Tavish. If I don't say, it's not real." Her eyes moved around the room before settling back on me. "But it is, isn't it?"

"Yes." I touched her hand. "You did everything you could to protect the family, Shumi."

"I never told. I never said what Bobby did to me." A rasping breath. "Everyone loved Amma and Pitaji so much, and most of the time, everything was perfect. He loved me, he *did*—he always wanted to know where I was, was always interested in my life, kept track of all my friends and called me throughout the day to say hi."

To hear of her twisted view of a healthy love made me hurt for the girl she'd been, unloved and emotionally abandoned.

"It would've hurt Amma and Pitaji so much if I'd told. Brought such shame to the family."

My stomach churned at the reminder of Rajesh and Sarita's perfect image, but aloud I said, "They're not around to feel that shame anymore . . . and Diya will drown in her thoughts if she doesn't get answers."

Our eyes met, a quiet understanding passing between us of Diya's fragile mental state.

Then Shumi sighed. "Okay. Okay."

I didn't celebrate yet. She could still backpedal. "Shall I call Ackerson over?" I'd seen the detective talking to Ajay and the elder Kumars in the waiting area. Probably hoping to find some way to get Shumi to open up.

"Yes. Just her and you, not my family." A hardness to her as she said the last.

Two minutes later, when she began to speak, I realized I'd been wrong about her on one critical point. There *was* something Bobby could do that would turn her against him, and he'd done it the night of the party.

"I was pregnant. I did a home test, then another, told Bobby straightaway and he hugged me and spun me around and brought me pink roses." Rough, husky words. "I was so happy—and really doing my best not to show it at the engagement party because that was Diya's moment and I wasn't going to steal it.

"I thought we'd wait till I was past the first trimester to tell the family . . . though I'd probably have slipped up with Diya." Her voice losing volume with each word. "Then Bobby hit me in the stomach that night, after we got home from the party, and I started bleeding. It had stopped by morning, but I knew my precious baby was gone." It came out flat, as if her anger was so deep that she couldn't bear to feel it.

"He still made me go to Amma and Pitaji's that morning, pretend everything was okay. It was like he didn't even care that he'd murdered our child, like it meant *nothing* to him."

"Here." I put the straw to her lips so she could drink some water, give herself a break from the emotional grindstone.

"Thank you." An automatic polite response before she drank.

After she was done, she went right back to it, as if now that she'd started, she had to finish. "I was outside looking at the lake with Diya while he spoke to Amma and Pitaji. When we walked back in, they were lying on the floor, and he had a knife in his hand." Her breathing sped up. "He shoved Diya so hard she fell against something— maybe a table?—and got dazed. That's when he stabbed me."

"Do you know why your husband turned violent?" Ackerson asked.

"I didn't know till we got home the previous night, but his finance person had called him before the party, told him that he'd run all the numbers again but there was no choice—he'd have to file for bankruptcy."

I thought I was good at wearing masks, but Bobby had given not a single hint of stress or panic that night, just a big brother there to celebrate his sister's engagement. Making plans for a fishing trip, standing beside his father while Rajesh bragged of his accomplishments, kissing Diya on the forehead with protective tenderness.

Her voice gone raw, stripped down to the core, Shumi said, "Bobby was *so* proud. He loved that he could give me the life we had, loved that even though he hadn't had the grades to do medicine, his parents boasted about him being a successful businessman." A gulping sob. "He loved how Diya looked up to him."

There was more.

Shumi had managed to stay conscious long enough to see Bobby attacking Diya, then leaving her for dead, as he'd left Shumi.

"Blood in my eyes, everything red, Diya's dress turning the same color." Horror in her face as she moved her hands as if trying to stanch her bandaged wounds. "I don't know about the fire or about going into the lake. I didn't see. I don't remember."

"That's fine, Shumi," Ackerson said. "What you've given us is plenty."

"Do you know about Rhiannon?" Shumi asked in a sudden burst. "I believed him when he said he didn't have anything to do with her death. I always believed him." Her sobs were heartrending. "He was my husband." A whisper wrapped in tears. "I believed him."

I put my arm around her, looked at Ackerson.

Who said, "I think we're done here for now." She stepped out, her phone in hand, but she was still nearby when I left Shumi ten minutes later.

Her family had rushed in after the detective left, but she'd leaned into me instead, so I'd stayed. Until, at last, she fell into an emotionally exhausted sleep. Her mother had looked at me. "She trusts you, a near stranger, more than she trusts us." It was less an accusation and more a confession.

There was nothing I could say to that, because it was true.

So I'd said nothing, just touched Ajay on the shoulder before I left.

"What will I tell Diya?" I said to Ackerson when we met by the empty waiting area outside the ICU. Knowing her brother had done this, annihilated their whole family—it would destroy her.

White lines bracketed Ackerson's mouth. "I don't envy you. Men like that, I wish they'd just take themselves out, but they always murder the innocent, too."

"I read about family annihilation," I admitted now that I was no longer a suspect. "I couldn't understand how anyone could murder their entire family, was trying to figure it out."

"Psychobabble bullshit is that they're narcissists who believe no one will be able to go on under the circumstances, so death is the kinder choice." She twisted her lips. "At least your brother-in-law had the grace to end his own pathetic life, too. A lot of that kind—and it's nearly always men—flinch when it comes to their own life. Cowards."

I would've never used that word for Bobby, but what other one was there?

Coward. Killer. Murderer.

That was now Vihaan "Bobby" Prasad's final legacy.

"And to think," Ackerson said, "I was beginning to lean away from him as the suspect. He was in negotiations with a possible business partner—we spoke to the man, and he said that while things *were* dire with the business, it wasn't beyond redemption.

"Guy was willing to stump up the necessary cash for a majority stake, and they'd worked out what had gone wrong so it wouldn't be repeated. Had a whole five-year plan mapped out to not just put Elektrik Ninja in the black, but expand it into Australia."

"He'd have lost control," I said, thinking about how he'd monitored every aspect of Shumi's life, how he'd followed Diya when she went on dates. "Someone else would've been the boss."

Ackerson shrugged. "Yeah. You're probably right. It'll all come out in the inquest down the road, I'm sure. But on my end, the case is closed—Shumi's account explains everything. Bobby Prasad must have started the fire, then taken his own life, not realizing he hadn't managed to kill Diya and Shumi."

I decided to follow Ackerson's lead. No one, least of all my wife, needed to know my suspicions about her parents. Sarita, Rajesh, Bobby, they were all in the past.

As were Susanne, Jocelyn, and Virna.

It was done. Finished.

# CHAPTER 66

Private notes: Detective Callum Baxter (LAPD)
Date: Nov 2
Time: 02:08

Things are finally starting to come together. We might not have physical evidence, but even the DA thinks this much circumstantial evidence will bury the bastard.

I'm not giving up on the physical evidence, though—eyewitness testimony might be notoriously unreliable, but the professor gave me a whole new window of time to check for movements in and around the route. Thank fuck the tech guys who got all that footage last December were as anal as usual and went back an entire day.

We're still shit out of luck when it comes to some footage we didn't know to get at the time, but it won't matter if I can pin him on at least some of the footage we do have. Because he *lied*. Not once, but in every interview. It's all on video.

# CHAPTER 67

Sarita, Rajesh, and Bobby's joint funeral three weeks later was a somber affair.

Shumi hadn't wanted Bobby anywhere near his parents, while Diya remained in a state of shock, not able to process the events of that horrific day—but in the end, there hadn't been a choice.

The remains were in such bad shape that some fragments were mere bone shards. There was no way to know which piece belonged to which family member without DNA testing each and every fragment—if the DNA was even there to find. The experienced forensic anthropologist the cops had asked to consult on the case was of the opinion that some of the shards were simply too small or too damaged to differentiate using any of the usual markers.

All three were as linked in death as they had been in life.

The Hindu priest—or pandit, as Shumi had called him—who officiated over the ceremony gave a speech about parenthood and the love parents had for a child, and it was only then that Diya stirred.

She, like Shumi, was yet under medical care at the hospital. The doctors had authorized their attendance at the funeral service only because the counselor who was working with the women said it would help with closure.

"He's right," my wife said dully, the dark shadows under her eyes all but purple. "The pandit." A painful inhale, a slow exhale. "My parents did love Bobby that much. I think they'd forgive him his day of insanity."

I thought of a child locked in a small room under the stairs, of a boy crying because his exam results weren't a hundred percent. It seemed to me that the Prasads had expected perfection from their only son—and what Bobby had done was about as far from that ideal as it was possible to get.

But if believing in their forgiveness gave my wife peace, then I wasn't going to argue. Because in the months and years that lay ahead, she'd have to come to terms with her own complex emotions toward her brother as well. "Yes," I said quietly. "From what I saw of how he was with your parents, I don't think they could do anything but forgive him."

She leaned her body into me from the wheelchair we'd parked near the end of the front row of seats, with me acting as the bookend. Shumi sat next to Diya, her brother Ajay next to her, alongside their parents.

Diya's hand was interlocked with Shumi's.

The rest of the padded chairs in the large room were filled by friends and strangers both. No more family, Diya the sole survivor of both her maternal and paternal lines. The funeral home's overflow room—the service fed into it via a television screen—was also full, and there were people standing in the parking lot listening to the service through the hastily arranged loudspeaker system.

All but a rare few were here to pay their respects to Sarita and Rajesh.

I'd spotted Richard and another one of Bobby's friends in the crowd, but no one spoke for him . . . at least not till the very end, when a red-faced Richard got up and walked to the podium that had been opened only to a strictly limited short list of people. Richard had a quick conversation with the funeral director before the solemn man waved him to the microphone.

"I know no one wants to hear good things about Bobby," he began, to a stir of whispers from the audience, "but you know what? Even if he lost his mind at the end, he was a good friend to me, and to many of you, and that should be remembered. His parents would want that, too."

His voice hitched. "They were always *so proud* of him." The tears rolling down his square-jawed face stopped the whispers, as others began to cry, too. "So, yeah, I think they would've forgiven him— after giving him one hell of a bollocking for what he'd done."

A hint of laughter in the crowd at the blunt speaking.

"I don't know what went wrong in Bobby's brain that day," Richard said. "But I'll remember him as the friend who never let me down, the man who quietly donated five percent of his profits to the city's food banks, the son and brother who would do anything for his family, and the business owner who took a pay cut so he could keep on several long-serving employees.

"I love you, mate, and what happened that morning, it wasn't the you we all knew. I'm going to remember the you from before."

# CHAPTER 68

Private notes: Detective Callum Baxter (LAPD)
Date: Nov 18
Time: 23:47

Got it! Clear evidence of malfeasance, with transfers from Virna's accounts at times she simply couldn't have authorized them. In one instance, she was under general anesthetic in the hospital for a minor procedure.

Added to that, the bastard's own accounts show a constant pattern of dives into the red, only to be topped up with a transfer from Virna's accounts. She might even have gifted him some of that money. But not all of it. Some of it, he took.

We're not ready to charge him yet, but his days of freedom are numbered.

# CHAPTER 69

Violet Long turned up a week before Diya was set to be released from the hospital. She still had the same blunt-cut bangs as in the photo I'd seen, though her bob was now asymmetrical and her cheekbones could cut glass. Diya's fellow event planner wore an ankle-length dress in an antique cream with small needlework flowers of a dusty pink.

It hung on her gaunt frame.

"Violet!" Diya, mobile now though still healing inside, got up to give her a hug. "You came."

Violet hugged her back with careful arms. "I was so ashamed that I couldn't even attend your family's funeral that I really ramped things up with my counselor." A hot flush on her cheeks.

Hearing her while being able to see her made me realize her face was partially paralyzed; that was what had caused the slur I'd taken for intoxication. The haircut, asymmetrical on purpose, was to help minimize the appearance of it when she wasn't speaking. It worked; I hadn't noticed at first glance.

"You have nothing to be ashamed of," Diya said fiercely. "It must be so hard for you being back in the hospital." Another hug before she drew back and said, "Oh, where are my manners. This is Tavish, my husband."

"Hi, Violet, nice to meet you in person."

"Same." When she smiled, the left curve of her lips tugged slightly down—and I realized she hadn't had the paralysis in the photo I'd seen in the newspaper.

This was a lingering result of the assault.

Anger stirred within, but I stuffed it deep down. I would never ever mention my suspicions of Sarita and Rajesh to Diya—my wife was barely holding herself together right now, a fragile glass bird who'd shatter with a single new blow.

"You two want me to grab you coffee and snacks from the café?" I asked, figuring they didn't want me hanging about while they chatted.

Diya beamed at me while tugging Violet toward her hospital bed so they could sit on it side by side, in front of a window that gave them a view of the hospital's sloping green grounds. "That'd be perfect. You know my order. Violet?"

"An almond milk flat white, one sugar. Thanks."

With Shumi having been discharged two days earlier, there was no Ajay wandering the halls, but he called me while I was waiting for the coffees. "How's it going?" I asked. "Shumi doing okay?"

"Fine—except I think she's going to murder our mum." A pause. "Oh man, how could I say that?"

I could almost see his mortification. "It's just words, don't sweat it." Life had to go on. "They're fighting?"

"No, the opposite. Mum is *hovering*—like she's trying to make up for all the years in between." That he saw so clearly was a testament to Ajay's inherent empathy; it would have been in his best interests not to see, to pretend his elder sister had experienced the same loving childhood as him.

"Shumi's already told me that she's moving in with you and Diya wherever you go, until she finds a place of her own. I thought I better give you the heads-up in case, you know, you'd rather she didn't." Youthful awkwardness. "I could talk to her . . ."

I'd been looking forward to having Diya to myself at last, but I couldn't abandon Shumi. Not when the idea of being stuck in a house with my own mother while I was vulnerable and recovering from injury was my personal nightmare.

Mrs. Kumar might have good intentions, but it was too fucking late. "Tell your sister she'll be welcome."

"Thanks, man."

Grabbing the drinks the barista had just slid over in a little cardboard carry tray, along with the brown paper bags that held the treats I'd picked up for the two women, I went back to the ward, arriving just in time to overhear Violet say, ". . . never told you, but I did get a couple of weird cards before I was attacked."

I hesitated outside the curtain the women had pulled around the bed to create a bit more privacy. Diya was in a room with three other patients, each of them in their own little curtained cubicle.

"What do you mean, weird?" my wife asked now.

"They were generic floral cards, but inside someone had written that you weren't what you seemed, and that I needed to stay away from you for my own good. Same message in different words in both cards."

Diya sucked in a breath. "Why would someone do that?"

"I figured maybe a competitor. I had several others approach me looking for a partnership, but I turned them down. Honestly, I forgot about them until just last week, when my counselor made me do a deep dive into the events of that entire month."

"That's pretty awful," Diya said, "knowing that someone dislikes me so much."

"I really think it was a dumb attempt to open up the partnership spot," Violet reassured her. "I wasn't going to tell you at all, but I want you to watch your back when you return to work."

The other woman paused. "My counselor thinks I'm too paranoid these days, but they never caught my attacker. Knowing that person is still out there . . . it's part of why I have such a hard time leaving the house. I can't help thinking that they could be waiting for me around any corner."

"Oh, Violet, I'm so sorry."

I went to back off, not wanting to interrupt what seemed to be an emotional moment, but a nurse came by just then and said, "Knock, knock," at the curtain before peeking inside. "Won't be long," she told the women. "Just have to chart your blood pressure."

I entered a moment later. "Your waiter's here!"

The rest of the conversation was light and carefree, but Diya told me about the cards after Violet left. "Do you think she's right? That it was just some disgruntled competitor?"

"Yeah," I said, because I could tell she needed reassurance. "Especially given the timing, with the two of you in partnership negotiations."

Nodding slowly, Diya leaned back against her pillow. "Tavi?"

"Yes?"

"I've been thinking . . . we have to take Mum and Dad and Bobby home. To Ani. She's been waiting such a long time."

# CHAPTER 70

Private notes: Detective Callum Baxter (LAPD)
Date: Nov 19
Time: 15:17

I thought Perez was punking me when he showed me the marriage certificates. No one could be that stupid. But then again, he did get away with it for years. But, yeah, this is it, the last nail in the coffin.

We'll be putting handcuffs on the bastard in a matter of days.

# CHAPTER 71

S ix weeks after Diya walked out of the hospital, and I continued to dream of the horror of that day, continued to grapple with the idea of Bobby being so consumed with his own image that he'd destroyed his entire family.

I'd probably never understand.

Diya, still mentally dazed and in psychic shock over the events that had forever altered the course of her life, sat quietly beside me on the sofa with its view of Lake Taupo. I'd rented the house with its sweeping views of a lake far bigger than Tarawera, then driven all three of us here through the night hours.

The renewed media storm that came with the revelations about Bobby had passed while the women were in the hospital, Ackerson turning up for most of the questions. The media must've known it'd be a bad look to hound a grieving family member, so they hadn't attempted to beard me, and the only articles about my past had been in the gossip rags.

When contacted by one of those rags during the tail end of

November, Detective Baxter had, surprisingly, come through for me with a blunt "No, Tavish Advani isn't a person of interest in the Musgrave case."

Five days later, he'd called me and said the last words I'd ever expected to hear. "I owe you an apology. I *did* get tunnel vision with you when it came to Virna, and didn't look hard enough at Jason."

A pause before he'd added, "I still don't believe you about Jocelyn Wai, but as far as the department is concerned, you're no longer under investigation in any capacity."

It was my father who'd filled in the gaps about Jason's headline-making arrest for the murder of his mother, having weaseled the information out of his contacts. "Some witness saw him tinkering with Virna's car the day before the accident.

"Virna was right there with him, offering him a glass of iced tea. Pretending to fix Mom's car while setting her up to die." Pure disgust in my father's voice. "Word is the man has two wives, two sets of kids, a champagne lifestyle with both families—and, despite appearances, his finances are in the toilet due to a string of bad investments."

I'd told Diya about Jocelyn that night she'd asked about my nightmare, but we'd never talked about Virna. I knew she had to know, however. We lived in a world of search engines and information at our fingertips—if she hadn't done the search herself, her family or friends would have.

That she'd never once brought it up with me told me all I needed to know: Diya trusted me.

*It hurts when you fall that far, that fast. I felt my bones break when I hit the pavement.*

Jocelyn's vengeful ghost ran her long red nails over my spine, but I shook off the sensation, shoving her into the past where she belonged. Behind a locked black door where I couldn't hear her scream as she fell.

My phone flashed.

When I glanced at it, I saw a new alert on the name Andrea Smithy-Carr. She was finally having her moment in the sun—and in doing so, fueling the interest in the Prasad family all over again. Her constant appearances and accusations had led to the reporters becoming emboldened in their attempts to reach Diya and Shumi. Two had tracked us down to the short-term rental I'd found for us in a quiet suburb of Rotorua, going so far as to knock on the door.

So I'd spirited them away in the night.

I'd hesitated on choosing a property with a lake view, but both women had mentioned how much they missed the peace of the lake, so I'd taken the risk—the city of Taupo itself was only a short distance away, so I'd figured I could always switch over to a place without this view if they didn't like it.

As it was, they'd both spent the sunny hours after our arrival sitting out on the deck chairs, watching the sun glitter on the water. Neither had wanted to talk much, and I hadn't forced it—though there were a number of important things about which we had to talk.

Shumi and Bobby's home had been used either as collateral for a cash injection into the business, or to guarantee a business loan—I wasn't sure of the details, but I knew it was currently tangled up in the bankruptcy proceedings. It wasn't looking like Shumi would see anything out of it once all was said and done.

The end result was that the Lake Tarawera land was the only thing tying either woman to that region, and it would sell once put on the market.

But the sale wasn't necessary.

Rajesh and Sarita had left their only surviving child a rich woman—and Diya had already decided to sign over half of her inheritance to Shumi.

"It's what they would've wanted," she'd told me. "They loved her, thought of her as another daughter."

My wife still couldn't understand how Bobby could've done what he had, no matter the evidence. She kept returning to the subject each time we were alone, her expression a dark cloud. "I knew my brother. He didn't hit girls or women. I hate that people are saying that about him."

I hadn't pointed out that Shumi herself had confirmed Bobby's tendency toward domestic violence. Diya was already heartbroken; if it made her feel better to pretend the world had it wrong, so be it. And she wasn't hurting anyone else with her beliefs; she followed Shumi's lead where Bobby was concerned, never brought up her brother with the other woman on her own.

This time was for healing, for peace—and for privacy. I'd chosen a house on a hill, the lake some way in the distance, no neighbors close by to spy on us. Looking out at the lights of other houses reflected in the dark sprawl of Lake Taupo seemed to give Diya solace. My wife had been quiet today, but I'd felt her relief as we left Rotorua and its memories behind.

"We could plan our trip to Fiji while we're here," I murmured, very aware of the urn of ashes stored at our rental in Rotorua.

Quite frankly, I wanted it gone, but despite her words at the hospital the day Violet visited, Diya wasn't quite ready to let go.

Today, however, she nodded. "Yes, let's do that." She looked up. "I know I've been dragging my feet, but how I felt when we drove out today . . . I want them to have their freedom, too."

While we sat talking quietly in front of the large window that framed the view of the lake, Shumi hummed to herself in the kitchen.

She'd made me stop at a local grocery store on our way to this house and stocked up on supplies with feverish intent—including liters of milk for the chai she was now making. An excessive amount of chai for the three of us, even had I liked the stuff.

Shumi was too much bright chatter and a refusal to discuss anything that had happened. She'd been like that since the first few days after she woke up. Like she'd shut a door and wouldn't look behind it lest she see a monster standing there.

*I don't want to say.*

She'd gone from not wanting to say to not wanting to even think about the events of that bloody morning. The other day, she'd chirped about how Bobby had always brought her coffee in bed each morning, and how he'd never forgotten to pick up her special spices from a shop in Auckland when he drove up for a business trip.

"He was such a good husband," she'd said with every indication of sincerity.

I was waiting for her to snap, just collapse into a screaming mess of grief. But I was also glad that she hadn't yet—it gave me time to hold Diya, focus on her heart.

"Shumi's hurt bad," she whispered after her sister-in-law sang out that the chai was almost ready. "The last time she got like this, it was after Velvet, her miniature poodle, died. She loved her so much— Bobby gave Velvet to her on their one-year anniversary."

She swallowed hard. "When Velvet got hit by a car and died, she got like this. Smiling real hard and trying to do everything at once. She made two enormous pots of biryani, baked a cake, and was in the middle of mixing dough for naan when she just . . . crumpled onto the floor. Like her strings had been cut. And she rocked and rocked and cried."

"We'll be ready," I whispered, pressing a kiss to her temple. "When it hits her."

Diya nodded and settled back against me. "I just . . . I don't understand it," she said again. "Why would Bobby do that to our parents? To us? He never hurt me, not once in our whole life. If anything, he drove me crazy with his overprotectiveness."

I knew by now that she just needed me to listen, so that was what I did, stroking my palm over her shoulder and dropping kisses on her curls.

Diya's tears were silent. "My parents loved him, Tavi. He was their firstborn, the child that made them parents. And he loved them. Loved all of us."

"I know, baby."

She spread her fingers over my heart. "I was holding my pills the other day, thinking I could take a few extra and just make it all go away."

My heart kicked. "Diya, *no*." This was the first time she'd even mentioned the idea of suicide.

"I won't." A firm promise. "Because the next second, I saw my wedding ring and I thought, how could I do that to you? Leave you to grieve me, too?" She shook her head. "No, Tavi, we're in this for the long haul. Me and you." A look toward the kitchen. "I'll talk to Shumi about finding her own place. She already mentioned how she knows we probably want to be alone as a couple, so she's expecting it."

"Can't say I'm not ready." I ached for alone time with Diya, but I hadn't wanted to kick a woman at such a low ebb in her life, so had kept my mouth shut. "Ajay's being really good with her. Maybe they can salvage a bond. He might even want to stay with her for a while."

"I'm hoping that for her."

I stroked her back. "Have you talked to the therapist about your thoughts? About the drugs?"

"No, but I will." She looked up to give me a soft smile. "I'm not going anywhere, Tavi. I just . . . I just have bad moments."

"Do you want me to hold your drugs for you and just give you what you need for now? Until you feel steadier?"

I half expected her to be furious, but she nodded. "Yes, I think that's a smart idea. I don't want to do anything, but my emotions are all over the place. It's not only the grief . . . I just don't understand. Bhaiya loved me. He used to call me his tagalong when he was in high school and I wanted to hang out with him and his friends at the lake—but he never told me to get lost. He's the one who taught us how to swim, back in Fiji."

Then she laughed. "You know the irony of it? He was a great teacher, but a terrible swimmer himself. Got freaked going out into water where he couldn't touch the ground with his feet."

*He drowned my Rhi, my sweet girl. She was such a strong swimmer that he had to have held her under or done something else to her. She used to swim out to that far buoy and back without problem.*

I frowned. "I thought your brother loved the ocean."

"He did, but mostly the beach. He liked to pretend he was cool with the water when his friends were around, but he stuck to the shallows most of the time or talked people into going out on the four-wheelers instead of into the water.

"That's why I always *knew* he didn't hurt Rhiannon, no matter what anyone said. They found her way out by the buoy, tangled up in the rope. Bobby bhaiya could've never made it there."

# CHAPTER 72

## RHIANNON

*Y*ou want to come with me? I'm swimming out to the buoy," Rhiannon said.

No one else was around, everyone having either headed off for a walk or to go take a quick dip and then sunbathe. And while Rhiannon didn't mind swimming alone, it was more fun with company.

"Yeah, okay."

Rhiannon smiled and grabbed her towel.

# CHAPTER 73

C ups clinking in the kitchen.

Diya looked up, whispered, "Drink a bit of Shumi's chai, okay?"

I indicated the potted plant by the television. "It's okay—I already scoped out my next victim."

Her lips twitched, and I was glad to see a flicker of her luminous light. "You have no taste," she muttered, then wiped at her cheeks with her fingers to get rid of the evidence of our emotional conversation.

Trying to be strong for the sister-in-law who had lost everything overnight. All of Shumi's love, all her hopes, everything she was, had been tied to Bobby and his family. Without them . . .

"Here we go!" Shumi walked out with three cups and a plate of cookies on a wooden tray. "I got the chocolate raisin cookies you like, Dee. You should eat something."

Taking the tray from her, I put it on the coffee table. "This looks really nice, thanks, Shumi."

She smiled that too-bright smile, picked up a cup, and gave it to me to hand to Diya. The next one, she put in my hands. "Extra sugar, just as you like," she said.

"You're the best." Bringing it to my lips, I took a deep breath. The rich scent of cardamom flooded my nose—I liked the spice, just not in tea. "Too hot to drink right away, but it smells fantastic."

"My special recipe." She took her own cup and curled up in the armchair kitty-corner from us. "I had to make do with grocery store items rather than the blend that I make at home with fresh spices, but I did a taste test in the kitchen, and it's good."

Putting my chai on the side table, while Diya cradled hers in her hands, I picked up one of the cookies. "Diya?"

But she shook her head. "Not yet. The chai is what I need." She took deep inhales of the aroma. "It's the smell of home."

Shumi accepted a cookie when I lifted the plate in her direction.

Then the three of us just sat there staring out at the lake while I ate two cookies to stave off the inevitable need to force down the chai, and Diya sipped at hers.

Shumi took a bigger sip of hers just then. "It's not too hot now," she said to me, and since she was staring straight at me, I smiled and picked up my cup, then, girding my loins, took a sip.

Cinnamon and cardamom and other crushed spices laid a film on my tongue that I couldn't wait to wash out with water. "Wow," I said. "Can't believe you managed this with the ingredients you had."

"I had to grind it all up with a makeshift—" Her head spun to Diya, who'd put her chai aside and was getting shakily to her feet. "Dee?"

"I feel a little sick." She shot me a look when I started to rise.

*Oh.*

I let Shumi jump to her aid. "Do you want to go to the bathroom?" the other woman said.

Diya nodded.

I'd had a whole excuse lined up about how Diya hated having me see her be sick, should Shumi turn to me, but the other woman walked Diya out without giving me a second look.

I was up and off the sofa a second after they vanished around the corner, and by the time they returned, the poor potted plant had had a healthy drink of lukewarm chai—but I'd left a little bit at the bottom of the cup, the part thick with masala.

I wasn't stupid. I knew how to cover my chai-hating tracks.

The sound of voices in the hallway. "Baby." I rose when Diya and Shumi walked back in. "Are you all right?"

"Yes. Just stress, I guess." She came into my arms for a cuddle before taking a seat again and picking up her chai to finish it. "Did you already guzzle yours?"

"Hey, it's good." Retaking my seat, I met Shumi's eyes. "Thanks, Shumi."

She smiled, but it was wrong, all tight and fragile. *Shit.* The breakdown was coming. I squeezed Diya's hand between our bodies, and she squeezed back.

"Shall we watch some TV?" she suggested. "How about that matchmaking show, Shumi? You love Auntie Seema."

"Ugh, she's such a harridan." Shumi finished off her own chai. "And yet strangely watchable."

The two women shared a smile before Diya picked up the remote. Taking it from her, I said, "Man privileges," but what I really wanted was to ensure Diya didn't accidentally trigger a news channel.

Ackerson had tipped me off that at least two major journalists were determined to dig deeper into the story of the Lake Tarawera Incident, as it had become known—figure out all the layers of it. "One's even starting to wonder if Bobby could've been a serial killer—I feel for Andrea Smithy-Carr, but she's making my job very fucking hard."

Yet, despite the statement, there'd been an edge to her voice. And I knew Detective Ackerson was already looking into that possibility herself. Especially since she knew about Ani.

Those two specific senior journalists had been keeping the story alive on television, too—no knowing if tonight was one of the nights they'd feature the murders again from some new angle. It was mostly talking heads, but the last thing Diya and Shumi needed was for photographs of their family to be flashed on-screen.

It was even worse because the media had been using photos from the engagement party since the day of the murders. Those had been the newest photos and the easiest to acquire due to the number of guests who'd shared images online. The cynical part of me knew that the photos from the party also had the most mass appeal because of the contrast with the horrific events of the morning after.

One particular photo that included the entire family laughing and holding each other, everyone dressed to the nines, had become the lead photograph on all the stories. I wasn't in it because I'd taken it. I'd then immediately sent it to the entire family—and Sarita had apparently uploaded it to her public social media page early the morning of the fire, next to a photo of a toddler Diya wearing a floofy blue dress.

Can't believe my baby girl is engaged!

"Bobby liked to be the king of the remote, too," Shumi said just then, her voice strangely flat.

I shot Diya a look but she gave me a small shake of the head.

So I navigated directly to the streaming channel that hosted the show.

The two women focused too intently on it, their comments light, as if they had not a single care in the world. Shumi close to breakdown and Diya on edge waiting for it.

Diya began to get quieter ten minutes in and I wasn't surprised when she yawned and snuggled into me. Putting my arm around her, I glanced over at Shumi, who was also looking heavy eyed.

Good, maybe the other woman would sleep through the worst of the crash and we could all be fresh in the morning when we had to face the confronting truth.

I wasn't feeling exactly wide-awake myself, but I didn't want to leave Shumi alone, and she was still fighting sleep. So I kept on watching Auntie Seema try to match these men and women who . . .

. . . *humming.*

Someone was humming.

Mouth dry, I tried to lift my lids, but they felt sticky and heavy. It was the hint of smoke in the air that kicked my adrenaline into overdrive, giving me enough strength to push those damn lids up.

Disoriented, I stared at the blank television screen.

One of the women must've turned it off, I thought dully, before realizing I couldn't see either of them. And the room was pitch-dark except for the red power light on the television, and what little light fell through the windows from what felt like a strangely large moon.

*Humming.*

It stopped. Words came through, fuzzy and barely understandable, with patches cutting in and out, as if my brain was a radio that couldn't hold on to a signal.

". . . lied for you . . . let Bobby . . . always." A grunt. "Don't you know?"

The humming started up again.

I recognized it now. *Shumi.* That was the song Shumi had been humming while she made the chai. Was she in the kitchen making more things? Diya had said she cooked compulsively when grieving.

But when I looked toward the kitchen, it was to see that it, too, was dark.

"Diya?" It came out weak and near-silent.

Shoving up off the sofa, I tried to get to my feet. My knees collapsed under me, pain shooting through my kneecaps.

*Smoke.*

Curling on the carpet, licking its way into my air passages.

I coughed and began to crawl frantically toward that humming sound. With each little foot of space, I gained more of my strength. "Diya!" Louder this time, before smoke-induced coughing took over.

When I stopped coughing, I realized the humming was gone, the world silent.

My heart punched in my rib cage. "Shumi? Diya?"

The smoke was thicker now, a fog through which I could no longer see. I knew I should turn, smash out that big window with the view, and get outside—but not without my wife.

More strength in my body now, I crawled faster.

I saw her foot first. With that yellow nail polish on her toes that she'd put on with patient care last week. It had taken her a while, since she couldn't sit bent over for long periods, the position causing pain to internal organs that weren't yet back to normal.

But when I grabbed on to her foot, there was no response. "Diya!" Telling myself it was fine, that she was still warm, I quickly made my way to the top of her body, where I could check her breathing.

"Thank God." She was alive, her respiration even. "Come on, baby, we have to get out." Even as I struggled to sit up so I could drag her out, I yelled out for Shumi.

Nothing. And the smoke was growing thicker.

I fumbled for my phone, input 911, only to realize I'd fucked up. I was in New Zealand. My chest spasmed with the urge to cough as I canceled the call and input the correct local number for emergency services: 111.

Dropping the phone to the carpet on speaker, I got my hands under Diya. "Fire!" I yelled at the operator when she answered, blurting out the address straight after.

I didn't hear what she said in response. I had a firm grip on Diya now, was able to move her. "Shumi!"

"Why are you awake?" A very confused-sounding question.

# CHAPTER 74

## SHUMI

*S*humi sat inside a café on the opposite side of the road from the café where Diya and Violet had taken a seat outside, beneath the spreading branches of a leafy tree. Diya smiled up at the server who'd just delivered them their coffees.

A double-shot latte with soy milk.

That was Diya's order, had been for years except for when she wanted something more decadent and decided to go for a mochaccino.

Shumi didn't know Violet's usual order and didn't really care.

Taking a sip of her own spicy chai latte—it wasn't real chai, but it would do—she watched as Diya laughed at something Violet had said. Shumi's stomach clenched at the light in her best friend's face, at how she chattered so brightly to Violet.

Diya was pulling away from her again.

She'd thought it was over after Kalindra decided to move to Wellington before things got bad enough that Shumi had to act, but now Violet was here and they were constantly texting and calling, and Shumi knew that wasn't good for Diya's fragile mind and heart.

Her best friend needed Shumi to watch out for her, and for that, Shumi needed to be the closest person in her life.

It had been bad enough when Risha had lived with the Prasads, her room right next to Diya's. The only thing that had kept Shumi from acting was the knowledge that Risha was a temporary guest, one who'd be gone soon enough.

But Violet . . . Violet lived in Rotorua, was talking about becoming Diya's partner. They'd be working together day in and day out.

Her chai latte spilled onto the saucer as she put the double-walled glass down too hard.

No, she couldn't let this happen, had to act.

# CHAPTER 75

Diya's sister-in-law stood in the hallway, smoke curling up
around her calves as it rose toward the ceiling.

"What?" I shook my head to clear it. "Shumi, there's a
fire! We have to get out!"

"I know." Pure calm. "I was pulling Diya out. Now you've gone
and spoiled it."

I stared at her, my sluggish brain trying to make sense of what she
was saying. "Go open the door!" It was still some distance away, this
spacious vacation home suddenly too big. "I'll bring Diya."

"You're meant to be *asleep*," Shumi insisted. "I put in a double
dose to be sure."

My brain started to catch up with her words, with the way she
was just standing there, but it was already too late. Because Shumi
had a knife in her hand, a massive thing that she held firmly by the
handle. "I had to go to the kitchen to get this," she said, before coming toward me with the knife raised high. "It's not how I wanted it."

Having slid my hands under Diya's shoulders to drag her to the door, I couldn't evade Shumi's first blow. It went right through that vulnerable space beside my shoulder blade, a screaming line of fire inside and out.

"Shumi! Stop!" I shoved her off with that pained cry, but she dug in the knife and twisted.

"You're *meant to be sleeping*," she gritted out, right before I threw back my fist.

It made hard, direct contact with her face, and she tumbled backward, taking the knife with her.

Something splintered, broke.

I couldn't smell blood, the acrid scent of smoke and fire blotting out all else. Not hearing Shumi move, I hoped I'd knocked her out. I couldn't go over and check—given the gray soup of smoke, I might never find my way back to Diya. I could barely make out the route to the front door as it was.

Coughing, I pulled Diya up again despite the agony in my shoulder, and began to move.

The knife punched into my back again, and this time, it hit something bad. Something that made the taste of blood fill my mouth and threatened to take the air from my lungs.

"It's meant to be us!" Shumi screamed. "Me and Diya! It's always been meant to be us! *I'm* the one who looks after her!"

Barely able to hear her through the crackle of the flames I could now see roaring to life in the living room, I shoved back with my whole body.

It drove the knife in even deeper, but it also took her to the floor. Twisting, I went to punch her, just get this over with, but, free of whatever drug she'd used to incapacitate me, she was faster, slid away and kicked at my face.

My head snapped back.

"I did so much for her! I do *everything* for her!" Her voice was

343

hoarse, her words making no sense. "I keep her safe! They never understood her! They didn't deserve her!"

Coughing, the sound wet now, I felt my hand touch something. The broken leg of the fragile table against which she'd initially tumbled. Picking it up, I rose to my feet, while staying right beside Diya, and swung wildly, made no contact. "You killed everyone," I managed to cough out.

"She doesn't need anyone else! She just needs me!" A disembodied voice in the darkness.

Using the sound of her voice to pinpoint her location, I swung again. A fleshy *thwack* of sound.

Shumi screamed and kicked out, but I somehow managed to avoid it this time. She was coughing now, yelling. "You ruined everything! I won't let you take her!"

I swung while she was ranting. The contact was solid. A thunk followed by a thud that was her body falling to the floor. My vision hazy and my balance shot, I crashed to the floor on my knees and got my hands under Diya again. "Come on, baby." Blood bubbled in my mouth. "We're gonna make it."

I began to drag and pull, and with each wrench, felt another spurt of blood down my back. I blocked it out, focused on Diya.

My light.

My one good thing.

My salvation.

I would not let her die. Not my Diya.

The taste of wet iron filled my mouth.

# CHAPTER 76

## SHUMI

"Do you love me, Shumi?"

"Of course I do, Bobby." Shumi laughed. "You're my husband!"

Bobby, so handsome with his dark hair and that stubble on his jaw, his upper body bare as he stood by their bedroom window, turned to look at her. "Sometimes, I'm not so sure. I feel like you're just out of reach, no matter how hard I try."

"Oh, hush now." Shumi kept her voice soft, affectionate, because she did truly like him a great deal. "You know you were the only boy I ever wanted—having you love me is a dream come true."

In many ways, that wasn't even a lie. Without Bobby, she'd never have been able to stay so close to Diya, continue to keep her safe as she had since the day she'd first met the baby who'd laughed and grabbed at her hand, and who'd always loved her even when her own mother couldn't.

Shumi's mother pretended, but she wasn't a good actress. Shumi had figured out as a very small child that she meant nothing to her, was just a mouth she fed to keep up appearances. But it hadn't mattered because she *had the Prasads, who'd always been kind to her. Then had come Diya, this tiny and bright light who had toddled after Shumi and who had always wanted to play with her.*

*Diya loved Shumi in a way no one had ever loved her.*

*To stay close to that love, Shumi had been more than happy to stick tight to Bobby. He was handsome, and sexually, they were more than compatible. It was no sacrifice to have a hardworking and good-looking husband who took his time making sure she was always satisfied.*

*Ensuring it stayed that way was an easy matter.*

*She rose from the bed and walked to take his hands as the moonlight filtered in through the window. "I adore you, you know that," she murmured, looking up at him with the big doe eyes that always did him in. "I'm just . . . you've seen how my mum is. I think sometimes I get scared of how much I love you."*

*She swallowed hard. "Please don't stop loving me. It would destroy me."*

*"Jaan, meri jaan," he said, enfolding her in the warmth of his arms and holding her with that endearing gentleness of his; sometimes, she wished he'd be a little rougher, a bit more exciting, but in the grand scheme of things, it was a minor complaint.*

*"I could never stop loving you," he told her. "I tried so many times over the years when we were younger—I thought it was just proximity, that we'd grow apart. But it was and will always be you. My Shumi."*

*Kisses pressed to her temple before he slid his hand to her abdomen. "Any news?"*

*Shumi shook her head, her face downcast. "Got my period again."*

*"That's okay. We're young." He nuzzled at her. "And it's so much fun trying, isn't it?"*

*Giggling, she pressed a kiss to his chest, the curly hairs there tickling her lips, but she didn't answer with words. Because while, yes, it was fun having sex with him, they weren't actually trying as he believed—she'd had her* doctor put her on long-term birth control the day Bobby began to talk about having kids.

It wasn't that Shumi didn't like kids—it was that she had her priorities in life and knew she couldn't give a baby the time and attention it deserved. Not now, not when Diya needed her so much. First she had to extricate her vulnerable best friend from the clutches of her stranger of a husband, then she'd have to settle her down in the no-doubt emotional aftermath.

It wouldn't be hard. She'd been digging into Tavish Advani, had an entire dossier on the computer with all kinds of damning information. She'd thought about showing it to Rajesh and Sarita, but her in-laws didn't know how to handle Diya. They'd yell at her and demand things and then Diya would get rebellious.

Shumi knew her best.

Diya's heart was soft and generous and ready to love.

Shumi would have to go delicately, drop a little piece of information here, an ounce of doubt there, until Diya began to worry. Only then would Shumi show her the pages and pages of articles and other data she'd collected about Diya's new husband.

The Jocelyn Wai situation spoke for itself.

Everyone thought he'd murdered the woman; they just couldn't prove it.

It wouldn't take much for Shumi to make Diya understand that Tavish had targeted her because of her fragile mental state, that he got a kick out of hurting and controlling women.

Shumi knew exactly what to say to make Diya question her impulsive decision. After all, she'd made it without Shumi's counsel. In some part of her, she already knew she'd messed up.

Shumi just had to bring that awareness to the surface of her consciousness.

Once Tavish was gone and Diya back where she belonged . . . yes, Shumi might have a child. It'd keep Bobby happy, and he'd be a good father, would *pull his weight. Diya would be a wonderful aunt, too, the baby bringing them even closer together. Perhaps she'd even suggest Diya move in to help Shumi with the baby. Such a loving reason. One that made sense in every way.*

*Diya would finally be where she belonged: under Shumi's loving care.*

*Life would be perfect.*

# CHAPTER 77

They told me later that they found me on the lawn on my front, with a huge knife sticking out of my back and an unconscious Diya beside me. I'd have died if I hadn't made that frantic call to emergency services.

My luck, it seemed, had finally come in.

"Jesus Christ, I fucked this one up." Detective Ackerson, who'd come to visit me at the hospital, put her hands on her hips, her suit jacket flared out. "But in my defense, your batshit sister-in-law did a good job of looking as innocent as Mother Teresa. She's still protesting her innocence even though she got caught on that emergency call as good as confessing to it all."

"Any chance she'll escape the charges?" I winced as I tried to make myself more comfortable in my seated position on the bed. "She didn't actually say she murdered everyone."

"What she did say is plenty," Ackerson reassured me. "Her obsession with your wife, though . . ." She shook her head. "The word 'stalker' doesn't quite capture it. The shrinks are having a field day with her.

"Apparently, she thinks she's Diya's protector, the only one who understands her. Extreme maternal urges. I say unhinged, but, hey, I'm just a mum who never murdered my daughter's friends for daring to take her away from me."

I thought about Shumi's own mother, the complete lack of a mother-child bond. Because Shumi's obsessive attachment to Diya hadn't appeared out of thin air; it had been born in the cold abandonment of her own childhood. "Her family still supporting her?"

"Only one she's willing to see is Ajay. Poor kid. He's shattered."

I hadn't seen Ajay since the events in Taupo—I'd been in the hospital. That final knife strike? It had perforated my lung and nicked other things. I'd made it worse when I'd slammed into Shumi. "How is she doing physically?"

"Better than you." Ackerson folded her arms. "She only made it out because you called 111. Otherwise, she'd have died from smoke inhalation well before the fire got to her. House is only a little damaged—your sister-in-law had to make do with what she could find in terms of accelerants, and it wasn't much. I think the plan was to make it look like a terrible accident."

"A second fire?" I asked skeptically. "She really thought people would buy an accident?"

"Yeah, she was decompensating by the end. Shrinks say she wasn't prepared for the impact of losing the support structure of the senior Prasads as well as her husband. They propped her up in ways she didn't understand before she destroyed that structure."

It made sense; Rhiannon and Violet, those crimes had been so well planned that not even a droplet of suspicion had fallen on Shumi. The Lake Tarawera Incident, in contrast, had been a mess that I still didn't understand, while Lake Taupo had been a full-on psychotic fantasy that would have put the spotlight firmly on her even if it had gone exactly as she'd wished.

"What about the drugs?" I asked. "Where did she get those?"

"Plain old sleeping pills. Her doctor prescribed them to her for insomnia, but she must've stocked them away at her and Bobby Prasad's home—her family confirmed that she did go back after she was released, to get some clothes, personal items, that kind of thing." The cop scowled. "I hate shrinks but I can see why someone would need some head shrinking after this. You and your wife should get therapy."

I took a sip from the juice box Diya had left for me before she went out to get me a burger with every fixing imaginable. I was craving one like you wouldn't believe, and it wasn't like knife wounds meant I had to be on a bland invalid diet.

Ackerson crossed her arms over her chest, pinned me with her gaze. "Did you hear that both of Jason Musgrave's soon-to-be-ex-wives—though I guess only one is legally married to him—did a *Dateline* interview? Both redheads, so he has a clear type. They're pissed and planning to form a united front against the murdering bigamist."

I stared fixedly at the curtain around my bed. "Virna deserved better, deserved more." Warm, generous, kind, she'd spent forty years with a husband who barely paid attention to her, too busy with his business interests, had only begun to fly after he was dead. "What a waste of a life."

I caught Ackerson's nod out of the corner of my eye, but when she spoke, it had nothing to do with Virna. "Baxter says the original detective on the Jocelyn Wai case still thinks you had something to do with it."

"Joss was self-destructive," I said. "That's why she was with me—because I was self-destructive then, too. I was grieving the loss of the first woman I ever loved, was vulnerable."

In had swooped Joss like the vulture she was; she'd led an already struggling and grieving young man to the edge of the abyss, then nudged him over.

This time when her ghost tried to whisper in my ear, I shut it down.

Joss had *made* me who I'd been the night she died—a man who, after a year of her working on him, had finally been willing to walk deeper into dissipation, let the drugs dull his pain. What happened next was her fault. I'd only killed one woman in my life, and it wasn't Jocelyn Wai.

"She did drugs, got messed up, and went over the balcony," I said, my anguish over the death for which I *was* responsible a visceral thing that hadn't faded even after all these years. "It's that simple, but because she was beautiful and charismatic, people want to believe there's a greater story, that it's not the same sad and predictable one as that of the addict on the street."

A nurse bustled in. "That's enough," she said to Ackerson. "He needs to rest. Come back tomorrow if you want to interrogate him more."

"We're just chatting." Ackerson scowled, but the nurse was having none of it, and honestly, I was grateful.

Exhaustion had begun to wash over me in waves, and I was asleep a bare minute or two after the cop left the cubicle.

I dreamed of curls of smoke on the carpet, my mind filled with a whispering hum that said, . . . *lied for you.*

# CHAPTER 78

## SUSANNE

Don't go," said the beautiful boy she'd watched turn into a loyal, empathic man at her side. "Please, Suzi W."

He was the only one she'd ever let get away with calling her Suzi. She was Sue to her friends, Susanne to everyone else, and had always thought Suzi rather low-class. Until he'd made it fun and flirty and young.

Suzi W had gone dancing with her lover in a club so dark that no one could tell the disparity in their ages, and Suzi W had sat on the back of a motorcycle with her arms around him as he zoomed around Singapore.

Suzi W had lived.

Now Tavish's eyes filled with tears, his hands trembling as he clasped them around one of hers and lifted it to his mouth. "Stay a while longer."

She ached to do so, but the rest of her . . . there was so much pain. "Sometimes, Tavish, the doctors get it wrong." The last scans she'd had done had shown that the tumors were progressing as predicted—at a rate that would give her another year or so of a good quality of life.

But her body had decided different, and she didn't need a scan to confirm it. She could see it in the blood she was coughing up, in the fact that she couldn't breathe well enough to even climb two flights of stairs, when only a couple of months ago she could've run up them without a hitch.

"In a way," she said, "it's a blessing. No long decline but a quick fall." She ran her fingers through his overlong hair, pressed her forehead to his. "Thank you for what you've done for me."

He wouldn't meet her eyes.

Taking his jaw, she made him look and shook her head. "Don't you ever feel guilty for it. Because of you, I'll die as I wish." Not twisted up and covered in vomit because she'd taken the wrong combination of pills.

And not caught in some horrific in-between because she'd damaged her brain without managing to stop her body.

He, this man who'd grown up in a world where drugs were passed around like candy, so many beautiful people dead by twenty-seven that there was a terrible club named after them, had gotten his hands on something that would give her a sweet slide into the final nothingness.

She'd be found with her hair and makeup done, dressed as she wanted to be dressed when she was discovered—she'd decided on the dynamite red dress that was her favorite. Paired with hot red lipstick, of course.

Why not go out like the diva she'd been in life?

"I'm killing you." It was a rasp.

"No, Tavish. You're setting me free." Taking his hand, she pressed it to a part of her that should've been soft and smooth. "Feel that? It's a tumor." So small on the scans, it was now a hard rock she could feel through her skin. "This thing is eating me up until I won't be Susanne much longer."

His breath hitched, his throat moving. "You'll always be you."

Stubborn, loving man. "No, Tavish. Because I won't be able to maintain my dignity." That, to her, was worth more than life.

After kissing him one last time, she pushed at his shoulders. "You know what you have to do. Get that bag, get on a plane, and make sure you're on plenty of security cameras on the other side." She wouldn't end her life by *making his a hell. "I'll wait until you call me to say you've landed safely. Grace will be gone within the hour, too."*

*His hug was a jagged thing that hurt her because of how strongly he held her, but she didn't protest. Not for this final hug.*

*"Thank you for teaching me love." A rough inhale as he stepped back.*

*Oh, how she wished she could stay, and watch him grow ever deeper into his skin, fall in love with a woman who could walk with him through life, get married, have babies. "You'll make a wonderful husband and father, Tavish. Never ever doubt that. You just need to find the right woman."*

*A shaky nod.*

*"Safe journey," she said, drinking him in with her eyes.*

*He picked up his bag, looked back at her. "You, too, Suzi W."*

# CHAPTER 79

One week after the doctors released me, Diya and I sat on the white sands of the beach behind the Prasad family home in Fiji. Turquoise waters lapped at the shore, their foaming tops a pure white.

A coconut had rolled in to shore on one of those waves, and now it moved with each new reach of the water, attempting to stay on sandy ground rather than being pulled back in. Shells glittered on either side of us, but there was only white sand below, this beach the kind that featured in magazine shots.

Above our heads waved the fronds of twin coconut palms, the air balmy.

It was paradise.

And Diya's hand was as cold as ice in mine. "Hey." I rubbed at it with my other hand. "What's wrong?"

Leaning her head against my upper arm, the pale brown slopes of her shoulders exposed by the strappy top of her sundress, she said, "I was thinking about Shumi."

We hadn't seen Diya's sister-in-law since that night.

The wheels were still turning there, but it was starting to look like while she might be mentally ill, she wasn't insane in the legal sense. Ackerson was sure she'd known right from wrong when she'd done what she had, and was confident the medical investigators would confirm her feelings.

If so, Shumi would be going on trial for the murders of her husband and in-laws, and for attempted murder when it came to me and Diya. The charge relating to Diya had to do with her original stabbing, not the Taupo incident—because there, Shumi had intended to save her.

The prosecutors were keeping the arson and assault charges in their back pocket for now.

"My brother never hit her." Diya lifted the sand with her other hand before allowing it to whisper through her fingers in a glitter of silica. "She'll never convince me of that. If anything, he pampered her too much—would drive her anywhere she wanted, would wait in the parking lot while she went shopping though it bored him out of his skull, would call her back each time she texted him with some small question."

All things I'd taken to be controlling behavior could, I realized, be seen from a whole different lens—that of a husband so devoted that he'd allowed his wife to run roughshod over him.

"She always agreed with whatever he wanted."

"You know what I realized after Taupo?" Diya's smile was tight. "She always got her way in the end. The house they lived in? Bobby thought it was too big and old-fashioned. *His* first choice was a sleek modern town house. His car? He showed me all the booklets he'd picked up on a Jeep Wrangler, was excited about owning one. The fact they were even in Rotorua? Bobby always said he wanted to live in Auckland."

She dropped her hand to the sand. "You know what hurts the most? Bobby wanted a big family, was open about the fact that he wanted to start young so they'd be done young. But Shumi had difficulty getting pregnant, so he shelved his dreams—only it turns out she was on birth control all along. Mrs. Kumar told me by accident when we talked on the phone—she was thanking God that Shumi always kept up the birth control, because she couldn't imagine what this situation would do to a child."

I held her close, just let her speak.

"Ajay wants to believe her, so much. He told me about a set of bruises she allowed him to believe came from Bobby, but I remember those particular ones because I was there when she ran into the edge of the counter in the kitchen of the Lake Tarawera house."

Her voice shook. "It went black-and-blue, and I joked with her that her parents were going to think her in-laws were beating her. She laughed."

"She didn't want her family to like Bobby, remain close to him." Harder to maintain certain lies if all parties were in communication.

Diya's face crumpled. "She's a stranger to me. I have no idea what's going on inside her head."

"Ah, sweetheart." I held her tighter against me and considered whether to bring up the one thing that continued to niggle at me—I loved her, no matter what, could go through my entire life staying silent on the topic . . . but Diya couldn't. Her head was already a place wounded; she needed to get this poison out. "Baby, why did Shumi say she lied for you?"

Diya went motionless. "That wasn't on the emergency call tape."

"I called after she said that."

Breaking our handclasp, Diya hugged her arms around her knees and stared fixedly out at the waters of the land where she'd been born.

"Before you answer, I want to tell you about Susanne." I'd mentioned my first love before, but only in passing. Now I told her all of it—including what I'd done at the end. "I killed Suzi W."

Diya, her face awash in tears, grabbed mine in her hands. "No, no, you didn't, Tavish. She wanted to go. You *helped* her."

Hands on her wrists, I allowed my own tears to fall, the sobs wracking my body as I buried my face against her neck and released all the anguish I'd held inside for years.

The pain of it was unbearable.

And the release a searing exhaustion that took me to the sand, the two of us on our backs, Diya's head pillowed on my arm as we watched the coconut palm fronds move against the blue, blue sky.

I'd told her about my involvement with Susanne's death so she'd know that I trusted her to the core—and that she could trust me, but I didn't push her to answer my question. It had to be her choice.

So we just lay there, and I thought that Susanne would be happy for me.

*You'll make a wonderful husband and father, Tavish. Never ever doubt that. You just need to find the right woman.*

I silently told her that I had. I'd found her. To stand at Diya's side for a lifetime would be the most beautiful thing I could imagine.

"Everyone always blamed me for Ani," Diya said without warning, "but I *never* hurt Ani." Her voice rose. "I *loved* Ani. Ani was my baby. I called her that first—my baby Ani. My parents copied me because they thought it was so cute."

"I called Kamal," I said, my mind on the policeman who'd kept a family's secrets for decades. "While I was in the hospital. With everything that's happened, I wanted to ask him a question."

Diya was silent.

"I asked him why he'd been so certain that you were the one who killed Ani, why he didn't think you'd just been nearby and got hit by the splatter of her blood."

The man's voice had been broken when he said, "At first, Shumi took the blame." A hacking cough followed by "She was always the quiet one, the good one, the one who never got into any trouble. And Diya was the one with blood on her clothes and Ani's doll in her hands."

Another cough. "But Shumi was wearing a dark color. Dark brown or black, I can't remember, and Diya was in a light dress—the blood was so visible, and she had it on her face, too. Shumi . . . Shumi didn't."

He hadn't verbalized that she must've wiped it off, but we both knew that had to be the case.

"I thought Shumi was trying to protect Diya, but maybe, shocked by what she'd done, the poor child was telling the truth." No life in his tone. "And we showed her that she could get away with the worst evil if she was quiet and didn't make trouble. I *asked* her if it was really Diya, and was it a fight about the doll, and told her Diya wouldn't be in any trouble because she was so small. I *gave* her the story."

When the truth was that Shumi was so jealous of sharing Diya's attention that she'd taken it out on a vulnerable toddler. "Shumi's the one who told the adults you hurt Ani," I said now. "It was her. Not you. And not Bobby." The latter was more conjecture than fact, but it fit.

Diya sat up so she could look down at me, her expression stark and open. "I remembered after Taupo. I don't know why. I wasn't pretending after we lost Mum and Dad and Bobby."

"I believe you, baby," I said, wondering if it was the scent of fire that had caused the cascade of memory.

"I've always wanted babies of my own," she whispered, "but that morning my parents kept bringing up all my medications. All of it to stop me being crazy when I *wasn't* crazy!"

Her voice grew louder, but no one would overhear us here on this empty stretch of paradise. Not even Ravi and his family—they'd gone off to Labasa to do the grocery shopping and give their children a day out.

"They *made* me crazy," Diya whispered. "Always watching, always waiting for me to hurt someone else when I'd never hurt Ani in the first place. That morning, my father started asking about my pills, and if I was staying on top of my regime. Then . . . Shumi, it was Shumi, asked if I'd talked to you about not having kids. Because of course I didn't want to risk that with my psychiatric problems."

"Bitch."

Diya's eyes widened. "Yes, she is, isn't she? She couldn't even share me with my own children. And once she put it out there, my parents started considering it, and saying how Shumi was right, that with my history, I should remain childless. That a stressor like pregnancy could be dangerous."

Rising to a seated position beside her, I took her hand, wove my fingers through her own. "Instead, their own words created the stressor."

"I was so mad at them," Diya whispered. "I was so mad, Tavi."

The wind chimes danced in on a seaward breeze, a ghost flitting in and out of my vision as Diya fell into nightmare.

# CHAPTER 80

## DIYA

*T*ears blurring her vision, Diya pushed at her dad, never imagining that he'd do anything but grunt. He was so much bigger than her, her father who had always been there, so strong and solid.

But somehow, his balance was off.

When she pushed . . . he fell.

The crack of sound was loud, too loud, too wet. "Daddy?" she whimpered, staring at his crumpled form on the edge of the solid stone hearth.

"Rajesh!" Diya's mother ran to her husband. "Rajesh!" Chest heaving, she checked his pulse, looked desperately at his face, searched for any hint of life.

But when she turned back to Diya, Diya knew. "No," she said, backing away. "No, I didn't mean it."

Shaking, white-faced, Sarita gripped her dead husband's hand. "I knew I should've had you put away after you hurt Ani." A harsh denunciation. "But I loved you so much. You were my little girl, my baby."

*A hard shake of her head. "I won't make that same mistake again, won't let you hurt anyone else."*

*Cracks inside Diya, an expanding spiderweb of fracture. "Mum, I didn't mean it," she said on a sob. "I'm so sorry."*

*But her mother wasn't listening, was pulling out her phone.*

*"No one is taking Diya away!" Shumi ran out from around the kitchen counter where she'd been chopping up fruit for a platter.*

*The knife in her hand dripped fruit juice onto the carpet.*

*Diya stared at the red droplets. Her mum would get mad soon, she thought dully. She loved that carpet, liked to keep it crazy clean.*

*"It's necessary, Shumi beta." Sarita turned to cup her husband's cheek with one hand. "What will I do without you, my love?"*

*Diya's mind was fuzzy, her legs trembling, but she knew Shumi shouldn't be running at her mother with a knife. "Shumi, stop!" But she was too late, Sarita already screaming as Shumi punched the knife into her neck hard before pulling it out.*

*Red sprayed onto the ceiling as Sarita grabbed at her neck.*

*"Shumi, no!" Diya lunged for the knife, tried to get it away from her sister-in-law.*

*"This is for you, Diya!" Shumi refused to let go of the blade, her face speckled with Sarita's blood as she managed to break Diya's grip long enough to stab Diya's mother one more time.*

*Sarita collapsed onto the floor, but she wasn't out. She started to crawl to the open patio doors.*

*Desperate to help her mother escape, Diya went to grab the knife from Shumi again . . . and Shumi slipped.*

*The knife was curiously painless going into Diya's abdomen.*

*"Diya!" Sliding the blade free, Shumi looked from her to Sarita and seemed to come to a decision. "It's fine, it's fine, we'll call an ambulance," she said as Diya clutched at her stomach. "I just need to finish this."*

*Turning, she stalked toward Sarita with murderous intent.*

*Shumi was too strong. Diya couldn't beat her on strength alone.*

*She ran to the kitchen. Her flight left a dark red trail on the carpet, her fingers wet on the handle of the knife sitting in the block on the counter. Wrenching it out, she ran at Shumi, who was crouched over Sarita, stabbing her over and over.*

*Diya brought the blade down into Shumi.*

# CHAPTER 81

My heart thundered at the horror of what Diya was describing. "Where was Bobby during all of this?"

"He'd gone into the roof cavity to check for signs of rats. Dad was muttering about hearing scratching up there when Bobby and Shumi arrived, and Bobby rolled his eyes at me and whispered that he might as well go up so Dad would calm down."

A hiccupping sob. "It was such a Bobby thing to do. He knew how to handle our parents when they got to be too much. He used to do it for me, too—he's the reason I got my own suite in the house, rather than just a room with no other private space."

It was hard to understand her now, she was crying so hard, so I just rocked her for a while. "Catch your breath," I said, pressing a kiss to her temple. "We have all the time in the world."

"I don't know if Bobby heard the screams," she said when she could speak again. "One time I went up there, and I couldn't hear anything because of all the insulation. Even if he did and tried to come down, the hatch was so far away from where he'd have been at the time . . . and that high . . . the smoke once the fire started . . ."

"Yes." Bobby hadn't stood a chance of escaping the rising hot air in the enclosed roof cavity.

"My mum, I tried to get her out, but Shumi . . ." Her voice caught. "Mum told me to run." A whisper. "I'd forgotten that. But at the end, I think she knew I hadn't hurt Ani, she understood that I hadn't meant to hurt Dad. She told me to run, 'Diya, beta, run!'" A scream as she repeated her mother's words. "But Shumi suddenly stopped fighting with me and left, so I didn't listen. I tried to get my mother out."

"She was setting the fire."

"Yes. I started to smell smoke and smell petrol. I looked over and saw that the cans of fuel Bobby had brought for the boat were missing . . . and that was when I realized my mother had stopped breathing, her heart quiet. I almost lay down next to her, I was so weak from all the times Shumi had stabbed me as we fought, but all I could think of was you calling me your light."

So she'd staggered out, somehow managing to escape the house Shumi had turned into a death trap.

"Do you think she'll tell on me?" Diya said. "About my father?" Sobs shook her shoulders. "I didn't mean to hurt him. I was just so mad, and always before, he'd just hug me tight when I tried to push him away. He was so strong; he never even staggered before."

"Shumi has no credibility at this point—it doesn't matter what she says." Whatever she said would be considered a transparent attempt to pass off her crimes as those of someone else.

But I didn't think she'd talk; her entire existence was tied to what she saw as her duty to protect Diya.

"I'm so angry still, Tavi." A whisper. "Mum and Dad destroyed me. I was just a depressed kid who'd witnessed the murder of her baby cousin, and they filled me with so many drugs that I learned to shove all my problems inside, never show them anything but a happy face. I knew if I didn't, they'd dope me up again."

"Did you stop taking the meds?" I'd never questioned that she was medicated—I'd seen the bottles, after all.

"Yes. A few months before we met." She pressed her lips together. "Am I crazy? Do I need to be on those meds?"

"We'll find a doctor you can trust to do an evaluation—and only if you want to," I said. "But what happened in that house? That's not your cross to bear." I wasn't about to let the woman I loved bury herself in guilt for another lifetime.

She'd borne that burden long enough already. "You didn't mean to hurt anyone, just struck out in self-defense like a cornered animal."

"Aren't you horrified?" she whispered. "Scared of me?"

"No. You'll never again be in that position, pushed and blamed for something you never did." I pressed a kiss to her hair. "I know you didn't hurt Ani. Now it's your turn to let it go, baby."

She went silent, both of us watching the waves roll in one after another. "Did she kill Rhiannon, too, do you think?" she asked a long time later.

"You were close friends with her, weren't you? I saw the letters you wrote her."

"I thought she was the most amazing person I'd ever met." She dashed away a tear. "Shumi never really had other friends, just me and Bobby. I didn't see how angry she was about Rhiannon—but I do remember how weird she was about Kalindra. Always wanting to be part of our group, to join us on every outing.

"I just thought she was lonely, so I went along with it a lot of the time even though it annoyed Kali. One time Kali found her tire slashed just before we were going to go on a road trip, but she figured that was her ex-boyfriend. I guess we won't know unless Shumi tells us."

Diya exhaled, the breath jagged. "I always felt guilty whenever I went out even after we'd all left uni—like to the movies or to dinner with Carolyn and the others you met at the party. So I nudged the plans to dates and times where I knew she was doing something with Bobby already.

"I felt so bad about it, but she was smothering me—it was so hard to make deep friendships because as soon as I did, she managed to be a part of them somehow. And then she'd subtly push at me to turn down invitations, and she'd start to tell my parents how this friend or that one wasn't good for me. I always thought there was something wrong with me, that I was being selfish in wanting friends who weren't enmeshed with Shumi or my parents."

"You did nothing wrong." I ran my hand over her curls. "I know she tries to call you when she gets phone privileges, but, baby, we have to let her go. She's toxic."

Did I feel sorry for the child Shumi had been?

Yes.

I'd been there, had experienced the pain and the bitterness.

But that pain and bitterness didn't absolve her of the evil of what she'd done. "She set this entire sequence of events in motion when she murdered Ani. And she didn't stop even when she saw what it was doing to you." Instead, she'd taken advantage of Diya's disintegrating mental health to dig her claws in deeper.

"I think she was mad at me for loving Ani so much." Diya's voice was a scrape, her throat raw. "In her head, I wasn't allowed to love anyone else. Just her. Only her." She clenched her hand in the back of my T-shirt. "She wanted to murder you, Tavi."

"Yeah, she tried and failed." I kissed her. "I'm here. *We're* here."

"We're here," she repeated, then exhaled. "I want to have a proper funeral ceremony for my brother. She made everyone blame him the first time and hardly anyone came for him, spoke for him. He deserves better."

"Whatever you want, baby." Looking at the ocean waves, I said, "Shall we walk?"

Diya took my outstretched hand and we walked together across the endless sand, the waves a crashing music in the background. But below that was the sound of the wind chimes, Ani's ghost a giggling companion as she raced down the beach ahead of us.

# ACKNOWLEDGMENTS

Every time I write a book and reach out to people for help with my research questions, I've been humbled by their generosity and kindness in sharing their knowledge. This book was no exception—and if there are any factual errors (and any artistic liberties taken), they are mine.

Huge thanks to Mamta Swaroop, MD, FACS, FICS, for answering my many (many!) medical questions when it came to all my injured characters. We met online years ago when she answered a medical question that I was struggling to find an answer to for another story, and were finally able to meet in person last year—and the conversation never stopped flowing. Sometimes, joyous friendships are born despite oceans and time zones, and this one is now set in stone!

Another huge thank-you to Maria Hurford for making sure I got the details of Rotorua Hospital's ICU setup correct. At times, luck plays a role in bringing people together, and this was the case with Maria and me—we were talking at a gathering hosted by another friend when I realized that Maria had over a decade's worth of experience working in Rotorua Hospital's incredible ICU! Maria answered every question I had with infinite patience and told me things I didn't even know to ask about. I feel very lucky to know her.

A massive thank-you to my editor, Cindy Hwang, and the entire team at Berkley, who always go above and beyond to ensure my books are the best they can be. As I write this, we're about to close in on twenty years of working together, and it's been all-around brilliant.

A forever thank-you to my wonderful parents, Vijay and Usha, who brought me up-to-date on the details of Labasa Airport and the island of Vanua Levu for this book. These two have crisscrossed the island and gone down many a winding road—and also brought us back mouthwatering handcrafted chocolate made from locally grown cocoa beans. Thank you for all that you do, Mum and Dad.

My amazing sister, Ashwini, saves my sanity on a daily basis—and also saves me from turning in books that have people putting their pockets into their hands. Thank you for so much, bestie!

And to Rene—thank you for driving me to Rotorua and back multiple times, endless sweeps of Lake Tarawera, and walks along Sulphur Point and Kuirau Park. I love being on the adventure of life with you.

Nalini
*Auckland, New Zealand*